**Innocence Lost – A Childhood Stolen**
Copyright ©2018 Philip Sherman Mygatt

## Photo Credits

**Cover Design: WillowRaven:** www.willowraven.weebly.com

**Auschwitz Gates: Shoah - The Holocaust**; United States Holocaust Memorial Museum; Mitchell Bard; Beate Klarsfeld Foundation (possibly Bundes Archives – unverified).

**ISBN 13: 978-1-79-071233-5**

## Dedication

I am dedicating this book to my dear sister, Cynthia Jane Mygatt Baker, who passed away on November 29th 2013, after a lengthy battle with ovarian cancer. She reminds me so much of Mira; a brave, courageous, and strong-willed woman who battled adversity without complaining. I miss her sparkling, enthusiastic spirit. I love you, Cindy, and I will forever miss you.

Cynthia Jane Mygatt Baker
March 29, 1949 – November 29, 2013

## The Gates of Hell

### Entrance to Auschwitz
### "Arbeit Macht Frei" — Work Sets You Free

## Foreword

This fictional story of a seventy-eight-year-old woman's memories recalled from her childhood; from farm, to ghetto, to Auschwitz, and finally to Israel, is not intended to be an historically correct account of events that took place during the unspeakable genocide sometimes referred to as *The Holocaust* or *The Final Solution*. If she could speak to us, I'm certain her memories may now be clouded by time; perhaps they are even too horrible to share, so the dates, times, and places may be slightly inconsistent with history, but what she endured as a young, Polish Jew would be her memories and hers alone, and this would be Miriam Kabliski Cohen's story, as I imagine she would have told us, if she could. I have presented her story in an interview format to make it more readable so she could speak in her own words, not mine.

Jews captured by SS and SD troops during the suppression of the Warsaw ghetto uprising are forced to leave their shelter and march to the Umschlagplatz for deportation.

**(See Appendix A at end of book for more information)**

## How I Met Mira

*On July 14ᵗʰ 1942, heartless, well-armed German soldiers with snarling dogs forcibly dragged my entire family and me from the safety of our beautiful apartment in Warsaw and crammed us into a cattle wagon along with eighty other suffering souls.*

*When we arrived at a terrifying place called Auschwitz-Birkenau, they immediately murdered my mother, my father, my innocent little brother, my aunt and two cousins, and burned their naked bodies in incinerators like trash, then unceremoniously dumped their deathly-grey ashes in random, wind-swept piles in a long-forgotten, weed-choked field only to be scattered forever by the uncaring winds of time. Only through a miracle did I survive. I want you to hear my story so the world will never forget. Those horrible people may have stolen my innocence and my childhood, but they can't steal my memories. So, let me begin.*

With those chilling words told to me in a frail but strong voice filled with emotion, Mira began recalling her close brush with death at Auschwitz; a story she has never told anyone before. It is a truly remarkable story, and one I had the privilege of hearing first-hand from this amazing woman; a story she has asked me to now share with you.

I met Miriam Kabliski Cohen quite by accident, and for me it was a life-changing event. My ninety-four-year-old widowed mother had recently moved into an assisted living facility in Venice, Florida, after my stepfather died in 2009, and Miriam was her next-door neighbour.

One day when I was visiting my mother, Miriam or Mira — as her friends and family called her — stopped by to visit. My first impression of her was of a small, white-haired lady who walked with a slight stoop and had a foreign accent that I couldn't quite place. She appeared to be in her late seventies and what surprised me the most as we started talking was that she was quite computer literate. She had her own active Facebook page, Twitter account and kept in touch with her large family through thoughtfully written e-mails.

After Mira had left the apartment, I asked my mother to tell me more about her. She told me that Mira was Polish and had been sent to Auschwitz during WWII, but that's all she knew. Since I was quite interested in WWII history, especially The Holocaust, I asked my mother to call me the next time Mira stopped by and I would like to hear more about her life.

A couple of weeks later, my mother arranged a meeting in her apartment. I didn't know what to expect as I wasn't sure if Mira wanted to talk about her childhood experiences. Our meeting started out pleasantly, but soon it became apparent that whatever had happened many years ago was something that she didn't want to discuss with a stranger, so I changed the subject because I certainly didn't want to make her uncomfortable by asking her questions about her past. She asked me where I worked, and I told her I was an author and that I had written several books, including one about WWII. The more we talked, the more she opened up, until she told me that she wanted to go back to her apartment and get something to share with me.

Within minutes, she returned with a well-worn leather satchel. Opening it, she started pulling out scraps of paper until there was quite a large pile on my mother's coffee table. When I asked her what were on the scraps of paper, she replied, "My story." As I picked them up and examined them, I noticed they were obviously written in a young person's handwriting and were in foreign languages; Polish and German I correctly assumed. As I was going through the scraps, she reached into the satchel, pulled out a well-worn rag doll, and handed it to me. "Meet Alinka," she said. Alinka's clothes were tattered and dirty, her bisque head was crackled and chipped, and one of her arms was badly repaired. However, when Mira reached over, took her back, and hugged her tightly to her chest, I got a brief glimpse of an eight-year-old Polish girl sitting across from me.

Over the next few months, we met many times in her apartment, and she introduced me to many traditional Polish dishes as she told me her story. After translating each of the dozens of notes she had written and videotaping hours of her talking about her life, we celebrated the end of our journey by eating one of her delicious homemade pączki and enjoying a glass of strong, black tea.

## Our Friendship Begins

I used over two-hundred-forty hours of conversations with Mira along with dozens of notes that she had kept hidden for more than seventy-years to write this story. My journey of discovery began when I arrived at Mira's small apartment on the morning of October 21st 2010, armed with my laptop computer and a video camera. She greeted me at the door and invited me into her crowded living room. Her living room was filled with the typical knickknacks we all seem to accumulate over the years; mementos of past events, places we have visited, and things we have cherished. Things that after our passing will be divided among the remaining family members and will eventually show up on some flea market table or in a thrift store with their meanings now lost to history.

Photographs of her family seemed to occupy every available space in her apartment, and before we started our first conversation, she introduced me to each family member. I took it as an honor, as though she was inviting me to be a part of her large, extended family. After exchanging pleasantries, she moved Meyer's hassock so I could set up my video camera and tripod. She said it was her late husband's favorite piece of furniture in the apartment because it was the only piece he could put his feet on without her scolding him. As I was setting it up, she excused herself and walked into her bedroom. Soon, she reappeared with her doll, Alinka, clutched tightly to her chest and settled comfortably on her couch with a hand-crocheted comforter draped over the back, and she began her story.

As a writer, I couldn't help but notice how Mira's demeanor and language changed over the course of our interviews. In the beginning, she spoke in a soft voice as she recalled her early memories of her life on the family farm in Poland. It was almost as though she was once again an eight-year old as she spoke in simple sentences like any eight-year old would, however, as she began to trust me and open up to me, I distinctly noticed her language maturing into that of a confident adult.

Oftentimes she would pause as she searched for just the right word to express her feelings, and sometimes when she couldn't express it in English, she would say the word in German, Hebrew, Yiddish, Polish or some other foreign language and we would scramble to the computer to translate it into an appropriate English word.

Something else that intrigued me was her insistence that I use the British spelling for certain words. As she proofread my written transcriptions of her interview, she would often correct my spelling for words like *traveled*, which she insisted should be written *travelled*. I would make her corrections, but my spell-checker continued insisting on wanting to correct it. When I confronted her with her 'errors', she would just smile and tell me to look it up in the *Cambridge Dictionary* and as usual, she was always right; much to my embarrassment. I thought I had her stumped when I mentioned that she allowed me to use the word *check* when it should have been spelled *cheque*. She smiled and said that she never did like spelling it that way; it looked funny. Typical Mira! When I asked her why she wanted it done that way, she would just laugh and tell me to wait until the end of her story and if I was as smart as I thought I was, I should be able to figure it out. A challenge I now present to you.

We never started out with any goal in mind other than to talk about her life's experiences and perhaps write a small book she could share with her children, grandchildren, and great-grandchildren. However, the more I wrote, the more we both understood that her story was something she needed to share with more than just her family. It was a story she needed to share with everyone. Therefore, with Mira Kabliski Cohen's kind permission, I'd now like to share her story with you.

## Mira Begins to Tell Me Her Story

On July 14th 1942, heartless, well-armed German soldiers with snarling dogs forcibly dragged my entire family and me from the safety of our beautiful apartment in Warsaw and crammed us into a cattle wagon along with eighty other suffering souls.

When we arrived at a terrifying place called Auschwitz-Birkenau, they immediately murdered my mother, my father, my innocent little brother, my aunt and two cousins, and burned their naked bodies in incinerators like trash, then unceremoniously dumped their deathly-grey ashes in random, wind-swept piles in a long-forgotten, weed-choked field only to be scattered forever by the uncaring winds of time. Only through a miracle did I survive. I want you to hear my story so the world will never forget. Those horrible people may have stolen my innocence and my childhood, but they can't steal my memories. So, let me begin.

I was born sometime in the spring of 1932 in a tiny village in southwestern Poland; however, I'm not sure it even exists anymore. It was just a cluster of maybe five or six houses and the nearest town was called Zelów. My parents couldn't remember the exact day I was born, so in my third year, my father decided they would celebrate my birthday on Erev 15 Nisan since that was the first night of Passover in 1932. For my third birthday, my parents gave me a very special doll my father had bought in Łódź, and I named her Alinka after my best friend in the village. We hardly ever celebrated birthdays with presents; instead, my mother would cook us a special supper, sometimes with meat.

After the war, I tried to confirm my actual birth date, but, unfortunately, my birth probably wasn't recorded, and even if it had been, my entire village's marriage, birth, and death records were undoubtedly destroyed when the Germans swept through there in late September 1939. I eventually did some research and discovered that Erev 15 Nisan on the Hebrew calendar that year was April 20th on your calendar, so that became my birthdate.

My father, Lev Kabliski, was a very scholarly man from a fine family in Łódź. He had studied languages in college, and he could read and understand Greek and Latin. He could also write and speak Polish, Yiddish, and Hebrew. Our village was too small to have a school, so my father taught my two brothers and me by oil lamp after we had finished the daily chores on the farm. My older brother, Lev, was six-years older than me and my other brother, Chaim, was three-years younger than me. Although my father was a very smart and educated man, my mother was a plain, simple woman who had grown-up in the village and had never attended school. My parents met one summer when my father came to visit some distant relatives who lived in a nearby village. My grandfather thought it was important for his children to spend some time in the country working on the land and to get away from the hot summers in Łódź.

After my father had graduated from the Higher School of Social and Economic Sciences in Łódź, he returned to the village, married my mother, and started a family. He enjoyed living the simple life in the country rather than living in the city. He was also a very religious man, and he made sure we celebrated every Jewish holy holiday and festival, and believe me, we never missed one.

Life in the village was simple. We had to be completely self-sufficient since it was a day's journey to the nearest town. I fondly remember the first time my father hitched the horse (it looked more like a mule) to the farm wagon and took me into Zelów. How proudly I sat next to him as we travelled down the small dirt track towards town. The families in the village took turns going into town to get supplies, and this was my father's turn. The first thing I remember was seeing the tall buildings from a distance. I had never seen anything like that before, and I watched in amazement as they grew bigger and bigger the closer we got to town. It was nothing like anything I had ever seen before, and the confusion, noise, and crowds overwhelmed me. By contrast, our village was peaceful and quiet, and I never knew such a place existed outside my small world.

I mostly remember the people walking down the streets. They were all dressed so differently. Some looked like peasants while some looked as though they were dressed up in their best finery, headed somewhere important. The only people I was familiar with were our neighbours in the village, and they were all peasants. I think this was the first time I realised a larger world existed outside the village, a world populated with different kinds of people. To me, it was an eye-opening trip.

After we had loaded up the wagon with supplies, we stopped at a little roadside cart to get something to eat. We sat in the wagon under a tree and enjoyed our meal. It wasn't much, just a couple of *gołąbkis*. I tried to be careful as I ate mine, and my father laughed when the meat juice dripped all over my dress. I was horrified; my mother wouldn't be happy. She wasn't, but my father took the blame.

Our farm wasn't large; just an old horse, a milk cow, a flock of chickens, rabbits, some sheep, and three or four cats who lived in the barn. Every time my father milked the cow, the cats would come begging, and my father would squirt milk into their open mouths. After they were satisfied, they'd go out into the sunshine and groom themselves trying to get every drop of milk from their faces and whiskers. It was fun to watch them.

My brother Lev was the most wonderful person in the world. Being my big brother, he always tried to protect me, especially when I went out to the hen house to collect eggs, and the mangy rooster attacked me. He just shooed him away and laughed, but I never thought it was funny.

The villagers shared a common garden in the center of the village. It provided vegetables for the community, and it was also a gathering place for them to get together and work. Most of the villagers were uneducated and illiterate, so sometimes after we had finished the gardening chores, we would all sit around in a circle. My father would then tell stories about far-away places he had read about, and we were all delighted and amazed to hear such places even existed.

Nothing very exciting ever happened in our village. The only big event I can remember is when the rabbi from the synagogue in Łódź visited our home. He was my grandfather's best friend, and he spent the night with us. I remember overhearing him and my father talk about what was happening in Germany, and how bad people, *anti-Semites* he called them, had come to power.

## My Family

My two brothers, Lev and Chaim, were amazing. Lev was such a handsome man, and as far back as I can remember, he was my protector. Whenever I had a problem, I'd always go to Lev, not my parents. He and I had a very special bond. Chaim was my little baby brother. Sweet little Chaim! Such a dear, sweet, innocent, little boy; an angel.

Life on our small farm was difficult. You might wonder how there could be so many things to do on such a small place, but believe me, Lev and my parents worked from sunup to sundown. If they weren't doing something on *our* farm, they were helping the neighbours on *their* farms. Ours was a tightly knit community. Four families were Jewish and two families were Christian, but I don't think they ever discussed religion. The two Christian families joined the Jewish families for our festivals, and we joined them for theirs. When I was three-years old, we even celebrated Chanukah and Christmas at the same time. Regardless, December was a wonderful month of the year. Full of festivities and fun.

Lev was tall, and he had a wonderful head of coal-black hair. I still remember watching him chop wood. He didn't wear a shirt, and I loved watching his muscles as he swung the ax and split the wood. I can still see him now. Every now and then, he would look over at me and wink, and I knew that was his way of telling me he was watching over me. Sometimes I'd go over to the water bucket by the well and bring him back a dipperful of water. When he had finished drinking, he poured what was left over his head. That always gave me a big laugh.

Lev was never as curious about learning as I was. He never showed any interest when my father sat by the coal-oil lamp after supper reading his books. My father told me what was in the books would be my key to the outside world, my way of escaping the village. It would also be my way to learn about magical places I could never begin to imagine.

Chaim was more of a momma's boy. Since he was younger than me, he was always the baby. My mother still treated him like a baby long after he was walking, and he was always holding her hand. One of my fondest memories was watching him and my mother walk out to the chicken house to collect eggs. They would always hold hands, and he would carry a little wire egg basket in his other hand. If I close my eyes, I can see them as though they were right here. Chaim was such a sweet boy. I don't think he would ever hurt any living thing. Bugs fascinated him. Sometimes he sat in the dirt and stared at the ground. When I'd go over to see what he was doing, he would just be watching ants going about their business.

When I was about five-years old, my mother told me it was my job to take care of Chaim. She said I was a big girl now. That meant I had to make sure he ate his meals, kept out of trouble, and went to bed when he was supposed to. As you can imagine, he and I became quite close, almost as though I was his second mother. Every time we went for a walk, he would hold my hand; he always had to be touching someone.

Before we ate dinner, my father would take a piece of bread in his hand, break it, and hold it up so we could all see it. He'd then bless the meal: *BA-RUCH A-TAH A-DO-NOI ELO-HAI-NU ME-LECH HA-O-LAM HA-MO-TZI LE-CHEM MIN HA-A-RETZ (Praised are*

*You, Adonai our God, Sovereign of the Universe, who brings forth bread from the earth).* He had a nice voice, and it was always comforting to hear him say the blessing. At our Passover dinner, his voice would soar over everyone else's, although my brother Lev had a beautiful voice, too.

When I was about five or six-years old, my father thought I should learn how to read Hebrew. He had tried to teach Lev, but he was never interested. It was fascinating to discover how strange marks on a piece of paper could have sounds and stranger yet, to see how those sounds came together to make words. *Aleph, Beth, Gimel, Daleth, He, Vav, Zayin, Heth, Teth, Yodh, Kaph, Lamed, Mem, Nun, Samekh, Ayin, Pe, Sadhe, Qoph, Resh, Shin, Sin, Tav.* My father used a little stick to point at each letter as I memorised it. The first Hebrew word I learned was *Adonai.* Literally translated, it means 'my Lord'.

The Jews have a wonderful tradition that centers on a Jewish child learning their first Hebrew words. It's usually done on *Shavout*, one of our religious festivals. It's filled with rich ceremony that's been passed down from generation-to-generation, and it usually involves a rabbi, some honey, a honey cake, a slate, and a hard-boiled egg. Jewish tradition says that a child who licks honey from a slate and eats honey cake and a hard-boiled egg on the first day of class will immediately understand that the Torah is 'as sweet as honey'. Unfortunately, we didn't have a rabbi, a slate, a hard-boiled egg, a honey cake, or even some honey. Instead, my father put a piece of sweet candy on my tongue as I repeated the word *Adonai.*

My father told me when he reads the Torah, that whenever it mentions what you would call God, he substitutes the word *Adonai* instead. He told me it was a Jewish tradition never to refer to God using the Hebrew word *YHVH.* He said they called it The Unutterable Name, and he would teach me more when I got older. The second

Hebrew word he taught me was *Av*. It's spelled *Aleph Kaph*. It means "Father".

I learned to read Hebrew before I learned to read Polish. Most of my father's books were written in Hebrew, so there wasn't a need to learn how to read Polish. Since most of our community was Jewish, everyone understood Hebrew, although my father was the only one who could read and write it. All the Hebrew prayers and ceremonies were verbally passed down from generation to generation, sometimes with unexpected consequences. The only time I needed to know how to read Polish was when we went into the city. All the signs in the city were written in Polish. At first, I struggled because Hebrew is written and read from right to left while Polish is written left to right, just like English. My father used to laugh as I tried to read the Polish words from right to left. "No, no, no," he would say. "Think Polish. Think backwards." His feeble attempt at humour.

Our family spoke mostly Polish with a few Yiddish words thrown in to spice up the soup as my father used to say, and Hebrew was our religious language. Having grown-up that way, it was just natural to know both languages. When the men of the village got together, they often spoke Yiddish. I don't know if you know it, but there are many different Yiddish dialects. I think the dialect in our village was called *Poylish*, but as I learned later, most Yiddish speakers can understand one another, even if they speak different dialects since there are enough common words that it usually isn't a problem. Although Yiddish is related to what they call Old High German, it's a much different language, although they both share common words. Knowing Yiddish was a big help with learning German, something that played a big role in my upcoming life.

I know I sometimes seem to skip around from topic to topic, but when I start talking about one thing, it triggers other memories. It's like following a winding path; I never know when I start, where it will lead me. I hope I'm not boring you. Tell me if I am. Okay?

Going to Łódź was a big event. My father's parents lived there, and when I was six-years old, we went to Łódź to celebrate Passover. We hitched our ancient horse to the wagon and rode into Zelów. It was mid-April, and the weather was quite hot, as I remember it. My mother made me wear my blue dress; it was the only dress I owned. It was more of a cold-weather dress than a warm-weather dress, and I was uncomfortable. When we got to Zelów, we left the horse and wagon at a stable and walked to the railway station. It was a small station, and we waited outside for the train to arrive. I can still remember hearing the train long before I saw it. As it got closer, the noise got louder and louder, and then I saw a tall column of black smoke in the distance. When the locomotive finally came into view, it truly frightened me. I thought it was a fire-breathing dragon, so I ran inside to get away from it. As it drew up alongside the station, it made the whole building shake. I was terrified, but my brother Lev came in and got me. I told him I didn't want to go outside, but he said he would protect me. After we had boarded the train, I sat as far away from the window as I could and when it started with a lurch, I grabbed onto Lev's arm and tried to crawl into his lap. He just laughed and put his arm around me. That was the first time I took a ride in a train; however, it wouldn't be the last.

## Life on the Farm

We were all so excited to ride the train to visit my father's family in Łódź for our Passover celebration. I even enjoyed myself after a while. When we arrived, we took a trolley car to my grandparents' apartment on *Grabinka Ulica*. The street connected two main streets and it was lined with three or four story apartments. The trolley-car stop was a couple blocks from their apartment and we walked the short distance. It was as though I had landed in a fairy tale place. Lev and I held hands as we walked along the busy streets as I stopped in front of every store and gazed into the windows. Lev literally had to drag me down the street by my hand. There were windows with fresh fish sitting on beds of crushed ice and bakeries with freshly baked pastries and big loaves of bread enticingly displayed in the windows. Moreover, the aroma of those freshly baked goods as we passed by their open doors made us want to stop and sample one of everything! There were also meat shops with big chunks of meat hung from hooks in the windows. The streets were busy with people, horse-drawn wagons, motorcars, and trolley cars. It was a magical place. I later learned we were right in the middle of what would later become known as the Łódź Ghetto; a terrible place where the Germans trapped and eventually liquidated thousands of Jews, including my father's entire family.

My grandparents' apartment was small. After all, there was only *Dziadek* and *Babka* Kabliski living there. My grandfather was a very intelligent man. He had studied law in Warsaw and graduated from the university with honours. He and my grandmother moved to Łódź shortly after they were married and he started a small law practice that had spanned many years until he had retired soon after I was born. They had five children, all boys, including my father, and every one of them had graduated from college. Uncle Addam was a lawyer in Warsaw. Uncle Efrayim was a physician in Łódź and lived nearby. Uncle Emanuel had something to do with accounting, but I never knew him that well as he and his family had moved to Berlin many years ago. Uncle Schmaiah was a rabbi in Poznan and he hardly ever visited. There must have been some kind of a family problem because nobody in the family ever talked about him. When I asked my father about him, he smiled and told me Uncle Schmaiah had died many years ago, but my mother told me he hadn't actually died, he just wasn't part of the family anymore. I never bothered to ask and I never met him. I later found out he died in Bergen-Belsen. That was a concentration camp somewhere in Germany.

Sometimes it's so difficult to talk about my family. When I do talk about them, I try to think of them only during the 'happy times' when they were all alive. That's why I think it's important to include *their* story as part of *my* story. Put them in a place where they are healthy and happy, once again.

This was the first time my entire family had visited my grandparents in Łódź and it's something I fondly remember. They lived on the third floor and there was a small balcony overlooking the street. My grandmother used to grow some vegetables in big pots on the balcony, mostly tomatoes. She also had one or two rose bushes which she would bring inside in the cold weather. Uncle Efrayim, his wife and three, small children joined us for Passover dinner. My brother Chaim, my three cousins, and I went out onto the balcony. It was a beautiful, sunny day, and the roses were in full bloom, but the tomatoes were still small and green.

Some of the rose petals had fallen onto the balcony floor and we decided to play a game. One-by-one, we each tossed a rose petal off the balcony and watched as it floated down to the street below. If the petal landed on top of a person, we got one point; if it landed on a standing horse, we got two points; and if it landed on a moving horse, we got three points. I don't think anybody scored any points, but several passersby glanced up at the balcony to see where the rose petal shower was coming from and we ducked out of sight. The game ended when my grandmother came out onto the balcony and scolded us, but she was smiling.

Passover dinner was wonderful. There were twelve of us crowded into their small apartment. The adults sat at a large table my grandfather had set up in the middle of the living room and the children sat wherever they could find a space to sit. Our family had always celebrated Passover; however, it always seemed as though there was more ceremony than substance because we lived on a farm and had to be self-sufficient. We just couldn't go to the supermarket when we needed something like people do nowadays.

The Passover Seder is a time for friends and family to come together and celebrate the Israelites' exodus from slavery in Egypt. It's a tradition we Jews have celebrated for centuries; a way of reminding ourselves what it was like to be slaves, to pass along our traditions to future generations, and to make sure we are never slaves again. We Jews are commanded to carry on the tradition because there is a passage in the Book of Exodus that says, "*You shall tell your child on that day, saying, 'It is what the LORD did for me when I came out of Egypt.'*"

We'd all gather around as a family and my father would read from something he called the *Haggadah*. It talks about the Israelite's exodus from Egypt, has special blessings, rituals, commentaries from the *Talmud*, and special Passover songs. He used to read it first in Hebrew and we could understand some of it, but not all. Therefore, he would retell it in Polish. The Passover Seder ceremony is quite involved.

All I remember about Passover Seder at my grandparents' apartment was that it was wonderful, but the next time we were all together, it was under much different circumstances. I'm not too sure I want to talk about it anymore, so is it all right if we take a break?

##### #####

*Author's note:* *We took a short break, sat on Mira's balcony, and talked about the weather, her grandchildren, and her beloved New York Yankees. Being a Red Sox fan myself, you can be sure our baseball conversations were lively, and I was amazed at her knowledge of the game as she knew every player on the Yankees, their batting averages, and what position they played. After a few minutes, she got up, and I followed her back into her living room.*

##### #####

After the Seder meal, my grandmother, aunt, and mother went into the kitchen to do the dishes and straighten up. My two brothers, my cousins, and I crowded back out onto the balcony and tried to find some mischief to get into. Chaim wanted to pick some green tomatoes and drop them from the balcony, but Lev stopped him and said it wouldn't be a nice thing to do. My grandfather, my uncle, and my father sat down in the living room and began a serious conversation over glasses of strong, black tea.

I was bored, so I drifted into the living room and quietly sat in a corner. It made me feel grown-up to be sitting there with the adults. My father glanced over and saw me sitting there, and he motioned for me to come over and sit down next to him on the settee. That made me feel extremely important.

The main topic of discussion was about the National Socialists coming to power in Germany. Many called them Nazis, but I never remember anyone in our family calling them that. My grandfather called them *bandyci*. That's a Polish word meaning *thugs, hooligans,* or *gangsters* in English. My father said that war with Germany was inevitable, but the Polish Army would crush them like a horse stepping on a nasty bug. My Uncle Efrayim wasn't as confident as my father, and he wondered what would happen to the Jews living in Poland if the *bandyci* overran our beautiful country.

That was the first time I had ever heard the word *war* mentioned, and it was difficult for me as a young farm girl to begin to understand what it meant. When I asked my father what *war* was, he said it was when two countries couldn't agree to be friends, and they decided to settle their differences by fighting. He explained it by telling me it was like when the neighbour's rooster came into our barnyard. Our rooster would come running out of the barn and they would fight, however the fight wouldn't last very long, and the intruder usually ran back into the neighbour's yard. If that's what war was like, it didn't seem too bad. After all, the cockfight only lasted for a minute or two, the vanquished would flee home, and nobody got hurt.

My father was more concerned about what would happen to the Jews if the *bandyci* prevailed. He argued they were *anti-Semites* and the Jews wouldn't be safe, and that was the first time I had ever heard that word. When I asked my father to explain, he said an *anti-Semite* was someone who hated Jews. For me, it was hard to understand how one person could hate another person, let alone hate an entire group of people. The word "hate" was something I didn't understand; it was a very unfamiliar word to me.

My grandfather argued that the world wouldn't stand by and let the *bandyci* take their hate out on the Jews; after all, this was the twentieth-century not the time of the Pharaohs, and if the world wouldn't protect us, God would because He'd never let His chosen people be persecuted and enslaved again. Let the *bandyci* come, he argued; God and my grandfather would protect us. He said if the *bandyci* ever came, we were all welcome to come live with them in Łódź, and we would be safe there. I left there that day filled with dread and uncertainty about the future; however, I knew we would always be safe with my grandparents in Łódź.

## The Rumbles of War

I can't say 1938 was a good year for us. My father appeared to change after we returned home from our Passover Seder in Łódź. He used to be quite outgoing and engaging, but I could tell something was troubling him as he became more and more withdrawn, and spent a lot of time visiting with the other men in the village. The mood in our village was also ominously dark and somber, even though the sun would be shining brightly there was always a dark cloud hanging over our village.

Sometime before Hanukkah that year, I overheard my mother and father having a serious discussion about something they called *Kristallnacht*. My father said that the German *bandyci* had gone berserk and had attacked Jewish synagogues, businesses, and buildings throughout Germany.

I couldn't understand everything they were saying, but I knew it was serious when my mother started crying. It was the first time I had ever seen my mother cry. She was such a strong woman, and when I saw her crying, I knew they were talking about something quite serious. My father travelled to Łódź a few times after that, and his mood darkened with every visit. I started to become very afraid, but I didn't know why, and it was obvious that our Christian neighbours' attitudes about the four Jewish families living in our village had also changed. It wasn't anything I could put my finger on, but there was just something about their demeanor when they were around us, and then they began to avoid us, whenever possible. They still helped in the community garden, but they didn't speak to us, and it was as though we had even stopped existing

I was just a seven-year-old child, and the only knowledge I had of the outside world was through my father's eyes, and he always tried to protect me; shield me from the bad things that were starting to happen around us. He didn't let anyone in the family know that the Germans were starting to make threats against their neighbours, and their leader's speeches were getting more and more outrageous. Pardon me if I refuse to say his name, but he was the *Bies*, Satan himself, and I'm sure you know whom I'm thinking of.

As time went by, my father spent less time working around the farm, and more time reading his *siddur* while wearing his prayer shawl. As the chores around the farm began to suffer, Lev and I had to work even harder to keep up with things, but no matter how hard we tried, life on the farm began to deteriorate. Watching my mother suffer, too, was hard on all of us, and it was as though she was beginning to disappear right before our eyes as she started losing weight, and began to age far beyond her years. Sometimes at night I could hear her crying after we children had gone to bed, and I wanted to comfort her, but I didn't know what to do.

I also watched my brother, Lev, grow into a man in a very short time. It was as though one night he went to bed as a boy and woke up the next morning as a man. Can you imagine? A man at twelve-years old! Taking care of the farm and the family was such a huge responsibility for such a young man; however, he appeared to grow taller and stronger with each new day. Chaim was too young to be as affected as we were, but I noticed as time passed, he slowly lost the sparkle in his eyes. Sometimes he would disappear, and I would find him hiding in a corner of the barn, and it was obvious that he'd been

[26]

crying. I tried to comfort him, but I didn't know what to say, so I would just take his hand and walk him back to the house.

The winter of 1938-1939 was particularly brutal and our family greatly suffered. The sun didn't shine for weeks, and it was quite cold, although there wasn't much snow. Since our father hadn't spent much time preparing the farm for the upcoming winter, we had to make do with what Lev and I had been able to accomplish.

We didn't have as much firewood or food as we should have, so it felt as though we were cold and hungry the entire winter, and sometimes we had to make hard decisions about taking care of our animals. Once we had to kill all our lambs to feed our family, however I couldn't do it, so Lev had to. I held my hands over my ears so I wouldn't hear their terrified screams when they realised what was about to happen. After a while, the barn became strangely quiet, and I cried myself to sleep that night snuggled next to Chaim who didn't want to know what had happened. I didn't have the heart to tell him why we had fresh meat on our table that evening.

When spring finally came, my father just wasn't interested in taking care of the farm, or his family. Sometimes he didn't even get out of bed, and all the farm chores fell onto us children, so we did the best we could, but it just wasn't the same.

My father went to Zelów many times over the summer to talk to the rabbi at the synagogue, and every time he came home, he would take my mother into the kitchen, and I could hear them talking. I could never quite hear what they were saying, however all I know is that when they had finished talking, my mother would walk out of the kitchen crying, her apron held to her face to shield her emotions from us children.

My father would often meet with the other men in the village, and their discussions were always very animated, and I sensed they were talking about something that greatly disturbed them, but I was too young to understand what they were discussing.

The summer that year was exceptionally dry, and the crops withered and died before we could harvest them. We were extremely worried about how we could make it through the upcoming winter with such a meager harvest, and everyone in the village suffered as much as we did. Some talked about leaving the village, moving to Zelów, and living with their families. However, when I asked my father why people were talking that way, he said they were weak. We were strong, and we would stay right here; we'd be safe staying right where we were. I never questioned him; I always felt safe when I was with my father.

I spent a lot of time with my pet lamb. I named her *Biały śnieg*. That means *White Snow* in English. She was the cutest little thing I had ever seen, and she followed me around like a puppy, and sometimes we even let her come into the house. My mother wasn't too happy about that, but she knew how happy it made me.

Since we had to slaughter most of our animals the previous winter, we only had a cow, a horse, two sheep, some starving rabbits, my lamb, and several chickens left.

Sometime in early September 1939, a stranger rode into our village, and he was in a real hurry. He galloped into the center of our village, tied his horse to a tree, jumped down, and started shouting. Soon, the villagers came running from every direction to see why he was shouting, and my father came running out of our house, too. My mother and I wanted to go with him, but he told us to stay right where we were.

I watched from a window as the stranger reached into one of his saddlebags, pulled out a large sheet of paper, and started reading. As he read, the villagers became very agitated. They began shouting and pointing their fingers at the stranger, however he just kept reading and pointing at the document in his hands. When he was finished, he rolled up the document, hurriedly stuffed it back into the saddlebag, mounted his horse, and rode off in a cloud of dust, leaving the villagers yelling and shouting at each other.

What news had the stranger brought that had caused so much concern? I couldn't even begin to imagine. After what seemed like forever, my father and Lev rushed back into our house, and when they came into the front room, my father took my mother into the kitchen, telling us children to stay where we were. I asked Lev to tell me what news the stranger had brought, but he said our father would tell us after he had talked to our mother.

We three children sat nervously waiting for our father to return and comfort us. Within a few minutes, he walked back into the room, and we could hear our mother softly crying in the kitchen. I can remember it as though it was yesterday, as my father stood in front of us in the front room, and I wanted him to stand tall and brave, but it appeared as though he had suddenly shrunk, and he just stood there, shoulders hunched, head down, bent over like an old man, and his demeanor was so frightening, it terrified us.

Wringing his hands as though he didn't know how to begin, all he said was, "I wish I could tell you good news, but I can't. The stranger said the Germans have invaded our country, and we're at war," and with that, he turned and walked back into the kitchen, a defeated shell of a man.

## War Comes to My Village

War. "What is war?" I once again asked my father. How was an eight-year-old peasant girl supposed to know what war was? As before, my father told me that war is a disagreement between countries, but the poor people living in those countries are the ones that are always hurt. I'm sure he wanted to spare me the gruesome details and what the future probably held for Poland.

Strangely enough, in the next few weeks the war actually bypassed our village, however, from time-to-time, we could hear loud noises, like explosions, over the horizon, and once a large swarm of airplanes flew over our village, but other than that, life appeared normal.

One day a large caravan of gypsies came through our village and asked if they could set up camp nearby, but the men in the village told them they had to keep moving on. My father had once told me that the gypsies stole children and whatever else they could find, so I just stared out the window at them. They didn't look like thieves, but they were dressed differently, and I thought it would be fun if they could stay and I could visit them, but I didn't want to be stolen. So, I was happy when they moved on.

My father didn't say much more about the war, but he told us that each one of us needed to pack a bag in case we had to leave the village in a hurry. I couldn't imagine leaving our village as it was the only home I had ever known, and I didn't want to live anywhere else, but I had to do what my father told me.

About four weeks after the stranger came riding into town, we saw a large dust cloud on the horizon, and it was coming our way. We could also hear lots of noises; creaking noises, roaring noises, noises I had never heard before. The noises got louder and louder as the dust cloud got closer and closer to our village.

Within a few minutes, a strange vehicle, one like I've never seen before, came driving into the center of our village, and there were two men in the front and eight men riding in the back. They had funny hats on their heads, and they were all carrying gun, guns like my father used to hunt wild boar, but these guns were bigger, more menacing. I didn't know why these strange men would be visiting our village; after all, the war had passed us by a while ago.

It wasn't until much later that I learned these were German troops who followed in support of the blitzkrieg troops, and they were the scavengers who looted the villages, stole what food and supplies they could, and shot anyone who tried to stop them. They kept whatever they stole even though they were supposed to be provisioning the advancing troops, and their orders were to leave nothing but scorched earth in their path.

Soon after they arrived, a large number of trucks pulled into the village behind them; more armed men jumped down and started rounding up our villagers. My father told us all to stay in our house and not to step outside until he found out what they wanted, as we all watched while they rounded up the village men. I watched through the window as old Mr. Szydło limped out of his barn and started walking towards the others. One of the soldiers shouted at him, and when he didn't move fast enough, the soldier ran over, grabbed him by the back of his shirt, dragged him to where the others were standing, and forcefully threw him onto the ground.

Soon, I saw Mr. Stępniak come running out of his barn with a pitchfork in his hand, and he ran right at the soldiers, but before anyone could say anything, one of the soldiers shot him dead. Right in his own barnyard! I can still see the bullet hitting him in the middle of his chest, and then there was a splash of blood as he pitched backwards and fell onto the ground still tightly clutching the pitchfork in his hand as the red blotch on his crude, peasant shirt grew larger and larger. He coughed once, a large glob of red blood flew from his open mouth, and then he lay still. I was hypnotised, frozen in place, and I didn't understand what had just happened, but I couldn't stop watching.

His hysterical wife ran to his side, and one of the soldiers grabbed her by her hair and roughly threw her to the ground, but as she tried to get up and help her husband, the soldier kept throwing her to the ground. Finally, he put his heavy boot on her chest and pinned her to the ground as many of the nearby soldiers laughed, watching her flailing her arms and legs trying to get free.

There was a lot of screaming and shouting. One soldier, who appeared to be in charge, was yelling at the assembled villagers, however I didn't know what language he was speaking, but I assumed it was German. There was also a tall, striking man standing next to the German, he was dressed in a different uniform, and he was much calmer than the others. Every time the German said something, he would say something to the village men, so I can only assume that he must have been a Polish soldier who was translating. Whatever he said apparently calmed the men down, and if it hadn't been for his soothing manner, I'm sure the Germans would have shot everyone right there.

It was obvious when the German officer had given all the orders he was going to give; he swept the village men towards their houses with a wave of his arm, and it was as though he was sweeping flies off a horse's hindquarters.

My father ran back to our house as it was obvious he was greatly distressed. When he came into the front room, my mother ran over to him. "What's happening?" she asked.

"We have to leave. Now!"

My mother fell to her knees, grabbed his legs, and started sobbing. "They can't do this, Lev. This is our home."

My father, who had once been reduced to a defeated shell of a man, now stood up straight and proud. "Tell the children to gather their things. I'll get the horse and wagon." His demeanor was so commanding that there wasn't any panic as my mother got up off the floor, straightened her simple, peasant dress, and said, quietly, "Children. Go, gather your things."

I ran into my bedroom and grabbed the small satchel I had packed right after the stranger had ridden into town. As I rushed out of my bedroom for the last time, I turned and took one last glance. To my horror, my doll Alinka was still sitting on my bed propped up against my pillow, so I ran back into the room and swept her up into my arms. She and I would make the journey together.

When we all ran out into the yard, we saw that my father had already hitched our horse to the farm wagon and was pulling it up next to the house, and there was a lot of commotion around our barn. When I looked over, one of the German soldiers was dragging our cow out of the barn, but she didn't want to move. Two more soldiers ran over and started pushing her from behind, but she started bucking and kicking, and the soldiers were greatly amused by her antics. Finally, with a lot of pushing and shoving, they got her into one of the trucks, and her loud mooing voiced her displeasure at such rough handling.

Soon, a soldier came out of the barn carrying one of our young lambs. It bleated its annoyance, but the soldier also roughly threw it into the back of one of the waiting trucks as another soldier came out of the barn dragging our ram by his horns. He, too, loudly protested and dug his feet into the dirt, but he was no match for the determined soldier, and he went into the back of the truck kicking all four legs.

The last soldier came out of the barn carrying our ewe, and I could see the terror in her eyes as she struggled to get free. Before he had a chance to throw her into the back of the truck, another soldier ran over to our barn with a lighted torch and threw it onto the thatched roof, and the roof instantly erupted into a mass of red flames, white smoke, and crackling noises as though the gates of Hell had opened and spewed forth its nightmarish terror.

Where was my lamb? Where was *Biały śnieg?* The last thing I remembered was tying her to her stall so she wouldn't run away. Had someone taken her, and I hadn't seen them? Then, I heard her terrified bleating in the barn. She was still in the barn; she was still tied to her stall, and the barn was going up in flames, and I had to save her! I jumped down from the wagon and started running towards the barn, but my father grabbed my arm and dragged me back onto the wagon. "She's in God's hands now." I was frantic as I didn't know what to do. She was calling out to me; calling me to come save her, and I couldn't. It was the most helpless feeling anyone could imagine.

Then, there was a loud noise, a kind of thumping sound, and the entire barn erupted in flames as I heard *Biały śnieg* scream, once, and then she was silent. The only sounds left were the loud popping noises as the barn collapsed into a mass of flaming wreckage, and the sounds of the other villagers' animals being dragged and pushed into the waiting trucks.

As we all watched in horror, a soldier ran up to our house with a torch and tossed it onto the roof, and our entire life, our farm, and the land we worked so hard to tame, all went up in flames. The entire village; all up in flames. My father started the wagon, and we drove away without looking back, with the soldiers' laughter still ringing in our ears; mocking us, taunting us, haunting us, forever.

I often wake up in the middle of the night and hear *Biały śnieg* screaming, and I can't do anything about it. I saw and heard many horrible things after that, but that's the one thing that has haunted me all my life. I'll take it to my grave with me. Poor *Biały śnieg's* one, terrified scream. Where was I when she needed me?

## The Beginning of My Long Journey

Without turning to look back at our burning farm, my father flicked the horse's reins, and we started down the dirt track leading away from our village. Some of the other families in our village had already left, and some were still loading their wagons. My mother and father sat in the front of the wagon, and Lev, Chaim, and I rode in the back. We hadn't been able to save much from our house as we were only able to take the small bags we had already packed. I rode backwards in the wagon leaning against Lev and watched our small, burning village disappear into the smoky distance. As I looked around, all I could see were columns of smoke from other nearby burning villages, and it was at that moment that I remembered what my father had told me, and I finally began to understand what *war* truly was.

Soon, we joined many families from other villages, and we didn't know where we were headed; we only wanted to get away from those bad people and get somewhere safe. From time-to-time, we had to pull over to the side of the roadway and stop to let the long line of German trucks pass us, and many of the German soldiers spat on us as they passed. I couldn't understand why they hated us; we hadn't done anything bad to them, so why were they punishing us?

At lunchtime, my father steered our wagon off the road and down a small dirt road leading to a small farm that, like all the others, had been destroyed. There was a large tree in a nearby field and we stopped, got down from the wagon, walked over, and sat down under it. My mother opened a small cloth bag, and we shared our first meal as refugees, and it wasn't much; one loaf of bread and two hard-boiled eggs for the five of us. My brother Lev walked over to the well near the destroyed farmhouse and drew some water, but it really tasted foul. However, it was the only thing we had to drink, so we drank it, and tried to keep it down.

Although I was afraid and still mourning the loss of my dear lamb, it seemed like an adventure, at least that's how I tried to look at it. After all, we were all still together, we were taking a trip, and I knew my father and Lev would protect us. After we had finished our meager meal, we rejoined the other families on the dusty road, and their wagons stretched as far as the eye could see. Not only were there wagons filled with people and whatever they could salvage, but many others were pushing wheelbarrows full of their possessions, some were pulling small wagons, some were pushing bicycles with large bundles tied to them, and some were walking and carrying large sacks over their shoulders.

It was a very hot day, and the road was dusty, especially every time a caravan of trucks passed us, however the only thing we could taste was the dust that covered us. Lev took my mother's shawl and made a little tent to shelter Chaim and me from the sun, but nothing could protect us from the dust. Even now when my son takes me over to Sebring to visit my family, I ask him to avoid the back roads he likes to take. Although it's nice to drive through the orange groves and smell their wonderful fragrance, many of them are dirt, and they always bring back memories of our flight from our village.

Before it got dark, we pulled our wagon out into a field where there were several other families who had also stopped for the night. We parked our wagons in a circle, and someone built a large fire in the middle as my father and Lev unhitched the horse and led it to a nearby stream to drink. While they were gone, my mother reached into her bag and took out a few vegetables, mostly turnips, if I remember right, and there was also a loaf of bread and not much else. Fortunately, she had packed a small, black pot, and we were able to have boiled turnips and bread for dinner.

There were quite a few children our age, and we played in the nearby field while the adults gathered around the fire and talked. The one thing I remember about that night was how dark the sky was and how many stars there were. Also, how red the horizon all around us was, and I guess those must have been other villages burning in the distance. It was as though we were sitting in a dark hole surrounded by a ring of fire.

Lev, Chaim, and I slept out under the stars that night, and as we lay on a blanket, Lev pointed out the Milky Way and some other heavenly constellations. He was so smart, and I don't know how he knew everything he did; I never saw him read a book. I remember I went to sleep that night amazed at the universe that God had created, but I was also mad at Him for what had happened to us. However, my father had taught us that God was all-powerful, and He had a plan for each of us, however I just didn't know what that plan was, and my father was never able to explain it when I asked; he just told me to trust in God.

Finally, after three grueling days on the road, our caravan approached the city of Łódź, and although there had been many battles around the city, it appeared to be mostly intact. Every now and then, we could see remnants of the German blitzkrieg, but for the most part, it was as though the war had passed it by. The only difference was there were German soldiers everywhere; some were marching towards town, and some were riding in trucks. Everywhere we looked there were lines of refugees just like us making their way into the city, and I wondered where they were going to put everybody.

As my father guided our wagon into the city towards my grandparents' apartment, the streets became more crowded, and it was difficult for us to make our way through the congested streets. The minute we turned down *Grabinka Ulica*, I felt safe because everything was so familiar, and it looked just the same as when we had visited there to celebrate Passover with our family. My father tied the horse to the railing in front of my grandparents' apartment, we unloaded our meager possessions, and then made our way up to their third floor apartment.

*Dziadek* and *Babka* had seen us arrive, and they greeted us at the door. It was a joyous reunion as we all hugged and kissed, and after we had greeted one another, *Babka* and my mother went out into the kitchen while my father and *Dziadek* sat down in the living room and started a serious discussion.

After we had all gathered around for our evening meal, my father said the blessing, and then he said he had an announcement, and as we all leaned forward in anticipation, he declared, "*Dziadek* and *Babka* have graciously asked us to come live with them." We were safe!

## My Grandparents' Apartment in Łódź

My grandparents' apartment was quite small as there was only one bedroom, and they shared a bathroom down the hall. A kitchen and living room were the only other rooms. Our first night there was quite confusing as we all tried to settle in, and our entire family slept on the living room floor even though my grandparents had graciously offered their bed to my parents. It took a couple of days to figure out the final sleeping arrangements.

Although our living quarters were cramped, we made do, and we quickly settled into a daily routine because having a routine made life easier. In the morning, *Babka* and my mother would walk down to the local marketplace to buy the day's meals. The apartment didn't have an electric refrigerator like we have now; instead, they had an old-fashioned icebox. Unfortunately, after the war started, there weren't any more ice deliveries, and they had no way to store their perishable food for more than a day or two before it spoiled, and sometimes we had to eat the spoiled food if we didn't want to go hungry.

As the days dragged into weeks, there was less and less food available in the marketplace, and we often had to barter; money meant less as time went by. *Babka* and my mother had to barter away most of their jewelry and the family silver just to keep the family in food, however, the only thing they refused to part with was the family's menorah. It had been passed down through the family for many generations, and although it probably wasn't worth a lot to anyone else, *Dziadek* swore he would only part with it over his dead body. Much later we learned it was the only thing they had taken with them when they were deported to Chelmno, and the Germans undoubtedly confiscated it before they murdered them in the gas vans. That was all in the future; a future that in our wildest dreams we could never imagine.

*Dziadek* and my father spent a lot of time in the synagogue praying and meeting with the other men in the neighbourhood. Often, when my father took me with him, I overheard their conversations, and my father argued that the Germans would continue persecuting the Jews and would try to eliminate them from their domain altogether. My grandfather was more pragmatic as he argued that the Jews were crucial to the very fabric of the country's society. After all, they were the bankers, the doctors, the lawyers, the professors, and the merchants. How could Polish society survive without them? My father countered that someday we would have to face the fact that the Germans would eventually figure out a way to liquidate the Jews all together. My grandfather admonished him for his views, saying that his negative attitude would only result in what he predicted, and it was *his* position that the more the Germans had to depend on the Jews, the more valuable they would be; to destroy them would be suicidal. Making themselves indispensable within the community and to their tormentors would surely be the Jews' solution to their current plight.

I'm not sure I understood words like *solution, liquidation, persecution,* and *social fabric.* These were concepts I had nothing to compare with, and they were only words, but words that filled me with dread only because they greatly upset my parents and grandparents. As time passed and things changed in what would eventually become known as the Łódź Ghetto, I began to understand the meanings of those words and what they meant for my family and for me, and for all the Jews. However, for the time being, these events were some time in the future.

The local synagogue had set up a meeting place in the basement for the children. None of us three children had ever attended school because there wasn't even a school within many kilometres of our village, and the only teacher we ever had was my father. Imagine my surprise the first day we walked into the synagogue's basement and saw the children reading, writing, and learning Hebrew. It was as though we had walked into an alien world. Even though my father had taught Lev and me the basics of reading and writing, the other children my age were so much more educated than either of us, and we truly felt like country bumpkins right from the start. However, Chaim didn't care. He just played with the other children his age, and he was so happy to be with them, that every day when we left the synagogue, it was as though he had left the sad Chaim back in our village and had been reborn a happy child.

In the afternoon, we all gathered in a large circle, and someone would read us stories from the Torah. As you may already know, the Torah is the first five books of the Jewish Bible, and Christians know it as the Old Testament. I already knew some of the stories because my father had shared many of them with us children, but I never tired of hearing the story of Moses and how he led the enslaved Israelites out of Egypt, across the Red Sea, and finally to the Promised Land.

The Jews were, and still are, a great people; God's Chosen People. We still struggle to exist, and to this day I don't know why we are still so persecuted, and that's why I think it's important to talk about Moses. As a child, I knew how the Israelites must have felt, because even though we Jews weren't slaves in the true sense, we were still being isolated and persecuted, and what we needed was a modern day Moses; someone who would lead us to *our* Promised Land. To me, Moses was like your Christians' Jesus, and being the naïve child I was, I truly expected him to show up in a flowing robe and long beard and once again lead the Jews out of slavery.

After we had fled Łódź, the Germans presented a man named Mordechai Chaim Rumkowski as a modern day Moses, but he turned out to be the *Diabeł,* the Devil. I'm sure he tried his best to save the Jews, but he wound up leading them to God's Promised Land. Not on earth, but in Heaven; a journey he led himself in person as he, too, died in the gas chambers; just a mortal man like all the others who died alongside him.

As time passed, the streets in our neighbourhood became more and more crowded, and many of the newcomers weren't peasants, like us. They were more sophisticated, more educated, and their clothes were much finer than ours were, and they looked more like city people than country people. One day I overheard my grandfather and father talking in the living room, and they were talking about how the Germans were rounding up Jews from nearby towns and crowding them into the old part of the city where we lived. Why would they do something like that? It didn't make sense to either of them. If the Jews were what *Dziadek* had called the *social fabric* of Polish society, what happened to their towns after they had left? It was all too confusing to me, and unfortunately, my father claimed that what he had predicted was coming true. The Germans were up to something, and it wasn't good, and I was surprised when *Dziadek* began to agree with him.

## My Family Flees Łódź

After we had been in Łódź for a few months, life started to become very difficult as there was less food on our table, and the synagogue stopped their daily classes. My father said the local Jewish leaders didn't feel safe having so many children in one place at the same time, although he didn't tell me what they were afraid of. I truly missed our daily classes, and Chaim missed playing with his friends, so, as before, he began to retreat into himself, just as he had done back in our village. I would often find him hiding under my grandparents' bed in the middle of the day, and I tried to cheer him up, but I didn't know what to say to him.

[42]

The Jewish leaders were still under the impression the more they made themselves useful to the Germans, the better their chances of survival, and it was a hope many in the community, including *Dziadek*, still clung to. Our leaders had even set up factories in our neighbourhood to help the German war effort where sometimes they would often work outside in the streets making ammunition and other war materiel. In the meantime, my father had even started working in a print shop where they printed propaganda and other official documents for the Germans.

The Germans had started requiring the non-Jewish, Polish citizens to carry ID cards that they had to show at the many checkpoints the Germans had started setting up throughout the city. It was beginning to become more difficult, if not impossible, for the Jews to travel outside the boundaries of the old city, and their ability to move around the city was becoming more and more restricted every day, and it reminded me of how the Egyptians had enslaved Moses' Jews.

As the restrictions became more stringent, the local Jewish authorities set up a council to provide the communities with some sort of government since the Polish government had collapsed during the Blitzkrieg, and the Germans controlled the government they had put in place to replace it. The local council assigned a leader for each block in the neighbourhood, and they reported to the council. For the time being, it was an informal group of leaders attempting to maintain control over the neighbourhoods, however the Germans eventually learned of its existence, put it under their control, and called it the *Judenrat*.

Our block leader was a well-respected member of our neighbourhood named Doctor Zedeck, and he had been a professor at the Lódz University before the war. I can still see him as though it was yesterday. He was always dressed very elegantly in a fine suit complete with vest and a beautiful pocket watch he kept on a long gold chain in his vest pocket. When Doctor Zedeck talked, people listened.

Soon after the council was formed, Doctor Zedeck called a meeting of all the neighbourhood men in the gymnasium of the now-closed school. When *Dziadek* and my father returned from the meeting, they appeared quite agitated, and it was apparent that something was truly bothering them.

We all gathered in the living room and *Dziadek* told us that the Germans had ordered all Jews to wear a yellow Star of David on their outside clothing to identify them as Jews. My father said it was an insult to the Jewish people, and he would refuse to wear his; however, *Dziadek* said he should consider it a badge of honour. After all, wasn't he proud to be a Jew, one of God's Chosen People?

My father said he was proud to be a Jew, but he didn't need to announce his pride to the despised Germans as his Jewishness was something he felt deep within himself, and it was between him and his God; not between him and the Germans.

My mother convinced him it was in the family's best interest if we all went along with the council's 'suggestion', however the only stipulation he insisted on was that the yellow Star of David would be kept out of sight in the apartment. All outside garments would be secreted away when we weren't wearing them.

It was about that time I overheard *Dziadek* and my father discussing that maybe it would be in the family's best interest if we left the city while we still could. *Dziadek* thought as long as the Jews living there made themselves indispensable, they would be allowed to move about without too many restrictions. My father argued that every day he saw more and more restrictions being imposed on the city's Jews, and he feared it wouldn't be long before the Germans isolated the neighbourhood from the rest of the city and wouldn't let anyone in or out. It eventually turned out my father was right.

Once he had convinced *Dziadek* that he needed to spirit his family away to safety, the two of them spent a long time planning an escape route; a way to leave Łódź and journey to Warsaw to stay with family there. The biggest obstacle we faced was coming up with ID cards identifying us as non-Jews, and although my proud father didn't want to hide his Jewishness, he swallowed his pride for the sake of his family's safety.

Because of the shortage of everything in the neighbourhood, there was a very active black market, and you could get practically anything as long as you had something of value to barter for it. My father had been able to use his job at the printing shop to print counterfeit ID cards for the wealthier residents who wanted to flee, and although he doubted they would be successful in their escape attempts, he couldn't refuse their offers. The forgeries were a crude attempt at duplicating the necessary cards, but the purchasers were desperate to leave the city, and hopefully, the country. Now he was faced with the fact that his family's safety depended on how well his forgeries passed the Germans' scrutiny.

The first obstacle was coming up with photographs of each family member to put on the counterfeit ID cards, and since only officially-appointed photographers were allowed to take photographs for the cards, they were closely controlled by the Germans. In addition, the photographs were printed on a special photographic paper that had swastikas embedded in the emulsion, and each photograph also had a special stamp in the lower right-hand corner that was the Nazi Party's symbol; an eagle on top a wreath encircling a swastika. Hidden within the wreath, and engraved in letters so minute one had to use a magnifying glass to see them, were the words "Ein Volk, ein Reich, ein Führer".

Fortunately, one of the older men working in my father's print shop had been a master engraver at the Polish National Mint, and he had secretly been working on duplicating the despised mark. Although he was close to finishing it, my father would have to wait a few days before it was completed. In the meantime, he needed to find a way of duplicating the special photographic paper.

Someone in the print shop had been able to obtain an original ID card with the unique photographic paper and dreaded stamp, but nobody could figure out a way to copy the emulsion. They tried every method they could think of, but none of the results was good enough to pass even casual inspection. Without the special paper, any attempt to forge passable ID cards was doomed right from the start.

Just when my father was about to give up, someone in the print shop was able to smuggle some of the photographic paper into the shop, however there was only enough paper for a few dozen photographs, but that was better than having none at all. No one but my father was willing to attempt to use the ID cards to escape the city, and although he wasn't certain they would pass scrutiny, he knew he had to try, or face what he knew was the neighbourhood's ultimate fate. The five sheets of paper cost us our horse, but the horse had become useless to us anyway. We even had offers to slaughter him and sell him for meat; however, we were afraid someone would steal him for just that purpose, and we wouldn't benefit from the transaction at all, therefore, the horse had to go.

One sunny day in early spring, everything had fallen into place. The engraved seal was complete, my father had the necessary photographic paper, and the forged, blank ID documents were practically impossible to distinguish from the real items. All we needed to complete our charade was a new name; a name that didn't sound Jewish, an occupation for my father, and some nice clothes for the photographs. We needed to look like a well-off, middle-class Polish professional family, but our current wardrobe didn't make us look the part. So, my grandmother bartered with a local family for some nicer clothes for the five of us. We all put on our new clothes and headed for the local photographer, but we made sure to wear our coats with the hated, yellow Star of David. He looked so handsome in his new suit, vest, tie, and shoes, and although the overcoat he had to borrow from my grandfather was a bit too large for him, it helped him conceal the fact that he had hidden the bulky package containing the special photographic paper under his dress shirt.

Fortunately, when we entered the photographer's shop, we were the only ones there, and the photographer warmly greeted us. "Welcome to my humble studio, Mr. Kabliski."

"No, no. Mr. Greenburg. We're the Bednarczyk family, and we're here for our portraits," as my father winked at him.

Mr. Greenburg returned his wink. "Then welcome to my humble studio, Mr. Bednarczyk," and from then on, we were the Bednarczyk family.

I often wondered why my father had chosen such a difficult last name for our family. If anyone had asked me to spell it, I would have had great difficulty, however the biggest problem we faced was if someone had asked my little brother, Chaim, his last name. Would he even be able to pronounce his new name?

One-by-one, Mr. Greenburg led us into his studio in the back of his office and took several portraits of each of us, and when he had finished developing the film, he and my father would choose which ones to print on the precious photographic paper. Mr. Greenburg's effort cost us our farm wagon, but what good was a farm wagon without a horse?

Within a few days, we had our new ID cards, and even my grandfather was impressed as the Bednarczyk family, led by my father, now a civil engineer, was prepared to start the next leg of its journey, hopefully to safety.

## Our Departure for Warsaw

It wasn't until much later that I found out my father's decision to leave Łódź had almost caused our family to break up. My grandfather and father thought it only made sense to leave, while my grandmother and mother thought it would be sheer suicide for the family. What if our charade was discovered? What fate would the family suffer?

Although the adults didn't express their feelings in front of us children, we often lay in bed at night and listened to them arguing in the living room, but, finally, it was settled. Our flight from Łódź was sealed, however we had to wait until my father could buy five railway tickets to Warsaw.

Buying the tickets was risky. First of all, my father had to make his way to the railway station outside the Jewish neighbourhoods which meant that while he was still in the neighbourhood, he would have to display the despised yellow Star of David on his clothing, so he and *Dziadek* developed a plan they hoped would work. *Dziadek* knew a back way out of the neighbourhood, a route where my father would be less likely to encounter the German soldiers. Right before he left the neighbourhood, he would remove his jacket with the yellow Star of David and hide it somewhere where he could retrieve it on his return home.

The next problem he faced was using his fake ID card to purchase the railway tickets as well as presenting it to any German soldier who demanded to see it. I remember the day he left my grandparent's apartment on this treacherous journey and the goodbye embrace he shared with my mother seemed endless, as though she were trying to prevent him from leaving. However, with a kiss and embrace for each of us children, he opened the door and left. I didn't know how dangerous this journey would be, however I could tell from my mother's emotional goodbye that we might never see him again.

Waiting for his safe return felt like an eternity as my mother and grandmother sat on the couch holding each other tightly and our grandfather sat in his chair, smoking his pipe, and reading his *siddur*. Although we children sensed something important was happening, we knew that time would pass more quickly if we kept occupied, so we went outside and played with our friends.

Within a couple of hours, we saw our father walking down the street, his jacket with the dreaded yellow Star of David casually draped over his arm. We ran up to greet him, and he picked each of us up and gave us a big hug. He tried to lift Lev, but Lev was almost as big as my father was, so he just gave him a hug, and with a large grin on his face, he told us to follow him upstairs to our apartment; he had some good news to share with us.

When he walked through the apartment's door, my mother and grandmother got up off the couch in anticipation as my father tried his best to put on a grim face. I thought my grandmother and mother were going to faint from fear, but he quickly reached into his trouser pocket and waved five railway tickets in the air. My mother started crying as she ran up and gave him a huge hug and kiss, and *Dziadek* just looked up from his *siddur* and said, "Good work, Son."

There was great excitement around the dinner table that evening as my father relished telling his story of how he had managed to purchase the railway tickets right under the Germans' eyes. Leaving the neighbourhood wasn't a problem, in fact he had only encountered one German soldier on his way to the railway station, and all he asked him was where he was going; he didn't even ask to see his ID card. When he got to the railway station, the ticket clerk had asked to see his ID card; however, it appeared to be more of a formality than an interrogation. Maybe having a German soldier stationed nearby was why the clerk even gave it a passing glance. Although the ID card hadn't actually passed close inspection, my father felt as though it hadn't aroused any suspicion, either.

It was decided over dinner that the family would leave on the coming Sunday because everyone agreed there would be more families travelling on the weekend, and we would more easily blend in with the other passengers on their way to Warsaw. In addition, my grandfather and father assumed the Germans would be more relaxed on a weekend, and they wouldn't question a family of five walking down the street.

The Saturday night before we left our dinner was very solemn as *Dziadek* recounted the story of Moses leading the Jews out of Egypt. He said that my father was a modern-day Moses leading his children out of bondage and into safety, and although the journey would be perilous and fraught with dangers, he would provide us safe passage to the Promised Land.

Everyone was up early on Sunday morning in anticipation of leaving. Grandmother fixed us a special breakfast, and she also made lunch for our journey, which my mother wrapped in her scarf and put into her travel satchel. Since we knew we would be questioned along the way, it was important to have a believable cover story; one that made sense, and more importantly, one we could all remember.

Since we had relatives who lived in Warsaw, (Uncle Addam lived there with his family) our story was that we were going to Warsaw to visit his family. Which, in fact, was true, but it was more than just a visit; hopefully it would be a permanent move. The only problem my father faced was if he were quizzed about our relatives, what would he tell them? After all, Uncle Addam was Jewish and lived in a predominately Jewish section of Warsaw. Would the inquisitor know Warsaw well enough to know the address was in the Jewish section? Since Warsaw was a big city, and there were many neighbourhoods and thousands of streets, we hoped, if questioned, it would be by a German soldier who wasn't that familiar with the city.

If we *were* stopped and questioned, my father had already decided that he would say he didn't know the exact address; only that our relative would be meeting us at the railway station in Warsaw, and he hoped that answer would satisfy the questioner. We also had to appear to be a family who was only going for a short visit, so we couldn't pack all the belongings we had brought from the farm, in fact we could only bring three sets of clothing, and everything else we would have to leave behind. Of course I brought Alinka; she went everywhere with me.

Finally, it was time to say our tearful goodbyes and I sadly remember taking one last look at *Dziadek* standing there in the doorway of their small apartment with his arm around *Babka's* waist, and little did I know it would be our last goodbye. They looked so small and frail standing there, and they seemed to have aged way beyond their years during our stay with them, and now I know it must have been a terrible imposition on them, but they never complained. They were very stoic, loving, and supportive, and I still miss them so.

As we walked out the door for the last time, my father promised to visit from time-to-time, but everyone knew it was a promise he would never be able to keep; I think they did it for us children. So, with a final hug and farewell, my father closed the door behind us, our stay in Łódź ended, and our journey to Warsaw began. The moment we walked out into the sunshine and started down the street, it felt as though we had already been liberated because it was as if we had walked out of a dark room into the light, and the fear of the great unknown immediately vanished. I know it's hard to describe the feeling, but I think the Jews must have felt that way when Moses called upon God to part the Red Sea, and they escaped from Egypt.

We were a happy group as we made our way to the escape route my father had used when he had bought the railway tickets, and as we got closer, the streets got narrower, and there was no one in sight. At the end of the street there was a small field separating the Jewish neighbourhood from the rest of the city. It wasn't a park, it was more like an empty field where maybe a building had once stood, however before we dared cross the field, we removed our jackets with the yellow Star of David and threw them into a nearby trashcan. We knew they wouldn't go to waste since people had already started picking through other people's trash looking for scraps of food or anything else of value they could use to barter for food.

We passed other families on our way to the railway station, and they acknowledged us with smiles and friendly greetings, and although we saw some German soldiers along the way, none of them gave us a second glance, nor asked to see our ID cards.

We got to the railway station before the train to Warsaw had arrived. It was a beautiful sunny day, and we felt safe sitting among the other families waiting for its arrival. My father bought some drinks from a sidewalk vendor, and we all sat in the sunshine and enjoyed our freedom. Several German soldiers walked through the station; however, they hardly gave us a glance as we seemed to fit right in with the other travellers. We were quite comfortable as we sat there, but my father was on edge; as though he was keeping a watchful eye on us lest we betray our true mission.

Finally, we heard the train approaching in the distance, and this was only the second time I had ever ridden on a train, and like the first time, the train reminded me of a fire-breathing dragon, however I wasn't afraid of it this time. Everyone waiting in the station got up, gathered their belongings, and walked out onto the platform. We had to wait until the arriving passengers had gotten off the train before we could board, and while we waited, German soldiers with enormous dogs walked up and down the platform, but I think they were there more for show than to harass people. The soldiers looked so smart in their starched uniforms, brass insignia, and ribbons, and it was only later that I learned to despise and fear them.

Our family boarded the third coach from the locomotive engine, which was sitting there making hissing noises amidst clouds of steam and smelly, black smoke. It was a hot day; all the coach windows were open, and the odors from the coal-fired locomotive filled the already stuffy railcar making it hard to breathe. I can still close my eyes and smell the smoke, however, at that time, it was just another part of our wondrous journey. It was only later that I would associate it with something horrible; something so frightening that even now when I smell smoke of any kind, I have to run away. Smoke, to me, is an evil thing.

After the coach was loaded, and before it had departed the station, the conductor walked down the aisle asking the passengers for their tickets with two German soldiers following behind him, closely observing everything he did. Occasionally, they would ask the passengers to produce their ID cards, which one of the soldiers would closely examine while the other scrutinised the owners, and then they would move on. When they arrived where we were sitting, my father handed our tickets to the conductor while the two German soldiers watched over his shoulder as he looked at the tickets, and then punched them with a ticket punch. I know my father was quite relieved, although the ID cards had yet to pass their first test.

Finally, the locomotive started making loud banging noises, the big driving wheels started to turn, and we started on our journey with a jolting lurch. We were finally on our way to Warsaw!

## Our Arrival in Warsaw

To me, our trip to Warsaw felt more like a vacation outing than an escape. Of course, being a small child, I couldn't fully understand why we had to leave Łódź, but as we got closer to Warsaw, I could tell by the way my parents were acting; it wasn't just another happy family outing.

Chaim didn't want to sit still, and he kept getting up from his seat and running up and down the coach's center aisle. My mother had to keep getting up and drag him back by the hand to where the family was sitting. Once he bumped into a German soldier who was walking down the aisle, but the soldier just patted him on the head and smiled as my mother retrieved him, once again. I don't think he even knew how dangerous his little game was for all of us.

As I remember it, it was a beautiful day; the sun was shining brightly, and there wasn't a cloud in the clear, blue sky. Most of the countryside we passed through appeared untouched by the war, even the farmers were working out in their fields, the villages we sped through looked normal, and other than an occasional destroyed farm, it was as though nothing had changed.

The train stopped several times before we got to Warsaw, and each time it stopped, one or two German soldiers walked up and down the aisle, glanced at the passengers, and checked some of their ID cards. Every time they passed by where we were sitting, my father would glance over at my mother and give her a look that obviously warned her to keep us children under control. Fortunately, they never asked my father for our ID cards.

The railway coach was filled with what I can only describe as an electric tension, which only increased as the train approached Warsaw. Passengers who had been engaged in lively conversation for most of the trip were now silent as they blankly stared out the windows as we passed through the Warsaw suburbs.

This was the first time any of us had seen any large-scale destruction from the war, and many of the outlying neighbourhoods we passed through were nothing but rubble. Where buildings had once stood, there were now only piles of bricks and other debris, and neighbourhoods that used to be filled with hustle and bustle were now more like cemeteries, the piles of rubble their tombstones. Some streets had been cleared, leaving narrow paths as people wandered aimlessly down them as though they were lost, and from time-to-time, we'd pass piles of rubble with people picking through the debris. Whatever were they looking for?

My mother and father glanced nervously at one another, and I could almost read their minds. Why had they left the relative safety of Łódź and brought us to this place? It was a decision that once made, couldn't be unmade.

As the train got closer to the center of Warsaw and our final destination, the railway station, we saw less destruction, although it was apparent there had been major battles throughout the city. As the train approached the railway station, the atmosphere in the coach became more relaxed, like the air being let out of a balloon, and there was a collective sigh of relief as the train crawled towards the station.

Finally, the train came to a noisy halt in Warsaw's central railway station. As we glanced out the windows, we could see that part of the station had been destroyed, and it looked as though they had tried to build a partial roof over what remained of the building. We got up from our seats and joined the other passengers as they made their way to the coach's exit, and there was a lot of noise and confusion as the passengers stepped down from the train cars and onto the wooden platform.

My father led the way down the coach's narrow aisle with Lev right behind him, and my mother followed closely behind him holding Chaim and my hands. I clutched Alinka to my chest as we shuffled our way to the exit as everybody and everything around me appeared to grow larger as I grew smaller. I wasn't used to being in the middle of such crowds and confusion, and suddenly I became terrified. It's hard to explain; I had been afraid before, but there was suddenly something ominous, something dangerous surrounding us, and I hoped my father hadn't brought us to a bad place.

When we finally stepped down onto the railway station platform, our family closed ranks, and we stayed as close to each other as possible. Even Chaim seemed to sense the danger as he tightly clutched my mother's skirt while my father looked straight ahead and tried to appear as anonymous as possible. There were German soldiers on the platforms with fierce-looking dogs on leashes, and whenever one of the dogs walked up to Chaim and sniffed him, he let out a shriek and buried his head in my mother's skirt.

The German soldiers at the station weren't nice like the ones on the train, and they never smiled as they roughly pushed their way through the crowds, sometimes knocking people to the ground. The dogs acted just like their masters; they snarled, growled, and barked incessantly. Even today, when I hear a dog bark it takes me back to the day we arrived in Warsaw and that wasn't the last time fierce dogs would play a terrifying role in our lives.

We finally made our way out of the station and onto the busy street where there were many horse-drawn wagons waiting. Even the horses appeared agitated as they snorted and nervously stamped their hooves on the cobblestone pavement. The drivers shouted out, offering to take the arriving passengers to their destinations. Now, whenever I fly somewhere, step outside the terminal, and see the line of waiting taxis, I can still hear the horses snorting and the sounds of their hooves stamping on the cobblestones.

My father walked up to one of the wagons and handed the driver a piece of paper where he had written Uncle Addam's address. The driver took one look at the slip of paper and raised his eyebrows in a questioning way, and with a frown on his unshaven face, he asked my father if he was sure that's where he wanted to go. My father confidently assured him the address on the paper was correct, and satisfied with his explanation, the driver indicated with a nod of his head that he wanted us to board his wagon. My father helped my mother up into the back of the wagon, as Lev followed her, and then my father lifted Chaim and me up into his waiting arms. With an athletic leap, my father jumped up and joined us as the driver snapped the horse's reins, and we headed towards Uncle Addam's apartment and the next leg of our journey.

## Uncle Addam's Apartment

I wish I had a camera to capture Uncle Addam's expression when he opened the door. "What are you doing here?" he asked.

"Didn't you get my letter?" my father answered.

"We haven't had any mail delivered here for months," he laughed. "Come on in." And, with that unexpected welcome, the Kabliski, I mean, the Bednarczyk family, safely arrived in Warsaw.

Oh my, what a joyous occasion it was. It was the first time any of us had been to Uncle Addam's apartment, and to me it was like walking into a royal palace. There were beautiful paintings on the walls, carpets on the floor, and there was even a grand piano by the tall windows in the living room. The rooms were light and airy with high ceilings, and the enormous rooms made me feel very small, but happy.

This was the first time I had met Uncle Addam's family, but they made us feel at home the instant we walked through the front door. Uncle Addam was a big man with a dark, black beard that tickled when he bent down and hugged me, and that's what I remember most about him; his beard and his laugh. I used to sit on his lap and play with his beard; it was thick and wiry, and I loved to run my fingers through it. He would just sit back and laugh. Uncle Addam was always laughing, and you couldn't help but feel better when Uncle Addam was in the room.

Aunt Ania was just the opposite of Uncle Addam. She was slight, serene, and quite pretty, and when she was in the room, you knew she was there; you just felt her presence even though she didn't speak a word. She always was flitting around the apartment doing something; straightening the drapes, rearranging the beautiful picture books Uncle Addam had placed on the living room table, picking up after the children, or doing something in the kitchen. I'm not too sure I ever saw her sitting down except at the dinner table, and then she appeared to be in perpetual motion, jumping up and running back and forth into the kitchen.

My two cousins were named Aaron and Adiya. Adiya told me her name meant "God's ornament" in Hebrew, which she thought was special, which she was. Aaron was about my age, maybe a little bit older. Such a serious boy and very grown-up for his age! He always enjoyed sitting with the adults and being a part of their conversations rather than playing with us children, and he loved to play the big piano by the window. There was a funny little machine in a box on top of the piano that had a little pendulum inside it, and when you turned it on, it went tick, tick, tick, and you had to try to keep time to its rhythm. They called it a metronome and we were more fascinated with the metronome than we were with Aaron's playing, although he was quite accomplished. It was the first time I had even heard a piano being played, and the top of the piano was on a hinge, and you could lift the top and prop it open. We used to love to stand on a small stool and watch the little hammers strike the exposed piano wires as Aaron hit the keys, and it was amazing to watch and listen to at the same time.

Adiya was really fun to be with. She and I hit it off the minute we laid eyes on each other, perhaps it was because she was much more like her father than her mother. She had a wonderful twinkle in her eye, and it was hard to figure out if that twinkle was a humourous one or a mischievous one; perhaps both. She was just a year older than me, and her bedroom was like a wonderful castle filled with dolls and toys. We used to put a blanket over some chairs and make a tent, and then we would then crawl under there with a whole family of her dolls and make up wonderful stories; stories that took us outside Warsaw and to faraway places where everything was beautiful, and everybody was good to each other. She once told me she didn't like to leave the apartment because people out there didn't treat her nicely, and because of that, her bedroom had become her sanctuary.

Although their apartment was large, it wasn't large enough to fit us all comfortably without some rearranging. My mother and father slept in the guest bedroom, and the bedspread was somewhat frilly. At first my father objected, but my mother reminded him we were guests, and we were lucky to have a bed at all. After all, there were people sleeping on the streets; maybe he would like to trade places with them, and he never complained after that.

I slept in a big bed with Adiya where we would pile as many dolls on top of the bed as it would hold, and then we would crawl under the covers and giggle. Boy, how we both loved to giggle. We didn't even have to say anything; we just looked at each other, and that was enough to get us to giggling so loud that Uncle Addam would often come into the bedroom and tell us to go to sleep. When we were under the covers, we felt safe; a place where nobody could hurt us, or even find us.

More than anything else, I remember Adiya's laugh; it was infectious. I hope the gas chamber walls where she died still reverberate with her spirit. Wouldn't that be a fitting tribute? Those *skurwysyn* can take our lives, but they can't take our spirits, and I know Adiya's spirit still lives on, if only in my memory.

I'm sorry. I really didn't want to go there, but it's hard to keep the happy memories alive without letting the bad ones take over. It's a real struggle for me sometimes to only look at the bright side of my life and not let the demons in, and if I let that happen, *they* would win; those nasty people who stole our lives and our families. I hope that in the end, good will prevail over evil, but we always have to be on our guard that it never happens again.

[60]

# Innocence Lost - A Childhood Stolen

You know, sometimes I feel as though I'm surrounded by ghosts. I know that sounds somewhat silly, but I often sense my family's presence in the room with me, and when I do, I sit back, close my eyes, and I can hear them; Uncle Addam's laugh, Adiya's giggle, my little brother's childlike voice as he clung to my mother's skirt, Lev's strong voice trying to sound like a grown man, and the reassuring tick, tick, tick of the metronome droning on and on as the piano's little hammers struck the wires, making glorious music.

Aaron's bed was big enough for two, but Lev didn't feel comfortable sleeping in the same bed with his cousin, so he slept on the floor. Lev had a bad habit of snoring when he slept, and sometimes when Adiya and I were hiding under the covers telling stories, we would be interrupted by Lev's snoring in the other room. She and I'd break out giggling so hard we thought we'd wet our pants.

Sometimes we'd get out of bed and sneak into Lev's room just to see what it looked like when he snored, and once he woke up. I guess our giggling must have awakened him, and he sat straight up and looked at us, and we ran screaming back into our bedroom, jumped under the covers and giggled. He then sneaked back into our room and jumped on top of us under the covers. We screamed so loud we woke up the entire family, and Uncle Addam came running into the bedroom to see what was causing the commotion. We thought he was going to punish us, but he just stood by the side of the bed and laughed, and that was the last time we sneaked into Lev's room even though his snoring grew louder after that. Maybe he was just doing it to get back at us. Now I long to hear that irritating snoring, just one more time.

## The Warsaw Ghetto Begins to Trap Us

I can't say life at Uncle Addam and Aunt Ania's was wonderful, because it wasn't. Although it was good to be with our extended family, it was becoming more and more difficult for my mother and Aunt Ania to find enough food to feed all of us, and as time went by, food became scarcer and scarcer, and most of their day was spent walking around the Jewish neighbourhood looking for somewhere to buy food. The shop windows were mostly bare, and the lines outside the stores that did have food often stretched around the block.

Some farmers from outlying areas were able to bring some fresh vegetables into the neighbourhood in their wagons, but as soon as they parked along the street, unruly crowds anxious for anything to eat, mobbed them. Quite often fights broke out between otherwise peace-loving neighbours; such was the urgent need to have food to feed their families.

There were also rumours that the German occupiers were beginning to cordon off the old Jewish neighbourhoods from the rest of the city, and some were beginning to call it a *ghetto*. Although the Germans hadn't blocked all the streets, there were fewer and fewer ways to get in and out of the neighbourhood as time passed. My father was concerned, but as long as we had our counterfeit ID cards, he said if things got bad, we could leave and find somewhere else that was safer. That is, up until he tried to pass through one of the security checkpoints with his ID card. When the German soldier had asked him for his ID card, my father handed it to him, the soldier took one look at it, laughed, and stuck it into his pocket. My panicked father turned around and rushed back to the apartment; he was crushed.

Although the adults tried to shield us from what was going on, we often overheard them talking about what was happening throughout the old Jewish neighbourhoods. There were even rumours that the

# Innocence Lost - A Childhood Stolen

Germans had started to force families from their apartments and send them out of the city, and other rumours abounded; if only they had been turnips, instead. Some people said they were sending families out into the country to settle on farms, while others said they were sending them to special camps the Germans had set up throughout the country. Whatever their destination, nobody who left the city ever came back to tell us where they had been.

The uncertainty and the way the adults were behaving terrified us children, and we didn't feel safe anymore. We seldom left the apartment, and when we did, we were always with an adult who hovered over us like a mother hen hovers over her chicks. Although Adiya and I still snuggled under the covers, we seldom giggled like we had at the beginning; we just lay there and held each other closely until we went to sleep.

Whenever we played under our makeshift tent, we would make up stories about how we'd protect our little dolls and how they'd be safe as long as they stayed nearby. Even Alinka seemed to understand she was in great danger, and she clung to me more tightly whenever I held her. She was my connexion to the good times, and I never wanted to let her go.

One day we heard a lot of commotion in the street outside the apartment, and we ran to the window and looked down into the street where a large crowd had gathered. There were three German soldiers with snarling dogs, and there was an elderly man lying in the middle of the street. The Germans were kicking him with their boots and calling him bad names as the dogs snapped at him and tore at his clothes as he tried to cover his head with his arms, but the Germans just kept kicking him until he stopped struggling. When he lay still, two of the soldiers picked him up under his arms and dragged him through the crowd with his bare feet leaving two bloody trails behind him. He was moaning, so I knew he was still alive, and later, when my mother asked someone what he had done to deserve such treatment, they said he had stolen a beet from one of the street vendors and tried to run away. That was his punishment for stealing just one beet. Can you even begin to imagine that?

Before the Germans had invaded our country, Uncle Addam had been a very important lawyer within the community, and people came from all over to seek his advice. He had a wonderful office in an impressive building, and several dozen people worked for him there. After the invasion, he wasn't able to practice law anymore, and he had to close his office and let his people go. I know it pained him as I could see it in his eyes when he talked about it, and although people still knocked at his apartment door and asked for help, the only thing they could offer in payment was some jewelry or things to eat. Uncle Addam said it was difficult to take anything from them as he knew they, like us, were suffering, but he also knew he had to take care of his family and us, too. Over time, the knocks on the door became fewer and fewer until they stopped altogether.

As time passed, the crowds on the street below also thinned as there just weren't as many people as usual. The mood in the neighbourhood had turned dark and foreboding like the storm clouds that occasionally formed in the sky near our farm right before the wind, rain, and sometimes hail crashed down on us. Even the mood in Uncle Addam's apartment grew dark and somber, too, and after Aaron stopped playing the piano, someone had removed the metronome and put it away. My father said its ticking reminded everyone that time was growing short and like the others, we would have to leave soon, however nobody realised how soon it would be.

## A Horrible Day

July 14th 1942, began as a beautiful day. At 8:00 AM, it was already hot and humid, but there was something in the air that didn't feel quite right. Maybe it was because it was so peaceful, and even the birds in the trees along the street had stopped their chattering. A silence, an ominous silence, hung over the neighbourhood. It must have awakened my father because as soon as he woke up, he walked out onto the balcony overlooking the street, and looked up and down the street trying to determine why it was so quiet.

All of a sudden he turned, ran back into the apartment, and rushed to Uncle Addam and Aunt Ania's closed bedroom door. When he got there he knocked loudly and within moments I heard Uncle Addam's irritated voice ask what he wanted, and my father yelled, "Addam! Quick. Get dressed and come out onto the balcony with me."

It didn't take long for him to come running out of the bedroom, shirtless and fastening the top of his trousers, and they both ran out onto the balcony. The commotion had awakened us children, and we wanted to see what was happening, but they sternly warned not to come out onto the balcony. Although we were all curious, the tone of their voices kept us in our places.

As we sat there frightened, we could hear the distant sound of many trucks coming down the street, and they growled like savage animals; I don't think I've ever been as frightened as I was then. I was even more frightened than I had been when the Germans came through our village and burned our farm down.

The truck's brakes squealed as they pulled up in front of our apartment, and the only other time I had ever heard anything like that was when old Mr. Szydło had strung up a pig from a tree and slit its throat. That's the only thing I could compare the sound to; it was the sound of death.

[65]

There were lots of men outside shouting in German, and I could hear the sounds their boots made as they jumped out of the trucks and started running up and down the street. My father and Uncle Addam ran back into the apartment and told my mother and Aunt Ania to gather all the children and wait in the living room, and they tried vainly to appear calm, but the fear in their eyes gave them away.

Within minutes there was a loud banging on the apartment's front door; it was insistent and urgent. Uncle Addam calmly walked to the door and opened it. There were two enormous German soldiers standing in the hallway with rifles in their hands, and they told him that we had only five minutes to gather our things and leave the apartment. I sensed Uncle Addam wanted to resist, perhaps protest, but I'm sure he knew it would be to no avail, so he closed the door behind him and walked back into the living room. My mother and Aunt Ania started crying, but Uncle Addam said they needed to be strong, and they should try to think of everything they needed to take with us.

Aunt Ania walked up to Uncle Addam and tugged at his shirtsleeve. "No, no, Addam. They can't do this to us. This is ours; they can't take it away from us. We've worked so hard to make it our home, our sanctuary."

Uncle Addam gently put his arms around her and looked straight into her teary face. "Ania, our time here is over. Go gather our things before Satan comes back for us."

Aunt Ania and my mother left the room to pack what few belongings they could for our journey to an unknown destination. Adiya and I watched as Aunt Ania took off all her jewelry except for her gold wedding band, put the jewelry into a box, and hid it on the top shelf of her closet where she could find it when they eventually returned to the apartment. I'm sure now the treasured gold wedding ring she wore when we left the apartment wound up melted down into some gold brick along with countless other stolen wedding rings.

You don't know how many times I've relived those five minutes as I still wonder what must have gone through the adults' minds as they tried to take a lifetime's worth of memories and cram them into a small carpetbag. What would I take if someone burst into my little apartment today and told me I had five minutes to gather up my things? I know every time Meyer and I moved into smaller apartments, I agonised over everything we owned, trying to weigh how important each thing was to us. What to take and what to leave behind?

As it turned out, those carpetbags filled with a lifetime of memories wound up in a heap outside the gas chambers, or wherever they dropped them; their importance now lost to history. What would I find if, by chance, I happened upon a secret place where they had been stored ever since? What would I find as I opened each bag? Would the meaning of their contents be lost even to me? Me? Someone who had gone through those horrible times and had survived. I think I'd hold each thing in my hand trying to sense what the long-dead owner had felt when they were forced to make those hurried decisions; the same ones my mother and Aunt Ania had to make on that terrifying day. What to take and what to leave behind? To this day, I still don't know what my mother packed; what she had decided to take, and what she had decided to leave behind as her carpetbag filled with those now-unimportant decisions was probably left outside the gas chamber's doors as she held my little brother Chaim's hand and joined him in death. Maybe someday I'll find it, and then I'll know. I know the only thing I took was my doll, Alinka.

As my mother scurried about the apartment gathering up our things, I heard my father and Lev having a heated discussion in the living room. Lev said he wanted to stay behind and join the resistance that had started to grow in the ghetto; however, my father was quite adamant in telling him that once all the residents had been evacuated, the German troops would sweep through the neighbourhood and flush the resistance fighters out of their hiding places like rats out of their nests. Lev said he would rather die fighting for his freedom than to be loaded into a truck and sent to an unknown destination.

"Who put this nonsense into your head?" my father asked.

"It's not nonsense. It's the right thing to do. My friend Meyer Cohen and I have already talked to the resistance leaders, and they even have some weapons they are willing to give us," Lev insisted.

Hearing heavy footsteps in the hallway outside our apartment door and knowing our tormentors would soon be knocking on our door, my father gave Lev a quick hug. "God be with you, Son," as Lev quickly embraced my mother, Chaim, and me. He then turned and ran into the back bedroom to escape through the window just as the loud knocking on the door announced our tormentors' return, and that was the last time I ever saw my beloved brother.

Years later after I had encountered Meyer Cohen, quite by chance, he told me the last time he had seen my brother, Lev was running through the sewers beneath the city trying to escape the pursuing German troops, and only with an amazing stroke of luck was Meyer able to escape. He told me that he and Lev had come to a branch in the sewer where they had to decide which way to go. Right or left. Meyer thought they had a better chance to survive if they split up, so Lev went one way and Meyer the other; one to freedom and one to his certain death. Lev would be happy to know that Meyer and I've been together ever since that fateful day we met in Munich. Maybe now he knows, now that Meyer has gone to join him; God bless them both.

## We Begin Our Death March to Auschwitz

When Uncle Addam opened the apartment's front door, the same two German soldiers were standing there, and this time they had a very vicious dog with them that was tugging at his leash trying to bite them. "*Raus, raus. Schnell, schnell,*" they shouted. "Out, out. Quickly, quickly."

Uncle Addam shouted for everybody in the apartment to hurry and come to the front door. Aunt Ania was in their bedroom looking in the mirror, straightening her hair and her dress, and with one quick glance behind her, she walked out of the room and closed the door behind her.

Chaim was out on the balcony looking down at the commotion on the streets below watching as our nearby neighbours came streaming out of the buildings lining the street. Some were dressed as though they were going to a party while some looked as though they were still in their nightclothes as it was still quite early in the morning.

My mother was sitting on the couch, clutching her carpetbag tightly to her chest, and it was obvious that she'd been crying, but the only remnants of her tears were the wet streaks running down her cheeks. I don't think she understood what was happening; I know I didn't. It was so surreal, almost like a dream as those horrifying events slowly played out their unfolding tragedy.

My father walked over to my mother, helped her up from the couch, hugged her sweetly, and escorted her to the front door. When we had all assembled by the door, one of the soldiers stepped into the apartment and roughly pushed my father in the back with his rifle to get the family moving. Uncle Addam led the way, followed by Aunt Ania, who was holding Aaron and Adiya's hands, followed by my mother who was holding Chaim's hand. She tried to hold mine, but I wouldn't let her; I was a big girl now, and I wanted to leave the safety

[69]

of Uncle Addam's apartment with my head held high, and with dignity. Such a stubborn child, I was. If I only knew.

As we walked down the stairs, the soldier behind my father kept pushing him in the back with his rifle, shouting *"Raus, raus,"* and he kept bumping into me. I had to grab the railing to keep from falling, and I could hear the heavy sounds of footsteps above us on the stairs as the upstairs neighbours followed behind us. That, and the sound of doors slamming, people shouting, and dogs barking. You know; it's funny how our memories play tricks on us; what we remember the most and how we remember them.

What I remember most were the sounds, the noises. It was as though my sense of hearing was so finely tuned that I could hear the wings of a hummingbird from way across the street, and even now as I lie in bed and try to sleep, I close my eyes and hear those sounds playing over-and-over in my head, and no matter how hard I try to forget them, they won't go away. They won't let me forget, even though sometimes I wish I could, but then again, I need to hold onto them; the good memories and the bad memories. Someday the last survivor of The Holocaust will join the other six-million who went before them, and our voices will be silenced forever. That's why it's so important for me to tell *my* story, because I never want *my* voice to be silenced; even after I'm long gone.

When we got down to the street, the first thing I can remember is how bright the sun was, and how good it felt on my face since we hadn't been out of the apartment for quite a while because it wasn't safe. The streets were now crowded with German soldiers, snarling dogs, trucks sitting there idling and spewing forth their noxious fumes and people; *our* people. They were the friends and neighbours we saw out on the streets when the streets were friendly.

# Innocence Lost - A Childhood Stolen

The German soldiers were so unruly; they pushed and shoved us towards the waiting trucks, and one elderly gentleman who was dressed as though he was going to the opera, dropped his glasses onto the pavement. A soldier standing nearby ground them into the concrete with his hobnailed boot. "You won't need them where you're going, old man," he said in perfect Polish. Was he one of *us,* or was he one of *them*?

Finally, we were next in line to board one of the waiting trucks, and there were already many of our neighbours sitting on the crude wooden benches lining either side of the truck's open rear bed. Kind hands reached down to help us up; Aunt Ania, Adiya, Aaron, my mother, Chaim, and me. When one of the German soldiers who was helping push us up into the truck raised my mother's skirt and peeked under it, my father reached around and punched him hard on the shoulder. "Pig!" he shouted. The soldier swung around and hit my poor father in the face with his rifle butt, knocking him to the pavement, bloodying his face and knocking out two of his front teeth.

"I should kill you right now, you insolent Jew. Don't you know your place? Where do you think you are? The Promised Land? Maybe I should shoot you right now and hasten your journey," as he spat in my father's face.

My father didn't say anything; he picked himself up from the pavement with as much dignity as the occasion could muster, climbed into the truck, and sat down next to my mother. She took off her headscarf and tried to wipe the blood from his face, and it was then I realised this trip was different; this was a trip to Hell. I was just a young, uneducated, Polish peasant girl who grew up on a farm far from anything dangerous, and I couldn't even begin to imagine what was going on, and even now as I look back on it, it still puzzles me although now I know the truth.

# Innocence Lost - A Childhood Stolen

We sat in the back of the truck for the longest time waiting for the others to be loaded with their human cargo. The sun was hot, there wasn't any shade, there wasn't any water, either, and we were all uncomfortable. After what felt like hours, the long line of trucks started moving; actually, it started crawling at a tortuous pace. The truck jerked every time the driver shifted gears, and if it hadn't been such a terrifying time, it would have almost been humourous watching the truck's occupants move back and forth in unison like the chorus line at Radio City Music Hall. That endless line of trucks carrying their occupants to slaughter like the trucks that used to pass our farm loaded with cattle staring out at us with innocent looks on their faces; if cattle can have looks on their faces.

It took forever to arrive at the railway station; the same railway station where we had arrived several weeks earlier, only now the waiting train's coaches were replaced by cattle wagons, their doors slid back, their mouths wide open — waiting to devour the new arrivals.

There was such confusion as the trucks stopped with their "dying pig" brakes making that awful sound, once again. The trucks quickly disgorged their passengers and then headed back for their next load of doomed souls, and as we all stood in line next to the waiting cattle wagons, one-by-one, they rudely shoved us into the already crowded wagons until there were at least eighty people packed tightly together. By the time the wagon was fully loaded, there wasn't any place to sit, and we all stood there packed like kippers in a tin. Then they slid the doors shut and bolted them closed. I can still hear the sound they made; a rumbling sound as the door slid on its overhead tracks, a loud thud when it was firmly closed and in place, and finally a metallic sound as the bolt was snapped shut sealing the car's occupant's fate. Where were we headed? If I had known then what I know now, I should have thrown myself under the departing wagon's wheels.

# The Cattle Wagon

It took a while for my eyes to adjust to the dim light in the cattle wagon since the only light came through several, small openings near the ceiling which were covered with some kind of wire mesh. It struck me as peculiar they thought they needed to cover the openings; they were so narrow even a small child like me couldn't even begin to fit through them.

As I waited for my eyes to grow accustomed to our surroundings, I was enveloped in a sea of noises. There were people moaning, people crying, whispered conversations, and loud shouting as people banged helplessly on the wagon's rough, wooden walls. Someone nearby started screaming; a high, piercing scream that passed right through me like an electric shock and I had to cover my ears. Soon, the screaming turned into a loud gulping; a choking sound as though the poor soul couldn't catch their breath, and it reminded me of when my father and I used to fish in the small pond in our village; how the fish gasped for air as they lay dying on the nearby bank where my father had casually tossed them.

Suddenly, I felt my mother's gentle hands on my shoulder. "Be brave, Mira. Be brave."

I took her hand and squeezed it three times. Our secret little way of saying, "I love you." She squeezed mine back, and it was comforting to know that even though I was in such a terrible place, my family's love still surrounded me.

I felt the sorriest for Chaim as he stood next to me clutching our mother's dress, and he was shaking so hard I thought he might shatter and break. I know he was terrified, but there wasn't anything I could do for him. Poor sweet Chaim; he was someone who didn't have the heart to kill even the most annoying bugs that had infested our barnyard. Why would anyone even want to shatter such a soul? What had *he* done to deserve this cruel punishment?

I could hear Aniya's stifled sobs behind me, so I turned to see if there was anything I could do to comfort her. She was my best friend; someone who had brought joy and happiness into my life even under the most trying circumstances, and to see her standing there sandwiched between Uncle Addam and Aunt Ania with tears running down her face was more than I could bear. I handed my beloved Alinka to her to comfort her, she clutched her tightly to her chest, we hugged, and for a brief instant we were the only two people in the cattle wagon, and I knew the moment we touched, how much we truly meant to each other.

It took forever for the train to start moving, but finally, with two loud toots of the locomotive's whistle, our car lurched forward, knocking some people to the floor. The train made loud banging noises as each car in succession lurched forward and began its grisly journey. The noise, the confusion, the fear of the unknown; they overwhelmed me, but I had to stay strong.

I must say that the sound of the locomotive's whistle making a 'tooting' sound still haunts me as it tried to be a friendly 'toot', almost as though it needed to encourage the cattle wagons to follow it on its merry way. Sometimes when my great-grandchildren visit me, they watch a cartoon about a friendly locomotive named Thomas. Thomas has a friendly face, and he loves to toot his whistle, but I have to leave the room, and I'm sure they don't know why Grammy gets up and leaves the room; they never seem to ask anyway. Maybe they never even seem to notice. All they do is watch TV or play video games. Don't they ever have chores to do like we had to do on the farm?

The train crawled along at a dreadfully slow pace, and my father said it looked as if we were headed south; the morning sun was on the left side of the wagon, which my father said was east. My father and Uncle Addam were quite confused by the train's direction as Uncle Addam had told the family he thought we should have been heading west, towards Russia, to the countryside to settle on land the Germans had liberated from the Russians. Why, then, would we be headed south?

I can't even begin to describe the horror; what it was like to be crammed into such a small space with so many people. We had no water, no food, and nowhere to relieve ourselves. Even if they had put a bucket there for our use, we never could have made our way through the tangle of people to use it. Soon, the cattle wagon began to fill with the odor of people relieving themselves standing in place; such a disgraceful, embarrassing, dehumanising thing to endure.

After a while, I couldn't stand it any longer, and I told my mother I had to pee. She said I'd have to do what she had just done, so I stood there and peed down my leg. I wanted to cry as I felt its warm wetness trickling down my bare legs into my shoes, but my mother had told me to be brave, so I silently wept within myself. No tears, no sniffles, just a deep resolve within myself to survive at all costs. Survive to tell the world what *they* were doing to us, and if I could survive my ordeal, it would be at the expense of *their* defeat.

As the day wore on, the train stopped a couple of times out in the countryside, far away from the city, and they briefly opened the doors to let in some fresh air, but they wouldn't let anyone out of the wagons. Unruly German soldiers patrolled the path alongside the train with huge dogs who growled at the coach's occupants as they passed by.

Everyone in the wagon tried to push their way through the crowd to get near the door, and one elderly man actually fell out the wagon's door onto the ground. A nearby German soldier shouted a warning and helping hands quickly pulled him back to safety. It's funny now that I use the word *safety*. How *safe* was our wagon? Why hadn't the occupants flooded out when they opened the doors and try to run away? I'm sure many of them would have been killed, but maybe some of them could have escaped. Of course, the two times we did stop we were in the middle of open country with nowhere to hide.

Just as darkness began to envelop our cattle wagon, the train came to a noisy stop, and then it began to back up; very slowly. The locomotive tooted three notes, we came to a grinding, banging halt, and suddenly, bright lights flooded through the small windows like sunbeams, randomly illuminating one face here, and another face there; frightened faces, confused faces, and I sensed we had arrived at our destination, but where were we?

## Auschwitz

When the train finally stopped, our little family banded together; frightened souls clinging to one another, and although they didn't want to admit it, I could tell even my father and Uncle Addam were frightened as the tone of their voices when they tried to comfort us, was far from comforting.

Then I heard the sound of the cattle wagon's latch being opened, the door suddenly slid open, and the wagon was filled with a brilliant white light. It was so bright that people gasped and covered their eyes, and I was awestruck; I had never seen anything like *that* before.

# Innocence Lost - A Childhood Stolen

Our family was near the door, so we were one of the first ones out. There was a lot of shouting, dogs barking, and the peculiar and frightening huffing sound the locomotive made as it patiently waited for its human cargo to be discharged.

We all tumbled out in one tangled heap, and as we stood in line on the wooden platform trying to figure out where we were, my father and Uncle Addam reached up and helped our fellow passengers down from our filthy transport. Aunt Ania stood there like a beautiful statue even after the ordeal we had just suffered through. She was such a beautiful woman and both Aaron and Adiya still clung tightly to her dress, while my mother just stood there looking dazed and confused with Chaim's face buried in her skirts.

I watched in amazement as an endless mass of people tumbled out of the nearby cattle wagons. I don't know what other word to use other than *tumble;* it certainly wasn't an orderly exit as some people fell to the ground on top of others, some jumped down to the platform, and some were helped down by the other passengers. There was such confusion and the noise was overwhelming. I'd be lying if I didn't say I was terrified; I was.

I had once overheard my father and Uncle Addam talking about how the Germans were resettling the Jews or sending them to work camps, but they never talked about it to us children, and all I knew was that I was caught up in something I had no control over. I was like a leaf floating down a river at the mercy of the wind and the current with no control over my destination, and it's something no person should ever have to endure.

Most of the passengers were carrying small bags filled with their meager possessions, and my mother and Aunt Ania still clung to the carpetbags they had packed in the five minutes we had before evacuating Uncle Addam's apartment. The soldiers standing outside the cattle wagons shouted at us and told us to leave all our possessions behind, and when everyone had been rudely dragged out onto the crude wooden platform, a horde of emaciated skeletons dressed in ragged, black-and-white striped *pyjamas* descended on the foul-smelling wagons, climbed inside, and roughly threw the abandoned carpetbags filled with now meaningless memories down into waiting, horse-drawn carts to soon disappear along with their owners.

Mean-looking German soldiers patrolled up and down the growing line of frightened souls. There was a yellow line painted down the entire length of the platform and if someone stepped over that line, a soldier would run up and roughly push them back into the crowd, often knocking others standing nearby to the ground.

After my eyes had adjusted to the brilliant light, I could see we were standing on a long, wooden platform, and the light was coming from big spotlights mounted on tall poles lining it, and there was a tall fence with rolls of barbed wire strung along the top separating us from the buildings silhouetted on the horizon.

I felt as though we were in a long tunnel; the cattle wagons on one side, the fence on the other, the dark sky our ceiling and only one way to move; forward. It was all so confusing as German soldiers walked through the crowd and separated the men into one line and the women and children into another. Elderly men were forced to join the women's line. I was just a child; not much more than a metre tall and most everyone around me was much taller. In a way, it made me feel safe, practically invisible, and then the line started moving. Slowly. We shuffled our feet, rather than walking.

I made my way to the outside of the shuffling crowd next to the yellow line that defined our little, crowded world, and I tried to look towards the front of the line to see where we were headed, but all I could see was a line of people that stretched forever. I clutched Alinka tightly, her face to my chest as I didn't want her to witness what *I* was seeing; I had promised to protect her, no matter what. My mother held both Chaim's hand and mine, and Aunt Ania clung tightly to Aniya's and Aaron's. My mother clutched my hand so tightly I could feel her thin wedding ring dig into the flesh of my hand.

I felt sorry for my father and Uncle Addam who were in a long line of men standing across from us. My father still had my mother's silk headscarf tied around his head covering the large, bloody lump that had swelled up after the soldier had hit him in the mouth with his rifle butt. The headscarf was covered with his blood, and it was filthy after the ride in the cattle wagon. However, he never showed his pain; he stood proudly, his arm around Uncle Addam's shoulders, and I must say that I don't think I've ever been any prouder of my father than I was that day. He was bigger than anything nearby; bigger than the entire world in my eyes.

As we got closer to the front of the slowly moving line, I began hearing loud voices, and they were speaking in German. "*Sie. Auf diese Weise. Rechts. Sie. Auf diese Weise. Links. Schnell jetzt.*"

"You. This way, to the right. You. That way, to the left. Quickly now." A loud Polish voice shouted above their German, "*Lewa, prawa,*" *(Right, Left)* to direct them on their way.

There were several uniformed soldiers standing at the front of each line and when my father got to the head of the line, one of the soldiers said, "What have we here? Looks as though someone has tangled with a bear," as he roughly pushed my father towards the line of women, children, and elderly men on the left who were quickly disappearing into the dark unknown. He glanced back, blew me a kiss, and mouthed the words, "I love you," and that was the last time I saw him while Uncle Addam joined the line of men who were headed off to the right.

When Aunt Ania and my cousins got to the front of the line, the soldier took his rifle and without saying a word, steered them in the direction my father had just taken. Aaron broke free from his mother's grip, ran forward to my father, grabbed his hand, and unknowingly walked with him to their deaths. Of course, I didn't know that at the moment; I thought they were just going to get cleaned up.

Just as my mother, Chaim, and I got to the front of the line, one of the nearby dogs ran up and tried to snatch Alinka from my arms. He probably thought it was a toy and he was just being playful, so I screamed at him and held her as tightly as I could, but he viciously tore off one of her arms and ran back to his waiting master. I was horrified! Enough was enough. After all I had been through the past few days, everything came flooding to the surface, and I began to cry as I had never cried before. While I was rescuing Alinka from the dog, a soldier had roughly grabbed my mother's arm and forcefully pushed her towards the receding line of women and children.

Before I could react, I felt a firm hand on my shoulder, and then a nice looking man who was dressed differently than the others, kneeled down beside me. "What seems to be the problem, young lady?" he asked in Polish.

"The dog tore off my doll's arm," I said through my sobs.

"I'm a doctor. Why don't you let me fix her for you?"

"No. I want to go with my mother and brother," as I tried to tear away from his grip, and I was so terrified that I wet my already soiled underpants.

[80]

He grasped my shoulder much tighter. "No. You stay here. You can join them later," as he slowly got up, pulled me protectively to his side and continued his role in sorting the arriving passengers.

I stared towards the retreating line of women and children looking for my family, when all of a sudden, a small boy stepped out of the line, turned around, and waved at me; it was my dear brother, Chaim. He waved both his arms above his head and smiled, and I could even see his smile from where I was standing. Then a soldier roughly pushed him back into line and that was the last time I saw him, however that picture of him is frozen in my memory; his wave, his smile. He was such a dear, sweet, innocent boy.

It didn't take long for the lines of arriving passengers to be sorted and sent off in two different directions and before I knew it, everyone had disappeared into the dark night. When all its passengers had departed, the little locomotive 'tooted' its whistle, and the train slowly started pulling away as I watched the red light on the rear of the last car disappear into the gloom. Then one by one, the bright spotlights on top the poles started shutting off and the only illumination left was from the ever-present yellow lights that surrounded the camp.

Sometimes when I'm with friends they ask me what it was like to arrive at Auschwitz, and I'm not sure they realise what a sensitive nerve they have just struck. Sometimes when I lie in bed and close my eyes I mostly remember the noises; the sound the locomotive made as it obediently stood there making that peculiar and frightening huffing sound as though the labour of pulling the cattle wagons had totally exhausted it, the sound the cattle wagons' doors made as they slid open and the clanking sounds they made when they finally came to rest, the sounds of loud voices in many languages, the sound of dogs barking and people screaming as they yelled out loved ones' names in the confusion. It was awful, just awful!

The stench; the overpowering smell of urine and human feces spilling out from the cattle wagons' open doors, the smell of fear as it clung to the cattle wagons' occupants as *they* tumbled out into the unknown, the sweet odor of death from the other side of the barbed wire fence, and a very peculiar, smoky odor, almost like meat cooking coming from somewhere behind the distant buildings.

So you ask, what was it like to arrive at Auschwitz? I can only think of three phrases to describe it: *mass confusion, amazing efficiency,* and then *deathly quiet.*

Then my protector took my hand. (I later learned his name was Doktor Mueller.) "Let's go see what we can do to make your doll get better," as we started to walk away, and when we turned, something caught my eye. After the bright spotlights had been turned off, the sky had become dark, threatening, and ominous, and then I saw *them.* Two glowing, red, sinister, smouldering lights on the horizon; *Dem ruekhs oygn (The Devil's Eyes).*

## The Selection 'Process'

To this day, I can only suspect why Doktor Mueller chose *me. Me.* Of the thousands, no, tens of thousands of innocent children who paraded past him on their way to the gas chambers, he chose *me.* Perhaps it was just an accident, perhaps he didn't intend to choose me after all; perhaps when the dog attacked my doll it touched something inside him and made me a human, a real person instead of just another faceless face in an endless stream of anonymous, faceless faces; faces only familiar to those who loved and cherished them, but faceless to their tormentors. Maybe he thought if he saved just one soul, God would consider that on Judgment Day. He eventually explained why he took me out of the selection line, and although his

[82]

explanation hurt me deeply, I'd like to think he was just angry at the world, and he took it out on me. I'll never truly know why, now that he's gone.

All I know is that sometimes I feel so terribly guilty that I was the only person in my family to survive. Why? God has yet to reveal his special plans for me and maybe he never will. Perhaps, I'll meet Him someday, and then I'll hear His answer, face-to-face.

After the train had left, the terrified passengers continued on their journeys to their own personal fates and after all the bright lights had been extinguished, Doktor Mueller took my hand and led me through the tall gates guarded by armed soldiers and their fierce dogs. As we walked away from the camp towards his nearby house outside the tall, wire fences, I wanted to be with my family, and I felt left out, abandoned, and alone. I was certain they would soon be on their way to their new homes out in the country and more than anything else, I wanted to be with them. It was only much later that I learned that he was a Schutzstaffel (SS) doctor, one of many stationed at the camp who chose those who lived and those who died with a simple wave of their hand as soon as the new arrivals had left the cattle wagons and gotten into line.

As we walked away from the camp, I was surprised to see how different our surroundings were from where we had just been as we walked through a tidy neighbourhood full of small wooden houses set up off the ground on concrete blocks. Each house appeared friendly with its warm lights shining from their front windows, and it looked like a nice neighbourhood, or at least it was an attempt to appear so. I later learned this was the neighbourhood where the camp officers and their families lived, and many of them were the doctors who were responsible for what I later learned was called the *'Selection Process'*.

However, this was all new to me, as I held the stranger's hand and walked down the dirt street with him.

Soon, we came to a tidy house with flower boxes filled with red flowers that filled the night air with a wonderful fragrance, and they reminded me of the warm, sunny days I used to spend playing in the fields near our farm back in Poland. Those fields were filled with wildflowers full of colourful butterflies flitting from tempting blossom to tempting blossom as though they couldn't make up their minds. However, I wasn't back on the farm now, I was in a strange place about to walk into a strange house with a total stranger, and I suppose I should have been frightened, but for some strange reason, I wasn't. The word *strange* has so many meanings, doesn't it?

The house windows gave off a warm glow, a comforting glow, and it made me feel safe after all the terrible things I had just endured, and as we walked up the three stairs to the front porch, Doktor Mueller held my hand, and I clutched Alinka tightly to my chest. I can still remember my first impressions when he opened the front door and we stepped inside, and all I can say is that it was very white. Maybe that's the wrong word to use, but that was my first impression. White. Maybe I should just say that it wasn't colourful, it was quite antiseptic; bright, but cheerless like a hospital waiting room.

The living room was sparse; just a couch, two chairs, a lamp and a small table, almost as though nobody actually lived there. Doktor Mueller told me to sit and wait in one of the chairs while he went and talked to his wife, and then he turned, opened the door behind him, stepped through it, and closed it. Within moments, I heard a loud argument from behind the closed door, and it was obvious his wife was terribly upset about something, but I didn't know enough German to understand what they were saying. The only word I understood was *Nein (No)*, repeatedly.

In a few moments, Doktor Mueller came back through the door; his face was flushed and red and it was obvious he was quite upset. "My wife doesn't want you to stay here," was all he said.

I was confused; I thought that we were only coming here to fix Alinka's arm, so why did he think that I wanted to stay here? I wanted to be with my family; not stay here.

He walked over to my chair, took my hand, led me to the nearby couch, and I sat down next to him, my skinny legs not quite reaching the floor. "You have to forgive my wife," he apologised. "She just isn't quite herself since we lost Anna. Give her time."

*Time for what?* I thought. It didn't make any sense to me at all. In fact, nothing had made sense ever since the soldiers forced us to leave our farm and flee to Łódź.

We sat there for the longest time without saying a word. Just the three of us; Doktor Mueller, Alinka and me. After a while, the door slowly opened, and Frau Mueller slowly walked into the room. Forgive me for being judgmental, but first impressions are always the most important ones, and this was my first impression of Frau Mueller. What I noticed first was her hair. It was done up in braids, and they were coiled up on top of her head, and it reminded me of a giant snake coiled up, ready to strike. Her eyes were red, and it was obvious she had been crying. She was wearing a smock, a plain and simple outfit, and she wore brown, low-heeled, lace-up shoes, and if I hadn't known better, I would have taken her for a peasant woman.

She walked over in front of the couch and just stood there wringing her hands, looking down at the two of us, and without saying a word, tears began streaming down her face. Doktor Mueller did nothing to comfort her. Instead, he just sat there and said, "*Jah! (Yes),*" very sternly. Frau Mueller reached down, took my hand, said "*Kommen Sie! (Come),*" and led me out of the room.

[85]

## Sanctuary – Doktor Mueller's House

Frau Mueller led me out of the living room, through a small kitchen and into a back room which obviously served as some kind of utility room where they stored things and perhaps did their laundry. She dragged a large, round metal tub from next to the wall and placed it in the middle of the utility room. *"Sich ausziehen! (Get undressed),"* she said in a stern, commanding, voice. I just stood there, frozen as I didn't understand German, and I had never heard a word like that in Yiddish. *"Sich ausziehen!"* once again, but I still didn't understand what she wanted me to do.

Finally, she reached down and began unbuttoning the front of my dress. Now it was obvious that she wanted me to get undressed, but I was reluctant as I didn't know what she was going to do to me. *"Sich ausziehen, bitte,"* she repeated in a kindlier voice, quite unlike the voice she had used before. I began to undress as I thought I may have detected the beginning of a slight smile on her stern face although there was nothing warm and comforting about her. Nothing about her made me want to snuggle up next to her like I used to do with my mother.

When I had finally undressed and dropped my filthy clothes in a heap on the floor, she gingerly picked them up as though she didn't want to touch them; *"Müll (Trash),"* as she dropped them into a nearby ashcan.

*"Warten Sie hier (Wait here),"* and she left the room. Within a few moments, she returned with a tin bucket full of water. *"In der Wanne! (In the tub),"* she commanded as she pointed at the tub and as I gingerly stepped in, she immediately poured the bucket of water over my head. I shrieked; the water was icy cold. Then she reached over, picked up a rag and a bar of brown, laundry soap, and started scrubbing me from head to toe, but it wasn't a gentle scrubbing; it

[86]

was an angry scrubbing and it hurt. When she had finished, she took the bucket, left the room, and returned with another bucket of cold water that she once again dumped over my head.

Then she picked up a nearby, coarse towel and with angry strokes she began to dry me off, however it was too much, and I started to cry. If she had been my mother, she would have put her arms around me and comforted me, but Frau Mueller just kept on methodically drying me without saying a word.

When she had finished, she wrapped the towel around me and led me out of the room where Doktor Mueller was sitting at the kitchen table drinking something out of a tall glass. *"Es ist geschafft (It's done),"* as she led me down a short hallway and opened a door; a door decorated with colourful ribbons that lent much needed contrast to its drab surroundings. When she opened the door, it was as though we had stepped into a fairy princess' castle. It was beautiful; the bright colours, the dainty furniture, a lovely rug, and rose-coloured curtains hanging loosely in the windows; I was overwhelmed.

I immediately noticed a small desk set against one wall with many framed photographs of a young girl sitting on it. As soon as we walked into the room, Frau Mueller hastily walked over, picked each photograph up, put it into a drawer, and then walked over to what was obviously a closet door. When she opened it, I was amazed at how many beautiful clothes hung there. I had never seen so many clothes in my life; even when we had shopped in the clothing store in Łódź, I hadn't seen such a marvelous collection. The clothes were carefully arranged by type and colour starting with dresses on the left, followed by skirts, smocks, blouses, and jackets. It almost appeared as though someone had gone through the closet and had carefully measured the distance between each hanger and they reminded me of soldiers lined up neatly in a row.

[87]

Frau Mueller reached into the closet, took down a plain, muslin smock. *"Legen Sie es auf (Put it on),"* as she held it out to me. I turned my back, unwrapped the towel, and pulled the smock up over my head. It was clean, and it was such a welcome change after having to wear my same filthy clothes for days on end without changing them, especially after I had to wet my underpants in the cattle wagon.

When I turned around for her inspection, I expected her to soften and smile, but she didn't, instead she took my hand and led me over to a small bed covered with a beautiful patchwork quilt that was pushed up against the wall. She pulled the quilt down, neatly folded it at the foot of the bed, pointed at the bed, and I climbed in. The bed was so soft; it was as though I was floating on a cloud and I practically forgot where I was and what had happened to my family and me over the past few days. I was sure Doktor Mueller would patch up Alinka the next day, take me back to the resettlement camp, and reunite me with my family before we left for our new farm somewhere in Russia, and I hoped Frau Mueller would let me wear some of the beautiful clothes in the closet. Wouldn't my mother be proud when she next saw me!

Without saying a word, Frau Mueller picked the towel up from the floor, turned, walked out of the room, and for the first time in a long time I was alone. Alone, lying in a beautiful bed in a beautiful bedroom.

I had just started dozing off to sleep when the door quietly opened and Doktor Mueller walked into the room. *"Śpisz? (Are you sleeping?)"* he asked. I assured him I wasn't sleeping; I was just resting my eyes as he sat down on the side of my bed. "Did you forget something?" he asked as he brought Alinka out from behind his back where he had been hiding her and gently tucked her into my arms.

[88]

When I checked to see if he had mended her arm, "*Jutro* (*Tomorrow*)," he said in Polish.

He sat there on the side of the bed for the longest time without saying anything; he just stared out the window with a faraway look in his eyes as though he was seeing something that wasn't there. After a while, he patted me on the top of my head, with a terse "Good night," as he left the room.

In the middle of the night, I was suddenly awakened by the shrill whistle of the locomotive far off in the distance and it wasn't friendly this time, it was terrifying. Then I heard dogs barking, loud muffled voices, and bright lights came beaming through my drawn curtains; then deathly silence and it was something that repeated over and over again in the coming months. Where was I?

## A New Home

When I awoke the next morning, it took me a while to figure out where I was, and then I heard the locomotive's now shrill-sounding whistle, and I was suddenly yanked back into reality. I swung my legs over the side of the bed as I rubbed the sleep from my eyes and strained to listen for any sounds from the adjoining rooms, but my interest was only met with silence.

Soon, my curiosity got the better of me, and I wanted to know who the little girl in the photographs was, the ones Frau Mueller had hastily swept off the nearby desk. So, I walked over to the desk and opened the drawer where she had hidden them, took them out of the drawer, carefully studied each one, and I was immediately struck by how much she looked like me; she even had dark hair like me. In one photograph she was sitting on the ground in what looked like a park with a big dog sitting next to her and she had her arms around the dog in a loving way. Another photograph was of her, Doktor Mueller and Frau Mueller which had obviously been taken at some sort of celebration since Doktor Mueller was dressed in traditional *lederhosen* holding a beer stein in one hand, and Frau Mueller was dressed in a beautiful *dirndl;* a bodice, a blouse, a full skirt and an apron. It was much like the outfit that Julie Andrews wore in *The Sound of Music's* opening scene, and the little girl in the photograph was dressed just like her mother. It was such a happy scene. Was this her room, and was I sleeping in her bed? If so, I hoped I would meet her someday.

I carefully placed the photographs back in the desk drawer and walked down to the kitchen where I had seen Doktor Mueller sitting at the table the previous night. Frau Mueller was standing at the kitchen sink with her back turned to me, and when she heard me walk into the room, she quickly turned from what she was doing and let out a loud gasp as though I had startled her.

She then pointed at a chair next to the table, *"Sitzen Sie! (Sit),"* in a frosty voice. When I pulled the chair away from the kitchen table, it made a loud scraping sound on the floor, and Frau Mueller just stood there and frowned; it was as though there wasn't anything I could do to please her. What had I done to make her feel this way about me?

She walked over to the cupboard, took out a plate, put some bread, a slice of cheese and a small piece of ham on it, and placed it in front of me, and it was the first time I had a chance to eat anything since we had left Uncle Addam's apartment in Warsaw a few days earlier. I was famished, but I waited for Frau Mueller's permission to eat, as my mother had taught me to be polite when I was sitting at someone else's table. Frau Mueller looked at me, raised her eyebrows in a quizzical way. *"Essen Sie! (Eat),"* she commanded, and as hard as

I tried to take little bites and enjoy my breakfast, it quickly disappeared right before my eyes.

That appeared to please Frau Mueller. *"Mehr? (More?)"* she asked as I nodded my head and she got up from the table and refilled my plate. Although German was a new language to me, it seemed simple enough. *"Sitzen,"* sit, *"Essen"*, eat, *"Mehr"*, more, *"Warten,"* wait. I already knew enough of the language to be able to sit, eat, ask for more, and patiently wait until the plate was placed in front of me.

After I had finished my second breakfast serving, Frau Mueller got up from the table, walked over and took my hand, and it was obvious she wanted me to follow her as she led me back to the bedroom. When we got to the bedroom, Frau Mueller started opening drawers and closet doors in a frenzy of activity as though she was looking for something she couldn't quite put her hands on. Finally, she had assembled a complete outfit; underclothing, blouse, skirt and a pretty pair of black shoes, which she held out to me and it was obvious she wanted me to get dressed. So, I took off my muslin nightshirt and held it out in my hands in an attempt to have her show me where to put it, and she sternly pointed at a drawer in the bureau. I carefully folded it and placed it neatly on top of the other clothes in the drawer, and with a quick nod of her head she signaled her apparent approval.

I followed her out of the bedroom and back into the kitchen. When we got there, she went into the utility room and returned with a broom in her hand. *"Fegen Sie! (Sweep),"* as she handed the broom to me. I walked over into the corner of the kitchen with Frau Mueller closely following behind, and I started sweeping the floor. Occasionally she'd tap me on the shoulder and point to a speck of dirt I had obviously overlooked and although the floor appeared spotless to me, Frau Mueller must have had microscopes for eyes as she carefully directed my attention to the minutest bits of dust. When I had neatly swept the entire kitchen floor into one small pile, she walked back into the utility room and returned with a metal dustpan. After I had swept the tiny pile of dirt into the dustpan, she took me by the arm, led me back into the utility room, and pointed at the ashcan where she wanted me to deposit my little hard-won treasure. Believe it or not, we did every room in the house the same way.

When I walked into their bedroom to sweep, the first thing that caught my eye was a large picture hung over their bed, and it was a photograph of Adolf Hitler, if I may say his name, standing on a podium before a large crowd assembled below. It was obvious he was giving a speech, and he had his right arm extended in a salute that I would witness all too often in the future. Like the other rooms in the small house, it was quite sparse with few comfort items.

After we had swept the entire house, she led me outside and showed me how to water the flowers. It was a beautiful April day, the sun was shining, and we could have been most anywhere in any neighbourhood except for the tall barbed wire fence at the end of the dirt road with the tall wooden gates guarded by soldiers and their ever-alert dogs. This was the first time I had been outside since I arrived so I took time to notice my surroundings. On the other side of the tall fence I could see many buildings, most were two or three stories tall, and they stretched as far as I could see. Off in the distance I could see people milling about, but they were too far away so I couldn't see them very well. However, it was a very peculiar place, menacingly ominous, and on the horizon, I could see two columns of greasy, black smoke rising from behind the buildings.

When we had finished watering the plants and had picked off the dead leaves, we went back into the house where the rest of the day was spent doing meaningless little chores. The more I observed Frau

Mueller, the more it appeared as though she had a daily routine that probably didn't vary much from day-to-day, however I *did* learn quite quickly, that like Doktor Mueller, there was only one way to do things; *her* way.

When Doktor Mueller came home at the end of the day, he walked through the front door and went directly to the kitchen sink without touching anything. I peeked into the kitchen from where I was sitting and watched him remove the pair of grey, calfskin gloves he always wore, and then he painstakingly scrubbed his delicate hands with a stiff brush and a bar of brown, laundry soap. Several times, he held them up to make sure he hadn't missed anything, and it was as though he had touched something dirty that required his immediate attention once he got home, and he repeated this ritual *every* time he came home from work.

After he had dried his hands, he returned to the living room, gave Frau Mueller a quick embrace, a small peck on the cheek in passing, and walked over to where I was sitting on the couch. Before I continue, I'd like to describe how handsome he was. There wasn't a spot on his neatly pressed uniform jacket proudly displaying an Iron Cross and cinched tightly with a black leather belt. My, he was so handsome. He was rather tall, perhaps more than two-metres, thin but not skinny, with beautiful, dark black hair which he combed straight back from his forehead. Perhaps he combed it that way because he didn't want it to overshadow his fine, aquiline features. From time-to-time, I would catch him looking in the mirror and smoothing his hair, and I don't know why he was so fixated with his hair, because once he had every hair in place, he would then put his SS cap on top of it. The skull-and-crossbones emblem on his SS cap terrified me and I wished he wouldn't wear it, and perhaps Frau

Mueller felt the same as I did as she refused to allow him to wear it in the house.

He sat down next to me and asked me how my day had been as if I were his child, and he had just come home from the office. I told him I wanted to be with my family, and suddenly he got very serious. What he told me next sent shivers through my entire body.

## Doktor Mueller Formulates a Plan

Doktor Mueller moved closer to me on the couch and took my hand with his long, delicate fingers closed tightly around mine. "I've been thinking," he said. "I'm sure by now your family is on a train bound somewhere for a beautiful new farm in Russia, and we'll just have to wait until they get there and let us know where they are before I can put you on a train to rejoin them."

I was crushed! On a train bound for Russia? A train now speeding away from here taking them far away? How could they have abandoned me; left me behind in this awful place, and suddenly I felt alone, terribly frightened, and I began to cry.

"Why are you crying?" he asked.

Through my sobs, "I want to be with my family."

He pulled me closer and put his arm around me. "Mira. I don't think that's possible right now. Don't you like it here?" he asked.

I didn't know how to answer his question truthfully. Although I felt much safer sitting here in a comfortable house than I would have been on a train bound for an unknown destination, at least I would have been with my family.

"I *do* like it here and you've been very good to me, but I miss my family."

[94]

He squeezed my hand more tightly, "I want you to be with your family, too, and I think I have a plan that might make that happen sooner than you think."

That was welcome news. At least we'd have a plan; something to work towards and I sat there eagerly waiting to hear his plan. It took him quite a while to compose his thoughts, and as I stared out the front window, once again, the bright spotlights suddenly illuminated the night sky. Another train had just arrived.

"Do you want to hear my plan?" he asked.

"Oh, yes," I eagerly replied.

"Well, you have to listen carefully and you have to do everything I say."

"Of course I will. Please tell me your plan."

Doktor Mueller then began unveiling his plan as I sat by his side. "Mira, it's not safe to send you back to the resettlement camp by yourself. I'm sure you'd get lost, and you might never get to see your family again. You wouldn't want that, would you?" he asked.

"No, Doktor Mueller, I wouldn't."

"Do you like to play games, Mira?" he asked. Although I thought that was a strange question, I told him that I loved to play games, especially with my little brother, Chaim.

"So, let's play a game. Do you like to play make-believe games?"

"That sounds like fun," now that I had stopped crying.

Doktor Mueller then said something like this, although I might not be able to repeat it word-for-word, but to paraphrase it, "From now on we won't speak another word of Polish in this house because we're going to pretend that you're a young, German girl who is visiting us from the big city. From now on, you'll only speak German, think German, dream German, and act German. Can you do that for me?" as he patiently awaited my answer.

I just nodded my head as I didn't know how to respond.

"I know it will be hard for you at first, but I'll teach you how to speak and write German. It's not that difficult, you know, and I can bring books home which we can read together. I'll be your teacher, and I want you to practice your writing in a little scrapbook I'll bring home from work tomorrow. Every day I want you to write something down in German; something about what you did that day, and we'll go over it when I get home from work."

That sounded exciting to me because I never had any formal schooling back in Poland; the only way I had learned to read and write Polish and Hebrew was when my father sat down and taught me back in our village, and I truly enjoyed learning, especially new languages, so I welcomed his suggestion right from the beginning.

"Only one problem," he continued. "Your name. It sounds too Polish, too Jewish. If you're going to be a German princess, you need to have a German princess name. If we ever had another daughter, I wanted to name her Bernadette. Do you like that name?" he asked.

I thought Mira was a nice name and I didn't know why was it too Polish or too Jewish, so I just sat there and didn't answer right away. His plan sounded like a lot of work; a lot to remember, and now I had to remember a new name too? After a while I guessed that Bernadette would do if I had to have another name. "Bernadette Kabliski," I finally said aloud.

"No! Bernadette Schneider. That sounds more German. I had a friend named Schneider who had a daughter named Bernadette. I heard he was killed somewhere in Russia, and I don't know where his family is right now. So, if anybody asks me, I'll tell them you're his daughter, and we've brought you here for your safety."

That was a lot to remember, but now I realised I wasn't going to join my family any time soon and I had plenty of time to become

Bernadette Schneider. If I couldn't do it for myself, I'd do it for my new protector, Doktor Mueller.

## Doktor Mueller's Plan Unfolds

I was so excited about Doktor Mueller's plan that I could hardly wait for him to get home from work the next day. As promised, he brought me a little notebook and a brand new pencil. Of course, he had to wash his hands before he led me to the couch, sat me down, and taught me my first German lesson.

He handed me the notebook and the pencil, "Open the book and write what I tell you."

I eagerly accepted his wonderful gift, opened the book, and with pencil in hand, eagerly waited for my first lesson.

"Now," he said. "Write *Mein Name ist Bernadette Schneider (My name is Bernadette Schneider)*. Shall I spell it for you?"

"No, Doktor Mueller. I'd like to try it myself," and although I misspelled the word *Mein*, he corrected me, and patted me lovingly on my head.

After I had written my first German sentence, he told me to wait, and he rose from the couch and left the room. Within a couple of moments, he returned with a picture book in his hand, and it was only later I learned that he had hidden all Anna's books high on a back shelf in the utility room.

It was a beautiful book and it had a picture of kittens playing with a ball of yarn adorning its shiny cover. The title of the book was *Mein erstes Buch*, "My First Book" as I later discovered. The letters were written in a beautiful old German script, and they literally jumped off the page at me, and I was going to learn to read German! It's funny how clearly I remember that book, even after all these years.

Doktor Mueller opened the book to the first page to a picture of a black cat. He covered up the German caption with his hand. "What do you think this is?" he asked. "*Kot (Cat),*" I replied.

Doktor Mueller frowned, "Not Polish, German." I didn't know what to say, so I just shrugged my shoulders. "Do you want to guess?" he asked.

"No."

"*Eine Katze (A cat),*" and so started my interesting journey on my transformation from a Polish peasant girl into a German princess.

From then on, Doktor Mueller was a very kind and gentle man; extremely patient with me in a very loving way, and he never criticised me, he was always making sure to offer encouragement when I needed it. If I made a mistake, he would always correct me in a way that made me want to do better, not go off into some corner and sulk.

Don't get me wrong. I truly loved my father, but Doktor Mueller was the kind of man that any young girl would want for a father, and I came to love him like a father although it was only years later when I began to understand this uniquely complex and conflicted man that I began to have serious doubts about him, and who he really was.

After he went to work the next day, and after I had helped Frau Mueller with her endless little household chores, I got the picture book from my nightstand where Doktor Mueller had lovingly placed it the night before. I spent all afternoon studying the pictures and learning all the animals' German names, and when he arrived home and sanitised his hands, I led him to the couch where my first book was waiting for us. I picked the book up, opened the first page, covered the German word with my hand, and exclaimed, "*Eine Katze*". Then doing the same with the remaining pages, "*Ein Hund (A dog), Ein Pferd (A horse), Eine Kuh (A cow), Ein Schwein (A pig),*

*Ein Huhn (A chicken), Ein Schaf (A sheep), Eine Ziege (A goat),*" but I just couldn't remember the German word for rooster. Doktor Mueller took my hand away from the page revealing "*Ein Hahn*".

"Very good," he said. "Now get out your notebook and pencil, and let's write today's entry," as I ran back into my bedroom, retrieved the notebook and pencil, and rejoined Doktor Mueller on the couch. I sat there, pencil in hand, eagerly awaiting his next instruction.

"Now tell me Bernadette. What did you do today?"

"Well, I helped Frau Mueller sweep the house, water the flowers, hang out the laundry, and make the beds," hoping that was what he wanted to hear.

"You do that every day," he said, frowning. "Didn't you do something special today?"

I just shrugged my shoulders as I didn't know what he wanted me to say. "Okay. I'll help you. Write this down. *Heute las ich mein erstes Buch,*" as I wrote what he had told me, but he did have to help spell a couple of the words. "Now. Can you read what you just wrote?"

I was already familiar with *Mein Erstes Buch* since that was the name of the book. "My first book?"

"Yes, that's part of it, but what did you do today with your first book?"

"I read it," I shouted, bouncing up and down on the couch; I was so happy with myself.

"And when did you read your first book?"

"Last night?"

Doktor Mueller just laughed. "You didn't tell me that, Bernadette," he joked. "Rather than erase what you just wrote, let's pretend that you read it, when?"

"Today?"

"Good. So let's go through what you just wrote. *Heute* - today; *las ich* - I read. Now you finish it."

"Today I read my first book."

Learning German was going to be a snap, or so I thought until I realised that I had thousands of new words to learn as well as learning to navigate the complicated sentence structure the German language demanded. Anyway, it was a good start.

After we had finished our reading lesson, Frau Mueller walked into the room. *"Abendessen (Dinner)"*, delivered in a dry, emotionless tone, as we all walked into the kitchen for our evening meal.

To this day, I don't think I ever figured out Frau Mueller and why she acted the way she did towards Doktor Mueller and me. He once had confided that she hadn't always been that way, instead, she used to be a very happy, fun-loving person; warm, loving, gentle, and quite caring. It wasn't until after 'the incident' that she seemed to lose herself, but Doktor Mueller wasn't ready talk about it, yet. Since she and I were never close, it really didn't matter to me; I was just happy to be safe, warm, and quickly becoming a German princess.

## Doktor Mueller's Plan Begins to Unravel

The days slipped by in monotonous regularity, day after day as the Mueller household ran like a well-oiled machine without any frivolity or joy. The only joy in my day was when Doktor Mueller came home from work and spent time with me, and he even began coming into my bedroom at night and reading stories to me, in German, of course. Other than that, there wasn't any excitement in the Mueller household until the night we had an unexpected visitor.

One evening, just as we were about to sit down to our meal, there was a loud knock at the door, and Doktor Mueller got up from the couch where he was reading a book to me and answered it. I peeked around him to see whom he was greeting and I saw a man dressed in a fine uniform standing there, and he and Doktor Mueller were having a vigourous discussion. Shortly, Doktor Mueller invited the guest into our house.

My first impression of our visitor was that he was quite important, as he was impeccably dressed in a striking uniform and just the way he carried himself proclaimed his high-ranking position within the community.

Doktor Mueller walked him to over where I was sitting. "Bernadette, this is Commandant Rudolf Höss," he announced, and I froze; I didn't know what to do or what to say. What if I accidentally greeted him in Polish? However, I finally got up my nerve, *"Hallo"*, I said.

Commandant Höss just stood there and spoke to me in German as though I understood every word he was saying, but I didn't, and I patiently waited until he had finished speaking. It seemed as though perhaps he had just asked me a question, maybe he had asked how I was, so I just replied, *"Gut, danke (Good, thank you)."* With that, Commandant Höss gave Doktor Mueller a strange look, but he didn't ask me any more questions, and as the two sat down on the couch and continued their conversation, I went into the kitchen and helped Frau Mueller finish preparing our meal.

After Commandant Höss had left, Doktor Mueller came into the kitchen, took my hand, and led me back into the living room. He looked flustered, and he had a very concerned look on his face, one that frightened me as he sat me down on the couch and began talking to me in Polish, not German as I guess he wanted to make sure that I clearly understood what he was about to reveal to me.

"Do you know who that was?" he asked.

"Yes. Commandant Höss."

"Do you know who he is?"

"The Commandant?"

"Yes, more than that. He's the big boss of the whole camp, and he wasn't pleased."

I wasn't sure what he was trying to say and what had displeased him so.

"Commandant Höss asked a lot of questions about you, and I didn't have any good answers because I hadn't thought about those kinds of questions, so I had to make up a story. If he had discovered that you had arrived on one of the trains, he would have immediately marched you right out of here, put you back into the camp, and I might have even lost my job; we might even have to move away. So, listen carefully."

Doktor Mueller asked me to get my notebook and pencil, and then he dictated the following to me, which I carefully wrote down exactly as he told me.

##### 

*Author's Note: Mira got up and left the living room where we were sitting. Soon, she returned with the well-worn leather satchel she had shared with me the first day we had met. She dug down through the pile of papers and other memorabilia until she found what she was searching for. Taking out a small notebook, she handed it to me. It was well-worn; the pages were curled up with age and the covers were quite frazzled. "Here," she said, handing it to me. "My notebook."*

*I carefully opened it, making sure I didn't lose any of the loose pages that were stuffed haphazardly between the still-bound pages. I opened it to the first page. There, written in block letters, obviously in a child's handwriting were the words "Mein Name ist Bernadette Schneider". It was obvious that some of the letters had been erased and the spelling corrected, and in an instant I was transported back to the day Doktor Mueller had given this little book to Mira and a feeling of happiness and joy overwhelmed me. To think I was sitting here in a comfortable apartment, holding the journal a young girl had written as she struggled to survive her ordeal in Auschwitz, and it was a truly magical moment. After briefly glancing through it, I handed it back to Mira, and she leafed through it until she found what she was looking for.*

#####

Here it is. Here's what I was looking for. See here? See what I wrote down? Let me read it to you. It says: *Geburtsname (Birth name): Bernadette Schneider; Geburtsort (Birth place): Breslau; Geburtstag (Date of birth): 20 April 1932; Name des Vaters (Father's name): Sigfried Schneider; Name der Mutter (Mother's name): Bronislawa Skoczylas.*

Doktor Mueller told me that Breslau is a town in eastern Germany near the Polish border, and that my new pretend father, *Sigfried*, married my new pretend Polish mother, *Bronislawa*, in 1928, and that I had grown up speaking both German and Polish. That would explain why I spoke German with a heavy Polish accent.

He said that my father had been killed during the initial German invasion of Poland in October 1939, and my mother had sent me to live with my uncle Herr Doktor and my Aunt Frau Mueller where she thought it would be safer for me farther away from the battlefront.

After that brief start, Doktor Mueller and I would sit up late at night after Frau Mueller had gone to bed and we'd make up stories about my life growing up in Breslau. We concocted wonderful tales of adventure and misadventure and we often laughed so hard I'd almost fall off the bed; however, he told me it was important to believe the stories that we made up. He impressed upon me that they might be the difference between life and death, and although I thought he was just being overly theatrical, he was closer to telling the truth than I ever could have ever imagined.

## A Fleeting Year and a Trip into Town

Before I realised it, it was almost summer once again and nearing the first anniversary of my arrival at Auschwitz. Time flew by, and perhaps it was because Frau Mueller's house ran like clockwork. If I close my eyes and try to imagine it, I can almost hear the clock, like the metronome, ticking inside my head as our daily routines never varied except for my only visit into town with Doktor Mueller.

Although I didn't attend school (that would be too risky at the moment), I did read a lot of books Doktor Mueller brought home for me, and I wrote in my journal almost every day. It was amazing how easily I learned German as I discovered that I had a knack for learning new languages. It wasn't difficult at all, and that's why I decided to become a linguist and translator when I grew up. After a while I even started thinking in German and although I feared I might even lose my ability to speak Polish, I always safeguarded my mother tongue.

Doktor Mueller only took me into town on one occasion. Although the Germans called it Auschwitz, its real Polish name is *Oświęcim*. When Doktor Mueller asked me if I wanted to go into town, I was really excited as it would be the first time I had even gone more than a few steps from our house since I had arrived there almost exactly a year earlier.

[104]

By now, Anna's room had become mine, and I added little things every now and then to make it look more like mine, however I didn't want to change things too quickly as I'm sure Frau Mueller would have frowned on that, however slowly over time, it became my room. There were still things hanging in the closet she wouldn't let me wear, but I did just fine, and it didn't bother me at all.

On the appointed day, Frau Mueller dressed me in a little yellow dress with a white sash, and she even put a white ribbon in my hair. It made me feel quite special as I sat on the couch eagerly awaiting Doktor Mueller's arrival. Although it seemed like forever, I'm sure it wasn't long before he walked through the front door. "Is my princess ready for a ride in her coach?" he asked, jokingly.

I ran over and grabbed his hand. *"Ich bin bereit (I'm ready),"* in my best proper German accent. He just laughed and led me to the door, and when he opened it, I couldn't believe what was parked in front of our little house. It was a huge, black motorcar (I think it must have been a Mercedes-Benz). It was the biggest motorcar I'd ever seen, and it was shiny black, with two of those German flags flying from the front fenders; those red flags with the awful, black swastikas in the middle.

A driver was patiently sitting in the motorcar waiting for us, and when we approached he got out, saluted Doktor Mueller, and held the rear door open for us. I got in first and slid across the back seat, and when I touched the metal door handle inside the motorcar, an electric spark jumped from my finger to the handle and startled me. Doktor Mueller just laughed; he was in such a very good mood that day that he didn't even wash his hands when he first walked into the house; the only time that he ever did that, and to this day I don't even know why he was in such a jovial mood; he never shared that with me.

When we drove out the front gate and towards town, the two armed soldiers smartly saluted, but Doktor Mueller just stared out the window, didn't acknowledge them, and it was as though he was glad to get away from there.

As we approached the town, I began to see signs written in Polish, and I was thrilled. Although Doktor Mueller had asked me to forsake my Polish roots, I still yearned to connect with my true heritage and as we drove into town, I began seeing Polish words like *ulica (street), sklep (shop), wieś (village),* words that had meaning, words familiar to me and they were like friends waving to me as we passed by.

Gazing out the motorcar's window as we drove into town, I was confused by the locals' reactions when they saw the motorcar. Some just gazed at us with blank stares while others turned their backs to us, and when I asked Doktor Mueller why people reacted that way, he said they were ignorant peasants who didn't respect authority. I wasn't too sure if I understood what he was saying, but I shrugged it off at the time.

Right before we entered the main part of town, we crossed over a beautiful river. It wasn't very big, just a mere stream, but there were children splashing in the water and adults were standing as they fished from the grassy banks. It was so peaceful, so unlike the turmoil and chaos I had experienced not too far from there when I had first arrived, and I wondered if they knew about the nearby resettlement camp and what went on there. I so wanted to join them, but I'm not sure what Frau Mueller would say if I dirtied my beautiful dress.

Right after we crossed the bridge, the driver turned down a narrow road paralleling the river and after a short while we entered a wooded park hugging the riverbank. I noticed families having picnics on the crude wooden tables and there were several benches overlooking the river. When we were opposite one of the benches,

Doktor Mueller ordered the driver, *"Halten Sie hier! (Stop here),"* and the driver pulled the motorcar off the road and parked it.

After we got out of the motorcar, Doktor Mueller took my hand and we walked to one of the benches and sat down in the bright afternoon sunlight. I felt safe sitting there next to Doktor Mueller and listening to the nearby families chattering away in Polish since it had been some time that I had heard anybody speaking my mother language, and it suddenly made me realise how much I truly missed my family.

We sat there in silence enjoying being somewhere peaceful and serene, and when I looked over at Doktor Mueller, he had a faraway look on his face as though he was somewhere else, not with me. Finally, he began, "Sitting here reminds me so much of the time Frau Mueller, Anna, and I spent in Treptower Park when we were living in Berlin. It was on a beautiful river called the Spee and we spent many glorious afternoons there spread out on a blanket enjoying a wonderful picnic in the warm, afternoon sunshine. That was such a wonderful time."

I didn't know what to say. He was in his own private world, and I didn't know if he was inviting me to join him there or if he needed his privacy. Finally, I decided to step into his world. "Doktor Mueller. Please tell me about Anna. You hardly ever speak of her."

Doktor Mueller just sat there, silent as a statue and didn't speak a word, and just when I thought perhaps he hadn't heard me, he spoke in a far-off voice, as though he wasn't speaking directly to me, but to someone else; someone in the past. "It was August 25th 1940. Frau Mueller and I had just gotten to Auschwitz, and it was a beautiful, warm summer night. I can still remember it as if it was yesterday. The moon was full and the planet Venus hung in the sky like a brilliant diamond. It was such a marvelous spectacle that I called

Frau Mueller out onto the porch. 'Look,' I said, pointing skyward. 'That's Anna telling us that she's safe and happy back in Berlin, and that she can't wait to join us.'"

Doktor Mueller paused before continuing. "Only she wasn't safe. We had left her with relatives in Siemensstadt because we knew she'd be safe there, but those cowardly bastards had the nerve to fly over our beautiful city and drop bombs on it. We didn't think that was ever possible. How could they? However, they did, and one of those bombs hit the house where she was staying. Nobody survived and when we found out, Frau Mueller was inconsolable."

Doktor Mueller squeezed my hand even harder as he recalled that awful night. "She was supposed to leave on the train the next day and come join us, and we had her room all ready for her. After her death, we never even opened the door to her room until you unexpectedly arrived. It's too bad you never had a chance to meet her; she was a very special child. Frau Mueller had a difficult birthing delivery, and after that we knew she wouldn't survive having another baby, so Anna was our only child, and she brought such joy into our lives, and you remind me so much of her. She had a smile that could light up a room and she was so full of adventure. Mischievous at times, but she was always such an energetic and happy child."

I felt sorry for him and his loss, and I tried to be as grown-up as possible. I said something like, "That must have been such a terrible time for you. I can't even imagine how you felt."

Doktor Mueller smiled, "No, child, you can't even begin to imagine how we both felt after that. It was hard enough to leave Anna behind when we moved to this godforsaken place because we knew someday she would join us. At the beginning, I was reluctant to come here and help build the camp, but Herr Hitler was such a charming and charismatic leader and he made us feel good about ourselves;

made us believe that we, not the Jews, were the Chosen People, and it was our duty to help resettle the Jews somewhere far away, somewhere where they couldn't poison our pure, Aryan society. I really didn't believe what he was saying since I was always taught that we all had a right to exist peacefully with one another, and I was quite hesitant about becoming part of the efficient machinery that was sweeping the Jews out of Europe. However, I was drafted into the military when the war broke out and I had a duty to follow orders."

A lot of what he was saying was too difficult for me to understand as he was talking to me as one adult would talk to another. You have to remember that I was just a young child, barely twelve-years old, however I could truly feel his pain as he spoke.

"When Anna was killed, I began to understand that Herr Hitler spoke the truth. The *Jews* had caused her death; *they* had started the war just like he had said, and it was now my duty to make sure we sent them somewhere far away where they couldn't hurt us anymore."

"Is that where they sent my family? Somewhere far away?"

"Yes, Bernadette, somewhere far away."

"Will I be with them someday?"

"Not if I can help it," his curious reply. I wasn't too sure what he meant, but I could tell by his manners that he had just touched an angry place he kept safely concealed within himself and I didn't want to know any more.

We sat there in silence; him in his own world and me in mine, until he finally said, "Time to go," and we got up, he took my hand, we walked back to the waiting motorcar, and drove back to the camp in total silence.

## God Speaks to Me in a Dream

After we had arrived home, Doktor Mueller walked straight into their bedroom and didn't come out until it was time to eat dinner. When he finally joined us at the table, he just sat there and ate, silently, without saying a word to either of us. I'm sure he was still upset from talking about Anna, so I didn't say anything either as we three just sat there eating in silence, but it felt as though there was now a fourth person in the room with us.

After I'd gone to bed, Doktor Mueller came in, sat on the side of my bed, gently stroked my hair, kissed my forehead, and said, "I love you," then walked out of the room. I lay there for the longest time thinking about what we had talked about on the bench and I was mad at the Jews for killing Anna, but I didn't know whom in particular to be mad at. All the Jews I knew were good people just like my mother, father, brothers, and the rest of my family, and none of them would have ever dropped bombs on Berlin, so maybe there were some bad Jews I didn't know about; maybe it was *their* fault.

Before I drifted off to sleep, I got up and opened the window to let in some fresh air and I could see lightning off in the distance. Every time there was a flash, I could see two tall smokestacks outlined on the distant horizon, and when the sky turned dark again, there were two ominous, red glowing lights where the smokestacks had been an instant before.

It took a long time to get to sleep when suddenly I was transported back to Uncle Addam's apartment in Warsaw and I was standing, once again, in front of the apartment's door with my mother, my father, my brother, Lev, and my little brother, Chaim. My father knocked on the door and when it opened, it wasn't Uncle Addam who answered the door, it was a horrible ogre. His face was terribly disfigured, covered with warts, and he had two smokestacks

[110]

sticking from the top of his head, just like the Devil's horns, and his eyes glowed cherry-red, like burning hot coals, and with the beckoning of a bony and crooked finger, he said "Welcome. Please come in."

As soon as my father took his first step inside the apartment, the ogre opened his mouth and all I could see were flames, and my father stepped right into his open mouth followed by mother, my younger brother, Chaim, and closely followed by my older brother, Lev. When they had all stepped inside, the ogre closed his mouth and his eyes started to burn brightly in their deeply sunk sockets as greasy, black smoke started pouring out of the smokestacks atop his head. Suddenly I saw my family's souls swirling about in the unctuous, black smoke as it rose to the apartment's ceiling; then their souls disappeared, and in an instant they were gone forever. The ogre then turned towards me, wiggled his finger and said, "Your turn, child."

I turned and ran screaming down the hallway and out into the street, and the street was crowded with a multitude of animals dressed in grey coats adorned with yellow Stars of David. There were donkeys, mules, cows and goats with long beards, and they smiled at me with toothy grins full of gleaming, white teeth as men on stilts dressed entirely in black leather drove them down the street and cracked whips over their heads that made loud snapping sounds like gunfire.

As I made my way through the crowd, the animals rubbed up against me and they smelled of terror and fear and I was petrified. As soon as I broke free, I came upon a large crowd of people standing in a circle in the middle of the street, and there was a clown standing in the center of the crowd with a square mustache dangling precariously above his upper lip. He was juggling newborn babies as the crowd cheered him wildly while raising their arms in salute, and when he dropped one of the babies, throngs of new mothers ran towards him, tears streaming down their faces, their newborn babies held out beseechingly to him, "Take my baby," one shouted. "No. Take mine," another shouted.

I was horrified, and I ran up to him and screamed at the top of my lungs, "STOP! You can't do that," but he just looked down at me, smiled, and thousands of butterflies flew out of his mouth, but they weren't butterflies, they were little yellow Stars of David with wings. They engulfed me and became tangled in my hair, and as they flew up my nose and into my ears, I ran screaming down the street batting them away.

When I looked down the street, I saw my mother, father, and my little brother, Chaim, standing there, their arms outstretched towards me, encouraging me to run faster. As I ran towards them, and just as I was about to be swept up in my father's arms, there was a loud thunderclap and they disappeared into three little piles of ashes at my feet, and as I stared down at them in horror, a radiant, white whirlwind glowing with the whitest light I had ever seen, came careening down the street towards me and it blew the three piles of ashes high up into the pitch-black sky where they instantly disappeared.

Suddenly, the whirlwind stopped spinning right in front of me and a beautiful man stood there dressed in alabaster-white, flowing robes that radiated a pure, brilliant light, and he looked down at me as he asked, "What can I do for you, child?"

I looked up at him. "Here. I don't want this anymore," as I handed him the yellow Star of David I had ripped from my coat.

"You *must* wear that," he admonished me; "It tells the world you're a Jew."

"I don't want to be a Jew anymore."

[112]

"Okay, if that's what you want, put it in here for safekeeping."

He then took a satchel from over his shoulder and set it down on the ground. "Here, child. Drop your star in here," as he opened the satchel, and when I peered inside, I could see millions of bright lights swirling about like lightning bugs in a jar, and as I threw my star into the open satchel, it instantly turned into a bright light just like the others and then rushed to join them.

The man then took my hand. "Can you keep a secret?"

"Yes," I replied, happy now that I was freed of my Jewish burden.

We turned around and suddenly two, large doors appeared before us. There was a sign over the doors shouting out "*Arbeit Mach Frei*", and as the doors opened with a loud screeching sound like a million souls shrieking, I peered inside and saw dozens of skeletons dressed in black-and-white striped *pyjamas*, their arms on each other's shoulders forming a circle, and as they danced around a huge pile of burning books, their bones made dry, clicking sounds. "Would you like to join them," he asked.

"No!" I shouted.

As we turned away, the doors slammed shut behind us, and suddenly we were standing on the top of a tall mountain looking down into a beautiful, peaceful valley, with twinkling lights brightly shining like stars. "Would you like to live here, instead?" he asked.

"Oh yes, that's beautiful," and just as the winged words flew out of my mouth like the butterflies had flown out of the clown's mouth, his swirling robes completely enveloped me, and suddenly I was surrounded by darkness. I screamed and awoke to find myself standing in front of my open window; the wind preceding the fast approaching thunderstorm was whipping the drapes around me and engulfing me as I collapsed on my bedroom floor, my nightshirt wet with my tears. I couldn't go back to sleep; I was too terrified. Had I just met God?

## I Discuss My Dream with Doktor Mueller

The dream so terrified me that I crawled into bed and pulled the covers up over my head. In the morning, there was a gentle knock on my door and Doktor Mueller walked into the room. "Are you all right?" he asked.

"I don't feel well," I lied.

Doktor Mueller sat on the side of my bed, took off his grey gloves, and laid the back of his hand on my forehead. "You don't feel like you have a fever. Are you sure you don't feel well?" he persisted.

"I have a tummy ache," and I turned my back to him and rolled over on my side, as he just gently patted my back, got up, and left the room.

When I finally felt like getting up, I got out my journal and wrote about my dream. I wrote *"Ich hatte einen schrecklichen Traum letzte Nacht. Gott sprach zu mir, aber ich könnte nicht verstehen was er meinte."* Translated it means, "I had a terrible dream last night. God spoke to me, but I couldn't understand what he meant."

My dream haunted me all day long and I couldn't wait for Doktor Mueller to arrive home that evening. Before I sat down on the couch in eager anticipation of his arrival, I put on the yellow dress I had worn when we went into town and patiently waited for him to walk through the front door. When he finally walked through the front door, he briefly acknowledged me with a slight nod in my direction, walked briskly into the kitchen, and washed his hands, as usual.

Shortly, he came back into the living room and sat down next to me. "You look as though you're feeling better. Any special occasion for getting so dressed up?" he asked.

"I have something very important to talk to you about."

Doktor Mueller listened patiently as I told him about my dream in great detail, and occasionally he would ask me to repeat what I had told him, however he appeared to be listening intently. When I had finished, I asked him, "What does it all mean?"

My protector sat there silent, thinking, and finally he spoke. "What you just told me has to be very terrifying for a young girl like you, and I'm sorry it happened. I'm not sure what it means; it all seems so jumbled up and confusing, even to an adult like me. I think you're right when you said God was speaking to you. God *does* work in mysterious ways and perhaps this was his way of revealing the truth."

"The truth about what?" I asked.

"Auschwitz."

His one-word answer startled me and it didn't even begin to satisfy all the questions I had rattling around inside my head; it only added to them. The ogre, the smokestacks, the herds of animals being driven by the leather-clad stilt walkers, the juggler, the newborns, the three piles of ashes, and the bright light clad in pure-white robes. None of that made any sense to me, neither did anything else in my dream, and neither did Doktor Mueller's puzzling, one-word answer. The only thing that made any sense was my not wanting to be Jewish anymore, so perhaps that was the decision God wanted me to make.

After a long pause, I finally asked him, "Doktor Mueller, why do you hate the Jews?"

"It's a long story, Bernadette, and you don't really want to know, *do* you?"

I reached over and took his hand, "I'd like to know, Doktor Mueller. It's important for me to understand why you feel that way."

He gently squeezed my hand and smiled, "It happened a long time ago and it's not important now. Maybe I'll tell you sometime, but not now."

I wasn't about to let him get away with that answer, so I persisted. "No, I want to know *now*, not *later*. Please." I said in my most pleading little girl's voice.

He exhaled a loud sigh, "If you insist, but it's not a very interesting story."

"I insist," now more than ever determined to try to understand why Doktor Mueller felt that way about the Jews.

Soon, he began to tell *his* story. "I grew up in a small town in eastern Germany close to the Polish border. My father was German, and he worked for my grandfather in a local clothing store, and my mother was Polish, and we spoke both German and Polish in our household, so I grew up speaking both languages. My father was a hardworking man, but he had one weakness; he loved to gamble, however he wasn't very good at it and he wound up owing the local moneylenders a lot of money. When he couldn't repay the debt, they came to our house, beat him up so badly that he stayed in bed for weeks, and he never truly got over it."

He had touched my heart. "That's awful, but what does it have to with the Jews?"

"The men who beat him up were Jews; nothing more than vicious thugs and my father said they were no better than the moneychangers Jesus had driven out of the temple. He said the Jews were only interested in one thing; money, and they were all greedy leeches and many people had suffered because of the Jew's voracious appetite for wealth and power. When Herr Hitler spoke, he repeated the same things about the Jews that my father had incessantly drilled into my head, and what he said made sense to me. I bore witness to what the Jews had done to my father, and now I realised they had done the same thing to others. So, it wasn't difficult to convince me that all Jews are greedy and evil."

"Do you feel that way about me?" I asked.

"No, of course, not, Bernadette."

"But I'm Jewish, too."

"You're different. I know you as a person, not as a Jew, and I'm sure there must be some good Jews, like you, out there somewhere."

"Then why are you resettling all the Jews? You just said not all Jews are bad and you, yourself, acknowledge that many of them are good, honest people, like my family."

My question appeared to confound Doktor Mueller as he hesitated for a moment, "There are just so many Jews that it's impossible to judge each one; separate the good ones from the bad ones. The only way we can make sure we get rid of the bad ones is to resettle them all. Unfortunately, the good Jews have to suffer because of what the bad ones have done to us. Doesn't that make sense to you? It does to me."

"Is that why you don't want me to be Jewish anymore? You don't want me to suffer because of what the bad ones did to you?"

"Bernadette, I think God answered that question in your dream. Remember when you threw your yellow Star of David into the satchel and you told him you didn't want to be Jewish anymore? He didn't judge you; He just said if that was what you wanted to do, it was up to you, and that you will always know in your heart who you really are and who you want to be. If you want to stay Jewish in your heart, stay Jewish, but just don't let it show. That would be too dangerous right now."

"But when will I know who I truly want to be?"

"When the time comes, you'll know the true answer," and with that, our conversation ended and I knew he was right. When the time came, I'd know who I was, and would I choose to be Mira Kabliski, Mira Bednarczyk, Bernadette Schneider or maybe even Anna Mueller?

## Frau Mueller

Frau Mueller was never a part of my life; she was there, but she really wasn't there and although she went through the motions of daily life, she never appeared to be connected to it. Even Doktor Mueller appeared to notice. As I became more fluent in German, he began to rely more and more on me for conversation as he and Frau Mueller hardly spoke anymore. I felt sorry for him, but there wasn't much I could do for him; I was just a child trying to be as invisible as possible since I was never allowed outside by myself, and the small house soon became my prison as much as the resettlement camp would have been, but, of course, I still didn't know exactly what went on there.

Eventually, Frau Mueller began spending most of her days in bed, and when I questioned Doktor Mueller about her, he'd just raise his eyebrows as though he had already accepted her strange behaviour as just another normal part of our dysfunctional, daily lives.

I'm not too sure when my taking over Frau Mueller's place started. Over time I had just begun to assume Frau Mueller's household responsibilities, one small chore at a time, starting with me doing the laundry, then watering the flowers, then I began fixing my own meals when Doktor Mueller was at work, and finally I wound up doing all the cooking.

Whenever I'd knock on her perpetually closed bedroom door, she would just say, "Go away," so I finally gave up altogether. The only time she left her bedroom was when she needed to go to the bathroom, and when she did and I tried to talk to her, she wouldn't even acknowledge me; she just moved like a zombie. I was getting quite worried about her, but Doktor Mueller didn't appear to be as concerned as I was, and it was as almost as though he had even stopped caring, himself.

Now, whenever Doktor Mueller came home, he would rush into the kitchen to wash his hands, as usual, but instead of going into their bedroom to check on Frau Mueller, he would ask me to join him on the couch, and we would have interesting talks. One day I got up the courage to ask him what he did at the resettlement camp as it was something he never had wanted to talk about, it was a topic he always carefully avoided, but I was curious.

I remembered the night my family and I had arrived at the camp, and how they had so efficiently separated the women, children, and elderly into one group and the men into another, and there were uniformed men at the head of each line. As each person approached them, they steered them in one direction or the other, and although I didn't want to admit it, Doktor Mueller had been one of those who were involved in making that fleeting, life-changing decision.

I was curious, "Tell me what you do at the camp, Doktor Mueller."

"Why do you ask, Bernadette?"

"I'm just curious about what goes on in the resettlement camp. You hardly ever talk about it and I truly want to know," I persisted.

"Do you really want to know the truth?"

"Of course, I do," wondering why he hadn't told me the truth from the beginning.

"Do you remember when we talked about trying to separate the good Jews from the bad Jews? Well, what I do is try to separate the healthy Jews from the sick Jews, because we send the *healthy* Jews to resettle the land we took back from the Russians, and we send the *sick* Jews to the hospital to make them all better."

I know now he probably didn't want to reveal the truth to me; that would have been too painful, probably for the both of us, however I've come to forgive him for that awful lie, but I know it was probably because he loved me. Maybe he even believed it himself; although it wasn't until much later when we had the same talk as adults that I finally discovered how he truly felt.

Strangely enough, it was the first time he had mentioned the Russians and I wasn't sure what he was talking about. "What do you mean by resettling the lands you took back from the Russians? Did they just give the land back because they're nice people?"

"No, child. We're at *war* with the Russian dogs and we're at war with the British and the Americans, too."

"Doktor Mueller, I thought the Germans were fighting the *Jews*. You never told me about the others."

My question appeared to irritate him. "Does it make any difference, Bernadette? It's all a Zionist plot to take over the world. See, it has even infected the British and the Americans, and it's a worldwide epidemic that will soon plant its evil roots everywhere and strangle the life out of everyone in our beautiful country. That's why we have to send the Jews somewhere far away; somewhere where they can't spread their evilness and it's in their best interest too, you know."

Just when I was about to contest Doktor Mueller's abrupt answer, Frau Mueller walked into the room. She was still in her nightclothes, and she looked pale; gaunt and drawn. "Heinrich, I need to talk to you," she said in a dry, scratchy voice.

"What is it?"

"Not here. In the bedroom," as he got up from the couch and followed her out of the room.

They were gone for quite a while and when Doktor Mueller finally returned to the living room, I asked, "Is she all right?"

"She said she doesn't feel well," was all he said.

The next morning started like any other day as Doktor Mueller went to work, as usual, and I started my daily household chores, as usual. There wasn't anything special about the day, as I remember it, that is until I took Frau Mueller's lunch to her. When I knocked on her bedroom door, my knock was met with a disturbing silence. So, I knocked again; more loudly this time. Still no response. When I opened the door, I could see her lying in bed, asleep, or so I thought, so I set the lunch tray on her bedside table and gently shook her shoulder trying to wake her. However, when she didn't wake up, I grabbed her hand and vigorously shook it, but she still didn't wake up and her hand was cold and lifeless. It was then that I realised, much to my horror, that she was dead.

I didn't know what to do. Except for when the soldier had shot and killed Mr. Stępniak in our village, this was the only other time I had seen a dead person, let alone touch one. Frau Mueller's face was ashen grey and her lips had started to turn purple, and I couldn't stand to look at her. Even in death, she still intimidated me, so I pulled the covers up over her head, ran out of the room, and slammed the door behind me.

What should I do? Doktor Mueller had warned me never to leave the house alone, and even if I could, I didn't know where to find him. So, I went into my bedroom, pushed a chair up against the door, and stood in front of the window all day waiting for Doktor Mueller to return home. Me, alone in a small house with a dead person in the next room. I was terrified, and I was so glad to finally see him walking up the dirt street in front of our house.

When I heard the front door open, I ran out my room into the living room and when he walked through the front door, I ran up and grabbed onto his uniform.

"Don't touch me. I need to wash my hands," he sternly admonished me.

I continued tugging at his sleeve. "Frau Mueller! Frau Mueller!" I stammered.

"I need to wash my hands," he insisted, so I let him go into the kitchen and perform his daily ritual, and when he finally returned to the living room where I stood trembling, he asked in a gruff voice, "What about Frau Mueller?"

"She's dead!"

He showed absolutely no emotion as he protectively took my hand and we walked to the closed bedroom door. When he opened the door, we could see Frau Mueller lying on the bed covered with her bedspread shroud. I almost expected her to jump up and surprise us, but she didn't. Doktor Mueller walked over, pulled the bedspread down, and we saw that her entire body had started to turn a dark colour, and both arms were bent up at the elbows up as though she was begging an invisible something to come down and save her.

"*Sie ist tot (She's dead)*," he said without any emotion. "Go to your room and stay there until I tell you it's all right to come out. Make sure to draw the drapes and stay quiet as a mouse," he commanded and I did exactly as he ordered.

It wasn't long before I heard a motorcar pull up in front of the house, two car doors being slammed shut, and I overheard Doktor

Mueller talking to our visitors, but I couldn't understand what they were saying. When I heard the front door close a second time, I disobeyed his orders and peeked out my window through the drawn drapes. Two men were loading something into the back of a stretched-out motorcar and I assumed it was Frau Mueller. Soon, the two men closed the back of the motorcar, shook Doktor Mueller's hand, patted him on the back, and drove away.

Within a few moments, Doktor Mueller came into my bedroom, and I expected him to be crying, but he wasn't. He just came over and hugged me. "It's just the two of us now, Bernadette," and that was the last time we ever talked about Frau Mueller.

I later learned he had sent her coffin on a train to Berlin to be buried in the family plot, but the train never arrived, and we just assumed that Frau Mueller's coffin had been destroyed along with the train on its sad journey. I know it's not a nice thing to say, may God strike me dead, but I never did like her, anyway.

## Doktor Mueller's Downward Spiral

After Frau Mueller's death, nothing changed around the Mueller household as I had already become the head of the household and other than not having to take care of her, my role remained pretty much the same as before. However, Doktor Mueller began acting detached, as though he had stopped caring, and it was as though he was just travelling through life, not participating in it.

The day after Frau Mueller died, he took all her personal things and put them in the back room. Her clothes, her jewelry, her shoes, her pictures; everything except for a pair of her warm, fleece-lined winter boots he saved out for me as he just swept the house bare of Frau Mueller, and he started drinking more than he should have. In fact, I can't remember a time after that when he didn't drink himself into a stupor before bedtime, and he would fall asleep in the chair in the living room after dinner, however, I didn't dare disturb him until bedtime. Then I'd have to shake him awake and help him stagger into his bedroom where oftentimes he would just collapse on the bed in his uniform and fall asleep.

In the morning, I'd hear him get up while I was still in bed, stumble around in the kitchen fixing his simple breakfast, however I waited until I heard the front door close before I dared get up. Only once did I confront him in the morning and he was so grumpy and mean to me after that, I just avoided him altogether in the morning.

Don't get me wrong, we still had our conversations when he came home; after he washed his hands, of course. That part of his daily routine didn't change, and we tried to keep the conversations light and non-confrontational, but sometimes we talked about the world and what a terrible place it had become. We never talked about the Jews again since he had already made his point, and I didn't want to risk getting on his bad side by arguing with him.

I didn't keep many secrets from Doktor Mueller, only one, in fact. When I had told him about my dream when God talked to me, Doktor Mueller had told me it was all right to be Jewish in my heart, just not to show it, and although I had told God in my dream that I didn't want to be Jewish, I thought it was very important to set aside a part of me in a secret place to honour my heritage.

Although my family had celebrated every Jewish holy holiday and festival, it was hard for me to know all the sacred dates on the calendar and besides, there wasn't even a regular calendar anywhere in the house. Therefore, I decided Alinka and I would just celebrate Hanukkah as I knew Hanukkah was celebrated sometime in late

November or early December, so I decided I'd wait ten days after the first snowfall and then I'd start the celebration.

In anticipation of the upcoming celebration, I tore a piece of paper out of my journal and drew a menorah without any candles, just like the one my father kept stored in the living room. My father liked to play a little game with us children as Hanukkah approached. There was a bookcase in our living room where my father kept his books and after Hanukkah was over, he would put the menorah on the very top of the bookcase. A few days before the beginning of the next Hanukkah, he would put it on the top shelf and then every day after that, he would move it down one shelf at a time until it was time to put it on the table next to his reading lamp. The anticipation as we watched the menorah move downwards, shelf-by-shelf, was overwhelming.

So, in honour of my father's little game, I drew one candle on my menorah each day in anticipation of the upcoming Hanukkah until all nine were in place. Then, every night during *my* Hanukkah celebration, I would draw a flame on each candle and recite the only Hebrew prayer I knew; the one my father used to recite before every evening meal. I know it wasn't the proper *brachot (blessing)*, but I was sure God would take into account that I was just a twelve-year-old, uneducated, peasant girl; however, I'm certain He appreciated my attempt. At least I tried, didn't I?

Sometime before Hanukkah in 1944, probably in October, there was a great commotion in the resettlement camp and as I ran to my bedroom window and peered out, I saw a line of trucks entering the camp with mean-looking German soldiers sitting in the back with their rifles clutched tightly to their chests. When Doktor Mueller returned home that night, I asked him what was happening as he seemed quite upset. However, he abruptly said he didn't want to talk about it, although after a couple of drinks, he loosened up a bit. He told me that some of the bad people at the resettlement camp had revolted, had destroyed some of the buildings, and German soldiers had to come in and restore order. He said it was an ominous sign, and even worse, the Russians were drawing dangerously close, too, and if the Russians overran the camp, he said they would kill everybody, including us, and we needed to start thinking about leaving Auschwitz before it was too late.

That was a lot to absorb in just one frightening sentence, and what he had just told me greatly upset me, because after all the hardships I had endured since the Germans had come through our village and burned it, I felt safe in Doktor Mueller's house, and just the mention of leaving it for unknown destinations was overwhelming.

## Escape from Auschwitz

When Doktor Mueller returned home on the fourth day of *my* Hanukkah, he appeared more upset than I had ever seen him, so much so that he didn't even go into the kitchen to wash his hands; he just took off his gloves and threw them onto the couch. "We have to talk. Now!" he said, and his demeanor frightened me.

I sat down next to him and waited to hear what I knew was going to be bad news. "We have to leave here, soon! Things are getting quite bad and the Russian wolves are at our doorstep."

Russians? Wolves? It was all terribly frightening; suddenly my safe haven had become a dangerous place. How could that be?

"Where will we go?" I asked.

He paused. "I truthfully don't know, but I've been thinking about it for quite some time now, and I think my plan might work. I've heard our troops are retreating on all fronts, and from what I hear, their retreat is extremely disorganised, but extremely dangerous, so I'm not too sure we could even make it through our own lines without being shot and we'll need to come up with a convincing story if we're stopped and questioned."

Retreating? Disorganised? Dangerous? Being shot? Such frightening words. So, we sat on the couch and began to hatch our plan. We finally decided to leave the next morning dressed as Polish peasants. Doktor Mueller and I would pose as displaced refugees fleeing to the west and we hoped our Polish language would be good enough to convince any potential adversaries.

As you might imagine, I didn't sleep much that night and before I went to bed, Doktor Mueller gave me a small carpetbag to pack my things. I couldn't take much; just Alinka, my journals and a spare set of clothing. When I told him what I had packed, he said he was afraid that if the Germans stopped and searched us, they would find my journal written in German. We talked about it, and I told him how much the journal meant to me, so we decided if that happened, I'd just say it wasn't mine; I had just found it along the way and wanted to keep it out of curiosity. We hoped our inquisitors would accept that explanation as we knew the Germans were in full retreat, and they wouldn't have the time to stop and search every refugee; they'd be more interested in saving their own lives.

It was in 1944 on Christmas Day eve when we left our little house outside the resettlement camp for the last time. Doktor Mueller had picked that night because he said the darkness of the new moon would help us escape detection. It was bitterly cold, so I put on two layers of clothing under my heavy jacket; however, Frau Mueller's winter boots were a bit large for me, so I put on an extra pair of socks to help make them fit more snugly.

Doktor Mueller wore a pair of tattered, worn gardening overalls over the top of two layers of underclothing and although he looked more like a Polish peasant than a German SS doctor, he still looked like Doktor Mueller to me. I hoped his disguise would hold up on our long journey. He packed a rucksack with as much food as he could carry and slung it over his shoulder, as we knew the journey would be long and food would be difficult to find along the way.

Before departing, I sat patiently on the couch waiting for him to go through the house and make sure everything was in order. Part of Doktor Mueller's plan was to leave a note saying there had been a family emergency and he would have to be away for a few days, however, we wondered if the authorities would buy that explanation, and if they did, for how long? Hopefully, by that time, we would have been able to blend in with the other refugees and be as far away from Auschwitz as possible.

Finally, it was time to leave. It was late at night and without looking back, we closed the door behind us, walked down the front steps to the frozen dirt road, and left the resettlement camp behind us for the last time. As we left the house, he stopped, took my hand, and said, "From now on you will be my daughter, Anna. Anna Mueller. Can you remember that?"

Hearing that made me happy. Doktor Mueller had just claimed me as his own daughter; his very own daughter and now I felt as though he and I were truly a family. My feet didn't even touch the ground as we continued down the crusty, snow-covered road. "Oh yes, Father. That would make me very happy, indeed," as we left Auschwitz as father and daughter, and watching the resettlement camp slowly vanish behind us in the distance, we disappeared into the safety of the moonless, star-studded night, hand-in-hand.

[128]

## The Beginning of Our Perilous Journey

As we left the neighbourhood, we could see many buildings in the resettlement camp were burning, and it appeared that the whole camp was engulfed in flames as though the Germans were trying to destroy it. Doktor Mueller said, "I think we're leaving just in time, Anna" and we never looked back.

Right before we left the house, Doktor Mueller took his beautiful pair of grey, calf-skin gloves he wore every day and hid them in the back room where nobody could find them. Then, on the way out of the house, he dug his hands down into the flower pot on the front porch and rubbed his beautiful hands in the dirt. "It makes me look like I work with my hands," he said in a joking way.

As we departed, we had to make sure we stayed away from the camp's wire fence because our silhouettes would have been highlighted against the burning skyline. Instead, we walked away from the camp between the other houses and into the surrounding woods. There was quite a bit of snow on the ground and since there wasn't any moonlight to guide us, it was difficult making any headway through the underbrush. Every time I lifted my foot to take another step, my foot almost came out of my oversized boots and it wasn't until we had stuffed weeds into them that was I able to walk more comfortably.

When Doktor Mueller thought we were far enough away from the burning camp, we headed towards the road. Through the trees, we could see truck headlamps moving down the road, away from the camp. It was so confusing; the burning camp, the fleeing trucks; however, it wasn't until later we found out that the big boss of all the resettlement camps, Heinrich Himmler, had ordered the complete destruction of the Auschwitz camp before the Russians overran it, and we had fled just in time.

[129]

When we finally approached the road, we saw that it was deserted except for an occasional truck, and as we started walking towards the town of Auschwitz, whenever we saw a truck approaching, we'd duck back into the woods and hide. Eventually, we joined a group of other refugees walking down the road and we finally stopped playing our little hide-and-seek game since we felt secure now that that we blended in with the others.

Our little ragged band of travellers silently trekked on down the snow-covered road; in fact, I can't remember anyone saying anything, even to one another. We all marched along in silence; our faces briefly illuminated by the approaching vehicles headlamps, and when the vehicles passed, we once again disappeared into the inky-black night.

When we crossed the bridge right before town, the bridge Doktor Mueller and I had earlier crossed in his big fancy motorcar, our little group turned down the path leading to the small park where he and I had sat on the bench and had our first serious talk, and we could see several campfires amongst the trees with other refugees silhouetted by the glow from the small fires.

We tramped through the newly-fallen snow trying to find a place to sit down near one of the fires to keep warm and we eventually found a place to sit down on a log someone had obviously dragged through the snow and placed by one of the fires. There were three or four others sitting nearby and our small group soon joined them. If I had to guess, I'd say there were probably fifty or sixty people of all ages gathered in the park sitting around the fires; mostly older people.

Once everybody had made themselves comfortable around the fire and had taken the chill out of their bodies, someone started a conversation and that conversation was soon joined by others until everybody in the group was talking at the same time. It was hard to listen to any particular conversation as usually the loudest speaker quickly drowned out the rest. The conversation centered on the fact that everyone certainly feared the Russians far more than they feared the Germans. It was the generally expressed opinion that the German occupiers had treated the local Polish population with some degree of respect, although they could be brutal at times. The Russians, on the other hand, were seen as uneducated, ruthless thugs who destroyed everything in their path, raped women and children, and had no respect for human life.

Both Doktor Mueller and I were surprised at how easily we had slipped back into our native Polish tongue as it had been quite a while since we had stopped having our conversations in Polish and had replaced it with German, and it was comforting to once again be thinking and speaking in our mother tongue.

Once we had settled in around the fire, Doktor Mueller opened his rucksack, took out a small loaf of bread, some hard cheese, and offered them to me. Others nearby hungrily looked on, but he didn't offer them any as we needed every scrap of food he had packed if we were going to survive. We found that to be common among the fleeing refugees; food was hoarded, not shared, and even gold coins were often refused when offered for food.

We all spent a cold, restless night huddled around the dwindling fire even though every now and then someone would get up, walk into the woods, and return carrying some firewood, which they'd toss onto the fire. The fire would flare up briefly, and then once again start to die out. Some of our group had brought blankets with them, but we hadn't, so we did the best we could to stay warm. Eventually, Doktor Mueller traded our last small loaf of bread for two blankets, but for the time being, we had to content ourselves with trying to keep warm with what we were wearing.

The new morning dawned bright, but incredibly cold. Some of those nearby had already departed, some were still sleeping on top of the snow, and some were already stirring, trying to shake the cold from their bodies. One of the nearby men retrieved a small pot from his rucksack, walked down to the frozen river, chopped a hole in the ice, and filled it to the rim, and as soon as he got back to the warmth and safety of the now blazing fire, he set in on a rock near the flames and waited for it to boil. Doktor Mueller dug out a couple of mugs from his rucksack along with some black tea, and our new friend gladly shared his hot water with us as we enjoyed two steaming hot mugs of tea. Doktor Mueller offered him a small piece of hard cheese in return, which he gladly accepted and shared with his wife, who returned our small gift with a toothless grin.

After everyone around our campfire had awakened, lively conversations began ricocheting around the fire pit. Overall, there were fourteen of us sitting there trying to figure out what to do next, however I was the only child amongst the group. We all agreed that we should travel towards Germany where we could eventually find the protection of the Allied forces approaching from that direction, but nobody knew how far we'd have to travel. Right now, we were caught in the middle of fleeing German troops with the same goal in mind; get away from the approaching Russians. While some in our group said the Allies were not that far distant, others said they might be hundreds of kilometres away; a journey fraught with dangers as we would undoubtedly get caught up in the cauldron of three well-armed armies, meeting somewhere in the middle. Regardless of where the Allies, the Russians, and the Germans currently were, we all decided we'd have to try; staying in Auschwitz was not an option.

## The Grueling Trek Westward

What we didn't realise until later as we sat around the campfire in the park outside Auschwitz discussing our options was that the Allies were a lot farther away than we had thought. In fact, they hadn't even made much, if any, progress in their push into Germany itself. In addition, unbeknownst to us, what the Germans called *Unternehmen Wacht am Rhein (Operation Watch on the Rhine)* and others called The Battle of the Bulge had begun roughly a week before we left the resettlement camp. The German troops leaving the area in the trucks were reserves rushing back to Germany to fill the vacuum created by the frontline soldiers flooding into Belgium to fight in Hitler's last, suicidal attempt to crush the Allied armies. All this, of course, was unknown to us as all we focused on heading west towards safety.

If we wanted to get anywhere near the Allied troops, we'd have to cross through the rugged terrain of southern Czechoslovakia, then across northern Austria, and finally into what we hoped would be the safety of Bavaria. Doktor Mueller said the majority of the Bavarian people weren't happy with Germany's participation in the war, and they would probably be friendlier to arriving refugees than would others in other parts of Germany. Once we had arrived in Bavaria, he said would could drop our Polish cloaks and be true Germans, once again. Had he already forgotten I was Polish, not German?

Our ragged band left the warmth of the campfire by mid-morning, however only twelve of us decided to move on; one elderly man and his wife decided to stay in the park as they were too old and sickly to join us on our perilous journey. As we walked through the center of town, there was hardly anybody on the streets, and either it was too cold for them to leave the warmth of their homes, or they were afraid to be caught up in the confusion of the departing troops. Either way, we felt exposed and vulnerable as we constantly needed to step out of the streets so we wouldn't be run over by the large, noisy trucks passing by, filled with uniformed troops headed west.

It quickly became obvious we'd soon have to make a decision which way to head; north, south, or west. One of our group, a man who appeared to be more educated than the others, had a map of Poland, that he carefully removed from his rucksack and spread out on the ground. The other men huddled over it while the women and I tried to peer over their shoulders, although I'm not too sure any of us could read a map. However, it made us feel involved, part of the decision-making, though none of the men ever asked our opinions, and it was that way throughout our entire journey; the men made the decisions and the women unanimously agreed.

Some of the men wanted to head north on the main road towards Tychy, some argued it would be shorter if we followed the road south towards Kety, while others wanted to head due west over mostly unimproved back roads towards Pszczyna. It was obvious if we stayed together as a group, we would have these types of discussions many times in the future, however, it was finally agreed that it was better to head south towards Kety. Most of the trucks were headed that way, and logic told us that they would be headed towards the Allies' front lines and away from the Russians, and this only made sense as we began our long journey headed south.

Walking along the busy highway was difficult as we had to make sure we stepped out of the way of the passing trucks as they sped by, just inches from us. Every now and then, a truck would hit a pothole filled with ice water and splash it up on me until my pant legs were stiff with ice. Fortunately, I was wearing another pair of pants under them, so I didn't get nearly as soaked as I could have.

It felt as though we had walked for many kilometres, although I'm sure it wasn't actually that far, when we came upon a farm truck that had slid off the road into a snow bank with the driver desperately trying to free the truck by spinning the rear wheels, but to no avail.

One of the men in our group walked up to the driver's side window and had a rather animated discussion with him. Finally, he walked back to where we were standing and delivered the driver's proposal. If we could help free his truck from the snowbank, he'd let us ride in the back of his truck as far as Kety, his final destination, and it didn't take long for us to free him from the snowbank. When he was finally freed, we thought for a moment he had lied to us and wouldn't stop to let us get on the truck, but he did, and we all climbed aboard.

The ride into Kety was uncomfortable since the road was in bad shape due to all the winter traffic, and we bounced from deep pothole to deep pothole and by the time we arrived in Kety, I was sore from head to toe. When we finally arrived in the center of Kety, the driver stopped and signaled he wanted us to get down off his truck, however, one of the men in our group told us to wait while he got down and talked to the driver. I'm not too sure what type of negotiations took place, but the driver agreed to let us stay in his barn for the night. With that, our bumpy journey continued a few more kilometres until we turned off onto a snow-covered road, not much more than a narrow track, and the truck slid from side-to-side as the driver drove through the heavy snow covering the track. Finally, we saw a light in the distance and as we drew closer, we could see it was coming from a crude farmhouse with a small barn sitting behind it.

When the truck stopped in front of the house, the driver got out and led us to the barn. It was small, and the air was foul, but at least we had a roof over our heads for the night. Doktor Mueller and I shared a few pieces of stale bread, some dried meat, and hard cheese for dinner. Our surroundings weren't nearly as comfortable as they had been around the campfires, but we had already put quite a distance between us and Auschwitz, and we fell asleep feeling proud of our second day's progress.

## We Approach Bielsko

We awoke in the farmer's barn the next morning, our bodies stiff from the cold and empty bellies and it would have been nice if we could have made a small fire to warm our hands with the flames and fill our bellies with a nice mug of tea, but there wasn't anywhere nearby to build one, so we just made due. One of the men in our group walked over to the farmhouse and knocked on the door. When the farmer answered the door, he didn't invite him in, and after a short discussion, our new friend returned to the barn with the distressing news that the farmer wanted us to leave as soon as possible. His wife was quite upset with our presence; she was afraid we would murder them and steal the truck. I think it's quite funny as none of us was armed and murdering them was the last thing on our minds; on mine, anyway. All I was interested in was a warm bed with a nice cup of hot chocolate sitting on a nearby nightstand and just thinking of it made me smile. In fact, a cup of hot chocolate was constantly on my mind, but for the time being it was just a dream; it would be a long while until I was finally able to satisfy my hot chocolate craving.

When we all finally got going, we had to walk back down the long track to the highway and the sun's blinding brilliance forced me to shield my eyes from the glare reflected from the snowy fields along our route. It took more than an hour to make our way back to the highway because walking along the rutted track was difficult, and my feet were starting to get blisters from walking in Frau Mueller's oversized boots.

When we finally got to the highway, it wasn't nearly as busy as it had been the previous day, and it made it easier for us to walk along the edge of the highway without having to jump out of the way of passing trucks. By late afternoon, we were on the outskirts of a large town named Biala situated on the Biala River right across from another town called Bielsko. They were both ancient cities dating back to the twelfth or thirteenth centuries. At least that's what Doktor Mueller told me, however, to be quite honest, I hadn't heard of either town, but he said they had once been part of Germany, although they had become part of Poland when Silesia was divided between Poland and Czechoslovakia in the 1920's. Just strange-sounding names to me at the time.

When our ragtag band of refugees finally stopped on the outskirts of town, we could plainly see a stately spire atop the tallest building in town. We were all tired and weary from our journey and we needed to stop and rest, and although we had all been together for almost two days, we had hardly begun to know one another. Nobody was very interested in making idle conversation; everybody just intently focused on putting one foot in front of the other; that and eating. Otherwise, there wasn't an opportunity to get to know one another as we all just trudged silently along on our journey to unknown destinations.

One man definitely stood out from the others, and he was a bear of a man; he definitely towered over us all. He had introduced himself as Jaroslaw, and he introduced his wife as Gergana. He had apparently become the unofficial team leader and he was the man who had negotiated with the snow-trapped farmer. I'm sure his muscular shoulder was the main reason we even got a ride into town.

Jaroslaw and Gergana's farmhouse had been destroyed in the early part of the war when the Germans had first invaded Poland, and they had moved in with her parents on the outskirts of Auschwitz until both parents had taken ill with the flu and died. Rather than stay there and face the approaching Russian hordes, they had decided to flee westward and, like us, find refuge behind Allied lines. It always struck me as strange that people in their situation would just up and leave the security of their home and start on what could turn out to be a thousand kilometre journey on foot, with no plans, no preparation, and no destination.

As we sat there resting, Jaroslaw spoke up, for the first time. "We need to make a plan," and it was so out of character for him to speak up, that it startled everyone sitting there.

"What kind of plan do you propose?" someone asked.

"That's simple," he replied. "How we're going to survive and how we're going to find our way to safety."

"That's easier said than done," another voice joined the conversation.

Soon we were all engaged in lively discussion as everyone wanted to talk at the same time and it was as though once the conversation dam had been broken, words were flooding out like water through its breach.

The conversation focused on several important topics. First, where were we headed? Second, should we stay together as a group or split up and go our separate ways? And, third, what should we do about food?

After much discussion, the group finally came to a unanimous decision. We would continue westward until we were safely behind Allied lines, as a group, and we would immediately begin sharing our food supplies. It wasn't an easy decision to come to; some objected, but the more levelheaded members prevailed and if we were going to work together as a team, we needed to bond, and we needed to begin with everyone introducing themselves; personal stories would come later.

Although everyone already knew his name, Jaroslaw, being the generally accepted group leader, began. "My name is Jaroslaw Tomaszewski and my wife's name is Gergana," and when Jaroslaw introduced her to the group, she smiled and directed a very endearing little wave of her hand in everyone's direction.

One-by-one they introduced themselves, and even today I can close my eyes and see each one of them as they introduced themselves to the group. I have to name them in order, otherwise, I get totally confused. There was Dariusz and Ghila Jaworskia, Tadeusz and Ladislava Chmielewski, Bronislaw and Rachyl Wojciechowski, Kazimeirz and Feidhelm Kucharski, Doktor Mueller, and me of course. Polish names are sometimes a challenge, aren't they?

## A Dangerous Journey into Bielsko

As we sat in a circle on the outskirts of Bielsko getting to know one another, the topic quickly turned to the next leg of our journey. It was apparent that we didn't have enough food or supplies to continue much farther and we'd have to soon find shelter for the night, and hopefully, replenish our rapidly dwindling larder.

Doktor Mueller said Bielsko was a dangerous place to stop because the population was overwhelmingly German, even outnumbering the native Poles, and he feared what might happen when Germany's defeat was imminent. Would the Poles rise up and drive the hated Germans out of their city, or would the Germans try to eliminate the Poles and burn their city as they retreated towards the Fatherland with the retreating German troops? He said it wasn't a good idea to be caught up in that conflict; we should bypass the city and find a safer place to rest.

Jaroslaw disagreed with Doktor Mueller. He argued that we were all exhausted, the women in our group had suffered the most, we were almost out of food, and we should take a chance and head into Bielsko. There was much disagreement amongst the group, however they finally decided Doktor Mueller should go into town by himself to see if it were safe for the rest of us to follow. Doktor Mueller was the only person in our group who spoke both German and Polish, so he was the obvious choice, and I often wondered what the group had thought when it was first discovered he could also speak German. Would his multi-national heritage be enough to satisfy their curiosity? They never asked, and he never needed to explain. Strange isn't it; what *is* and what *isn't* important when you're only concerned about your own safety?

It was already late in the day, it was beginning to get dark, and we were at odds as to whether we should camp out for the night and wait until the morning or if he should leave immediately. It was finally agreed it might be safer for him to undertake his risky journey under the cover of darkness, so he left right away, and we built a small fire and huddled around it for warmth and companionship.

We waited forever for Doktor Mueller's return, but we finally saw a light approaching us in the distance; a torch and two men. As they drew nearer, we could see it was Doktor Mueller being led by an armed man holding a torch, and when it was obvious their mission was friendly, we quickly besieged them with questions. The man spoke to us in Polish and he told us he was a member of a local armed resistance group, and they called themselves *resistance fighters*, but I always called them *partisans*. I didn't like the word *fighters*; it just reminded me that we were in the middle of a terrible war and *partisans* was a far more pleasing word.

The *partisan* told us the German troops had pulled out of Bielsko a few days before our arrival when they knew the Russians would soon overrun the city. After the German troops had left, the local Polish population had taken up arms and started a bloody rebellion against the majority German population now that their protectors had fled. After that, Bielsko had become a terribly dangerous battleground between the two opposing groups and it probably wasn't safe for us to continue our journey into town.

Hearing that was a great disappointment to our weary band of travellers and we pleaded with him to find us safe shelter for the night; somewhere out of the miserable cold. We even promised we would leave before the sun rose the next morning. So, with great reluctance, he agreed to lead us into town, but we'd do so at our own peril as he warned us that if we were confronted by armed opponents, he'd have to protect himself before he would protect us.

As we cautiously approached Bielsko, we could see many buildings burning and we could hear sporadic gunfire echoing down the ancient, narrow streets that crisscrossed the city, and it was quite frightening to a young girl like me, but Doktor Mueller held my hand as we followed our guide into the city.

When we got into the outskirts of the city, our guide extinguished his torch and telling us to stay behind, he would quickly dart down one of the darkened streets, vouch for its safety, and then wave for us to join him. We tried to be as quiet as possible as we hugged the buildings lining the streets as we zigzagged our way towards the tallest building in town. It was obviously a church, however as we approached the building, it looked more like a fortress than a church. The main part of the building was constructed of large stones and it had a tall tower rising up from the fortress flanked by two smaller towers, and I have to say that it was quite imposing.

The guide led us to a small wooden door in the rear of the fortress, knocked on it three times, and the door slowly opened just a crack. He then exchanged words with the person inside and finally the door opened wide, revealing a man dressed in a long tunic, obviously a holy man of some kind.

"Quickly," he said as we stepped into St. Mikolaj Church and he led us through the dimly lit sanctuary illuminated by many lighted candles and to another door, which he opened with a large key hanging from his tunic.

"Down here," as he motioned us to follow him.

The open door revealed a stairway leading down to another closed door at the bottom, and Father Tadeus led us down the narrow stairway holding a lighted candle in his hand. When he got to the door, he used another large key to open it, revealing a large room filled with religious objects of every sort. By the dim light of his candle we could see parts of what was obviously a Christmas Nativity crèche, religious flags stacked against an opposite wall, statues of saints, and other assorted religious objects, and it was quite spooky; especially with all the life-sized statues.

Father Tadeus handed the candle to Doktor Mueller and walked back up the stairs as we all just stood there, not wanting to move until we had more light. Soon, Father Tadeus returned with several candles, set them up around the room, lit them, and we finally relaxed. What concerned me the most was when he left the room, it sounded as though he had locked the door behind him, and if anything bad happened, we would be trapped there.

We tried to make ourselves as comfortable as possible, however the room wasn't as cold as outside as the only warmth we had was from each other and whatever heat the small candles contributed. Father Tadeus soon returned with a large pot of hot soup and two loaves of bread. He apologised that he didn't have more to offer, but it was far more than what we'd had on our journey, so far. When Father Tadeus left us and closed the door behind him, the click of the latch being locked behind him was an ominous sound.

We all took turns passing the pot around amongst ourselves and as we did, I noticed the men took small portions while they encouraged their wives to take all they wanted. It wasn't the last time I was encouraged by such kind consideration on their parts.

Soon, it was time for us to blow out the candles and try to get some sleep. I wanted to put Alinka in the Nativity Manger, however Doktor Mueller told me it would make God mad at us and we needed His loving kindness and help now more than ever.

In the middle of the night we heard a great commotion in the upstairs sanctuary, and there was a lot of shouting and loud crashes as heavy objects hit the sanctuary floor directly above us. Then it got very quiet and since none of us had a watch, or any other way to tell the time, it was difficult to know what time it was, but I guessed it was in the middle of the night.

It was loud enough to wake everyone around us and they all sat up in alarm. Fortunately, we had left one small candle burning and we used it to light the others nearby. Jaroslaw got up and tested the door, however it was still locked. There was great debate as the men in the group discussed what we should do next. Several wanted to start banging on the door to alert someone above us that we were trapped below, while some thought it best to wait for Father Tadeus' return. Finally, they decided to wait until the shortest candle had burned to a stub and if help hadn't arrived by that time, we would make as much noise as possible. Obviously, nobody went back to sleep as we silently awaited our fate.

## Escape from Bielsko

Right before the smallest candle had burned itself out, we heard a key being turned in the door's lock, and the door opened to reveal Father Tadeus; his tunic torn, and his face bloodied. He quickly stepped inside and closed the door behind him as the men in our group got up from their seats and surrounded him. Bronislaw Wojciechowski stepped out of the group, walked up to Father Tadeus, and protectively put his arms around him. "Tell us what happened, Father," as his wife, Rachyl, walked up beside him, took a handkerchief from her pocket and gently wiped the blood from his battered face.

Father Tadeus smiled at her kindness. "They ransacked the church in the middle of the night."

"*Who* ransacked the church?" someone asked.

"*Thugs.* They broke into the church and stole everything. Anything of value, even the icons from the walls, and they smashed all the furniture and stole what little food we had left. I've nothing left to share with you."

Doktor Mueller stepped up and joined the Wojciechowskis as they tried to comfort Father Tadeus. "Is there anything we can do for you?"

"No," he replied. "But I appreciate your concern. However, I'm more afraid for your safety than I am for my own. The streets are filled with thugs and armed men killing each other and you wouldn't stand a chance if you tried to escape here."

His stern warning greatly distressed everyone in our group, however although we knew we were probably safe where we were, we couldn't remain there. Not only were we out of food, but we knew that the thugs might return soon, discover our secret hiding place, and we needed to leave as soon as possible.

"What about the man who led us here last night. Do you think he may help us escape?" Dariusz Jaworskia asked.

"I don't know, and it's probably not even safe for *him* to be on the streets, but I'll try to get word to him. In the meantime, you're welcome to stay here, but I can't vouch for your safety. The tradition of the church being a sacred sanctuary is a thing of the past. Sad, isn't it? Even God must be shedding tears for our plight." With that, Father Tadeus went back upstairs, leaving us to ponder our next move. At least he didn't lock the door behind him and that gave us some comfort.

We sat in the dimly lighted storeroom for quite a while as the silence was only occasionally interrupted by the sound of someone's empty stomach rumbling its unfulfilled protest. Finally, there was a loud knock on our dungeon's door as Jaroslaw cautiously approached it; its unknown signaler standing on the other side. When he opened it just a crack, someone on the other side rudely shoved it open, knocking Jaroslaw to the floor, and we all panicked.

A tall, heavy-set man with a long, black, knotted beard and filthy clothes pushed his way inside, and it looked as though he hadn't washed in a long time. He also carried a large rifle. "*Polski? (Polish?)*" he shouted at us in a gruff voice. No one dared answer, because if the reply was *tak (yes)* and he was German, he would probably kill us all right there, however, if the reply was *Niemiecki (German)* and he was Polish, we would have all shared a similar fate.

We waited as our fate hung on that one-word answer as Jaroslaw got up from the floor and stood right in front of the stranger, just a few inches from his face. *"Polski,"* he said proudly, as he waited for the bullet to tear into his chest.

*"Dobry! (Good),"* the giant of a man exclaimed as he dropped his rifle to the floor and embraced Jaroslaw in a bear hug. Jaroslaw was a big man, but the stranger made him look like a midget as he lifted him completely off the floor.

In the heated discussion that followed, the stranger, whose name was Przemyslaw, told us that the man who had guided us to safety the previous night had been killed as he tried to make his way back to the partisan camp after delivering us to the church. We all felt terrible for his loss as he had given his life to save ours and we will be forever grateful to him for that.

Our dead guide and Przemyslaw belonged to a group of Polish partisans who had been harassing the German troops ever since Germany had invaded their country. With the Russians approaching and the German troops in full retreat, they had infiltrated the city and encouraged the Polish residents to rise up and drive their German neighbours out of town. Although the partisans were still camped just north of the town near the Biala River, they hoped to move into town once it had been finally cleansed of Germans.

He offered to lead us out of town and to the safety of their camp where we could get something to eat as we quickly gathered our meager belongings and followed him up the staircase into the church. When we walked into the sanctuary, we were horrified by the damage. What had once been a peaceful, beautiful, safe space was now littered with debris. The altar was stripped bare of all its contents, someone had pushed it down the steps, and it was lying among the smashed church pews. Father Tadeus was walking around in a daze trying to collect all the prayer books and hymnals trying to put everything back in order, and we wished we could remain behind and help, but it was far too dangerous for us to stay a moment longer. Each one of us walked up to Father Tadeus, embraced him for a moment, thanked him for his hospitality, and then we followed Przemyslaw out the back door.

When we stepped out into the bright sunlight we were shocked to see the destruction surrounding us because we had arrived at the church the previous night after dark and we hadn't noticed the nearby devastation. Now, we were surprised to see many of the buildings lining the streets had some kind of damage from recent fighting and the streets were littered with personal belongings people had dropped in their haste to escape the mayhem.

Przemyslaw led us down several narrow streets until we neared the Biala River and when we got within sight of the river, he led us down a narrow alleyway into a small courtyard where there was a horse-drawn cart and a horse tied to a nearby tree. Przemyslaw walked over, untied the horse, and hitched him to the cart and when he had made certain that the horse was securely hitched, he told us to climb into the cart. There was barely enough room for the twelve of us, but somehow we managed to lie down close together and he covered us with blankets to keep us warm and out of sight.

After we had travelled a short distance out of town and were in a more secure area, he stopped the cart and uncovered us. By that time, we were stiff from lying in the same position, so we all got down from the cart and walked around just enough to limber up. Finally, we climbed back into the cart, jostled around until we could all get comfortable in sitting positions and once again, we were on our way. We followed the river for several kilometres on a dirt track until we turned into a dense forest lining the riverbank and after a few minutes we heard voices and laughter coming through the trees, when, suddenly, two armed men stepped out from behind a tree and blocked our passage.

Once they recognised Przemyslaw, they stepped aside, and let us proceed. Soon, we came to a large opening in the forest with a blazing fire in the center of the clearing surrounded by dozens of similarly roughly-clad men. Some were cleaning their weapons, some were eating, others were just relaxing and talking to their friends, and we soon realised that we had finally arrived at the partisans' camp.

## The Partisans' Camp

The first thing that struck me about the partisans was how happy everyone appeared to be as I'm sure the last five years had been hard for them and Germany's impending defeat was obviously bringing great joy and happiness to the group.

The cart stopped just outside the fire pit and friendly hands reached up to help us down. One of the partisans, a particularly handsome young man who looked somewhat familiar, stretched out his arms to me, but I said, *"Nie! (No),"* and pointed at Doktor Mueller. The partisan exhaled a hearty laugh and stepped aside as Doktor Mueller gently brushed him aside, walked over and lifted me out of the cart, and it felt good to be on solid ground again, especially after our bumpy ride.

As I walked towards the welcoming fire, I looked around and noticed many tents pitched amongst the nearby trees, and it looked as though they had been there for a while. As soon as we all were seated around the fire, a partisan beaming a toothless grin brought us some real china mugs, and he was followed by another carrying a pot of steaming, hot tea. It felt good just to hold the warm mug in my hand as it was still bitterly cold outside, and feeling the hot tea run down into my empty stomach felt even better.

Our new surroundings lifted everyone's spirits as we began to know our new hosts. The partisans felt Germany's defeat was imminent, but they weren't sure if they would welcome their Russian liberators or not. It was the partisans' consensus that the imminent Russian occupation might be as intolerable as the German's since over the years, Poland had served as a buffer state between the two countries and had suffered greatly as the two opposing giants had used Poland, rather than their own homelands as an unwelcome battleground.

Someone asked, "Are you hungry?" and you can imagine the laughter as we all answered as one. The meal they served us was one of the best I had ever eaten and it even included a tasty meat stew with real meat (although I dared not ask what kind of meat it was. Deer, I told myself.) There were loaves of dark bread, more mugs of hot tea and someone even opened a box of sweet candies they had been saving for a special occasion, or so they said.

Although it was still mid-afternoon, many of us were exhausted because we hadn't gotten much sleep the night before when the thugs had ransacked the church, and when one of the partisans saw me yawn and start to fall asleep on Doktor Mueller's shoulder, he got up from the fire, took my hand, and gently led me to a nearby tent. When he parted the tent's flap, I must say I wasn't impressed as I had expected to see a real bed inside; after all, they had been there a while, however the bed was just a mound of hay with a blanket thrown on top. How I longed for my comfortable bed back in Auschwitz, but compared to what I had been sleeping on since our departure, it was as comfortable as any bed in the finest hotel.

It was so comfortable I didn't wake up until the next morning, and what woke me were the loud cries of the jays as the partisans threw breadcrumbs to them, which they fought over dearly. I've never heard such a racket in my life and as always, there was a dominant member of the flock who somehow muscled his way through the crowd to snatch up every crumb, often from the mouth of one of his comrades. No matter how hard the laughing partisans tried to toss a crumb to the other jays, the dominant jay knew right where they were going to throw it, and he was always in the right place at the right time. The partisans would even try to fool him by pretending to throw a crumb in another direction, but the smart old jay would just sit there, cock his head, and I could almost hear him say, "Nice try," as he claimed his hard-won prize.

I was the last one out of bed and I wondered if the adults had sat up all night around the fire and visited, but I'm sure they hadn't. A mug of steaming, hot tea and a piece of dark bread spread with sweet fruit jam started my day off just perfectly and as I sat there and enjoyed my breakfast, there was great debate around the fire as to where our group of ragtag refugees should head. The partisans offered us shelter for as long as we wanted to stay as it was their opinion the town would be free of most Germans within a few days as the German residents fled with the retreating troops. They offered us the finest houses in town; assuming their occupants had fled and if not, they would make sure they had. Many in our group were tempted by the offer, but others wanted to continue their journeys westward.

Nikolas, the partisan's charismatic and outspoken leader, walked back to his tent and returned with a large map of Europe. We all drew closer as he unfolded it and laid it on the ground. He began by poking his finger at a spot in southwestern Poland. "We're here," he began. "I've heard someone wanted to journey on to Bavaria," as he poked another finger on a spot in southern Germany, then he poked a couple of other spots on the map. "This is Prague and this is Vienna. Do you know how far it is from here to Bavaria? I'm sure it's at least nine-hundred kilometres. Are you all crazy?"

I looked over at Doktor Mueller for confirmation; he just looked back at me and winked. I was sure he had a plan that he hadn't shared with me yet, however as it turned out, he didn't. I'm sure if he had confided that to me in the beginning, I would have never left the comforts of Auschwitz.

## Danger – We Flee the Partisans' Camp

As we sat around the fire planning the next leg of our journey, a horseback-mounted rider came crashing through the nearby woods into the camp's clearing, shouting, "*Szybko! Szybko! (Hurry. Hurry.)* German tanks are headed our way."

Nikolas rushed up and grabbed the horse's reins, "Tell me what you saw."

"Five tanks and two-dozen soldiers are headed down the river road right towards us," the rider breathlessly shouted down from his lathered mount. "They're only two kilometres from here."

Nikolas quickly took control, "Hurry. Go warn the others," as he slapped the nervous horse on its flanks and sent the messenger galloping on his way as the other partisans quickly gathered round. "Guns and ammunition first," he ordered and we were quickly engulfed in a great commotion as the partisans ran to the nearby tents and grabbed whatever they could in the short time we had before our camp was discovered.

"Quickly," Nikolas shouted, encouraging us to hurry as we heard the approaching tanks knocking down trees in the distance as though they were matchsticks. It took a while to get organised (probably longer than Nikolas wanted), but we soon started walking single-file through the thick snow covering the forest floor and it was immediately obvious that the partisans had carefully planned their escape route as some of them headed off in one direction, while others fanned out through the woods in other directions, leaving confusing tracks that would be hard to follow if the Germans decided to pursue us.

It was difficult for the women in our group to keep up with the others, and their husbands half-dragged and half-carried them through the thick snow cover, as the partisans kept urging us to hurry, but they were never mean or cross about it. In fact, several of them got on either side of the women and helped carry them towards safety.

As we got farther from the camp, the clanking sounds the tanks made receded into the distance although we weren't sure if the German troops had decided to pursue us on their own. After all, we had left a blazing fire in the camp and it wouldn't have been too hard for the Germans to figure out we were still close by. Hopefully, they would just think we were a group of refugees, not armed partisans. Walking through the crusty snow was grueling and every now and then we'd stop and rest, but it wasn't long before we got up from our temporary resting places and continued our exhausting trek.

I was one of the lucky ones; Doktor Mueller carried me on his back for most of the way and although I'm sure I was quite a burden for him, he never complained. He seemed to be only concerned about one thing; not revealing his identity to our fellow travellers or the partisans, because if they discovered he was an SS doctor who worked at Auschwitz, they would have probably killed us both on the spot. Because of that, I barely spoke a word on our entire journey and if someone asked me a question, I'd always answer in as few words as possible. I'm sure they must have thought I was terribly shy, which coincidentally I just happened to be, but not for the reasons they may have thought.

After we had walked a few kilometres, we entered what may have been a swamp in the summer, but was now an impenetrable, crusty thicket. Someone said it was near the Vistula River, which didn't mean much to me then, as Nikolas led the way, being careful not to bend or break the slender willows forming the almost impassable obstacle lest he leave a track the German troops could easily follow. Hopefully, the snow that had started falling would eventually erase all traces of our escape route.

We made sure we stepped into the footsteps of the person ahead of us; not only was it an effort to mask how many of us there were, but it also made our going a lot easier because the thicket's icy crust made it practically impossible to make any headway. Nikolas, who was leading the way, suffered greatly, and we all tried to avoid the whip-like motion the bent willows made as the person in front of us pushed it out of their way and then released it. More than once Doktor Mueller was hit in the face by saplings being snapped back into his face, followed by *"Sorry,"* from the person in front of him.

We slowly made our way through the thicket until we came to a clearing filled with snow-covered mounds and when Nikolas walked up to one of the mounds and brushed away the heavy snow cover, it revealed a crude thatched hut. Others did the same until we were standing in the middle of what was obviously one of their abandoned camps, and at least we'd have a roof over our heads for the night.

As we gathered pine branches from the nearby forest to make comfortable beds, we could hear loud explosions coming from the direction of Bielsko, and it was obvious that the German tanks had entered the town and were engaged in a heated battle; probably with the armed Polish residents. Hopefully, the German troops would soon grow tired of fighting street-to-street in alleyways too narrow for their supporting tanks to navigate and would continue on their hasty retreat from the pursuing Russians.

Realising the Germans probably hadn't followed us, Nikolas told the partisans to go out into the forest and collect firewood to make a fire. Soon, we had a blazing fire in the center of the camp where one of the partisans had uncovered the long-abandoned fire pit. At first, the fire gave off dense plumes of grey-black smoke, but once it was burning brightly, it produced hardly any smoke that might reveal our new hiding place. Only once when someone threw some green pine boughs onto the fire, did Nikolas have to sternly admonish one of his comrades.

While we were occupied making ourselves comfortable, one of the partisans rifled through the snow-covered cooking hut and uncovered a rusty kettle someone had left behind. It took a while to melt some snow until we had a kettle of boiling but rusty water, and I never realised how much snow you have to melt to get just a little bit of water. Someone would fill the kettle to the brim with snow and would only get enough water to fill half a teacup and we all watched eagerly as they kept shovelling in mounds of snow which disappeared right before our eyes.

Finally, as I mentioned, we had a kettle of hot water, and fortunately, one of the partisans had thought to put a couple of mugs and some loose tea in their rucksack, so we shared some hot tea and some crusty black bread someone else had dug out of their rucksack. It wasn't much, but we were all grateful to have something, *anything*, to eat.

We spent a restless night huddled together in the thatched huts and we awoke the next morning to discover our fire had been extinguished by the fresh snowfall that had blanketed the camp while we slept. We were now faced with two choices; one was to stay where we were until we felt we could safely return to the camp outside Bielsko or we could head back right away. There was great discussion amongst the partisans, but they finally agreed to head back immediately since we no longer heard any explosions coming from the direction of Bielsko as they assumed, quite correctly, that the Germans had moved on.

It was even more difficult retracing our steps through the thicket as the willows were now covered with snow that exploded in huge white puffs as we pushed them out of our way, and we were all soon covered from head to toe with white, powdery snow. By late afternoon, we wearily arrived back at our original campsite to find it had been destroyed. It was obvious the tanks had deliberately crushed anything of use so we decided to keep moving into town and when we arrived on the outskirts of Bielsko, what we discovered truly shocked us.

## Return to Bielsko

As we approached Bielsko, we could see many fires burning and dense columns of black smoke soaring into the winter sky outlining St. Mikolaj's tall spire, and it was apparent there had been heavy fighting within the city, and we wondered how the lightly-armed residents had fared against the greatly feared German tanks, however it didn't take long to find out.

As we headed towards the center of town, there was carnage everywhere and many of the old buildings that had stood there for centuries were now reduced to piles of smouldering rubble. The streets were filled with destroyed vehicles of every type; there were dead horses still attached to their destroyed carts, and every now and then we came upon a corpse lying in some unnatural, grotesque position, sometimes with missing limbs.

Approaching St. Mikolaj Church, we were relieved to see it had been spared, although several of the nearby buildings were still on fire. The square in front of the church was now littered with the remains of what had once been barricades and were now piles of squashed rubble as though they were flattened by a heavy hand. We assumed from the litter that the citizens had made a futile attempt to fight the Germans behind their flimsy barricades only to be run over by the tanks.

Through the open front doors of the church we could see it was filled with people, however it wasn't until we had stepped inside did we realise it had been turned into a temporary hospital and morgue. There must have been at least one hundred people lying on the sanctuary floor. The smashed pews had been pushed up against the walls to make room for the wounded and dying, and Father Tadeus was going from person-to-person administering prayers and too often, last rites. Nikolas, the partisan leader, handed his rifle to a nearby companion, walked up to Father Tadeus, embraced him, the two of them then walked over into a corner, and began a lengthy discussion.

When Nikolas finally rejoined our group, he repeated what Father Tadeus had told him. When the Polish citizens realised the German tanks were approaching the town, they had set up several barricades in the square in front of the church and waited patiently, and as the German tanks entered the square, the citizens began firing their meager weapons at the approaching tanks and the German troops following safely behind them. The battle was over in just a couple of bloody minutes and the square was left littered with their destroyed barricades and dozens of dead townspeople. Father Tadeus had run out into the square when he first saw them building the barricades, implored them to disperse, and hide until the Germans had passed through town. Bielsko wasn't their main objective, he argued, and if they let them pass through town without any opposition, the town would be spared, however, they wouldn't listen, and they, along with the town, had paid dearly for their folly.

It was obvious there weren't enough people to tend to the wounded, so without asking, we all started helping. The men in our group helped move the 'walking wounded' to make room for the new arrivals, and Doktor Mueller started tending to the more seriously injured people lying on the cold, sanctuary floor. The women went out to the well in the center of the square and brought back buckets of water to help cleanse the wounds, and I so wanted to tell everybody he was a doctor, but I held my tongue lest I reveal our masquerade.

I followed Doktor Mueller from patient-to-patient and helped him as best I could, however, many of the wounded were beyond help, and we didn't have any medicine we could give them to ease their pain. We just bound their wounds, tried to reassure them, and then moved on to the next sufferer. Most of the wounded men tried to be as brave as possible, but every now and then one of them would cry out in pain, and one of the women would walk over, kneel down, and try to comfort him. Sometimes just a woman's gentle touch was all they needed to help them bear their unbearable pain.

Father Tadeus appeared to be everywhere all at the same time and as he prayed over each victim, I realised, that although he was a Catholic priest, *his* God was the same as *my* God, *Adonai;* the one my father had told me about back in our village; he and I just had our own unique ways of acknowledging Him. I knew different religions believed in a common God, but being in Father Tadeus' presence strengthened my belief that He was a part of *everyone's* life.

Many of the people lying on the sanctuary floor were covered entirely by blankets, or some other covering, as I assumed they were beyond saving and someone had covered them to retain their dignity. When Doktor Mueller came to a blanket-covered body, he would gently lift the blanket, check the person's pulse to make sure they were dead, and then move on to the next. When he raised one of the blankets I was horrified as I saw that the body under the blanket was that of a young girl, probably about my age. She was beautiful; her face was angelic, there wasn't a scratch on her, and I wanted to shake her and tell her to wake up, but when I tugged at Doktor Mueller's sleeve, he just shook his head and pulled the blanket back over her face. Her face still haunts me to this day.

When we had done as much as we could, we all gathered in the front of the church near where the altar used to stand before the church had been vandalised. Although their larders were mostly bare, some of the remaining townspeople had graciously responded to the crisis and brought hot food into the church. Father Tadeus treated us to a splendid meal of hot tea, *bigos, pierogis, gołąbkis,* and bowls filled with steaming, hot *rosół* and it was the best meal I'd had since we celebrated Frau Mueller's last birthday, back when she was 'normal', and it was even better than our first meal in the partisans' camp.

Every now and then one of the neighbours would bring in another basket of food and set it nearby, and we were all so tempted to gorge ourselves, but we felt we had to watch our manners. After all, we *were* in a church.

When we had eaten as much food as we dared, we all sat in a circle and relaxed. Soon, Nikolas, the partisan leader, walked up and sat down next to Doktor Mueller. After exchanging pleasantries, he got straight to the point. He said the German troops who had come through the city and had caused so much damage, were probably the last remnants of Hitler's fleeing armies, and the fighting was over, for the time being. We all knew the Russian Army would soon be on the outskirts of town although we didn't know when, but we knew it was inevitable, and how they would treat the townspeople was questionable, but the remaining town leaders had overwhelmingly decided to welcome them with open arms.

Nikolas said most of the German townspeople and Jews had either already fled or had been forcibly removed. When he mentioned the Jews being forcibly removed, I cringed. Clearly, there was still much hatred for Jews, even here in this out-of-the-way place in southern Poland and I wanted to speak up, but Doktor Mueller gave me a warning look that sealed my lips.

Nikolas slowly got up from our circle, stood, and lectured us as though he was delivering a sermon to a congregation during a Sunday service. He said he was certain the Russians wouldn't be interested in occupying Bielsko; instead, they'd be more focused on pursuing the fleeing Germans all the way to Berlin. After they had passed through town, he assured us things would quickly return to normal, the town would rebuild itself, there would be peace and harmony, and the partisans could disarm, disband, and return to their families. If he only knew then what we now know to be the truth.

As his sermon ended, he slowly looked at each of us, individually, and said something like, "I want you all to stay here and join me as we rebuild our glorious town. You will be safe here, we will guarantee your safety in a nice place to live, and you'll all enjoy a prosperous life if you decide to stay."

Satisfied he had made his point, he crossed his arms and just stood there waiting for some sign that we understood his offer. We all just sat there and looked at each other, not knowing what to say, when Jaroslaw finally broke the logjam. "Thank you for your generous offer, Nikolas. However, I think we're all quite tired now, and I'm not sure we could make a good decision the way we're feeling. Why don't you let us get some rest and we'll talk about it again in the morning?"

When we had all nodded our agreement, Nikolas smiled and said "So be it. Please get some rest, and we'll talk about it tomorrow. I know my friends and neighbours will always remember your kindness," as he turned and left the sanctuary.

## We Make a Difficult Decision

Although the first time we had slept in the basement storeroom I was filled with anxiety, this time I slept like a baby with Alinka clutched tightly to my chest. So much had happened since we had left Auschwitz and yet it had only been a few days, however, we still had many more days ahead of us until we reached the Allied lines.

The next morning, we went upstairs into the sanctuary to see if there was anything we could do to help the poor people who had spent the night lying on the cold floor. There were fewer people there as either they had gotten better and returned home, or they had died, and I hoped it was the former.

Father Tadeus greeted us with a warm smile and a pot of steaming, hot tea as our group huddled off in a corner of the sanctuary and we tried to make ourselves comfortable. We knew

[160]

Nikolas had asked us to make a difficult decision, but we hadn't had any time to discuss it amongst ourselves. Although it would be each person's own decision as whether to stay or move on, just talking amongst ourselves appeared to sway the group first one way and then another. Of course, I didn't take part in the discussion; I was just a child.

None of us had any destination in mind other than we wanted to stay ahead of the advancing Russian Army, and I'm not too sure it was even that; I just think people were tired of war, and the thought of being caught once again between the two armies as they brutalised each other was too much to bear. Many in our group thought staying in Bielsko might be a good idea, and they reasoned that since the German Army was in full retreat, the Russians had no reason to destroy the town, and perhaps they would pass right through town and not even stop.

Others said they had that heard Russian troops were beasts that raped the women and shot the men. To many, they were uncivilised mongrels direct from the Russia steppes; barbarians who had no regard for human life; uncouth animals, someone called them. Since the majority of our group were Polish peasants or working-class people, they had nothing in their past to fear. Doktor Mueller on the other hand, was a German SS officer who, if discovered, would be treated badly, perhaps even killed. Therefore, he just sat and listened to the others, and he didn't offer any comments one way or the other; he had already made up his mind.

Sometime in mid-morning Nikolas rejoined us and he was in a very jovial mood, happy now that the Germans had fled Bielsko and his partisan comrades could soon rejoin their families and resume their normal lives.

He pulled up a nearby chair and sat down and although he began the conversation by making small talk, we all knew what was on his mind, but we waited for him to bring up the subject. Finally, the discussion turned to the future, however before he asked anyone in the group as to what they had decided to do, he went on for quite a while talking about Bielsko in glowing terms and what the future held. He made it sound like the Promised Land; the Land of Milk and Honey and I must confess it was quite the sales pitch.

As before, the discussion centered on how the victorious Russians would treat the local population, how nobody expected them to fight their way to Berlin and then just return to their homes in Russia. Instead, everyone expected them to be occupiers, not liberators; however, what a Russian occupation would be like was the great unknown.

Although Doktor Mueller was German, his mother was Polish, and she had been a great influence in his life. She had ingrained in him the memories of how Poland had suffered through the years of war and conquest at the hands of the Austrians, Germans, Prussians, and Russians, and he fancied himself as quite a historian and an authority on the matter.

When it was finally his turn to speak, he spoke with great eloquence about the Polish struggles and how Poland had even ceased to exist until after the end of World War I. He reminded the group how the Russian conquerors had forced Polish citizens to work in the mines in Siberia and how they looked down upon them as a source of manual labour, so why would they treat the Poles any different this time, he asked.

Nikolas listened attentively until Doktor Mueller had finished, and then he stood up and addressed our group. Now was different, he argued. In the past, Russia had been ruled by czars and they had exploited the working class, but now the Communists were in power and they *were* the working class. Why wouldn't the Russians treat the Poles as hard-working brothers, not slaves?

Others voiced their opinions, but overall they agreed that Nikolas' proposal to stay in Bielsko was a generous one. Finally, Nikolas went around the group, one-by-one, and asked whether they would stay and one-by-one, they all agreed to stay. Doktor Mueller was the last one he asked and when Nikolas asked him whether we intended to stay or not, he paused for a moment, put his arm protectively around me, and said, "We'll continue on." With those few simple words, he had sealed our fate; unlike the others, our journey had just begun, not ended.

## Father Tadeus' Escape Plan

After the group had come to a decision to remain in Bielsko, a lively discussion began among us, and even those who were usually very quiet became energised by their decisions and everyone began to make plans about starting their new lives in Bielsko.

Doktor Mueller and I only sat there and listened as we were now the outsiders, not part of the group anymore, because we had decided to continue our journey and not stay. I say *we*, although it was entirely Doktor Mueller's decision. We *had* talked about it the night before and I had supported his decision, although I didn't have a clue as to what lay ahead in our journey. So far, our journey had been extremely difficult, I hoped things would get better, and as long as Doktor Mueller was my protector, I felt safe; we had truly become father and daughter. Sometimes I felt guilty for thinking about him that way, but I'm sure my real father would be happy to know I had a protector, and I couldn't wait to tell him about our adventures when we were finally reunited on our farm somewhere in Russia.

As the conversation finally began to quiet down, Nikolas took the members of our group off into a corner of the sanctuary and had a private conversation with each of them, which we only assumed involved making plans for their resettlement in Bielsko. Many of the houses in town had been deserted by the fleeing German residents and he appeared to have become the self-appointed, local real-estate broker, however we never did find out what they had to give him in exchange for their new homes; we were never part of that conversation.

Although we had only been together as a group for a short time, we had all endured such hardships together that we felt as though we had known each other for a lifetime, and leaving them behind and starting on our own again would be sad, but friendships born during wartime were often short-lived, and always ended too soon.

As we sat by and watched our little group dissolve before our very eyes, Father Tadeus came over and sat down next to Doktor Mueller. "So, I hear you and your daughter have decided to move on," he began.

Doktor Mueller smiled, "Yes, Father. Although we'd love to stay here, our journey won't end until we have found safety behind the Allied lines."

"I'm sure you'd be safe here," Father Tadeus countered. "There are so many wonderful things about our beautiful town. Well, it used to be beautiful before the war, but I'm sure it will be beautiful once again, and I'm certain the Russians can't be nearly as bad as the Germans." Doktor Mueller winced at his negative comment about the Germans, but kept his silence.

I knew he had already made his decision, and once Doktor Mueller made up his mind, there was no way he would even consider changing it. Doktor Mueller then crossed his arms across his chest; his way of letting him know how solid his position was. "Thank you, Father Tadeus, your offer to stay here is a generous one and a heartfelt one at that, but I have to think about our future, and I truly think our future lies somewhere in Bavaria, not Poland."

"So, you speak German, do you?" Father Tadeus' question was a curious one and I'm sure Doktor Mueller wasn't expecting it and I could tell by his reaction, that he didn't know how to answer.

I wish I could have been inside his head and listen in on his thoughts as he sat there and mulled over his answer. Finally, he spoke, "That's a curious question, Father Tadeus. Why do you ask?" An obvious attempt to buy some 'thinking' time.

Father Tadeus leaned over and said, in a whisper, "I have a plan in mind to get you safely to your destination, but you'll need to be able to speak some German. As it is, the journey could turn out to be extremely dangerous, but knowing some German would be helpful."

Doktor Mueller drew him closer and whispered into Father Tadeus' nearby ear, "*Ja, ich kann etwas Deutsch sprechen (Yes, I can speak a little German),*"

Father Tadeus' smile spread entirely across his patched up face, "*Ich dachte so. Mit einem Namen wie Müller, ich dachte Sie könnten etwas Deutsch kennen. (I thought so. With a name like Mueller, I thought you might know a little German).*"

That was the only conversation they had in German as they once again began speaking in Polish, but I sensed Doktor Mueller's response had greatly pleased the Father.

One-by-one, our new friends gathered up their meager possessions and followed Nikolas out of the church to their new homes and as they departed, we all hugged and agreed that someday we would all get together again and celebrate our successful flight, but we never did.

After our entire group had left the church, leaving just Doktor Mueller and me with Father Tadeus, he asked us to join him in his church office. As we followed him into his office, we were in for quite a shock as I don't know what I had expected, but I know what I saw *wasn't* what I expected, if that makes any sense. His office was stacked to the ceiling with everything imaginable. Because vandals had ransacked the church the first night we had spent in the church's basement, his office was now crammed full of anything of value he could salvage from the wreckage, and the only open spot was a thin mattress in one corner where he slept guarding the nearby church's treasures against further looting.

He walked over, straightened up the blankets on his makeshift bed, and offered us a seat. Once we had made ourselves as comfortable as possible, he started. "I apologise for the mess, but I needed to have a private conversation somewhere out of earshot of the others. I hope you don't mind." Doktor Mueller assured him that he understood the circumstances and appreciated him offering us a quiet place to talk.

Father Tadeus continued, in German, and that was a huge surprise to both of us. "Heinrich. With a last name like Mueller, I assumed you must be of some German ancestry and I guess I was right, wasn't I?"

"*Ja. Mein Vater war Deutscher und meine Mutter war Polnisch (Yes. My father was German and my mother was Polish),*" Doktor Mueller said in his proud, Bavarian-accented German.

Father Tadeus leaned back against the wall behind his mattress and seemed to relax. "I'm certain not too many of my parishioners

[166]

realise I was raised in Munich, myself. Like you, Heinrich, my father was German and my mother was Polish, and I have to admit I really took advantage of the best of both worlds. I truly enjoyed my father's love of good German music, and I also enjoyed my mother's wonderful Polish cooking, too. It was because of her I went into the priesthood and it's a decision I've never regretted. I even requested a parish in Poland so I could work to bring the German and Polish populations together under God's roof, and to some extent, I was successful, that is until this dreadful war started and people started taking sides."

"That must have been painful for you, Father," Doktor Mueller interjected.

"Heinrich. I tried my best to calm the waters, but there was nothing I could do, and you can't even begin to imagine the horror as I watched my parishioners fight and kill each other in the streets right in front of our church. My parishioners! The ones who had joined together under God's roof to celebrate our Holy Communion, wonderful midnight Masses on Christmas Eve in our beautiful candle-lit sanctuary, weddings, funerals; you name it. We were truly a wonderful congregation and then this war ruthlessly devastated us."

Doktor Mueller took a moment to ponder Father Tadeus' emotional reply. "Tell me, Father. How did you feel about the situation, having a German father and a Polish mother? That must have been difficult for you, wasn't it? Did you ever have to take sides?" he asked.

"It's curious you should ask me such a question of me, a Catholic priest! Well, I certainly know God doesn't have favourites; one nation over another, one religion over another, one people over another, one person over another, as I truly believe that anyone who believes in Him is an equal in His eyes. I'm certain He even embraces the non-

[167]

believers, knowing their souls can be saved in the end. However, I'm human, just like everyone else, and I must admit I've had many doubts in my moments of weakness. It was difficult listening to my German parishioners confess how badly they had treated their Polish neighbours and much of what they said made sense, and then I'd hear their Polish neighbours' confessions about their transgressions against their German neighbours and what they said also made sense to me. Clearly, I'm not in a position to judge them, only God can be their judge, but I was often torn between one side and the other and many times I asked myself what I'd do if I were in their position. Do you know what? I never found an answer, although I got on my knees many times and begged God not to allow such violence come into His church."

Doktor Mueller pulled me closer to his side and put his arm around me. "Tell me, Father. You said you had a plan to help us safely on our way and ever since you mentioned that, I've been eagerly waiting to hear what you had to say."

Father Tadeus took Doktor Mueller's hand in his. "Please forgive me for rambling, but I thought it was important for you to understand my feelings about our situation before I unveiled my plan to you both. I'm not one to take sides, so what you may have done in the past makes no difference to me, no matter how harmless or grievous it may have been, as I truly believe that someday we'll all meet God and beg for His forgiveness, so I'll leave that conversation up to you and Him. However, tell me, Heinrich, are you a religious person?"

"Not really, Father," Doktor Mueller replied through pursed lips.

"Too bad, because if you accept my plan, you'll have to get religion quite quickly," Father Tadeus chuckled.

Doktor Mueller nervously returned his laughter, "Hopefully, I'll have a good teacher," as we both carefully listened while Father Tadeus revealed his escape plan. It was interesting, but would it work?

## Father Heinrich's Unveiling

We both sat there entranced, listening to Father Tadeus' plan and it soon became apparent he'd been thinking about it for quite a while and as his plan unfolded, it became obvious it was his own personal escape plan if he ever had to flee Bielsko.

In the middle of his explanation, he got up and rummaged through the piles of clutter in his office until he found what he was looking for. He then walked back, sat down next to us, and spread a large map of Europe out on the floor. It had many towns circled in red ink with a handwritten sheet attached to it.

He pointed at one of the circled cities, "Bielsko." His finger then followed a line of red-circled cities moving west on the map. "Frýdek-Místek, Čadca, Trenčín, Trnava, Bratislava, Graz, Klagenfurt, Bad Reichenhall, Rottach-Egern. I personally know most of the parish priests in these towns, and it had been my plan to leave Bielsko, move from town-to-town, and stay with them until I reached Bavaria. Now my plan has become your plan; I've decided to stay here and help rebuild Bielsko."

Doktor Mueller looked confused. "I'm not too sure what you mean when you say *your* plan has now become *our* plan."

Father Tadeus removed the handwritten sheet from the map and handed it to Doktor Mueller. "This is a list of the towns I've mentioned, the name of the Catholic church in each town, and the name of the priest who was there the last time I was in touch with them. Many of them were in my seminary class back at the Priestseminar Berlin and we've kept in touch throughout the years and although I'm sure some of them have moved on since then, I'm likewise sure that many of them may have stayed."

"I'm not too sure how this will be of any help to us," Doktor Mueller interrupted.

"Since you said you weren't a religious man, I doubt if you know the history of the Catholic Church within the German National Socialists' state and in the countries they've overrun, and I have to admit it hasn't been a pleasant relationship. Since they came to power, they've tried to close all Catholic schools, shut down the Catholic press, and they have imprisoned thousands of priests, nuns, and scholars on mostly trumped-up charges. Fortunately, most churches were left unmolested if they kept a low profile and didn't try to influence their congregation against the State. Even our Holy Father, Pope Pius XII, has tried to maintain cordial, if not sometimes highly criticised relations with the National Socialists. The Russians, on the other hand, have all but crushed the Catholic Church in Russia, and I dare say not one Catholic church exists there today."

"That's an interesting history lesson, Father, but what does that have to do with us?" Doktor Mueller asked.

"Forgive me; I guess I *am* a bit long winded. You should hear my sermons," Father Tadeus joked. "What I'm trying to say is that you could find sanctuary in any of these churches as long as they haven't been overrun by the Russians. After that happens, I'm not too sure if they could offer you the same protection, however until then, I'm suggesting that you stop at these churches along the way for shelter and security. I'll give you a Letter of Introduction to take along with you and I'm sure my fellow priests would welcome you both with open arms."

Doktor Mueller picked up the map and studied it at length. "It looks as though you've planned your escape very well, Father, and if I had to guess, it looks as though each of these towns is a day's travel apart by motorcar. Was that a part of your plan?"

"Precisely, and I'm impressed that you've already picked up on that part of my plan. Each town gets you one day closer to Bavaria and what would have been my final destination, Rottach-Egern. It's a beautiful town on Lake Tegernsee, and that's where I grew up. In fact, I took my First Communion in St. Laurentius Church right on the shores of the lake, and it's such a beautiful, tranquil town in the heart of the Bavarian Alps. It's a destination I'd highly recommend."

Doktor Mueller just laughed aloud. "That's a good one, Father. You've made your plans based on travelling in a motorcar, however what would it do to those plans if you were on foot, like us?"

"However you won't be on foot, Heinrich. What if you had the use of a motorcar?"

"A *motorcar*, you say? Is someone just going to walk up to us and hand us the keys to a motorcar, Father?"

"Wait a minute," Father Tadeus smiled as he got up and walked over to what had once been his work desk, but was now piled high with clutter. After rummaging around for a while, he came back to where we were sitting, and dropped a set of keys into Doktor Mueller's open hand. "Here. Take these, it's all yours."

"What's mine?"

"My *motorcar*, of course."

Doktor Mueller sat there stunned, not knowing what to say.

"The motorcar is my gift to you and your lovely daughter. I no longer have any use for it now that I've decided to stay here with my parishioners. Moreover, I've been hoarding petrol for quite some time now, it's enough to get you far along on your journey, and I'm sure the generosity of my fellow priests will overflow your petrol cans at every stop. With good luck, you'll soon get to see my beloved Lake Tegernsee and when you get there, you can leave the motorcar with my brother, and although I'm sure he'll ask many questions, I know he'll be glad to hear that I'm safe here in Bielsko."

Doktor Mueller reached over and hugged Father Tadeus. "Thank you for your generosity. I'm truly overwhelmed as I'm not too sure we could have made it any farther in our journey on foot. However, we can both look now forward to safely reaching our destination, God willing."

Father Tadeus laughed wholeheartedly, "I have to admit I don't even know how to drive a motorcar and if I actually had to put my plan into motion, I'd have to quickly learn to drive along the way, wouldn't I? I must confess, however, that it's not *my* motorcar; it's actually the *church's* motorcar. A wealthy parishioner left it to the church when she died and it's been sitting in a garage for years now. I barely know how to get the engine running, nothing more. One of our parishioners is a motorcar mechanic, and he stops by to take care of it from time-to-time, but other than that, it hasn't been on the road for quite some time."

Doktor Mueller leaned forward towards Father Tadeus and said in a low whisper, "It's been years since I've driven a motorcar myself, however there's no better time than to reacquaint myself with the finer mechanical aspects of safe and courteous driving, is there?" And I had to laugh, because whenever Doktor Mueller wanted to be humourous, he'd talk like that; use big words to drive home a simple point. Sometimes his use of words was so complex that the humour was lost somewhere along the way, and by Father Tadeus' reaction, this was one of those times.

"One more thing," Father Tadeus said as he sat back and looked at us both quite sternly. "I'm not too sure it would be a good idea for you two to travel dressed the way you are. I'm afraid people would be highly suspicious of someone dressed like you driving a nice motorcar since you both look like beggars, if I may say so. On the other hand, if you were wearing fine clothing, someone may take you for a wealthy traveller, rob you, and steal your motorcar, so I have an idea," as he once again got up and started rummaging through a pile in the corner of his office.

Shortly, he returned holding something in his hands. "Here. Try these on," as he handed Doktor Mueller a complete Catholic priest's outfit replete with a full collar shirt, black trousers, black ankle-length cassock, and a pair of black shoes and socks.

Doktor Mueller protested, "I can't wear those, Father. Wouldn't it be against the Church's rules?"

"What are rules in times like these? God doesn't judge us by the measure of our cloth, does He?" his humourous reply, one that went over Doktor Mueller's head as *his* previous attempt had done so shortly before.

Doktor Mueller still wasn't convinced, "I understand what you're saying, but how could someone like me pass myself off as a Catholic priest? After all I can't even begin to recite a Hail Mary or whatever you call it."

"That *would* be a problem, Heinrich, however I've thought this whole thing through and here's what I propose."

After Father Tadeus had revealed his plan, he asked Doktor Mueller to change into his new travelling clothes, and it took him a while to change; minutes filled with anticipation, but finally Doktor Mueller returned to Father Tadeus' crowded office. The man who had left the room dressed as a ragged Polish peasant named Heinrich

Mueller now returned as a handsome Catholic priest named Father Heinrich, and even Father Tadeus was surprised by his transformation. Perhaps his plan *did* have a chance of succeeding.

Father Tadeus made one more foraging trip back to what had been his desk and it didn't take him long to return with a book in his hand. "Here take this with you. It's the Prayer Book I used back in the seminary and I hope you don't mind, but it's filled with my pencil notes in the margins, and it's in German. The only thing I could give you from our church would be written in Polish and that wouldn't fit your new identity, Father Heinrich," as a smile lit up Father Tadeus' bloodied face. "If you want, I'll even stick some bookmarks in it where you can find our more useful prayers in case you are called to duty, however I must warn you not to perform any marriages as that could prove to be very upsetting if discovered."

After placing several bookmarks in the Prayer Book, he handed it to Doktor Mueller, and our newly frocked Father Heinrich beamed, although many years later he confessed to me how terribly guilty he had felt about assuming his new identity, as he said it had haunted him for a long time until he finally had decided to do something about it.

## The Motorcar

Father Tadeus got up from his seat. "Let's go meet your new steed." Another feeble attempt at humour that like his previous failed attempt went unnoticed, as we both got up and followed him out of the church. We cautiously walked down the narrow alleyway behind the church; the same alleyway we used when we had first arrived there. Father Tadeus led the way, and it was a gloomy day, quite chilly, in fact, and the smoke from the smouldering buildings mixed with the fog blowing off the river made it quite difficult for us to see. I covered my face with my scarf to protect myself from the obnoxious brew and I stuffed Alinka safely inside my coat.

We zigzagged across town through back alleyways and just when I was about to tell Father Heinrich I couldn't go any farther, Father Tadeus stopped in front of a large wooden building; a lopsided sign lettered "*Stajnie (Stables)*" dangled precariously over the two large wooden doors. "This is it," he proclaimed as he took a large key ring from his overcoat pocket and checked each key until he found the one he was looking for.

He inserted the large key into the door's crude lock, turned it, and the bolt slid back with a loud clack. Then he and Father Heinrich struggled to open the heavy doors and it was quite a struggle; the narrow alleyway was filled with debris, and it took some time for them to clear enough away so they could fully open the doors. Finally, with one great effort, they managed to open the doors wide enough to accomplish our mission; retrieve the motorcar.

As I glanced inside, it was obvious the stables hadn't been used for their main purpose in a long time, because the air was musty, the floor was covered with pulverised horse manure, and the stalls were empty, and to top it off, the motorcar was nowhere in sight. We three stepped inside and waited for our eyes to adjust to the dim light, and slowly, almost imperceptibly, a massive hulk at the far end of the stables started coming into view - the motorcar!

It was huge and it wasn't what I had expected, at all, although I didn't know what to expect, but I just didn't expect it to be that large.

As we drew closer, it grew larger, and I'd say from where the driver sat to the front of the motorcar was longer than our biggest horse cart back on the farm. It had immense wire wheels, a spare tire mounted on the passenger's side front fender, four doors and a huge trunk hung off the rear bumper.

Father Heinrich was as surprised as I was. "It's not what I expected, Father Tadeus. I expected something smaller, something easier to drive. It's huge. What is it?" he asked.

Father Tadeus apparently enjoyed our amazement. "Yes, it is quite large, isn't it? The only thing I know about it is that it's a 1933 Mercedes-Benz Nürburg 500, if that means anything to you, as it doesn't mean a thing to me."

"Me either," Father Heinrich replied. "You mentioned a woman donated this motorcar to the church, however I can begin to imagine a woman driving such a motorcar. In fact, I can't even imagine a man driving it. It looks as though it needs a full crew to manage it, not a lone driver."

"Well put, Father Heinrich. I didn't say she had *driven* it, I said she had *donated* it, and there's a big difference, you know. She always had a chauffeur drive her around town; she was quite wealthy, in fact, and those two were quite the sight to see. When we saw the motorcar coming down the narrow streets we'd have to jump out of its way and when it passed by, we strained to look inside to see Frau Heinkel, however she was so slight that often the only thing we could see was the top of her hat. The motorcar literally swallowed her up like the whale swallowed Jonah," Father Tadeus remarked. "Shall we get it going?" he asked as he opened the driver's door.

The minute he opened the door I could smell the mildew and it was overwhelming. "Pardon the odor. I had to keep the windows rolled up to keep the birds from making a nest inside, however I'm sure it will air out in time," Father Tadeus apologised.

Father Heinrich got into the driver's seat; Father Tadeus walked around to the other side of the motorcar, opened the passenger's door, and got in. They left me standing there, not knowing what to do. "Anna, get in," Father Heinrich commanded, however, I couldn't open the rear door no matter how hard I tried. Finally, Father Tadeus get out and opened it for me, and when I slid into the rear seat, it felt as though the inside of the motorcar was larger than my entire bedroom back in our farmhouse, and I couldn't imagine anyone wanting to drive around in something that enormous.

Father Tadeus fumbled around with his large key ring until he had found the motorcar's ignition key and he handed it to Father Heinrich, "It goes there," as he pointed to a slot in the dashboard.

Father Tadeus then took a book of out the glove box, turned to a page, and began to familiarise Father Heinrich with the various gauges and switches. I'm not sure how anyone could remember them all; petrol gauge, battery gauge, temperature gauge, oil gauge, windscreen wipers, running lights, heater controls, and the list just kept going on-and-on.

Finally, Father Tadeus said, "Let's crank her up," as I looked around inside the motorcar for a crank, whatever that was, however I didn't see one. Perhaps it was just another one of Father Tadeus' feeble attempts at humour.

Father Heinrich just sat there, not knowing what to do, until Father Tadeus finally said, "Turn the key to the right. Now feel around on the floor for a little button. It's on the left and that's the starter button. Just push down on it with your left foot until the engine starts, then let go."

It took some time for Father Heinrich to find the button, but when he finally did and pressed it, the motorcar started making a funny sound under the front bonnet. I'd call it a low growl, like *whirr, whirr, whirr,* and finally, with a loud cough, the engine started, immediately filling the stables with smelly fumes and startling a flock of barn swallows that bolted for the open doors.

"It's not a good idea to sit here and let the engine idle for too long; it's very dangerous, in fact, so let's try to move it a few feet towards the door," Father Tadeus' first attempt at being a driving instructor.

Father Heinrich protested. "I'm not too sure what to do."

"*You're* the one who said you knew how to drive. I've never driven a motorcar before. You should be my *teacher*, not my *student*, but do something, quickly, before we all suffocate," Father Tadeus pleaded.

I knew right then the next few seconds would seal our fate, as we'd either drive to Bavaria or we'd walk, and it was all up to Father Heinrich. Finally, he got up the courage to master our so-called 'steed' and with the engine roaring, he took the large lever between the driver and passenger's side, did something with it that made a grinding noise, we leaped forward a few metres, stopped, and the engine fell silent. "*Verdammt* clutch," he mumbled under his breath. I'm not too sure they even have clutches in cars anymore, but he told me it had something to do with making the motorcar move forward.

Anyway, he restarted the engine, did something with that lever and the clutch thing, and we proceeded to make our way out of the stables, two or three metres at a time, and if that was how motorcars worked, it would take us a long time to get to Bavaria, for sure.

After we had safely exited the stables enveloped in a blue exhaust haze, Father Tadeus led us to the rear of the motorcar and opened the huge attached trunk. Pulling back a blanket covering its contents, he revealed five petrol cans, a strong rope, a shovel, another blanket rolled up and tied with a string, some tools, and a couple of motor oil bottles.

After taking a few minutes to say our goodbyes, Father Tadeus handed Father Heinrich the map and the sheet of paper listing all our proposed 'church stops' along the way. "Good luck, and may God protect and speed you two along the way," were Father Tadeus' parting words; however, they weren't his *final* words. When Father Heinrich offered him a ride back to the church, his *final* words actually were, "No thanks, I think I'll walk," and with that farewell, Father Heinrich started the engine and we were finally on our way to Bavaria in our brand-new motorcar.

## The Hitchhiker

The first ten minutes of our motorcar trip were filled with a combination of sheer terror and outright laughter as Father Heinrich tried to master our 'steed', as Father Tadeus had called it. We both thought it humourous that Father Tadeus had called it that and I decided to call it our *Koń*, instead, as that means *horse* in Polish. Whenever I'd call it our *Koń*, Father Heinrich would say, *"Nein. Unsere Esel."* That was a new German word for me, and he teased me mercilessly until I just had to ask him what it meant. "Our *donkey*," he replied, and after that we called the motorcar *EselKoń*, our *"donkey-horse"*.

Once Father Heinrich had gotten used to the clutch thing and we could move along, slowly, without feeling as though we were riding a bucking bronco, he attempted to master the unfamiliar art of steering *EselKoń* through the narrow streets on our way out of Bielsko. More than once, he had to put *EselKoń* into reverse gear while making a terrible grinding sound in the process, back up and try again, and several times he almost knocked a nearby pedestrian to the ground.

However, by the time we had made our way out of the city, he had pretty well mastered the art of the so-called 'finer mechanical aspects of safe and courteous driving', and we began to relax. I was too small to sit on the front seat and see out through the enormous front windscreen, so Father Heinrich stopped and got the rolled-up blanket out of the trunk for me to sit on.

The road to Frýdek-Místek was mostly deserted as we seemed to be the only motorcar on the highway, which, by the way, was in good condition considering the type of vehicles that must have used it before us. When we stopped alongside the road to take a short break, Father Heinrich took out the map, studied it for a few minutes, and as he ran his finger down our upcoming route, he suddenly frowned. "Is something wrong?" I asked.

"I don't know," he replied. "It looks like the border to Czechoslovakia is up ahead, and I'm not too sure what kind of problems we might encounter there."

"That's okay. I'll just give the border man a big smile and he'll have to let us in." What was I thinking?

As it turned out, crossing the border wasn't a problem after all, as there was only one lightly armed soldier standing there, and he just smiled at Father Heinrich and waved us through without even stopping. We both breathed a huge sigh of relief, because if this was how things were going to be on our trip, we'd arrive in Bavaria in no time at all. Unfortunately, we didn't take into account that we were only a few kilometres into a very long trip, a trip through extremely dangerous territory where anything could happen, however if that had crossed our minds back then, we probably would have ignored the warning signs anyway.

The difference between Poland and Czechoslovakia was amazing. Where there had been widespread destruction throughout Poland, the Czech countryside appeared serene and peaceful as though the war had totally forgotten it, and as we drove through small villages with crude houses with smoke curling from their chimneys we noticed the cheerful Christmas decorations still hung in their windows, and they reminded me of my village back home. Father Heinrich said the countryside wouldn't stay that way for long; the Russian barbarians would eventually sweep through here and burn these villages to the ground, and it was sad to think about what war did to innocent people like those peeking out their windows as our motorcar passed by. If only we could snatch them up, stick them in the back of our motorcar, and whisk them to safety, but we just kept going; they, like our Polish neighbours, would have to fend for themselves and whenever we passed a farm with a barn, I thought I could hear *Biały śnieg* calling out to me, and I couldn't stop to save her. Poor *Biały śnieg*.

# Innocence Lost - A Childhood Stolen

After we had only gone a few kilometres into Czechoslovakia, we saw someone sitting up ahead in a snowbank by the side of the road, and from a distance, it was difficult to tell if it was a man, a woman, or a child, and the person's elbows were resting on their drawn-up knees, cradling their head down between their legs. As we got closer and slowed down, we could see it was a man dressed in tattered rags with cardboard boxes taped to his feet for shoes. As we drew alongside him, he lifted his head, looked right at me, and his face was filthy, the part I could see anyway, as the rest of his face was covered with long, black whiskers that were knotted like rats' nests, and he was such a pathetic sight.

Father Heinrich stopped the motorcar, and I rolled down the window. "Are you all right?" I asked in German. He didn't respond; he just stared back at me with a pained look that both frightened and touched me at the same time. "Are you all right?" I asked again, this time in Polish.

"*Jestem zimny, jestem głodny, a ja jestem zagubiony.* (I'm cold, I'm hungry, and I'm lost)," he hoarsely answered in Polish.

I looked over at Father Heinrich for his approval as I spontaneously asked the stranger, "Would you like to ride with us into the next town?" as Father Heinrich, fortunately, nodded approvingly.

The beggar tried to stand up, but he didn't have the strength to do it on his own, so Father Heinrich and I stepped out of the motorcar, got on either side of him, and helped him into the front seat. He hardly weighed anything, probably not even much more than my little brother, Chaim, and he was so filthy it was all I could do to touch him, but I had no other choice; Father Heinrich and I were a team, and we had to help each other.

I climbed into the rear seat and Father Heinrich got back into the driver's seat and before we continued on our way, I asked him, "Would you like something to eat?" However, the man didn't reply, he just barely nodded his head, so I dug down into our food bag, retrieved a half-eaten loaf of dark bread, and passed it over the seat to our new passenger.

You could tell he was starving, but he didn't wolf it down in huge bites, he just broke off little pieces and ate them slowly, one mouse-like nibble at a time, and I only assumed by his manners that food probably meant a lot to him.

"We're only going as far as Frýdek-Místek tonight, so you can ride there with us if you wish." Father Heinrich offered, as the man just looked up from his precious meal and vainly attempted to smile his gratitude, and after he had picked the last crumb from his ragged lap, he appeared to be in better spirits and looked as though he might join us in conversation, if offered.

It was obvious he was Polish, so Father Heinrich attempted to start a conversation in the man's native tongue. "Tell me, where did you start your journey? You appear to have come a long way."

The man quietly answered "Sobibor," with his head slightly bowed,

"Ah, Sobibor. A lovely town, I've heard," as Father Heinrich made a feeble attempt to keep the conversation alive.

"Not the town, Father, the camp."

Father Heinrich paused for a long time, his jaws tightly clenched. "The Sobibor Camp? Are you sure?"

"I was there, Father, I should know."

"You were at the Sobibor Camp? How in the world did you get from there to here?"

"I don't know, Father. All I know is that I killed a man," and I could tell by the pained look on his face this memory greatly troubled him.

"I don't understand," Father Heinrich protested. "You said you started in Sobibor, killed a man, and now we find you sitting in a snowbank in Czechoslovakia. I'm sorry, but none of that makes any sense to me."

Maybe it was the fact that the hitchhiker thought Father Heinrich was a real Catholic priest, maybe it was because he felt safe riding with us, or maybe he just needed to talk about it, but the words just gushed out of his mouth and once he started, he talked himself to exhaustion.

He said he had been a prisoner at the Sobibor Camp in eastern Poland for more than two years. Sometime in October 1943, a small group of prisoners carried out a well-planned revolt against their captors. They cut the telephone and electric lines and disabled the camp's motor vehicles, and some of them even broke into one of the guards' rooms and stole rifles and ammunition. Although their plan was well thought out, they hadn't planned for the arrival of a German truck near camp headquarters, nor had they anticipated the driver seeing a dead SS man lying there on the ground. Upon seeing a prisoner running from the building, the driver immediately opened fire in an attempt to kill him.

Just as this was happening, the Ukrainian guard commander appeared in the main square during roll call and the prisoners viscously attacked and killed him with axes, however, since the other prisoners nearby didn't know what was happening, they panicked as the now alerted guards opened fire.

The conspirators then broke towards the gates and fences and total pandemonium ensued throughout the entire camp. Some prisoners broke through the main gate and headed towards the woods, while another group broke through the fence and into a minefield. Many were killed, but some escaped by stepping on the bodies of their dead comrades.

Our hitchhiker said he was in a third group and they broke through the fence where they suspected there weren't any mines. Fortunately, they were right, there were no mines, but the guards continued firing in their direction, although they didn't pursue them. However, he never looked back; he just kept running until he had reached the relative safety of the nearby woods.

He knew they were out in force looking for escaped prisoners and he could hear the sound of small airplanes flying overhead attempting to discover their hiding places. Luckily, he and a friend finally met up in the forest with a small group of escapees led by a man named Pechorsky. Between all of them, they had four pistols and a rifle, however during the night, this small group met up with other groups, and by dawn they numbered over seventy-five well-armed escapees.

The next day they hid in the woods near a railway track and fortunately for them, the spotter planes didn't discover them. That night they headed north towards the Bug River, but on the way they met up with two other escapees who told them the Bug River crossings were heavily guarded

Under these circumstances, Pechorsky decided a large group had no chance of eluding the pursuing Germans, so he thought it was best to break into smaller groups and try to sneak past the Germans that way. Our hitchhiker stuck with the Pechorsky group and they finally managed to sneak across the Bug River and three days later, they met Soviet partisans from the Brest region and joined up with them.

He stayed with the Soviet partisans for almost two months as they sneaked behind the retreating German's lines, committing acts of sabotage in an attempt to slow the German's retreat thinking perhaps if they could slow them up enough, the Red Army would catch up and finally crush them. Sometime in late December the group was accidentally discovered in their overnight camp and in the ensuing gun battle, only our hitchhiker survived. Since then, he had been making his way across Poland and now Czechoslovakia on foot; sleeping wherever he could, stealing food whenever he could, and just trying to survive until he could reach relatives living in Czechoslovakia, and now we were playing a small part in his cold, lonely flight from brutal captivity to safety.

We both sat there mesmerised, listening to his story, and it was the first time I had ever heard anyone talk about camp life and how the prisoners were treated. I assumed the camp at Sobibor must have been a different kind of camp than the one we had just left in Auschwitz. It had to be different, because our hitchhiker said he had been at Sobibor for over two years and Auschwitz was just a temporary stopping off place before the Jews were resettled. Nobody stayed there for more than a few days, or so I thought.

When it appeared as though he had told his entire story and had no words left, Father Heinrich asked, "You mentioned that you killed a man and I assume you meant you and the partisans killed someone. It's war. I can understand that, although it's something the Church doesn't condone in the slightest."

The man sighed, "No, Father. I personally killed a man with my own hands the night we escaped because it was part of the escape plan. It's the only time I ever had to do anything like that, but I was the only person in the camp who was in a position to do what I had to do, and I've begged God's for His forgiveness ever since then as it

[186]

haunts me every waking minute, and it's even worse when I'm asleep."

"I'm sure God has already forgiven you," Father Heinrich replied. "But tell me why this particular act has haunted you so."

"He was a good man, Father, and I respected him more than any of our other captors and he just didn't deserve to die that way."

"Tell me. What did he do at the camp and why were you the chosen one?"

"I worked in the camp infirmary, Father, helping the camp doctor tend to the sick patients. I killed the camp doctor because we needed the hospital supplies as part of our escape plan," in a whisper so low we strained to hear his words.

"Did your doctor have a name?"

"Yes. Doctor Berger; Erich Berger," he once again answered in a whisper.

At the mention of Doctor Berger's name, Father Heinrich's face lost all its colour and I could see the muscles in his neck tense as he tried to control his emotions. I thought for a moment that Father Heinrich would give away our ruse; after all, what if he did? Only our hitchhiker would know our identity and what could he do to us? I also knew Father Heinrich well enough by this time to understand what he was thinking.

After a few moments of silence, he spoke up. "God will certainly forgive you for your transgressions, especially if you accept Jesus Christ as your Saviour," and I could tell he was proud of his reply; it sounded so priest-like.

The hitchhiker glanced over at Father Heinrich with an odd expression on his face, replied, "Father, I'm Jewish."

[187]

I wanted to laugh aloud; it was a small, but humourous moment in the middle of a serious discussion, however, I didn't dare make a sound.

"Well, we both believe in the same God, don't we? I guess Jesus doesn't really matter, does he?"

"No, Father, he doesn't, but thank you for your kind reassurance."

Just when he had finished thanking Father Heinrich, we pulled into the driveway of Kostel sv. Mikuláše Catholic Church on the banks of the Ondrejnice River in Frýdek-Místek.

Father Heinrich handed a loaf of dark bread and some hard cheese to our hitchhiker as he got out of the motorcar, "Good luck. May God protect and speed you along the way," as he walked towards the highway like a man who had just had a heavy burden lifted from his shoulders. I hope he made it home as I felt sorry for him, however, what he said about the Sobibor Camp still troubled me, and I knew I'd eventually have to ask Father Heinrich about it. Then, Father Heinrich turned towards me, "Hungry?" he asked?

## The Beginning of a Spiritual Journey

Father David met us at the front door of the church and after some confusion as to who we were and why Father Heinrich was dressed as a Catholic priest, he invited us in. Having a Letter of Introduction from Father Tadeus had already proved to be an asset.

The church was much smaller than the one in Bielsko, it was more out in the country than right in the middle of a city, and as soon as we walked into the sanctuary, I realised I was in a very special place. When we had first arrived at the church in Bielsko, it was after dark, Father Tadeus had hurried us to the basement storeroom, and we didn't have time to appreciate the beauty of the church's

[188]

sanctuary. Of course, by the time we got up the next morning the vandals had already ransacked the church, so we never did have a chance to appreciate its beauty.

This church was different; it was untouched by the ravages of war, its beauty was overwhelming, and the first thing that caught my eye when we walked into the sanctuary was a large, golden cross prominently displayed over the altar; a life-size figure of a man was hanging from it wearing a ring of thorns as a crown. I immediately felt sorry for him, and I wondered who he was and why he was hanging from a cross.

The altar was covered with a beautiful, tapestry-like cloth, and there were golden candlesticks set on either end, and as we walked down the center aisle, I looked over and noticed a little alcove on one side of the church with a small statue of a woman standing inside it. She was dressed in blue, flowing robes, she had a beautiful face, and there was a table set in front of her filled with many small, burning candles that made shadows that danced on the ceiling and the nearby walls. There were also ornate pictures hanging on the walls between the tall, stained glass windows, and the cross with the man hanging from it, the statue of the beautiful lady, the windows, and the flickering candles created a truly magical place, and then I realised this was another one of God's houses.

It still amazes me how people have different ways of honouring God, something Meyer and I often talked about it. *My* God was a caring, loving God who was intimately involved in our daily lives, and He was my protector, my confidant, my friend, a wonderful force that had created the smallest details such as the sound a butterfly's wings make as they fly through the air, the voice of a bar-mitzvahed boy the first time he reads from the Torah, and a newborn baby's cry the first time his mother cradles him in her arms; small, but important details to *my* God.

My late husband, *Meyer's* God, on the other hand, was an observer, not a micro-manager, and Meyer always argued that God had put us on this planet as an experiment; an experiment to see how we all got along together. If we did well, God would populate the Universe with people, however if we didn't do well, God would wipe us from the earth in an apocalyptic moment and start over with another experiment. Moreover, Meyer felt we hadn't done too well either, as he argued that if God were like *my* caring God, why would He allow wars, and why would He allow Muslims to kill Jews and Christians and vice-versa? Sometimes I had to admit he had some good points, but I liked *my* God better than *Meyer's*.

It's important to understand that walking into Father David's church was a turning point in my life, and I think it was also a turning point in Father Heinrich's life. From then on he became calmer, more subdued, and I also noticed some of his quirky habits began to disappear; like his obsessive hand washing, his need for regimentation and order, and the comfort of an unwavering daily routine. In addition, the farther we travelled away from Auschwitz, the more relaxed he seemed, as if wearing his priest's vestments brought him great comfort.

He also appeared to enjoy Father David's company as he did with the other Catholic priests we met along the way, and when I saw him sitting with other priests and having interesting discussions, discussions that were way over my head, he just fit in as though he belonged there. I no longer saw Doktor Mueller when I looked at him, I saw only Father Heinrich.

We truly enjoyed Father David's generous hospitality and companionship and when he invited us to stay for a few days, we accepted and stayed with him for almost a week. It was an island of calmness and we truly enjoyed it, but soon it was time to get on the road again. One of Father David's parishioners had filled two of our empty petrol cans and we finally bid a sad farewell to our new friend. Although it felt good to be on the road again, I sensed our journey had taken on a new dimension as it was not only now a road trip, it was also becoming a spiritual journey, one with an unknown route and destination.

## The Border Crossing

The next day we made good time after leaving Frýdek-Místek and we had intended to spend the night at St. Martin's Cathedral with Father Georg, but when we reached the outskirts of Bratislava, we were making such good time that we decided to continue until nightfall.

When we were about two kilometres from the Austrian border, Father Heinrich looked over at me. "The Austrian border is just ahead. I don't think we'll have any problems. Just sit there, and don't say anything unless someone asks you a question, and then only answer the question. Nothing more. Do you understand?"

I nodded my agreement, as I remembered how easy it had been to cross the border from Poland into Czechoslovakia; actually it was just with a wave of a hand, so I wasn't too concerned as borders meant nothing to me, they were just lines drawn on a map.

As we approached the border we could see there were quite a few vehicles in line waiting to cross, and several uniformed men, soldiers I assumed, were walking up and down the line with clipboards in their hands, questioning each vehicle's driver and occupants.

[191]

When the soldier approached our motorcar, Father Heinrich rolled down the window and the soldier walked up to the open window. "Where are you headed?" he asked in German.

"Rottach-Egern, Germany," Father Heinrich replied, trying to sound casual, although he later told me he had been extremely apprehensive.

I was fascinated as I listened to their rapid-fire, staccato-like exchange, just like a Ping-Pong match.

"Name?" he asked.

"Father Heinrich Mueller."

"And the young lady in the motorcar with you is?"

"Anna Mueller, my niece."

"Reason for your travel today?"

"To visit relatives and leave Anna with her family for her safety."

I was shocked as this was the first time I had ever heard any of that and I could tell Father Heinrich was making it up as he went along. Then the soldier asked the most probing question, the one I'm sure Father Heinrich dreaded the most, "Papers?"

There was a long silence as Father Heinrich composed himself, as though he was trying to come up with an answer. "Our papers were destroyed when vandals ransacked our church in Bielsko, we had to flee for our lives and in our haste to leave, I didn't give it a second thought."

The soldier frowned, "Unfortunately, Father, you can't enter our country without papers. That's not permitted."

"*I* understand, but *you* have to understand how little time we had to leave there, especially with my niece, who I was charged to protect after her entire family was killed in Berlin." Maybe he could play on the soldier's sympathy and loyalty.

"I'm sorry, Father. I sympathise with your situation, but I can't let you into our country without papers. Do you have *anything* to prove your identity? *Anything* at all?"

That was the question Father Heinrich was waiting to hear, the one question that required implementation of the second part of Father Tadeus' plan.

"The only thing I have is this letter from the Bishop of Warsaw in Poland explaining our situation and I hope that will suffice," as he reached into his cassock pocket, retrieved Father Tadeus' hand-written letter, and handed it to the soldier. Fortunately, Father Tadeus had made sure to write it in both German and in Polish.

The soldier stood there and read it carefully. "Sir. Could you please drive your motorcar over to that building and wait there?" as he pointed towards the small border crossing building sitting alongside the striped border pole marking the borders between the two countries.

Father Heinrich drove our motorcar out of line as the soldier walked alongside and parked it in front of the Customs building.

"Wait here," the soldier said.

Father Heinrich and I just looked at each other, not knowing why we had been singled out.

Within a few moments the soldier came out of the building and approached our motorcar, "Would you please follow me inside?" as he came around to my side and opened my door.

The three of us walked into the small building. The border office was sparse, practically empty except for one desk with a rather chubby, red-faced soldier sitting behind it.

"Please," as he pointed at the two wooden chairs in front of the desk facing him.

[193]

After we had sat down, he picked up Father Tadeus' letter from his cluttered desk. "It says here the Catholic Church is granting you safe passage as you travel through our country. Is that so?" the chubby soldier asked.

"Yes, sir. It's my understanding the Vatican has come to a mutual agreement with your government granting its clergy safe passage. Is there a problem?"

"No, Father. No problem at all. I was just curious, however if you don't mind, I'd like to ask your niece a couple of questions. If that's all right with you."

I hoped the look that Father Heinrich and I briefly exchanged wouldn't give away our masquerade as I don't know if you'd call it a desperate look or a surprised look, but it was a look charged with fear and uncertainty.

"I'm sure that would be fine," Father Heinrich nimbly recovered. *He* may have felt comfortable, but *I* was terrified.

The soldier leaned forward and looked directly at me. "Tell me, child. How old are you?"

"I'll be thirteen in April." *That was easy,* I thought.

"Your uncle said you lived in Berlin. Where in Berlin did you live?"

My mind went blank as I didn't know how to answer his question. Then I remembered the conversation Father Heinrich and I had on the park bench overlooking the river back in Auschwitz and without hesitation, I replied, "Siemensstadt." To this day, I have no idea where that came from; it just flew out of my mouth.

The burly soldier smiled. "Siemensstadt. A beautiful part of the city. I used to visit my grandparents there when I was just a child myself and we used to go to a nearby park on a river. I forgot; what was that park called?"

I hoped the guardian angel that watched over me would help me just one more time. "Treptower Park. It's on a beautiful river called the Spee. My family and I enjoyed many wonderful picnics there stretched out on a blanket. Every time I think about them, I get sad." — *Thank you guardian angel* —.

Father Heinrich reached over and took my hand and I'm sure the soldier thought he was comforting me, but I knew he was congratulating me.

My answers appeared to satisfy his curiosity just as the soldier who had stopped us, walked back into the office, and nodded his head affirmatively.

"You're free to go now, Father," as he got up from behind the desk and shook Father Heinrich's hand. "Corporal Bender will show you to your motorcar. If you don't mind, we'll put you in the front of the line. Have a safe trip and please make sure to stop and enjoy some of our beautiful scenery along the way. *Auf Wiedersehen*."

With that cheerful farewell, we walked back to the motorcar, hand-in-hand, and I'm sure Father Heinrich could feel my knees shaking. "You did well, Anna. Where did you come up with those answers? he asked.

"I don't know, but I think I felt *your* Anna's hands on my shoulder."

When he heard that, I thought he was going to break down and cry. "She's not just *my* Anna anymore, she's now *our* Anna," he said quietly.

We got back into *EselKoń* and fifteen minutes later we were in Austria with only one more border crossing to go, and it turned out to be quite a challenge.

## The Blizzard

We hadn't driven more than a few kilometres from the border into Austria when we saw the dark storm clouds beginning to form over the distant mountains. Father Heinrich pulled the motorcar over to the side of the road and retrieved the map from the rear seat. He studied it for quite a while before making what would turn out to be a bad decision. Pointing at a spot on the map, "Here's Graz," he said. "I think we can make it there and stay at the Mariatrost Basilica with Father Laurent, but I think I can shorten our trip if I take this side road to Eisenstadt. It doesn't look like a main highway, but it will probably shorten our trip by at least twenty kilometres, and perhaps we'll outrun the approaching storm."

I wish I had better map reading skills so I could have better understood his planned route, but I didn't, so I had to trust he was making a wise decision.

Turning off the main road, we headed towards the small town of Parndorf and then took the road towards Eisenstadt. Up ahead on the left, we saw a large, frozen lake, and right after we had passed through the small town of Purbach, the first snow flurries began hitting our motorcar's windscreen. The wind swirled the snowflakes around on the roadway in miniature cyclones making it difficult to see the roadway ahead. Father Heinrich slowed the motorcar down to a fast walk, trying hard to stay on the roadway. Then, the weather quickly deteriorated until we could hardly see a few metres in front of us. Now we were on an unfamiliar road with no place to stop, and I could tell Father Heinrich was becoming extremely agitated and when I tried to say something to him, he just answered in a very sharp voice, so I kept quiet.

Soon, the snow began to become stuck on the windscreen and Father Heinrich turned on the wipers, but they weren't of much help, and the inside of the windscreen started to fog up, too. Using his handkerchief, he tried to wipe the fog away, but that didn't help much either and before too long, our progress had slowed to a crawl. When he turned on the headlamps, they only made things worse as the driving snow reflected the light back into our faces and blinded us.

Suddenly, the motorcar slid into a ditch and no matter what Father Heinrich tried, we were unyieldingly stuck. He got out of the motorcar to investigate our situation, but he quickly returned and slammed the door behind him, but not before the inside was filled with the blowing snow. "I think we have a problem, Anna," his frustration beginning to show.

He explained we only had one of two choices: one was to stay with the motorcar, leave it running so we wouldn't freeze and wait for help, or we could try to find nearby shelter. Neither of the two choices was very appealing, however I hoped perhaps we could stay in the motorcar and keep warm until help arrived. But the howling wind and blowing snow would probably keep any foolhardy soul from venturing forth. The only other option was to leave the motorcar behind and try to find some nearby shelter.

Retrieving the map from the rear seat, Father Heinrich spread it out, the best he could, on the front seat between us. He said he figured we were somewhere halfway between Purbach and Donnerskirchen, but it was difficult to tell, so it might be a good idea to turn around and walk back towards Purbach; that would put the wind at our backs. At the most, he thought it would be about two or three kilometres, but he wasn't certain.

Looking over at me, he asked, "What should we do?" I thought that was a silly question to ask a soon-to-be thirteen-year-old child. After all, *he* was the adult; *he* should be the one to make that kind of decision.

As I sat there and tried to come up with an appropriate reply, my mother's words, "Be brave, Mira. Be brave," came back to me, and how I wished she could be here to help us now and although she wasn't, her comforting words were. "I think we should go find shelter," my answer.

Putting on his wool overcoat and stuffing Father Tadeus' Prayer Book into the pocket for safekeeping, Father Heinrich prepared to face the blizzard. I put Alinka inside my dress, wrapped my overcoat around me, pulled my scarf up over my head, and prepared to follow him into the white unknown. Although Father Heinrich was wearing the shoes Father Tadeus had given him, I only had a pair of low-cut dress shoes without any socks, which I had brought with me from Auschwitz. I wish now I hadn't accidentally left Frau Mueller's oversized boots back in Bielsko. When Father Heinrich got out of the driver's door and held it open for me, I slid across the front seat and stepped out into the blizzard, and the moment I felt the icy wind stinging my face, I knew we had made a bad decision. My almost bare feet stepping into the crusty snow reinforced that thought and I knew then that we were in real trouble.

It was approaching dusk and it was almost impossible to walk down the snow-encrusted roadway and by the time we had gone ten paces, *EselKoń* had disappeared in the mist, and we were enveloped in a great, blowing, white emptiness. We later learned it was one of the worst winter storms in more than a decade.

I did the best I could to keep up with Father Heinrich as I dared not get too far from him, because if we were separated, we probably wouldn't be able to find each other in the storm. He did the best he could to stay on the paved roadway, but sometimes we stepped off the roadway into slushy ditches and by the time we had been gone for only a few minutes, my feet were frozen. Every step I took was painful and I just wanted to sit down in a snowbank and go to sleep, but my mother's words, once again, kept coming back to me, "Be brave, Mira. Be brave," so I kept putting one frozen foot in front of the other.

Suddenly, Father Heinrich said, "Anna, I see a light off in the distance. Can you see it, too?"

As I peered through the whiteness, I thought perhaps I could see a light, but I wasn't sure, so I didn't answer him, instead, I just kept walking; mechanically, one step at a time.

Finally, he shouted, "It *is* a light! I can see a light up ahead. Let's hurry."

I'm not too sure what he meant by hurry; I was walking as fast as I could under the circumstances, but I did manage to keep up with him as he quickened his pace.

Within a couple of minutes, we could see the outline of a small farmhouse alongside the road with two brightly-lit, welcoming windows on the front. Father Heinrich took my hand as we ran the last few feet to the farmhouse's front door and when we were finally standing in front of our welcome refuge, he banged loudly on the door. Within moments, the door opened just a crack and I could see two friendly eyes looking back at us from inside. Upon seeing two snow-covered travellers knocking on his door, Herr Eberhardt opened the door wide and whisked us inside. We were finally safe from the storm!

## The Eberhardts

We stood for a moment just inside the doorway, stomping our feet on the entranceway rug trying to get the snow off our shoes and every time I stomped my feet on the rug, they hurt as I think they had begun to become frostbitten.

Herr Eberhardt walked over and helped Father Heinrich take off his long overcoat. "What in heaven's name are you two doing out in this weather? You could freeze to death out there," in a concerned tone of voice.

"Our motorcar went off the road and got stuck in a ditch. Thankfully, we found your house just in time; I don't think we could have walked much farther in this weather."

Herr Eberhardt looked down at my feet. "Why don't you take your shoes off, young lady, and come join me by the fire? Your feet must be frozen," as he knelt down and unbuckled my shoes. When he had taken them off, he shook them, and big clumps of ice fell out onto the floor.

"Come, sit," as he took my hand and led me to a chair by the blazing fire. The warmth of the fire felt wonderful and just as I was beginning to feel comfortable, he shook the grate making a flurry of sparks rise up into the chimney, and then he placed another lump of coal on the fire. I shrunk back in horror. The train, the coal smoke, the barking dogs, the tall chimneys; they all came back to me in an instant and I wanted to get up and flee.

Herr Eberhardt must have noticed my discomfort because he asked me, "Are you all right? Did I make it too warm for you?"

I didn't know what to say or what to tell him that would help him understand what I was feeling. "No, you just startled me," I lied.

When it was obvious I was once again comfortably settled, Herr Eberhardt dragged up another chair by the fire and offered it to Father Heinrich. Just as he was sitting down, Frau Eberhardt came walking into the room, wiping her hands in her apron. "Ernst, you didn't tell me we had guests," she said in a surprised tone.

"Hilda, I've just met them myself, although I have yet to even know their names."

Father Heinrich arose from his seat, acknowledged Frau Eberhardt, and introduced himself. "My apologies. I guess the warmth of your fire made me forget my manners. I'm Father Heinrich Mueller and this is my niece, Anna."

Herr Eberhardt shook Father Heinrich's extended hand. "Ernst Eberhardt and this is my wife, Hilda. Please sit. Hilda, perhaps our guests would like something hot to warm them," as he looked questioningly at the two of us.

"Do you like hot chocolate?" she asked.

I had been thinking about a cup of hot chocolate ever since we left Auschwitz. "That would be wonderful."

"And you, Father Heinrich? A cup of hot chocolate for you, also?"

"I think I'll join my niece. Thank you," Father Heinrich gladly accepted as he rubbed his cold hands together in front of the fireplace.

At first, we were too busy trying to get out of the weather and warm ourselves to overhear the radio in the background. However, during a break in our conversation and before Frau Eberhardt returned with our hot chocolate, Father Heinrich asked, "Is that Radio Berlin I hear in the background?"

"Indeed, it is. Why do you ask?" Herr Eberhardt asked with a slightly puzzled look on his face.

"We've been so out of touch since we began our journey that I was just wondering what the situation is with this terrible conflict."

"How long has it been since you've heard any news?"

"Probably since early December."

"My," Herr Eberhardt harrumphed. "You *do* have a lot to get caught up on, don't you?"

We both sat there fascinated as we listened to Herr Eberhardt bring us up-to-date with what had happened since we left Auschwitz.

Of course, his perspective was limited to what he had heard on Radio Berlin, but regardless of the obviously propagandised viewpoint, what he told us astounded us.

He said the Germans had launched a huge offensive on the Western Front sometime in mid-December, which we already knew, and it was aimed at a lightly defended part of Belgium in the Ardennes Forest. At first, progress reports were glowing, but he said that, lately, the reports hadn't been as enthusiastic, although Herr Goebbels had just recently addressed the nation and tried to sound optimistic, albeit unconvincingly so. Only time would reveal the truth.

In the middle of the discussion, Frau Eberhardt returned to the room carrying two steaming mugs of hot chocolate. "Ernst. Did I overhear you boring our guests with more of your political viewpoints?" as she handed the two mugs to us.

Just holding the warm mug in my hand made me happy and it reminded me of sitting around the fire in the partisans' camp holding the mug filled with hot tea.

"No, Hilda. I was just bringing our guests up-to-date. Father Heinrich asked, and I was just obliging him."

"Well, Ernst. I'm sure they are more interested in enjoying their hot chocolate than they are in listening to you ramble on about this terrible war."

Father Heinrich interrupted, "Please pardon my manners, Frau Eberhardt, but it's been a while since we've heard anything about what's happening and since we are on our way into Germany, I'd like to know what we might be getting ourselves into."

Frau Eberhardt smiled, "I'm sorry, Father. Forgive me for interrupting your discussion, however, it's just that I've grown quite weary of hearing about this senseless war and I just don't even want to be in the same room when it's being discussed. My apologies," as she turned and left the room.

Herr Eberhardt returned her smile, "Please forgive her. It's been a topic of conversation ever since 1938 when the Germans overran our once-peaceful country and it still frustrates the both of us how the government just handed it over to the Germans without a fight. Nevertheless, so be it; I'm sure they'll get their just due. Now where were we?" he asked.

Father Heinrich resumed the conversation. "So, from what you've already told me, Herr Eberhardt, it sounds as though the German Army is retreating from their Ardennes offensive and is heading back east to defend the Fatherland. Is that what you make of Radio Berlin's reports?"

"It's sometimes difficult to piece together the truth amidst the propaganda noise, but I'd say your assessment is probably more accurate than theirs."

"So, I'm to assume that the Allied forces are approaching the Rhine on the Western Front, but what about the Russians? Right now, I'm more concerned about them, than I am about the Allies."

Herr Eberhardt was eager to talk about the Russians' progress. "From what Radio Berlin reports, the German troops are fighting a courageous battle in a patriotic attempt to stop the Russian hordes from overrunning their country. They hope to win a major tank battle somewhere in Poland and stop them short of the border, at least that's what they said, and they also made a curious mention about the Russians overrunning a small town in Poland called Auschwitz. Why in the world would they mention such an out-of-the-way place? I've never heard of it, have you?"

Father Heinrich tensed at the mention of Auschwitz and I could tell it greatly distressed him, but I didn't know why. I just assumed it was because he was glad that we had left when we did, but it wasn't a happy reaction, it was a nervous one, and only later would I discover why.

Like me, Herr Eberhardt appeared to notice Father Heinrich's reaction. "What seems to bother you, Father? The tides of war turning against the Germans or the mention of Auschwitz?" I thought his question was an intelligent one, and I'm sure Herr Eberhardt might prove to be a formidable debate opponent.

"Neither, Herr Eberhardt," he lied. "I'm concerned for my parishioners back in Poland and also for Anna's family in Germany. What will happen to them both if Germany falls and the two giants crush and divide Germany as I am now certain they will?"

"I wish I knew, Father, but I don't," was Herr Eberhardt's candid reply just as Frau Eberhardt walked back into the room carrying two trays with dishes laden with boiled potatoes and bratwursts.

"I'm sure the two of you are hungry so I fixed something to eat. Ernst, enough talking about the war and politics," she insisted. "Why don't you two discuss this terrible weather instead?" as she sat the trays in our laps.

Our stay in the Eberhardt house had already been an interesting one, and the next day would prove even more so.

## Father Heinrich Makes a House Call

After filling ourselves with boiled potatoes and bratwursts, we sat around the fire for a while recounting our adventures and Frau Eberhardt even rejoined the conversation. She was more interested in my background; where I was from, if I had any brothers or sisters, general questions like that and I had to make up most of it, but I did make sure to include Lev and Chaim in my imaginary family. She appeared to listen attentively, but I knew she was just trying to make conversation with a little girl, and I hoped I wouldn't have to retell my story and make a clumsy attempt at remembering all the little details I had playfully included for Frau Eberhardt's entertainment.

Soon, it was time to turn in for the night as I was quite exhausted after our terrifying encounter with the blizzard and I welcomed the soft bed she offered me. The thick, down comforter made up for the cold trek my frozen feet had just endured; they were now warm and toasty, snuggled comfortably under the covers. Even Alinka enjoyed herself as she buried herself in my arms, and I fell asleep listening to the wind howling outside my bedroom window.

The next morning when I awoke to the smell of breakfast cooking in the kitchen below, I anxiously looked out my window. Although I could see the storm had abated somewhat, it was still snowing, and I was surprised to see that sometime in the middle of the night, Frau Eberhardt had evidently put a fresh set of clothing on the chair next to my bed. There was even a new pair of boots sitting nearby on the floor. When I asked her about it, she said she always kept extra clothes for her granddaughters when they visited her, and they had probably outgrown them, anyway. When I went downstairs for breakfast, she had even washed the clothes I was wearing when we had arrived, and she reminded me so much of my *Babka* Kabliski.

When I walked into the kitchen, Herr Eberhardt, Frau Eberhardt, and Father Heinrich were already sitting at the kitchen table enjoying a cup of coffee. Father Heinrich had told me how much he missed his morning coffee, and he said all the coffee had to be imported, mostly from South America, so it was a treasured commodity, saved only for special occasions.

Seeing me walk into the kitchen, Frau Eberhardt got up from the table. "It looks like our young guest has decided to join us for breakfast, and doesn't she look wonderful in her new clothes! Would she like some hot chocolate?" I didn't even have to answer that question; she already knew the answer.

Fortunately for Frau Eberhardt, the morning's breakfast conversation centered on the weather, the shortage of most everything needed for daily life, and family, and the war wasn't even mentioned as I'm sure she had already lectured Herr Eberhardt about permissible topics for our breakfast conversation; out of our earshot, of course.

As I sat there, enjoying a cup of hot chocolate and a piece of bread spread with fruit preserves, Herr Eberhardt began a conversation with Father Heinrich, which, although it didn't really begin as a question was, indeed, a question.

He sat back in his chair and looked directly at Father Heinrich. "I know this might be a huge imposition," he began. "I'm sure you and Anna are eager to be on your way and from what you've told me, you still have a long way to go, and I certainly don't envy you for that. Although it appears the storm has somewhat lessened, I'm not sure it would be possible to extract your motorcar from the ditch and get you safely on the way."

*Okay,* I thought to myself. I'm sure this conversation is headed somewhere, isn't it?

Herr Eberhardt continued, "In light of your current situation, it appears as if you and Anna may have to stay an extra day with us."

Was he just inviting us to extend our visit or was he still headed towards a yet to be revealed destination? Father Heinrich and I both sat there waiting patiently for his extended monologue to come to some logical conclusion.

"It would greatly please me if you would do Frau Eberhardt and me a personal favour before you leave."

Okay. He was finally getting somewhere.

"Our neighbour, Frau Friedrich, has recently taken ill. In fact, she hasn't been able to leave her house since before Christmas and I know she's a devout Catholic who hasn't been able to attend Mass for quite some time now. I'm sure she would be delighted if you could visit her today and say a special Mass for her." Then he sat back in his chair, crossed his arms across his chest, and awaited an answer.

This wasn't where we had hoped his rambling introduction would finally lead us and it was completely unexpected, so Father Heinrich sat silent, trying to assemble an answer that would satisfy our gracious host. "Herr Eberhardt, although my heart goes out to Frau Friedrich, however, I'm not at all prepared to say a Mass. I don't have the necessary items needed for saying a Mass and besides, the weather surely would prevent us from getting to her house safely."

Herr Eberhardt refused to be denied. "Tell me, Father. What special items do you need for a Mass? They can't be that elaborate, can they?"

Father Heinrich later confessed he hadn't attended Mass himself since he was a small boy, so Herr Eberhardt's questions posed a huge dilemma for him. Once confronted with such a dilemma, he said he felt he had to honour our host's wishes and he would try to do the best he could and thankfully, he still had Father Tadeus' marked-up Prayer Book for reference.

"Well, Herr Eberhardt, we would need some bread and some wine, to begin with. But pray tell, how would we get through the deep snow to Frau Friedrich's?"

Herr Eberhardt seemed relieved now that Father Heinrich had apparently agreed to his request. "Bread and wine will be no problem, Father, nor will safe transportation. I have just the solution."

I'm sure people staring out their windows and seeing their neighbour, a priest, and a young girl riding down the road on a farm tractor in a snowstorm was quite a sight, like a scene from a movie; a comedy, of course, and after one or two kilometres, we arrived at Frau Friedrich's house; a bit chilled and happy to be out of the weather.

When Herr Eberhardt knocked on her door and announced ourselves, a feeble voice from within invited us in. When we walked into the small living room, Frau Friedrich was sitting in a chair by the fireplace hiding somewhere deep within a fur wrap of some sort.

Herr Eberhardt walked up and gave Frau Friedrich a kiss on her forehead. "Frau Friedrich, I've brought you a present," as he motioned for us to step closer to where she was sitting. "This is Father Heinrich and his niece, Anna. They have sought shelter from the storm in our house, and when I mentioned you hadn't been able to attend Mass for quite some time now, Father Heinrich graciously offered to visit and say a Mass with you."

Not quite the whole truth, but close enough to satisfy even the most zealous critic, including Father Heinrich, himself.

Frau Friedrich appeared overwhelmed and I thought for a moment she wouldn't be able to continue, but I had greatly underestimated her spirit. Turning to Herr Eberhardt, she asked, "Ernst, would you please get my eyeglasses from my nightstand next to my bed?"

As he left on his mission to retrieve her eyeglasses, she turned towards Father Heinrich. "Tell me, Father. Where is your church?" she asked.

Perhaps she had finally stumped him; however, he quickly answered "Bielsko, Poland, Frau Friedrich. Why do you ask?"

"No reason, Father. I hope the Mass is said the same in Poland as it is in Austria."

"Ma'am. The Mass is said in Latin and I'm sure Polish Latin is the same as Austrian Latin," obviously attempting to inject some humour into the conversation. Frau Friedrich just smiled; it was obvious she already liked Father Heinrich.

When Herr Eberhardt returned with her glasses, he handed them to her and she adjusted them comfortably on her prominent nose. "I'm ready," she proudly exclaimed.

Father Heinrich nodded in my direction; my signal to uncover the basket Frau Eberhardt had packed for the Mass. Reaching into the basket, Father Heinrich retrieved the small loaf of bread, the miniature bottle of wine, and the wine glass she had carefully packed for our journey. Then, he reached into his cassock pocket and took out Father Tadeus' well-worn Prayer Book.

Turning to one of the marked pages, he studied it for a while and then started. *"In nòmine Patris, et Filii, et Spìritus Sancti. Amen,"* he began reading aloud.

Handing the book to Frau Friedrich, he pointed to the respondent's passage; however, Frau Friedrich casually brushed his hand aside, "Take back your book, Father. *Et cum spiritu tuo,"* she responded in a strong voice.

It was interesting standing there as a bystander watching the curious interaction between the two, almost as though she was the *instructor* and he was her *student,* as she patiently coaxed him through the Mass.

I know many Catholics who read my story may be appalled by the fact that Father Heinrich wasn't an ordained priest, shouldn't have said a Mass, and I'm certain they'll criticise him for turning such a sacred ritual into theater, however you have to understand the times to understand the circumstances. We were at war, we were trying to reach safety ahead of the advancing Russians, and Father Heinrich hadn't solicited the situation. In fact, he had made every effort to avoid it.

After we had left the Eberhardts and were once again on our way, we spoke briefly about the experience and Father Heinrich had the opinion, and I have to say I wholeheartedly agreed with him, that the words in the Bible, any Prayer Book, the Torah, or any other religious writings are God's words. It's not *God's* decision as to who can speak His words, over time it has become the *Church's* decision, instead. I think that's wrong, regardless of what others may think. I apologise, but since this is *my* story, I think I have the right to express *my* opinions.

Anyway, to continue; I'm sure Father Heinrich's attempt at saying the Mass in Latin had given great comfort (and entertainment) to Frau Friedrich. Afterwards, she told us that she had enjoyed our company and wished us well on our journey.

Herr Eberhardt, Father Heinrich, and I bade her farewell and rode back to the Eberhardt's on his tractor with mission thankfully accomplished.

After we arrived back at the farmhouse and were finally alone, I asked Father Heinrich how he had even found the courage to attempt such a feat. His only words were, "I felt Anna's hands on my shoulders the entire time."

## Graz, Austria

Herr Eberhardt and his wife wanted us to stay another night with them as they said they truly craved company, especially during the long, dreary winter days, but the snow had stopped and we needed to be on our way. When it was apparent we had made up our minds, Frau Eberhardt packed a small bag for me with an extra pair of clothes, socks, and warm mittens; something I dearly needed, and she also packed a small lunch for us; a loaf of dark bread and some cold sausages.

Herr Eberhardt bundled up, went out to the shed, and started the tractor. Father Heinrich put on his heavy overcoat over his cassock while I bundled up in my coat, scarf, new boots, and the new mittens Frau Eberhardt had thoughtfully given me.

With a hug and a cheerful farewell, we left the house and joined Herr Eberhardt on the waiting tractor. I was truly sad to leave them; they reminded me so much of my *Dziadek* and *Babka* Kabliski and as Frau Eberhardt stood in the doorway and waved goodbye, I knew, like them, I would never see her again. Afterwards, Father Heinrich and I talked about coming back and visiting them, but time and other more pressing matters always got in the way.

It only took just a few minutes to drive from the Eberhardt's house to where our motorcar was stranded and although I swore we had walked at least ten kilometres in the blizzard, it turned out to be less than two.

It didn't take long for Herr Eberhardt to attach the rear bumper of the motorcar to the tractor with a strong rope and with a deft touch, he slowly pulled it out of the ditch. It looked none the worse for wear except it was extremely dirty and the tires were caked with mud, however other than that, it appeared to be in excellent condition.

Father Heinrich wanted to send Herr Eberhardt on his way back home, but he insisted on staying until he was sure the motorcar started and we were safely on our way. It took some time for Father Heinrich to wash off the windscreen and brush the snow off the motorcar. The relentless wind had drifted the snow up against the driver's side of the car until it was completely covered, but Father Heinrich had finally cleared enough snow to be able to open the driver's side door.

I wanted to get into the motorcar with him, but he insisted I stay outside until he was certain everything was all right. Miraculously, the motorcar started up on the first try and he beckoned me to join him, however before I did, I ran over to Herr Eberhardt, climbed up on the tractor, and gave him a big hug. He smiled, kissed me on my forehead, and I ran over and joined Father Heinrich. After I had gotten into the motorcar, I turned and watched Herr Eberhardt and his tractor disappear down the road.

After we were comfortably settled, Father Heinrich turned and looked at me, "Shall we?" he asked.

"We shall," I replied and with that, we continued our journey and our playful little word game.

There were still some snowdrifts across the roadway, so Father Heinrich carefully had to navigate our *"Landgebundenen Überseedampfer (Dry land ocean liner)"*, as he sometimes referred to it, through and around them. There were no other motorcars on the road, just us, and after we had finally rejoined the main highway at Eisenstadt, the highways were clear of snow and ice.

When we were just outside Eisenstadt, Father Heinrich pulled the motorcar over to the side of the road and retrieved the map, once again. He studied it carefully and finally he said, "I think I've found a shortcut to Graz that might save us twenty or more kilometres. What do you think?"

I didn't need to answer that silly question; the expression on my face said it all, so he looked at me and said, *"Nein, Jah?"* An apparent contradiction of terms, but I knew him well enough to know what he meant.

I smiled and said *"Nein, Jah,"* as he put the map away and we continued on the main road to Graz.

Soon, the highway started to climb up over the mountains, and I was quite afraid at first because we didn't have mountains where I had grown up in Poland as I could see the roadway in front of us disappear into the clouds. That was something I had never seen before, and I glanced over at Father Heinrich to see if he seemed concerned, but he didn't appear to be, so I just looked out the window at the beautiful scenery below as the houses in the valley far below us grew smaller and smaller.

We passed through several small villages along the way, although we saw very few people, and the ones we passed glanced up as we sped by, but they never acknowledged us. I guess they were just going about their business and trying to stay warm. Although the snow had stopped, it was still quite cold outside, and I loved breathing on the inside of the motorcar's window, watching the frost form, and then use my fingernail to draw pictures or practice writing my German. Anyway, it helped distract my attention until we drove into the clouds.

Father Heinrich inched our way along the road through the fog as he tried to stay in the middle of the roadway, and several times we had to dodge other motorcars coming towards us as they had the same thing in mind, and I think I heard him say *"Verdammt"* a couple of times under his breath. I think that's quite humourous; a Catholic priest cursing under his breath.

Within a few anxious minutes we finally drove out of the clouds, and I could see that we were on the top of a very high mountain. Up ahead, and far below in the valley, was a large town, and I tapped Father Heinrich on his shoulder and pointed down at it. "Graz," was his brusque answer. I guess he was too focused on staying on the narrow, mountainous road to have more than a brief, monosyllabic conversation.

As Graz drew closer, one building in particular began to stand out from the rest. It had two tall spires on one end and a large domed roof on the other, and as before, I tapped Father Heinrich on his shoulder and pointed at it. He just shrugged his shoulders in a questioning way; no conversation this time. Whatever it was, I hoped we would have a chance to stop there; it was beautiful.

When we finally entered the outskirts of the town, Father Heinrich stopped alongside the narrow street, retrieved the map, and ran his finger down the handwritten list Father Tadeus had attached to it. "Ah, here it is," Father Heinrich exclaimed. "Graz. Mariatrost Basilica; Father Laurent," he read aloud. "Okay. Let's find Mariatrost Basilica. What do you think, Anna?"

"Let's," I squealed. I really loved adventures!

As we started driving down the street towards the center of town, Father Heinrich stopped and asked the first person we encountered where we could find the Mariatrost Basilica. He just pointed at the two spires rising up from the trees just a couple blocks away. So, we *were* going to get to visit the building I had seen from the mountain; *that* was the Mariatrost Basilica.

I was overwhelmed as we approached the Basilica. First of all, it was the biggest building I had ever seen, including some I had seen in Warsaw, and it sat on top of a small hill dominating the entire town from its lofty perch. The church was painted a cheery yellow with white trim, and it had a bright red tile roof. The twin spires on either side of the main entrance soared into the sky and were topped with two, tri-tiered crosses mounted on golden orbs. The great dome at the rear of the church had four oval stained glass windows. I remembered wondering if the outside was this impressive, what surprises would the inside hold?

Father Heinrich parked the motorcar in the small parking lot at the foot of the hill below the church, we gathered our things, stepped out of the motorcar, and walked up the narrow flight of stairs to the Basilica. The closer we got to the Basilica, the smaller I felt, and although the building was magnificent, it was *overwhelmingly* magnificent.

When we walked through the Basilica's main entrance, we had only taken a couple of steps, when we both stopped in our tracks. If I thought the outside of the Basilica was magnificent, its interior made it pale in comparison.

The nave was quite long, and it was flanked by two rows of hand-carved, wooden pews, and the entire ceiling was covered with beautiful frescoes depicting Biblical scenes too numerous to stop and examine; besides, my neck started getting cramped from looking up. There were also several alcoves projecting off either side of the nave that revealed their contents as we walked down the main aisle towards the altar.

I had expected to see a cross with a crucified man hanging above the altar, but, instead, there was an incredible, golden statue of what Father Heinrich told me was the Virgin Mary, and she was surrounded by shafts of golden rays radiating upwards towards the great fresco-covered dome, and there were two larger-than-life angels on either side of her, standing on pedestals between the four curved, twisted pillars supporting the dome.

The altar would have been an impressive sight by itself if it hadn't been dwarfed by its surroundings. It was constructed of grey-striped marble that matched the four plinths supporting the nearby columns, and there were also six, golden candlesticks sitting on the altar with another golden statue of the Virgin Mary standing between them. If that wasn't enough, there were two, life-sized, winged angels hovering about ten feet above the altar suspended on long chains hung from the domed ceiling high above.

As we slowly walked down the center aisle towards the altar, I peeked into the alcoves on either side. One alcove contained a dark cross with a life-sized Jesus nailed to it, and the wall behind him was faux-painted as though he was hanging in an archway with a scene behind it, perhaps a depiction of ancient Jerusalem. There were also red drapes painted on either side of the archway with a wrought-iron candelabrum set on the floor nearby with seven lighted candles. In addition, someone had placed a flower-filled vase at the base of the candelabrum.

Another alcove displayed a painting of the Virgin Mary with Baby Jesus in her lap, and they were surrounded by a flock of angels hovering over them. In addition, did I mention the gold? Everywhere I looked, I saw only gold; the entire nave shimmered with a golden glow as the sun streamed through the beautiful stained glass windows that made colourful patterns on the stark-white walls.

As we approached the altar, a priest entered the nave from a side door, he smiled, walked up to where we were standing, and shook Father Heinrich's extended hand, "Welcome to our Basilica. My name is Father Ralf, and yours is?" he asked politely.

"Heinrich Mueller and this is my daughter Anna."

Father Ralf recoiled slightly when he introduced me as his daughter and I could tell he was confused. "Excuse me for asking, but you have a daughter, Father Heinrich?"

It took some time for Father Heinrich to explain our situation, and the fact that he actually wasn't a Catholic priest, after all. After reading Father Tadeus' Letter of Introduction, he asked us to follow him, and he led us through the door behind him, as we walked down a long hallway past paintings of saints and religious icons. I wished I had the time to stop and look at each one; however, he appeared to be in a hurry to reach his destination.

We finally arrived at his office door after turning down numerous hallways and climbing several flights of stairs, and if we had to find our way back to the main part of the Basilica on our own, I hoped Father Heinrich was taking note of our meandering route.

After opening the door and inviting us in, he closed the door behind him, and offered us a seat across from his cluttered desk. The office was quite small, but other than the clutter on his desk, it was rather tidy; *efficient*, if I had to find another word for it.

When we were comfortably seated, he walked around the desk and sat down in the big, leather armchair, which I could tell by its well-worn blemishes, had seen its share of priests come and go.

Father Ralf began the conversation on a pleasant note, "Tell me, Heinrich, what brings you and your daughter to our Basilica?" he asked.

Father Heinrich took some time describing our journey, some of our adventures and misadventures, and shared our destination and the reason for travelling there; however, the only thing he didn't share was the fact he was an SS doctor fleeing Auschwitz ahead of the approaching Russian Army and fortunately, Father Ralf didn't ask too many probing questions. In fact, he appeared to be listening politely, but not really listening perhaps because it appeared as though he was formulating his next line of questioning while pretending to be paying attention to what Father Heinrich was telling him.

After Father Heinrich had revealed all he intended to reveal, Father Ralf leaned forward, placed his elbows on the desktop and cradled his chin on his thumbs. In my naiveté I assumed he was about to take us into his confidence, so I was quite surprised by his following remarks.

"Heinrich Mueller, or whomever you truly are, I have to tell you that I am deeply disturbed by your masquerading as a priest in this most holy of places. It's a blasphemous act that has no precedent during my tenure here as you essentially have the nerve to walk into my Basilica garbed as a Catholic priest, when in actuality you're nothing but a pretender. Nothing but a false, sacrilegious, miscreant dressed in holy garments, and I'm sure our Blessed Virgin Mary would have come down from her sacred perch above the altar and stripped them from you, if she could. I want you and your daughter to leave here immediately and never set foot in our Basilica again, dressed as you are. I'll have Brother Martin escort you through the rear door," as he pressed a button hidden somewhere among the clutter on his desk.

We both just sat there, stunned by Father Ralf's unexpected outburst, and I had to admire Father Heinrich's composure as he sat there like a schoolchild being dressed down for some horrendous act. I could see the muscles in his neck tense as his cheeks slowly flushed, but he maintained his dignity, and I have to say that made me love and respect him even more.

Within moments, Brother Martin arrived and unceremoniously escorted us from Father Ralf's office, and just as Father Heinrich was about to walk out the door, he turned, made the sign of the cross and said, "Bless you, Father." He then turned his back on his inquisitor and followed Brother Martin out the door and I think if Father Ralf could have put his hands on a nearby heavy object, he would have flung it in our direction, but, fortunately, he didn't.

Doktor Mueller and I never discussed our encounter with Father Ralf. Father Ralf's rebuke was an almost humourous aside; a pompous performance on his part from behind his desk in his holy sanctuary deep within Austria when compared to our frightful experience in the basement of St. Mikolaj's Church, our flight from the partisans' camp, the perilous border crossing, getting stuck in the middle of a blizzard, and our trip through the clouds,

Fortunately, we were able to spend the night comfortably in *Die Hungrigen Reisenden* (The Hungry Traveller Inn) compliments of the generous proprietor. As we were leaving the following morning, he called out to us as we walked out the door, "Please stop by and visit our beautiful Basilica and be sure to meet Father Ralf. He's a very interesting fellow, indeed."

Father Heinrich acknowledged his farewell with a brief wave of his hand, took mine, smiled, and we were glad to be finally leaving Graz.

## Klagenfurt, Austria

As we drove out of Graz, I think we were both pleased to see the twin spires of the Basilica recede in the distance and every now and then, I'd catch Father Heinrich chuckling to himself, and I wondered what humour he had discovered that I hadn't during our visit to Graz. I didn't dare ask, lest it remind him of the 'schoolboy' scolding he had received from Father Ralf. Why hadn't Father Laurent greeted us when we first arrived? It hadn't even occurred to us to inquire about Father Laurent and we never did find out if he was still there, or if he had moved on.

It was still bitterly cold, although the sun was shining brightly. Father Heinrich had hoped we could have refilled our petrol supply in Graz as he said we were running low on fuel, and he hoped we'd have enough left to make it to our next stop, Klagenfurt, and maybe to a warmer welcome, too.

For the first few kilometres, we headed north following a winding, ice-choked river on our left, but every now and then I could see some frigid water tumbling over the exposed, ice-covered rocks. The farther we travelled, the narrower the valley became until it was so confined that even the smallest ray of sunlight had a difficult time finding its way down to the valley's narrow floor. Finally, it widened as we approached the small town of Köflach where the road made a sharp left turn and zigzagged its way across the face of a steep mountainside for as far as we could see. As he had done many times before, Father Heinrich stopped the motorcar, got out his map, and studied it carefully.

"We're not going up there, are we?" I asked anxiously.

Father Heinrich tried hard not to show the apprehension I'm sure he must have also been feeling. "I guess so," he replied, trying to sound cheerful. "Hang on," he said, as we started up the narrow, twisting road.

It turned out to be not nearly as bad as we had anticipated. Yes, the road was narrow and the turns were countless, but it was paved and there wasn't any traffic. The biggest problem Father Heinrich faced, however, was navigating the big Mercedes around each corner; the motorcar was quite long and the curves extremely sharp and more than once, he had to stop in mid-curve, back up, and make a second pass.

We passed through several small towns with names like Edelschrott, Pack, and Prietenegg; towns that clung precariously to their lofty perches and I would never have wanted to live there, but I must admit they did have beautiful views of the valleys far below.

The next town we came to was called Wolfsberg and it was nearly the size of Graz. We parked the motorcar in a small square near the middle of town and got out to take a much-needed break. It wasn't really a square; it was actually a grassy circle in the center of town with an ancient castle standing on top of the highest hill overlooking the town.

We walked around for a few minutes, stretched our legs, and then we got back into the motorcar and enjoyed the last few bites of the cold sausages Frau Eberhardt had thoughtfully packed for us. On the way out of town, we passed by a strange looking compound. It was quite large, and it was surrounded by barbed wire with tall towers in the four corners marking its boundaries. Somehow it reminded us both of what we had left behind in Auschwitz. Some of the buildings had been recently demolished and there were piles of rubble everywhere. There were a few people standing outside, apparently not doing anything in particular other than enjoying the late January sunshine. We didn't pay much attention to it in passing; however, we later discovered it was Stalag XVIII, a prisoner-of-war camp housing Polish, American, and British POW's. It had been attacked by Allied bombers in mid-December with many casualties among the POW's and the German guards. Of course, we didn't know that at the time and if we had, I'm certain we wouldn't have stopped anyway.

Within a few kilometres the road disappeared into a hole in the side of the mountain directly in front of us, and I poked Father Heinrich's shoulder several times to get his attention as I pointed towards it. When he finally looked my way, he just smiled and turned on the motorcar's big headlamps. I didn't know what to expect, and I let out a loud shriek when he didn't stop the motorcar as he just let the hole swallow us up. "*Tunnel*," he shouted as he honked the big motorcar's air horns, just as a playful child would do. That was the first time I had ever driven through a tunnel, and I was glad when I finally saw the brightly-lighted exit up ahead. After a few anxious minutes, we finally exited the tunnel and once again, were out in the bright daylight. We continued for several more kilometres until the outskirts of Klagenfurt, Austria came into view.

Like when we had approached Graz, the tallest building in Klagenfurt was a church, probably our destination, St. Mary's Cathedral. It wasn't until Father Heinrich and I had begun our journey that I ever realised how many churches there were, especially Catholic churches, and they were usually the biggest building in town. Growing up in a small, Polish village, the tallest building was usually someone's barn or two-story house, if they were lucky enough to have a second story. Since our journey had turned into a more spiritual one and we were staying in Catholic churches, I became acutely aware of the churches and cathedrals in every town we visited. I discovered that even the smallest town had a church, and it was usually one of the nicest buildings.

Although the cathedral wasn't quite as large as the Mariatrost Basilica, it was still quite impressive. It wasn't until Father Heinrich had parked the motorcar in the side parking lot that I had an idea of how large it actually was. Like the Mariatrost Basilica, it had twin spires at the front with ornamented crosses growing out of golden orbs shaped like onions, and one of the spires had a large clock face on each side. Unlike the Basilica, the outside walls were made of stone with beautiful inlaid designs, and there was a painted fresco of a man carrying a staff with a child on his shoulder on one outside wall, and there were many headstones embedded in an adjoining wall next to an alcove containing a large wooden cross.

After we had parked the car, Father Heinrich walked around to the rear of the motorcar, opened the trunk, lifted each of the petrol cans, shook them to see how much petrol we had left, and they were all empty.

"Shall we?" he asked. This expression was becoming somewhat of a standing joke between the two of us as we had grown to know each other so well that our conversations tended to be minimalistic, usually confined to one or two words.

"We shall," I replied.

When we walked through the cathedral's arched side door into the nave, they were in the midst of celebrating their Sunday evening Mass, and we stood for a few moments absorbing our new surroundings. Like all the other churches and cathedrals, we had visited, this one had a personality of its own. Perhaps it reflected the period in which it had been built, perhaps it glorified one saint over another, or maybe it simply reflected the architect's attempt to build something that would blend in with the surrounding area, but each church was unique.

I'm always amazed at how these beautiful churches and cathedrals were built entirely by hand. Nowadays, when we drive into the city, all we see are the tall cranes and specialised machines they use to build modern buildings. What did *they* have back then? Any power tools, diesel-powered cranes, forklifts, bucket loaders, cement mixers, steel beams? No. All they had were hand tools, amazing ingenuity, and the sweat of their brow, and yet, the results were spectacular.

When Meyer and I travelled to Paris in 1972, we stood in the plaza in front of the Notre Dame Cathedral and tried to imagine what it must have been like back in the twelfth century when they dug the first shovelful of dirt to lay the foundations for what would become probably the most stunning building in all of France, perhaps all of Europe; in the *twelfth* century! Can you even begin to imagine a beautiful cathedral slowly rising from the Parisian mud flats bordering the River Seine, one block at a time? Imagine; one *stone block* at a time, a block chiseled from the roughly quarried stones one *chisel blow* at a time, and it's no wonder it took them almost two-hundred years to complete it.

Since the congregation was in the midst of celebrating their Sunday evening Mass, Father Heinrich and I sat down in the last row of pews trying to be as inconspicuous as possible. Father Heinrich dug into his cassock's pocket and retrieved Father Tadeus' dog-eared Prayer Book. Turning the pages to the now familiar section, he searched until he found where they were in the service, and we then joined in.

This was the first time I had been drawn into the heart of a Catholic Mass, and I have to say that it moved me. The pageantry, the marvelous interaction between the priests and the celebrants, the wonderful music that filled the cathedral all the way to its lofty frescoed ceilings and echoed off the cathedral's walls forever; they all filled me with a warm, fulfilling love like I had never felt before.

I had promised myself never to forsake my Jewish heritage, and I still haven't to this day, but there was just something about walking into the Catholic Mass that was overwhelming, and I think that moment reinforced my growing interest in religion and especially my love of languages. Being raised a Jew, I remembered the throaty beauty of the ancient, spoken Hebrew language and I contrasted that to the precise, meticulous resonance of the spoken Latin language; both in praise of *their* own God, our *mutual* God. I laughed as I recalled Father Heinrich's unconvincing attempt at speaking Latin during the Mass he had said at Frau Friedrich's house; it sounded nothing like I heard being spoken that day in the cathedral.

After Mass, the celebrants, mostly elderly women, walked slowly out of the cathedral as Father Heinrich and I stood off in a corner trying to be as inconspicuous as possible. Once or twice, one of the women looked in our direction, smiled, and we returned their polite gesture while we waited until the cathedral was mostly vacant.

There was still some activity surrounding the altar as several acolytes scurried about in their haste to renew the altar for the next celebration. A tall, stately priest stood nearby, engaged in a lively conversation with one of the acolytes, and he had already divested himself of his celebratory raiment and was now dressed in a long, black cassock similar to the one Father Heinrich was wearing.

When he noticed us walking up the nave's long center aisle, he turned and put his hand on the acolyte's shoulder as if to pause him in the middle of the conversation. He appeared to be surprised to see an unfamiliar priest holding a young girl's hand walking towards him.

When we got within a few feet of where he was standing, he walked down the three steps separating us, held out his hand in welcome, shook Father Heinrich's outstretched hand, and greeted us. "Welcome, Father, to St. Mary's Cathedral. I don't think we've met before. My name is Father Georg, and you are?" as he waited expectantly for Father Heinrich's answer.

As before, he started, "Heinrich Mueller, and my daughter, Anna. However, before you say anything, let's sit down and I'll tell you our story."

I could tell by the look on Father Georg's face that he, like Father Ralf, was surprised by his answer; however, he led us to a nearby pew, and the three of us sat down. Father Heinrich put his arm protectively around my shoulder as he retold our story for what must have seemed to be the thousandth time.

Father Georg listened patiently, and then he carefully read Father Tadeus' Letter of Introduction. Both Father Heinrich and I sat there anxiously waiting for his reaction and when he had finished, he handed it back to Father Heinrich. "Well, I must say, Heinrich, I was quite taken aback when I saw you and Anna walking towards me, and I didn't know what to make of your sudden appearance. But now that you've told your story and I've read Father Tadeus' letter, I can only say that you are most welcome to stay with us for as long as you'd like."

I watched as Father Heinrich's shoulders collapsed in relief since he had probably expected a 'school boy's' scolding and had received a warm welcome, instead. Maybe Father Ralf had been just an anomaly; perhaps just a bitter old man masquerading as a caring, loving priest.

I had to laugh when Father Georg said he hoped Father Heinrich hadn't performed any marriage ceremonies along the way; just what Father Tadeus had said. Thankfully, he didn't ask him if he had said any Masses.

Our stay at St. Mary's Cathedral was delightful. The food, the company, and the beautiful surroundings were a welcome respite after our disappointing visit to Graz and the only time the conversation turned serious was when Father Heinrich inquired about the war's progress. When he asked, the mood around the supper table suddenly became serious.

Father Teodor, who was the assistant parish cleric, appeared to be the one at the table who was the most informed. He said the German Army was in a hasty retreat after suffering a crushing defeat during the Ardennes Offensive, the Allies had regrouped, and the front lines were back to their original position before the Offensive was launched. When Father Heinrich asked where the front lines were, he replied "The Rhine River."

"*The Rhine River?*" Father Heinrich exclaimed. "Why, that means they're right on Germany's border. Do you mean to say the Allies are about to invade Germany?"

Father Teodor frowned. "I'm afraid so."

"They're closer than I thought."

Afterwards, I wondered how his words were interpreted by the others. Was he worried by the Allies' proximity or was he happy?

I know one thing he was happy about; somehow our five empty petrol cans were miraculously filled to overflowing, something that was difficult under the current circumstances. Father Heinrich explained one of the reasons for Germany's impending defeat was its lack of access to petroleum, especially since they had lost the Romanian and Caucasus' oil fields to the Allies. Petroleum not only fed the 'war machine', it also fueled the industries that supplied the German Army with everything they needed to wage war, including petrol for their vehicles. The only way they could produce petroleum products was synthetically from other raw materials and the Allies continuously bombed those processing plants. That made receiving the gift of more than one-hundred litres of precious petrol a pleasant and truly welcome surprise.

After we had retired for the night to our sparse, but comfortable sleeping quarters, Father Heinrich drew me aside. "I don't want to frighten you, Anna, but we truly *do* need to hasten our journey. I thought the Ardennes Offensive may have bought us some extra time to reach our destination, but now the situation has changed, and it's urgent we get there as soon as possible."

I went to sleep that night worried about what we were getting ourselves into, but I loved and trusted Father Heinrich, and I knew he would get us safely to our destination, *our* God willing.

## Salzburg, Austria

We left Klagenfurt and our new friends early the next morning. As with all our other goodbyes, this one was especially sad as our gracious hosts had more than made up for the rude treatment we had received in Graz, and we were reluctant to leave them. We knew the town had already suffered greatly during the war with over six-hundred residents killed in nearly four-dozen Allied bombing attacks. As we later learned, the German commander declared Klagenfurt an 'open city' in early May 1945 and the British finally occupied it on May 8th. Father Heinrich and I rejoiced when we heard the news, but that was still almost three months in the future.

Father Heinrich was eager to get on the road because we needed to quicken our pace to our destination; the Russian/Allied vise was beginning to apply pressure from both sides. When Father Heinrich had asked the Fathers at St. Mary's Cathedral where the Eastern Front lines were, they all agreed the Russian bears were already deep within Germany and in fact, they were almost to the banks of the Oder River, just ninety kilometres from downtown Berlin and the front steps of the Reichstag.

Father Heinrich took this as good news, although he didn't think it prudent to voice his opinion. It appeared the Russian's main objective was Berlin, far north of us, and the Allies' objective was into southern Germany, towards Munich, much closer to our destination. If that was so, we might just be able to reach the relative safety of

Rottach-Egern ahead of the advancing Allied Army and that made our dash to safety even more time sensitive.

Soon after we left Klagenfurt our route headed north, away from the nearby Italian border and into the heart of Austria towards Salzburg, perhaps our last stop before we finally reached our destination. As we sped along, we began to see a lot more damage as we headed deeper into the battle zone and the closer we got to Salzburg, the more apprehensive we became, however, in order to reach Bavaria, we had to travel north. We had no other choice; the treacherous Southern Alps formed an almost impassable barrier had we decided to head southwest, instead.

Several times Father Heinrich stopped the motorcar and referred to the now well-worn map, but no matter how hard he tried to find an alternate route, the route through Salzburg was the only one that made any sense.

It took us several hours to reach the outskirts of Salzburg and what we saw when we approached the city, amazed us. Almost half the buildings in the city had either been destroyed or heavily damaged; even the large castle overlooking the city had suffered damage from the recent Allied bombing raids. Then we saw it; the Cathedral of Saint Rupert and Saint Vergilius, our supposed safe haven, and even *it* hadn't escaped damage. Where there had once been a great dome, there was now only a circular, gaping hole exposing the chancel below to the elements. Fortunately, the twin spires were still intact as was the rest of the building, at least from our vantage point, however that wasn't what we had expected.

We made our way down into the city, carefully avoiding the piles of rubble cluttering the narrow streets. *"Verdammt,"* Father Heinrich exclaimed as he surveyed the damage. "How could they do this to Mozart's beautiful city?" I didn't know if he was asking me a direct question or whether it was just a rhetorical one and not knowing who Mozart was, I didn't know how to answer, so I didn't.

Like all the other cathedrals we had visited, the Cathedral of Saint Rupert and Saint Vergilius, or as the locals called it, the Salzburg Cathedral, was large, imposing, and beautiful, despite the damage. Before we could even get out of the motorcar, a priest standing nearby surveying the damage walked up to us and Father Heinrich rolled down the window as he approached.

"Greetings, Father. What brings you here?" the priest asked.

"My good friend, Father Tadeus, from St. Mikolaj Church in Bielsko, Poland said you might shelter us as we passed through Salzburg," Father Mueller replied without his usual 'Heinrich Mueller and daughter, Anna', introduction.

The priest made a feeble attempt at a friendly smile, "I'm sorry, Father. We're unable to provide you and your young travelling companion any shelter, not even for one night. Although the Cathedral appears mostly undamaged from the outside, the bomb that destroyed our beautiful dome did considerable damage inside and there's just nowhere to put you up. I'm sorry. What is your *final* destination?" he inquired.

The devastating news he had just delivered was something we hadn't expected. Except for Klagenfurt, most of our journey had been through relatively unscathed territory and we just weren't prepared for the challenge he had just presented us.

Father Heinrich attempted to be stoic. "Rottach-Egern, Germany is our final destination. Salzburg was only intended to be our final stopping-off place. Now, I'm not too sure where we should go from here."

The priest recoiled from Father Heinrich's answer. "*Germany? Germany*, you say? Don't you know the border has been closed for some time now? Only the German military is allowed to move across the border; neither civilians nor priests are permitted to cross. I don't know who sent you this way, but Salzburg may be a dead-end for you, not just a stopping-off place."

I knew Father Heinrich well enough to know he wasn't about to give up, not after everything we had gone through on our journey; it just wasn't going to end in Salzburg.

Reaching into the back seat, he retrieved the map and held it out the window towards the priest. "There must be some way we can cross the border other than on the main roads. It just doesn't make sense they would block every border crossing into Germany as there must be dozens of secondary roads into Germany. How could they possibly waste their dwindling resources guarding cow paths when they're desperately needed on both fronts?" he asked.

The priest took the map from Father Heinrich's hands. "If you'd kindly step outside, I'll show you the problem," as we both got out of the motorcar and followed the priest around to the front. As he spread the map out onto the motorcar's still warm bonnet, Father Heinrich lifted me up so I could see what he was about to reveal to us.

He pointed his finger at a spot on the map. "Salzburg," he exclaimed. "Notice how Austria sticks into Germany like a small dent near Salzburg, if you would, and Germany evens the score by sticking a small dent into our country just west of here. If you were to travel west, or even southwest from Salzburg, you'd bump into the German border. In fact, the border is only a couple of kilometres from where we're now standing."

"Are there any other options?" Father Heinrich asked.

"Not directly from here without making a detour. Follow my finger, if you will," as he outlined an indirect route that avoided both 'dents'. "Head south from Salzburg until you reach Bischofshofen," as he pointed to another spot on the map. "From there take the road that follows the river through Saalfelden," yet again another finger on the map. "From there continue following the road until you reach St. Johann."

However, he didn't need to point at the map; Father Heinrich had already found St. Johann and pointed to it.

"Good. Now here's the tricky point, so please pay attention. In the center of St. Johann there's a farm road heading due north. It's a small road and easy to miss as there aren't any road signs directing the way. When you first come into St. Johann, you'll be following a river off to your right. When you get into town, keep to the right, and soon you'll cross a bridge across that river. Immediately after that, you'll come to a 'Y' in the road. Take the left fork, and within a couple of hundred metres there will be a road off to the right. That's the road you'll be looking for."

The priest paused to let Father Heinrich absorb what he had just told him and to give him a chance to ask any questions, which he did, "I have just one question, Father. How do you know so much about this area? It seems so remote, not a place someone would likely visit."

"Good question, Father, but if you wait a moment I'll gladly answer your question, but before I continue, do you have any other questions?" and seeing that Father Heinrich had none, he resumed his directions.

"If you continue on a few more kilometres you'll pass through a tiny village called Griesenau, there are exactly three houses in the village, and my parents still live in the last one on the left. Please honk and wave as you pass by, and perhaps someday I'll be able to tell them why a huge Mercedes passed through our village and honked at them. After you pass through Griesenau, you'll continue through Einwall, Kohlental, Einschnait, Schwendt, and finally

Kössen, however you may pass through many of these villages without realising it, but you'll know when you arrive in Kössen."

Father Heinrich carefully followed the priest's finger along the map as he pointed out those landmarks.

"When you reach the center of Kössen, bear left as though you're going over the bridge, but don't cross over the bridge. Instead, take the small road off to the right. Continue on that road for a few kilometres and it will take you through a narrow valley with a river off to your left. You'll know you're approaching the border when you see a most unusual sight."

"What's that, Father?" Father Heinrich asked, now curious.

"It's called the Maria Klobenstein Kössen. It's a wonderful little chapel perched on the edge of a river gorge, and I guess its most famous attraction is the large split boulder called the Klobenstein. There's an old legend accompanying it, but maybe you can stop there and see for yourself. There is also a small building below the chapel enclosing a spring whose waters are claimed to have healing effects. The German border is only a few metres north of there, unfortunately however, the Germans have built a barricade of earth and rocks to block the road, however I've recently heard that the locals have dug a narrow pathway through it. If you're fortunate, there may be just enough room to squeeze your motorcar through the barricade. If not, you will have wasted a day's journey and several litres of precious petrol. I'm not sure what the road may be like once you get into Germany, but I remember it as being a pleasant road that follows a river, crosses over one tall, narrow bridge, and eventually goes over a mountain. That's all I remember."

It was a lot of information to absorb, but I was sure between the two of us, we could make things work. Father Heinrich thanked the priest, folded the map, and we got back into the motorcar. You know what? We never asked him his name, and I've often thought we should revisit Salzburg after the war and thank him, but we didn't even know his name.

When we got back into the motorcar, Father Heinrich handed the map to me. "Shall we?" he asked.

"We shall," my reply, and with that, he started the motorcar, and we headed off towards Germany's 'back door'.

## The Back Door

We departed Salzburg with an interesting mixture of adventure, frustration, excitement, and apprehension. To-date, our motorcar trip had been relatively easy, if you ignored being caught in a blizzard. The roads were relatively passable, the routes easily followed, and with very little traffic to bother us. However, our plans had now been turned upside-down, and we were headed off on an unknown route, through unknown country, and perhaps to another dead-end. To top it off, there was now a sense of urgency thrown in to make it more interesting, as if it already wasn't enough of a challenge.

If we were going to be successful in following the tedious route the priest had pointed out, Father Heinrich decided it was time to give me a map-reading lesson. Our only map was a Michelin driving map of Europe and it was rather large, and the only way we could use it in the motorcar was to keep folding and refolding it to expose only the portion of our travel, otherwise it would have taken up the entire front seat. Anyway, soon after we left Salzburg and Father Heinrich could safely pull over to the side of the road, he stopped the motorcar and handed the map over to me.

"Anna, do you remember much about what the priest just told us when we were looking at the map?" his first question.

[234]

Not much of it had made any sense to me as I hadn't paid much attention, but I knew Father Heinrich expected an answer. "Yes. I remember he said to honk when we passed the last house on the left."

Father Heinrich smiled, "That's very good, Anna, and I hope you don't forget to remind me," as I hoped my answer had been of some help.

If he was disappointed with my reply, he didn't show it, and thus began my first lesson in map reading. Even today, I can clearly remember his rapid-fire instructions; always hold the map so the direction of travel is at the top, keep your finger on the map to keep track of your current position, pick out landmarks along the way, and always know the name of the next town you'll be passing through. That sounded easy, however I pointed out to him that if you were holding the map upside-down as you travelled south, all the towns' names would be upside-down, also.

"Good point, Anna," his only reply. I'm not too sure if I understood his pointed remark since I was looking for a solution, not a compliment.

I had a feeling the first few minutes of our travel resembled a scene from a Laurel and Hardy movie. "Next town?" he'd ask as I turned the map around to read it while attempting to keep my finger on our current position, find the next town's name, then turn the map back around and try to reorient myself. My task eventually became easier when we finally headed west, and when we headed north, it became a snap. Of course, I was an old 'pro' by that time anyway. Too bad we hadn't headed north to begin with; that would have made it a lot easier for me from the start.

After a few mistakes and having to turn around and retrace our route once or twice, we finally arrived in St. Johann, where we stopped to take a break. There was an imposing mountain nearby, probably the largest one I had seen on our entire trip, and when I asked Father Heinrich its name, he relieved me of my map-reading duties, took a quick glance at the map, and told me it was called the Kitzbüheler Horn. I later learned this area became a popular skiing destination after the war, but skiing wasn't on our minds; getting into Germany was.

The priest's instructions on how to get through St. Johann and onto the right road were quite complicated. So, after we had gotten underway again, we stopped and asked a stranger for directions to Griesenau, the priest's home village.

When we told him our supposed destination, he exclaimed, "*Griesenau?* Why in the world would you want to visit Griesenau? Just a couple of houses. There's nothing there of interest."

"Well, we actually wanted to visit the Maria Klobenstein Kössen and we knew Griesenau was along our route."

"Ah, that makes more sense. You *do* know the road into Germany is blocked, *don't* you? You can't go any farther."

"Yes, we're well aware of that, but I appreciate your comments, anyway."

"*Auf Wiedersehen* and good luck. Take time to enjoy the beautiful scenery along the way. We're quite proud of it you know, and we're especially proud of our Maria Klobenstein Kössen. Make sure you drink some of the spring water, it definitely has miraculous properties," and with those parting words, we once again continued on our journey.

We already knew the road was blocked, but the priest in Salzburg had told us the local villagers had cleared a path through it. Hearing those words again from the stranger only reinforced our growing apprehension as we made our way towards Germany's 'back door'. If the barricade had been breached, wouldn't the man have told us so, or had the Germans blocked it once again? We wouldn't know until we arrived there.

The priest in Salzburg had been right. Many of the small dots on the map marked as villages were only a small cluster of houses, too small to be called villages, but perhaps the Austrians in their obsession with organisation must have felt they needed names. Fortunately, there was a small sign announcing Griesenau and we honked as we passed the last house on the left. An elderly man was outside clearing snow from the cobblestone walkway. We honked, he waved. Maybe his son would ask about us the next time he visited his parents, however, would his father even remember?

The roadway narrowed as we approached the Maria Klobenstein Kössen. Once we had turned onto the road at St. Johann, my map-reading duties were limited to announcing the small dots as we approached them, although I had to approximate our position for the lack of landmarks. Thankfully, there weren't any roads leading right or left, only straight ahead.

When we finally came around the last bend in the road and saw the church's spire rising from the trees, Father Heinrich shouted, "Anna, look up ahead."

"I know; it's the church we've been looking for."

"No. The road. It looks as though it's still blocked."

I had to admit from our vantage point it looked as though the dirt and rock barricade stretched completely across the narrow roadway with no apparent breach. However, as we drew nearer, I could see someone had forced a narrow gap on the left although it wasn't nearly large enough to squeeze our motorcar through it.

Father Heinrich pulled the motorcar up within a few metres of our last obstacle to freedom and we sat there for quite a while, just staring straight ahead, assessing our situation. Finally, he said, "Shall we?"

"We shall." My, by now, well-worn reply.

We got out of the car, walked up to the earthen barricade, and it was obvious someone had picked away at it enough to force a small path completely through to the road on the other side. It was also obvious there had been some recent activity as we could see footprints and narrow tire tracks in the frozen mud as someone had also apparently driven a horse cart through it as we could also clearly see frozen hoof prints.

We stood there a couple of minutes assessing our options when Father Heinrich took my hand and pointed at the ground, "Austria," he proclaimed. We then carefully picked our way along the narrow pathway through the barricade until we emerged on the other side. "Germany," he exclaimed as he pointed down at his feet. Then, pointing first in one direction and then the other, "Austria, Germany. Austria, Germany. Austria, Germany," he repeated. I think he was just psyching himself up, building up his courage to make a difficult decision, and I just stood there, entranced, watching him perform his little theater until finally he said, "*Genug* (Enough)," as he took my hand and we walked back to the motorcar.

I wasn't sure what he was up to or what decision he had just made, but I could tell by the confidence in his stride that he had just made one, and it was unquestioningly irreversible.

He walked to the rear of the motorcar and opened the trunk. Reaching in, he took out the shovel Father Tadeus had thoughtfully placed there, then closing the trunk with a resounding thud, he said, with shovel in hand, "We'll just dig our way into Germany."

I didn't know if I was listening to the ravings of a lunatic or a man possessed, but either way, I knew there was no stopping him, and I've often wondered what a passing traveller might have thought if they had accidentally happened upon a Catholic priest, replete with his floor-length cassock covered with dirt and mud, digging in a rock pile with a young, female companion standing nearby.

However, before he attacked his formidable opponent, he measured the width of the motorcar using the shovel handle for a measuring stick. The motorcar was exactly *Zwei Griffe (Two shovel handles)* wide. He then just stood there trying to figure out where to begin as his new mantra soon became, *"Zwei Griffe, zwei Griffe, zwei Griffe"* which he repeated under his breath with every shovelful as he had truly transformed into a man possessed. Once again, using his shovel as a measuring stick, he walked up to the barricade and tried to decide where to start and how much dirt he needed to move. As I recall, the barrier was about one *Griffe* high, three *Griffe* deep, and he needed to widen the existing path to about two *Griffe*.

When I later told Meyer about this escapade, he said "What? Was he crazy?"

"I think so," I chuckled.

Once he began attacking the barricade, he never even stopped to take a breath as he attacked it with the shovel and with his bare hands, throwing small rocks over his shoulder into the nearby river gorge, and I listened as they tumbled down the rocky banks and splashed into the icy water below.

When he was about halfway through, he stopped and walked over to where I was sitting on the front bumper of the motorcar. "I think we need to take a break, Anna. Why don't we go explore the church?"

His use of the pronoun *we* surprised me; *he* had done all the work while *I* had been taking a break the entire time, and *he* was the one who needed to take a break, not *we*.

However, feeling that *we* needed a break, he stopped digging, took my hand, we walked over to the church and down the narrow stairway leading down from the road. I have to admit the church was much smaller than I had expected; after all, the churches we had been visiting were cathedrals, majestic in their dimensions. This church was *much* smaller, but majestic in its own way, nestled on a cliff overlooking the Großache River gorge. It had a tall, wooden-shingled steeple topped with a cute little pyramid-shaped roof supporting a small cross, and there were three arched windows in the main building facing the road perched above a painting of the Virgin Mary nestled safely under a shelf projecting from the outside walls to protect her from the weather. When we got down to the main building, we tried to open the front door, however it was locked.

There was a pathway alongside the church leading down to a suspension bridge spanning the gorge and as we walked alongside the church we noticed a large boulder sitting near the rear of the church. Imagine my surprise when I got closer and noticed the boulder was cleft in two and there was a cobblestone pathway through the cleft leading up to a rear entranceway. Of course, I made a mad dash for it, ran up through the cleft, and turned around to see Father Heinrich standing below, laughing so hard he was bent over. It was good to see him laugh as I couldn't remember the last time he appeared to be having so much fun.

I skipped back down the cobblestone pathway and rejoined him. We continued walking and as we neared the suspension bridge we came upon a smaller building. It actually wasn't a building; it was more like a three-sided shelter. When we stepped inside, we noticed a pipe running through the back wall and there was water running from it. This must be the miraculous spring the priest back in

Salzburg had mentioned and I playfully put my hands under the spouting water which was icy cold.

Father Heinrich said, "Forgive me, Father," as he put his muddy hands under it, too. I know he felt bad washing his muddy hands in the holy, spring water, but he had no other choice. Perhaps the spring water would work miracles, because after he had cleaned his hands, I noticed how much he had damaged them attacking the rocky barricade. There were open cuts and gashes on his beautiful hands and most of his fingernails had been torn off, leaving ragged nubbins. He didn't say anything, but I knew they must have been paining him terribly.

We walked down the pathway to the suspension bridge and I gleefully ran across it. It was the first time I had ever been on a suspension bridge, and I have to say it was a lot of fun, especially as it swayed from side-to-side with each step. Father Heinrich just stood at the far end of the bridge and watched, and I yelled back at him to follow me, but he just smiled and waved his acknowledgement.

Finally, I tired of my little game and ran back to where he was patiently waiting. He nodded his head up towards the road, "Shall we?" he asked. My answer, of course, was obvious. Reluctantly, we trudged back up to the road and once again tackled our daunting assignment; unlocking Germany's 'back door'.

This time Father Heinrich assaulted the obstacle like a demon possessed. Maybe the spring water *did* have some miraculous powers as he once again began tearing at the rock-laden dirt pile with his bare hands, forsaking the shovel, grabbing handfuls of dirt, and flinging them over his shoulder.

Finally, a potential breach was in sight, but there was only one problem. A large boulder about the size of a laundry-tub was blocking our way; an unmovable object he had intentionally left in place as he dug around it. When he had heaved the last handful of dirt over his shoulder, he wiped his muddy hands on his cassock and stood back, surveying this final obstacle; how to move the 'verdammt' boulder.

Walking up to it, he put his shoulder against it and pushed as hard as he could, however the boulder remained firmly rooted in place. "Anna, the rope. Go get the rope," he shouted back to me. I ran around to the trunk, retrieved the rope, and scurried over to where he was standing. "I have an idea," he said hoarsely, still panting from his effort.

Tying the rope around the boulder as best he could, he walked back to the motorcar and tied it firmly to the front bumper. Getting into the motorcar, he started it, put it into reverse gear, and attempted to pull the boulder out of our way. However, no matter how he tied the rope to the boulder, the minute he tried to drag it away, the rope came loose.

I could sense his growing frustration. "We have to move that boulder, Anna, or all our efforts will be in vain and we'll have to retrace our steps. We're so close, Anna, so close," as he threw his hands up in despair.

I studied the situation for a couple of seconds, "Why don't we try pushing it?" I asked.

"I've tried, but it won't budge."

"No, Father, not with your shoulder, with the motorcar."

"Wait. Why didn't I think of that? It might just work," as he retrieved the shovel, picked up the useless rope, and threw them both back into the trunk. However, before we attempted to use our motorcar as a bulldozer, we stood there and planned our strategy, until finally, it was time to put our plan into motion.

Father Heinrich got into the motorcar and started it as I walked through the widened breach into Germany and guided him into the narrow passageway. His *Griffe* measurements proved to be fairly accurate as the big Mercedes slowly crept into the breach with only a couple of inches to spare on either side. Finally, the big, shiny front bumper was nudged up against the boulder, and he gunned the engine as the rear wheels began to spin furiously throwing up big chunks of mud and gravel in a noisy fusillade behind the motorcar, but the boulder only barely moved.

I signaled him to stop. Getting out of the motorcar, he surveyed his progress, got back into the motorcar, backed up a metre or so, then gunned the engine and smashed into the boulder with a resounding crash. Father Heinrich literally lifted off the front seat and hit his head on the motorcar's ceiling, but the boulder only moved less than a metre.

From then on, it was like watching a raging bull trying to lift his tormenting matador into the air. Back up, smash into the boulder, back up again, smash into the boulder again until finally, with one last Herculean effort, the boulder rolled over to the side of the road, tumbled over the precipice, splashed into the icy river below, and we were finally in Germany.

Father Heinrich stopped the now overheated motorcar, jumped out and pointed to the ground under his feet. "Germany this way, Austria that way, this way, that way," as he danced a little celebratory jig. We had finally breached the barrier and were now on German soil, but we weren't actually any closer to our destination; we had merely crossed the border, however we didn't really care, we felt as though we were invincible!

## The View from the Top

Had we thought it through, what we encountered next would have only made sense; however, in our haste to get into Germany, it had totally slipped our minds. If the road was blocked, why would there have been any need to maintain it? If someone had asked that question about the Austrian side, it would have been easy to explain; the Maria Klobenstein Kössen was a popular pilgrimage site visited annually by hundreds of pilgrims, so the roadway was always maintained in good shape. However, what was the need to maintain the roadway on the German side of the border? The next closest town, Schleching, was three of four kilometres north of the border with nothing in between. No reason to travel, therefore, no reason to maintain. We figured the tracks in the mud we had seen were probably made by smugglers moving goods across the border, and now we were stuck on a road that nobody had maintained in probably the last four or five years. What would we encounter up ahead?

None of that was on our minds, however, as the adrenaline of finally making our way into Germany undetected, still coursed through our veins, that is until we had driven about three or four hundred metres up the road and encountered our first of many washouts. There had obviously once been a culvert under the roadway directing the small stream running off the nearby hill under it and into the river. However, that culvert had long since washed away and now it was replaced by a small stream cutting across the roadway in its place.

Father Heinrich stopped to survey the situation. The ditch wasn't very wide, nor was it very deep, however he was concerned that when we tried to cross it, the motorcar's front-end would pitch down into the ditch and we'd be stuck. We finally decided that the only solution was to drag over nearby fallen logs and try to fill the ditch. That, along with several large rocks thrown in for stability would have to be our only workable solution.

Before we made our first attempt, we decided to have a strategy meeting to discuss our options, of which we only had three. One was to turn around and head back into Austria, the second was to drive very slowly across our makeshift bridge, and the third was to get a running start and attempt to leap the gap. Option three was our unanimous decision.

So, we backed up about twenty metres, Father Heinrich gunned the engine and we sped towards an unknown result and I held onto the door handle as tightly as I could, Father Heinrich held onto the steering wheel as the big Mercedes hit the first bump and literally flew at least a metre into the air and landed on the other side of the ditch with a loud 'thunk', making us hit our heads on the motorcar's ceiling. Father Heinrich immediately applied the motorcar's brakes, and we slid sideways to a grinding halt. We had made it!

We both took a deep breath, and my hands were shaking with a mixture of fear and excitement and although Father Heinrich's hands still tightly clutched the steering wheel, I noticed his were trembling, too. We just looked at each other and grinned.

After that, we leapfrogged from one stream-bordered 'island' to another as we endured six more harrowing and equally as challenging washouts. We were about to congratulate ourselves on a job well done when the bridge across the Großache River suddenly appeared as we rounded a bend in the road. Father Heinrich slammed on the brakes, and we stopped just short of the bridge.

The concrete bridge was narrow and stood high above the river and many of the metal guardrails lining both sides either had rusted away and fallen into the river, or were in sad disrepair. The bridge's surface appeared to be in good shape, although we couldn't be certain until we had inspected it.

Father Heinrich told me to stay in the motorcar while he got out and walked towards the bridge to inspect it, however before he dared step onto it, he went around to the rear of the motorcar and retrieved the shovel from the trunk.

He then slowly made his way out onto the bridge and using the shovel handle to tap on the surface, he tested it for weaknesses. He walked all the way to the other side; probably one hundred metres or more, turned around, and walked back towards the car, once again carefully checking every inch of the bridge's roadway under foot.

Finally, he opened the motorcar's door, slid in, and took a deep breath, "Anna, we have a terrible decision to make. I'm not sure the bridge can take the weight of the motorcar; after all, it's quite heavy. I've tested the bridge's surface and although many of the reinforcing rods in the concrete have been exposed by the weather and there are some small holes, it still does feel quite solid underfoot. The map shows that we're probably less than two kilometres from the nearest town, and I'm certain the roadway should be much improved once we arrive there. If we can get across this river, the only remaining obstacle is that mountain in front of us and if that's an antenna I see on top, it only makes sense the roadway leading down the mountain on the other side from there has to be passable. What do you think?"

I didn't know how to answer. Ever since we had left Salzburg, our journey had been incredibly stressful, and I had grown tired of our adventure a long time ago. The farther we travelled, it seemed the more obstacles were thrown in our way until it was possible we'd be stuck out in the middle of nowhere, forever. I pondered our options. Retracing our steps was out of the question and remaining here was also out of the question. There was only one option; forward at all costs.

However, I still wasn't certain. "Do you think it's safe to cross? If the motorcar falls off the bridge, we'll both be killed. Is it worth the chance?" I asked.

Father Heinrich reached over and took my hand. "Do you remember when you said you had a guardian angel looking over you and you felt as though her hands were on your shoulders? Remember I told you those hands were Anna's and she was now *our* guardian angel? Well, I feel her hands on my shoulders now, and she won't let us down."

Now comforted, I looked over at him. "Shall we?" I asked.

"We shall!"

Father Heinrich insisted that he, alone, drive the motorcar over the bridge and he told me if anything bad happened to him, I should hike over the mountain and into town to get help. I agreed, however I knew that was just a hypothetical situation; Anna was watching over us, and she'd protect us.

Taking my hand, he led me across the bridge; however, it wasn't at all like when I had walked across the suspension bridge back at the Maria Klobenstein Kössen. This bridge was ominous, not friendly, and I was extremely frightened even though he was holding my hand. Sometimes when I looked down at my feet, I could see the river far below through holes in the pavement and when he had safely delivered me to the other side, I stood and watched him as he slowly walked back to the motorcar. Would I ever see him again? Suddenly, I felt alone and abandoned, just as I had felt back in Auschwitz as I watched my family's backs disappear into the darkness on their way to the gas chambers, which I later discovered was their true fate. If anything happened to Father Heinrich now, I'd certainly die like them.

Suddenly, the big Mercedes came to life as I could hear him start the engine, then the big headlamps on the front flashed on, and I could feel their powerful beams reach all the way across the bridge to where I anxiously stood; now merely a spectator.

At first, it appeared that he started across the bridge very slowly, almost at a crawl. Although the bridge was narrow, it *was* wide enough for two cars to pass each other, but perhaps not two large Mercedes. As he became more confident, he quickened his pace until he reached the middle of the bridge, and then I noticed the bridge began to tremble and vibrate and several of the rusty guardrails snapped off and spiraled down to the riverbed far below. Just as he passed over the bridge's center span, the section of the bridge he had just passed over collapsed behind him and crashed down into the river below making a huge splash.

I think Father Heinrich immediately sensed the danger as he gunned the engine, the rear wheels began spinning and throwing off huge clouds of blue smoke, and he came careening towards where I was standing, helplessly watching the drama unfold. As he passed over each section, they too collapsed behind him, in slow motion, and crashed into the river below. It was as though an angry hound was snapping at his heels.

When he had finally reached the safety of solid ground, he slammed on the brakes, and the motorcar came to a screeching halt. The instant he stopped, his door flew open, and he jumped out and fell onto the ground. I thought he was having a heart attack. I ran over to him, "Father, Father," I cried out. "Are you all right?"

He just lay there in his muddy priest's cassock sobbing like a baby, and I didn't know if it was from fear, relief, or both. When he finally was able to compose himself enough to be able to speak, he got up and hugged me. "Thank God, you're alive. The only thing I could think of when I was crossing that bridge was if something happened to me, you'd be stranded here, alone, out in the wilderness. It was almost too much to bear."

It took some time for him to recover from his frightening experience and when his shaking knees were strong enough to support him, we walked over to where the bridge once stood. Now, only two sections of the bridge remained intact; the other six lay far below in the Großache River. Before we turned and walked back to the car, Father Heinrich said with a sly grin, "I think they'll need to repair it. Don't you?"

We got back into the motorcar and continued our adventure, however the poor Mercedes looked like a derelict; the front bumper was dented from its many battles with the boulder, the side running boards were badly damaged from our passage through the narrow 'back door', there were dents and scratches from the numerous leaps over the washouts, and the motorcar was caked in so much mud it was difficult to tell its original colour. However, it had carried us safely from one crisis to another, and we still had enough petrol to get us to our destination, Rottach-Egern.

The roadway on the other side of the bridge wasn't nearly as bad as we had previously encountered. Although it was unpaved, there weren't nearly as many obstacles to overcome like before and Father Heinrich paid little heed to them anyway, he just wanted to get to the top of the mountain as we literally flew up the steep rocky road, our rear tires spitting out rocks behind us and our spirits soaring as we neared the mountain's peak.

Father Heinrich *was* right. There *was* an antenna on top of the mountain and the roadway leading down to the valley below *was* paved. As we crested the mountain, he pulled the motorcar off to the side of the road just as the sun was just setting over the distant hills, and we watched as the lights in the houses in the valley far below flickered on, one-by-one. It was such a relief to have that part of the journey behind us.

We both got out of the car and watched the sunset and I stood in front of Father Heinrich, his arms embracing me protectively from behind. He said, "It's beautiful. Isn't it? Would you like to live here?"

"Oh yes, it's beautiful," and just as I replied, a gust of wind blew Father Heinrich's cassock around me, completely engulfing me as the sun set over the distant mountain; just like in my dream. Was this all just a dream, too?

## The Wiedemiers

The two of us stood atop the mountain for a long time. It was such a welcome relief to finally be looking down on German soil after our harrowing journey, especially the last twenty-four hours. As darkness surrounded us and one-by-one, the lights on the houses below in the valley flickered on, it soon became impossible to distinguish between the star-filled sky and the star-filled valley below us. The horizon's delineator had totally dissolved and it was as though we were somehow suspended in space between the two.

Finally, Father Heinrich patted me on top my head, "Shall we?" he asked.

"*Jah,*" I jokingly answered, and he appeared to get a great chuckle out of my unexpected response.

"*Gut,*" he said, dryly.

We walked back to the car with the red light on top the nearby radio antenna winking at us, welcoming us to Germany. We had successfully opened the 'back door'", perhaps for the last time, or at least until someone repaired the bridge.

The ride *down* the mountain was certainly more leisurely than our bumpy ride *up* the mountain, although I noticed every time the motorcar hit a pothole in the roadway, it shook and rattled like an old washing machine. It had certainly endured its torture well.

We passed through some small villages as we headed towards Schleching's welcoming glow on the horizon and when we drove into town, there was a light dusting of newly-fallen snow blanketing the trees, adding charm to this quaint Bavarian village. As we drove through town, we noticed a sign up ahead that read *Der Steinweidenhof Hotel und Restaurant* with a charming chalet nestled nearby on a small hill overlooking the sign. Father Heinrich exclaimed, "Shall we?"

Realising the humourous reaction to my previous response to this question, I replied, *"Bitte",* and that cemented the foundation for the little game I and significant others played for the rest of my life.

Father Heinrich turned the motorcar up the short driveway towards the chalet's welcoming glow and when we got out of the motorcar, I was quite surprised by his cassock's condition. What had once been mud was now a dried, dusty layer blanketing his entire outer clothing. However, between the two of us, we managed to dust him off as much as possible, although his cassock was still marbled with long, dirty streaks we just couldn't remove, no matter how hard we tried.

As we walked towards the hotel, he asked, "Have you forgotten something?"

I wasn't sure what he meant. "Only two of us to spend the night? I thought we were three," he remarked.

"Alinka," I shouted and ran back to the car to retrieve her, but when I looked in the front seat where she should have been, she wasn't there. I panicked. Had she somehow fallen out of the car during one of our many confrontations with the roadway from St. Johann and perhaps we hadn't noticed?

I looked under the front seat; she wasn't there. I looked on the back seat; she wasn't there, either. Just as I was about to surrender and accept the fact that she had been lost, I noticed the rolled-up blanket, the one I used as a booster seat, laying on the rear floor and when I lifted it up, Alinka was lying there crumpled up in a heap and looking quite forlorn and forgotten. Perhaps Anna's hands had been on her shoulders, too.

I swept her up in my arms, hugged her tightly to my chest, and rejoined Father Heinrich, who was waiting patiently for me by the Inn's front door.

When we entered the Inn there was no one at the front desk, so Father Heinrich picked up the little bell sitting nearby and politely shook it. It made a tiny, tinkling sound, and I wondered how anyone could hear it unless they were standing nearby. However, within seconds, the door behind the desk opened, and a middle-aged woman suddenly appeared.

It took some time for Father Heinrich to explain our situation and why we needed a room for the night. Frau Wiedemier stood there and graciously listened as Father Heinrich went on-and-on, telling his tale, mostly untrue. Finally, I nudged his leg; my signal for him to stop talking and start listening.

When it was apparent his tale had come to its conclusion, Frau Wiedemier smiled, "Father, you and your niece are welcome to stay the night as our guests. It's not often we have the opportunity to have a priest stay with us, and I'm certain after you both have a chance to get cleaned up, you'd like to join Herr Wiedemier and me for a late supper."

We both followed her down the hallway to our rooms; rooms, plural. I was going to have my own private room for the first time since we had left Auschwitz.

After showing Father Heinrich to his room, she took my hand and opened an adjoining door. "This is your room, Anna." The moment we stepped into the room it reminded me of when I had first stepped into Anna's room back in Auschwitz. It, likewise, was a princess' fairyland, and my new room was decorated entirely in pink. The bed's headboard was pink with hand painted flowers, twin pink nightstands, pink drapes, and two overstuffed, pink bolsters on top of the bed. I stood there frozen, overcome by pinkness. "Come, come," as she literally pulled me into the room.

Once we got into the room, she kneeled down in front of me and straightened my dress. "My, my," she said. "I do hope you have some fresh clothes in your bag; you're truly in need of a change, you know."

I hadn't given it much thought; we had been so focused on sneaking into Germany that we had overlooked our by-now shabby outfits. As she straightened my dress, her gentle touch brought tears to my eyes. No woman had lovingly touched me like that since my mother held my hand in the selection line at Auschwitz and I had forgotten how good a woman's touch felt. Frau Mueller had always treated me as if I were an object, not another human, and even Frau Eberhardt's kindness didn't satisfy my cravings for a mother's touch.

"What have we got in here?" Frau Wiedemier asked as she opened my threadbare carpetbag and pulled out the spare set of clothing Frau Eberhardt had thoughtfully packed for me, then she carefully retrieved my journal, which I had totally forgotten. When the bag was empty, she turned it upside-down and shook it as though there might be other contents, but there weren't and I could have saved her the effort if she had asked.

"Why don't I draw a warm bath for you?" she asked as she got up and led me into the adjoining bathroom. There was an enormous, oversized tub set up against a window overlooking the nearby mountains and as she was filling the tub with hot water, she told me she would lay out my one clean outfit on the bed for me, and that I should drop my dirty clothes outside the door when I had undressed. She then turned and left the room.

I ran over to the window and looked out at the snow-covered peaks protectively ringing the village, and then I suddenly realised Frau Wiedemier had left the water running and I didn't know how to turn it off. I had never seen a bathtub quite like that before, and I almost panicked until I realised the two little brass handles I had watched her turn when she began filling the tub, could be turned the other way to shut the water off.

When I climbed in and slowly sank beneath the warm water, it felt wonderful and it felt even better to scrub off the layers of dirt I had acquired along the way. As I watched the dirty water swirl down the drain, it was as though all our struggles disappeared along with it, and I felt like a snake must feel when it sheds its old skin; new, refreshed, and alive.

When I had dried myself off and walked back into the bedroom, my heap of dirty clothes was gone and had been replaced by a fresh new outfit, lovingly set on the bed. I quickly dressed and looked at myself in the full-length mirror and I liked what I saw; I had truly become a young, refined, German princess surrounded by pinkness, waiting to join her handsome prince and his Court for a late night supper.

I knocked on Father Heinrich's door as I walked past. "Who is it," he called out.

"Me," I answered.

"Why don't you go downstairs? I'll join you there," as I turned and headed for the dining room.

As I walked past the front desk, Frau Wiedemier intercepted me. "Excuse me, Fraulein; are you a guest here at our hotel? I don't think I recognise you," she inquired with a knowing smile.

Her words were as gentle as her touch, "I'm Anna. Anna Mueller," I replied, confused as to why she didn't recognise me.

"Well, Anna, why don't I show you to the dining room," as she walked around the front desk, took my hand, and led me down the hallway.

When we arrived at the dining room, my vision of being in a fairytale castle was completed. There was a single octagonal table snugly nestled in a bay window overlooking the nearby snow-capped mountains and Herr Wiedemier was already seated at the linen-covered table enjoying a short glass of schnapps. He got up when we entered the room, walked around the table, and pulled out a chair for me. *What a gentleman,* I thought.

As he pushed my chair closer to the table, he reached over, took a linen napkin sitting next to my dinner plate, and with a theatrical flourish, placed it in my lap. I sat there mesmerised, my hands folded neatly in my lap as I carefully studied the place setting laid out before me, counting the knives, forks, spoons, plates, cups and other unfamiliar objects with yet to be discovered functions.

Within minutes, Father Heinrich walked into the room. He had removed his dirty cassock and only wore the priest's shirt, collar, dark trousers, and shoes Father Tadeus had given him. His hair was neatly combed, and it was obvious he had shaved, although I had become somewhat attached to his previously stubbly face. After introducing himself to Herr Wiedemier, he sat down next to me, and deftly placed his napkin in his lap.

Frau Wiedemier left the room as we waited for someone to begin the conversation. Finally, Herr Wiedemier elected to start, "So, tell me, Father. Where are you and your niece headed?" he asked.

"We're on our way to Rottach-Egern. It's not more than a day's travel from here," he answered.

Herr Wiedemier scrunched up his eyebrows in a questioning way. "*Rottach-Egern*, you say. Are you certain that's your destination because if it is, you must be totally lost. There's no direct way to get to Rottach-Egern from here. Just where did you start your travels today?"

It was obvious he was confused by what Father Heinrich had just told him and I hoped he could come up with a plausible explanation. If we revealed our actual route, I'm certain he wouldn't have believed us, anyway.

It didn't take long for Father Heinrich's reply, which startled me. "We began our journey in Salzburg this morning. We were well on our way, however I believe we must have taken a wrong turn at Siegsdorf and when I noticed my error, I attempted a shortcut back to our planned route, but I took a wrong turn in Staudach-Egerdach, ran off the road, and finally wound up here at your door," he explained in one long, uninterrupted breath.

When I later asked him how he had come up with that convoluted story, he confessed that he had taken our well-worn road map to his room with him and had carefully studied it in case we were questioned.

Herr Wiedemier appeared to be satisfied with his explanation, "*Jah*. I see. I can understand why it might be easy to get lost nowadays, especially since the military has removed all road signs in order to confuse the enemy should they spill over into our beloved *Vaterland*. But how did you cross the border from Salzburg? I thought they only allowed the military, not civilians, to pass through."

I knew he had a ready answer. "I presented them with a Letter of Safe Passage from our Bishop in Warsaw. It's my understanding the Vatican and the German government have come to a mutual agreement allowing the Vatican's representatives, including nuns and clerics, to pass freely through Germany under the government's protection. The border guards weren't too happy about it; however, there was nothing they could do except to let us pass through."

The conversation then turned to local issues, the weather, our motorcar trip and although I'm certain Father Heinrich wanted to inquire about the war's progress, the Wiedemiers were our gracious hosts and he probably wanted to keep the evening's supper conversation light.

Soon, Frau Wiedemier entered the room carrying a large tray with four, steaming, supper plates filled with sauerkraut, Wiener schnitzel, and potato dumplings. Upon seeing this, my stomach reminded me it had been twenty-four hours since I had last paid any attention to it.

To say that supper was less than delightful would have been an insult. Our gracious hosts' company, the delicious food served in a beautiful setting, and Father Heinrich by my side, set the tone for the remainder of our journey.

I wasn't too certain what all the utensils were used for. Why did we need three forks, two knives, and two spoons? Not knowing what to do, I carefully mimicked Father Heinrich's manners and nobody appeared to notice.

As I sat there admiring Father Heinrich's perfect table manners, I couldn't help but think how much I truly loved him and how the conversation we eventually needed to have would hurt him, and probably me, too. Several times during our journey I had wanted to begin that conversation, the one we both knew was inevitable, the one we had both shrewdly avoided up until now. What did *he* do at Auschwitz, *what* kind of a camp was Auschwitz, and *why* had he taken me out of the selection line when I first arrived? However, it was now critical for us to flawlessly perform our carefully scripted roles in our little charade; our only chance of getting safely to our destination in Bavaria. We couldn't do it alone; we needed to be a team. Ever since he had rescued me from the selection line at Auschwitz, we had unconsciously honored a fragile truce; a truce we needed to honour in our dash to freedom and I fell asleep wrestling with the *answer*, and the *question*; surrounded by pinkness.

When we arose the next morning to go down to breakfast, we discovered our discarded clothes, newly washed and set outside our bedroom doors. Frau Wiedemier had stayed up after we had gone to bed and had washed our dirty clothes. She was such a remarkable woman. Not only had she washed our clothes, but when she had noticed Father Heinrich's damaged hands, she had brought him a homemade remedy made from lanolin and beeswax.

After saying a tearful farewell, we got into our derelict Mercedes and continued our journey and it wasn't long before we joined the Munich autobahn and headed towards Rottach-Egern. However, we noticed a curious thing along the way. There were many military vehicles on the autobahn, after all, that's why the National Socialists had built them in the first place, but they were headed *towards* Munich, not away from it. They should have been headed the other way; *towards* the front lines in the east, not *away* from them. That concerned us; perhaps the Russians weren't that far behind, which wouldn't bode well for us.

Finally, we departed the autobahn at Irschanberg and headed south towards Lake Tegernsee and Rottach-Egern. It was a great relief to get off the autobahn and away from all the military traffic and Father Heinrich said that from the number of military vehicles passing us, it didn't appear that Germany had totally lost the war, yet, anyway. It wasn't until after the war that we learned the staggering price the German military, and also the entire country, had paid to satisfy 'that man's' ego.

The frenzied pace of the autobahn traffic was soon replaced by the welcome lack of traffic on the scenic roadway leading towards Lake Tegernsee. There was a light dusting of snow on the ground; however, there were large herds of dairy cows out in the fields grazing on randomly-placed hay mounds. If this was going to be home, I already liked it.

## Finally, Rottach-Egern

We stopped by Lake Tegernsee's frozen shoreline right before we reached the outskirts of town as we had been so focused on reaching our destination; we hadn't discussed what we would do upon our arrival. The steeple of St. Laurentius Church on the horizon reminded us we had to come up with a plan, and quickly.

We needed to decide *who* we were, *where* we had come from, and *why* we were travelling to Rottach-Egern, and it took some time for us to hatch a plausible plan, one that would endure through our indefinite stay. Part of our plan was for Father Heinrich to forgo his priest's cassock for 'everyday' clothes as soon as possible although the only civilian clothes he had to wear was what he had been wearing when we had first fled Auschwitz.

When we had finally come to a mutual agreement, Herr Heinrich looked over at me, "Shall we?" he asked.

*"Natürlich! (Naturally),"* I replied, continuing our playful word game and he laughed, as before, as we headed into town.

We didn't know much about Rottach-Egern other than it was on the shores of Lake Tegernsee, the Catholic church was called St. Laurentius, Father Tadeus had grown-up there, and he had a brother whom we hoped still lived there. To make things more difficult, Father Tadeus had never told us his surname and we weren't even sure his given name was Tadeus; he may he picked that name when he was ordained. Honestly, we didn't have much to go on.

We got more than a few curious stares as we arrived in our beat-up Mercedes as we had hoped we could sneak into town without drawing a lot of attention to ourselves, but that hope vanished the moment we entered the main street. Rottach-Egern was larger than I had expected. It was situated at the southern end of Lake Tegernsee in a natural basin formed by several, large mountains on its western, southern, and eastern borders. After the war, it once again became a popular skiing destination.

The first stop was at St. Laurentius Church to establish our credentials, however when we tried to open the church's front door, we were surprised to discover it locked and Doktor Mueller thought that strange; we had never encountered that before. So, he knocked loudly; several times. Eventually, Father Wilhelm opened the door and when he saw us standing outside in the cold, he graciously welcomed us in.

The first thing I noticed when I stepped through the church door was how chilly it was inside, all the electric lamps had been turned off, and there weren't any candles lit anywhere. I think Doktor Mueller also noticed as he stamped his feet quite annoyingly to get the circulation going. Father Wilhelm must have noticed, too, as he offered his apologies, "Yes, it is quite chilly in here, isn't it? With this terrible war going badly for us, there just isn't enough coal to keep the furnaces going; my apologies. Why don't we go to my office, it's a bit warmer there," as he led us down the church's center aisle with Doktor Mueller and me following his lead, genuflecting our respect as we paused in front of the altar.

The warmth of his office was certainly welcome; the church's sanctuary was not only chilly, it appeared lifeless and uninviting without people sitting there lost in prayer, and perhaps that was the first time I realised the word 'church' didn't refer to a building, it referred to its members; the congregation, instead.

After we sat down by the welcome wood stove, Father Wilhelm asked, "So, what brings you and your young companion to Rottach-Egern? It certainly isn't to enjoy the weather," he joked. Thus began the telling of our tale; the foundation we needed to construct in order to build a new life in Rottach-Egern.

Doktor Mueller carefully followed the script we had written when we had stopped on the town's outskirts before our much-noticed arrival. He said his name was Heinrich Mueller and I was his daughter, Anna, and he had been a successful merchant in a small town in Poland called Tychy. When the Germans had invaded Poland in 1939, his business had been destroyed, their modest home leveled, and his dear wife, Gretchen, was killed. We had moved in with relatives living in nearby Auschwitz, however when we realised the Russians were about to overrun the town, we had once again fled and made our way west towards Herr Mueller's beloved Bavaria. When we stopped along the way at a church in Bielsko-Biala, Poland, we had befriended the local parish priest who had graciously loaned us the use of his motorcar only asking us to detour to Rottach-Egern to let his family know he was safe. It didn't occur to us until much later that our cover story might not have matched what we had told Father Tadeus, and we hoped he wouldn't return in the near future and uncover our deception.

Father Wilhelm patiently allowed Doktor Mueller to spin his yarn, uninterrupted, and when it was obvious he had come to its conclusion, he offered his comments. "I'm sorry for the loss of your wife and mother. I'm sure it was a terrible shock to the both of you and I offer my sincerest condolences. It sounds as though the past few years have been difficult for you, however I can assure you that although the Allied Armies are fast approaching, I can guarantee your safety if you decide to remain here in Rottach-Egern."

Doktor Mueller reached over and gently patted Father Wilhelm's shoulder in gratitude. "Both Anna and I appreciate your concern and your offer of safety, but as I mentioned before, our journey to Rottach-Egern is only to deliver a message, not to remain here." — *A little white lie flawlessly delivered from our script with utmost sincerity* —

"Ah, yes. Your mission. Tell me once again the reason for your visit?" he politely asked.

"Father Tadeus at St. Mikolaj Church in Bielsko asked us to let his family know he is safe and healthy. That was part of our bargain; he would lend us the use of his motorcar if we would deliver his message."

Father Wilhelm appeared puzzled. "You said his name is Father Tadeus and his family lives here?"

"Yes, that's what he told us. Is there a problem? I'm sure you must know him, don't you?" I could tell Father Wilhelm's question had greatly distressed Doktor Mueller. After all, our plans were based on being able to locate his family, establish our credentials, and use their connexions to start a new life in Rottach-Egern regardless of what he had just told Father Wilhelm. Now those plans were complicated by him not personally knowing our connexion, and we desperately needed that connexion to move forward with our plans.

"I must apologise, Herr Mueller, I've only served this parish for less than a year and the name just doesn't sound familiar to me. Would you mind if I phoned someone who may know him?"

It was just like the Germans; although they didn't have enough petrol to fuel their Armies, enough coal to heat their churches or enough food to feed a hungry population, at least their telephones still worked, and I still find that humourous.

Although we could only hear one side of the conversation, it was liberally sprinkled with a lot of *"Aha's"*, *"I see's"*, and *"I understand's"*. When the conversation finally ended, he turned towards us. "I think you're in luck. I may have uncovered your Father Tadeus. His real name is Konrad Degenhardt and his brother's name was Kristof. I use the word *'was'* because he was killed on the Eastern Front a few months ago. Such an unspeakable tragedy."

"I'm sorry to hear that, Father. I'm sure other families in your town have had that same unwelcome message delivered far too often. Tell me, does Konrad have any other relatives living here in town?" Doktor Mueller asked sympathetically.

"Only his brother's widow, Karen. I know her quite well, in fact. She attends our church quite regularly and I'm sure she'd welcome your message that her brother-in-law is safe. She runs a boarding house not far distant from here. Why don't I take you there," he offered, and soon the three of us were on our way to Frau Degenhardt's boarding house.

## Frau Degenhardt's Boarding House

I had to laugh at Father Wilhelm's remarks when he first saw our car as he said it looked as though we, too, had been caught up in a major battle along the way. I wanted to tell him it felt as though we had, but I didn't think it appropriate to reveal the finer details of our travels.

When we were all comfortably seated in the big motorcar, Doktor Mueller turned around and looked for me, lost somewhere in the huge rear seat. "Shall we?" he asked.

"*Warum nicht? (Why not?)*" I merrily replied as we renewed our little word game while Father Wilhelm looked questioningly over at Doktor Mueller, who just smiled and drove down Seestraße Street towards town.

By now, Doktor Mueller had relied on me so much to be his navigator that I made sure to note every landmark, every street name, and every change in direction and I've been that way ever since. My late husband, Meyer, on the other hand, was what he referred to as being "directionally challenged". Every time we stayed in a hotel, he would always, without exception, turn the wrong way upon leaving our room, and the one time he *did* turn the correct way, I patted him on the shoulder, congratulated him, and he walked right past the elevators without stopping. I *really* do miss him so. Dear Meyer; he was such a wonderful fellow.

We continued driving until we came to the main street and turned right and after a few more blocks, a left on Sonnenmoosstraße, a quick right on Obwerachweg, a left on Georg-Hirt-Straße, a few hundred metres, then a right onto a narrow driveway. I know you must think I have a wonderful memory for such a short trip, but it was a route I soon came to know by heart; from Frau Degenhardt's boarding house to the church and back.

[264]

Frau Degenhardt's house was set back from the street on a nicely wooded lot surrounded by what appeared to be flower gardens bedded down for the winter. The main house was a three-story chalet with a two-story addition set off to one side fronted by a summer patio. Typical Bavarian architecture. The second and third stories both had balconies bordered by wooden railings decorated with flower boxes, and it had a red tile roof, white walls, and reddish-brown shutters on all the outside windows. Although it was still the dead of winter, it radiated a warmth that's hard to describe.

Doktor Mueller parked the motorcar in the small parking lot in front of the house; we all got out and followed Father Wilhelm to the front door. When we arrived at the front door, he briskly rapped the doorknocker that was shaped like a large nutcracker, similar to the one in Tchaikovsky's, Marius Pepita's, and Lev Ivanov's ballet, *The Nutcracker*. When I finally had a chance to ask Frau Degenhardt about it, she told me she called it Herr Drosselmeyer after the nutcracker in the ballet and whenever someone would come to the door and rap the doorknocker, she'd say, "Let's go see what Herr Drosselmeyer wants."

It didn't take long for Frau Degenhardt to come to the door and greet us, and the moment I saw her, I knew we'd be friends. There was just something about her that instantly appealed to me. I guess I just must have liked her looks, and in retrospect, she reminded me so much of the actress Glenn Close and every time I see a movie with her in it, I see Frau Degenhardt, instead. So attractive, and yet in a masculine way. I would have guessed her to be around Doktor Mueller's age; late thirties, perhaps early forties, though not any older.

She welcomed us into her living room and offered us seats, and I sat down without thinking as did Father Wilhelm, but Doktor Mueller patiently stood there. Finally, Father Wilhelm realised he hadn't formally introduced us, so he quickly rose and formally announced us. The Germans *do* tend to be so formal, don't they?

Introductions comfortably aside, we all found our seats and Father Wilhelm plopped back down into the overstuffed chair, leaned back, and crossed his legs in what I thought was a most unpriestly manner. Doktor Mueller sat erect, both feet respectfully on the floor, his hands politely folded in his lap. I think Frau Degenhardt must have noticed Father Wilhelm's casual posture because she looked directly at Doktor Mueller and smiled coyly while nodding her head in Father Wilhelm's direction. If I hadn't known better, I think I had just witnessed an unspoken dialogue between them. Of course, what was I to know about love and chemistry? I was only twelve, going on thirteen.

After offering us refreshments, we shortly got down to the task at hand; delivering our message. I guess since this was *her* house and we were *her* guests, Frau Degenhardt felt the need to start the conversation. "What brings you two to Rottach-Egern and especially to my home?" she politely began.

Father Wilhelm began to answer her question, but Doktor Mueller interrupted him and I felt that rather rude of him, but he later explained he felt the need to establish our credentials right from the beginning, on *our* terms, not Father Wilhelm's.

He leaned forward as if to share a secret with Frau Degenhardt. "To begin, Frau Degenhardt, please allow me and my daughter, Anna, to personally deliver our condolences to you in regards to the loss of your dear husband, Kristof. It was something we hadn't expected to hear. Such a tragedy. However, we do have some welcome news to deliver. Your late husband's brother, Father Tadeus, is safe and healthy. It's been less than two weeks since we enjoyed his warm hospitality, and he wanted us to convey our best wishes to you and his brother. Unfortunately, he wasn't aware of *your* loss, *his* loss, too."

She smiled, "Thank you, Herr Mueller, for your kind words. They mean so much to me at such a sad time. I always thought I would see him again like so many other families that sent their sons and husbands off to protect *Der Vaterland* only to wait in vain for their safe return. However, life goes on, doesn't it? What are *your* plans for the future, Herr Mueller?"

"To be quite honest, Frau Degenhardt, we have no other plans other than to safely deliver our message. With the Allies fast approaching, I'm not too sure it would even be safe to travel until we know the outcome and I sincerely hope they treat us as occupiers, not as conquerors."

Frau Degenhardt's smile broadened, "Well put, Herr Mueller. Our future is *so* uncertain, isn't it? Ever since my husband's death, I can only attack *my* future one day at a time. Do *you* feel the same way too, Herr Mueller?"

I'm sure now that Doktor Mueller and Frau Degenhardt's relationship must have begun with that brief, yet pointed exchange of words and I sensed Doktor Mueller enjoyed his verbal parrying with her; after all, I had been his sole confidant and conversationalist ever since Frau Mueller's death, and I was glad to relinquish that role, or so I had thought at the time.

Doktor Mueller appeared to relax now that the formal part of our introductions had been efficiently dispatched. "It's timely you ask such a question, Frau Degenhardt. Ever since Anna and I started on our long journey, we ourselves only had one goal in mind; reaching here safely and delivering our message. I guess we, too, have been living day-by-day, one destination, one meal, and one safe night's rest at a time. Until you just mentioned it, I had never thought of it that way, however you're right, and I commend you for your insight."

Father Wilhelm, who had been left out of the conversation since its inception, interrupted. "If you don't mind, Herr Mueller, I feel it's my duty to return to the church and take care of church matters," as he uncrossed his legs and started to get up out of his comfortable chair. "Thank you for your hospitality, Frau Degenhardt, but I must ask you to forgive us for leaving so soon, even though you all seemed to be enjoying your conversation. However, I must ask Herr Mueller to drive me back to the church as I'm sure our guests are eager to be on their way, also."

Frau Degenhardt put out her hand as if to hold Father Wilhelm in place, half in, and half out of his chair. "Before you leave, Father, I have a suggestion. Since it's getting late and our guests have no plans for the night, I might extend them an invitation to spend the night here with me. That way they can start their journey tomorrow refreshed and renewed. Herr Mueller can drive you back to the church while I show Anna to her room."

A decision had been made and I felt that like Doktor Mueller, once Frau Degenhardt had made a decision, it too was irreversible. Doktor Mueller got up from his chair and walked over to Frau Degenhardt and gentlemanly took her hand in his, "Thank you for your kind offer, Frau Degenhardt. Anna and I would be delighted to enjoy your company for the rest of the evening; however, we'll need to be on our way first thing tomorrow morning."

I wondered where he was headed with this chivalrous act, but I also knew he didn't intend to leave Rottach-Egern in the immediate future.

## Frau Degenhardt's Interesting Boarders

The next morning the bright sunlight streaming through the sheer curtains woke me with a start and for an instant, I didn't know where I was, and then I remembered we were at the *end* of our journey and I was relieved we didn't have another day's motorcar ride facing us.

I could hear voices downstairs, and I assumed there were some early risers in the house, or perhaps Doktor Mueller and Frau Degenhardt had stayed up all night talking. When I had gone upstairs to bed the previous night, they had been quite engrossed in a serious conversation. In fact, they had barely acknowledged my *"Gute Nacht"* as I left the room.

I quickly got dressed; glad to start the new day off with a clean set of clothes, the ones Frau Wiedemier had stayed up late at night to wash and press after I had gone to bed.

Following the voices' trails downstairs, through the front hallway, and into the dining room, I saw Doktor Mueller and Frau Degenhardt sitting at the community dining table engrossed in a new conversation over a cup of tea and freshly baked almond brezels which I learned are made out of puff pastry dough and finished with toasted almonds, then shaped like a pretzel. However, they barely noticed when I entered the room. — *What in the world could still they be talking about?* —

Finally, a small cough caught their attention and Doktor Mueller politely arose, "Anna. Please sit," as pulled my chair out for me. "Frau Degenhardt got up early this morning just to bake us some fresh brezels. They're divine. Please join us."

— *Well, at least that answered one question. However, divine? Was he attempting to impress Frau Degenhardt with his impeccable Bavarian manners or was that a little inside joke for my benefit alone?* —

[269]

After my first bite, I had to admit the word *divine* might have been an understatement; they were *celestial* and in fact, I quickly helped myself to a second one.

After a few minutes, we were joined by one of Frau Degenhardt's boarders and I couldn't help but be surprised by his unexpected appearance; I didn't know anyone else lived there. I wish that I could have taken a photograph of him, something I could share with you, however I'll do the best I can to describe him. The elderly man who walked into the dining room, someone who was about to play a very influential role in my life, was dressed 'to the nines' as the British love to say. I would guess he was in his late eighties, slightly stooped at the waist, a monocle firmly planted in his left eye, and he was dressed as though he was headed to the Berlin Opera House to attend a performance of a Wagnerian opera.

His impeccable, blue-serge suit coat was buttoned smartly, concealing a matching vest that itself cloaked an immaculate white shirt topped with a stiff, cellophane collar securely anchoring a hand-tied, black bow tie. His shoes were shined to a high gloss, and they were topped by buttoned spatter dashes, and did I fail to mention he also wore sharply-creased trousers?

He nodded politely to acknowledge Frau Degenhardt and Doktor Mueller, and stiffly walked right over to where I was seated. He stopped short of my chair and as I turned to speak to him, he smartly clicked his heels, took my right hand to his lips, and planted a sweet kiss, much to my delight.

He then stepped back a respectable distance and once more clicked his heels, "Please allow me to introduce myself. I am Otto Felix Krumpfelder. Actually, Professor Doktor Otto Felix Krumpfelder, Ph.D., D.M.F, A.L., and all those other silly initials people put after their names to make themselves feel important.

However, I would be *honoured* if you were to call me Uncle Otto and I only offer that privilege to very special people, you know," as he winked at me. "And you are?" he asked.

I was so mesmerised by his amusing theater that I almost forgot he had asked me a question. "Anna. Anna Mueller," I politely answered.

He scrunched up his eyebrows at my answer, so much so that his monocle fell from his eye, but, with a flourish, he quickly put it back into place. "*Fraulein* Mueller, I assume."

I smiled at his obvious attempt to make me feel like an adult, "Professor Krumpfelder, I'm just a little girl. I'm only twelve-years old."

"Uncle Otto, please. You're my new *friend*, not my new *student.*"

I have to admit that I loved that man the minute he walked through the door, eccentricities included. Perhaps I fell in love with his *eccentricities* first and the *man* afterwards, but who knows? In the future, he and I would share many wonderful moments at the local library as he infused me with his love of languages, but I'm getting ahead of my story, aren't I?

To continue, Uncle Otto joined us at the breakfast table and after he had seated himself, he withdrew a white, linen handkerchief from his suit coat pocket, unfolded it, and carefully placed it on the table in front of him. Then, using his wrinkled hands, he lovingly smoothed it out from corner-to-corner and when he was satisfied with his handiwork, he set his teacup saucer on one corner, and his butter dish on the other as anchors. All in an effort to protect Frau Degenhardt's starched-white, linen tablecloth from any possible transgressions. This routine never varied for as long as I knew him. Later, when I stood at the ironing board ironing Meyer's handkerchiefs, it always transported me back to Frau Degenhardt's boarding house and the day I had first met Uncle Otto.

As Uncle Otto joined the others in lively conversation, I sat back and listened; entranced by his language, his wonderful words, and the way he stitched them together in a marvelous way. His speech was rhythmic, enchanting, melodic, and hypnotic. I don't want to besmirch his memory, however I do have to say that every time I hear my oldest grandson listen to what he calls 'rap' music, although I would probably hate the lyrics if I could understand a word of them, the way they're delivered are likewise rhythmic, enchanting, melodic, and hypnotic; just like Uncle Otto's manner of speaking.

Frau Stoffregen sat down right next to me before I even noticed she had entered the room. Perhaps I was *too* engrossed in Uncle Otto's conversation, and since I hadn't noticed her before she sat down next to me, my first impression was formed by only her waist-up appearance. The first thing I noticed was her jewelry. She wore a sparkling diamond ring on her left hand, a beautiful blue sapphire ring on her right, and her scoop-neck, formal, day dress was accented by a string of fine, beautifully-matched, pink pearls. Like Professor Krumpfelder, she was perhaps in her late eighties and she carried herself with great dignity. I could sense she had probably had lived an interesting life, perhaps world travel filled with meeting kings and queens, however I can't say I immediately warmed up to her. She was too formal, too untouchable, and too unhuggable, if that's a word. Whether or not, it accurately describes her. After we had introduced ourselves and had dispatched with the preliminary pleasantries, she cleverly ensnared me in conversation about her favourite hobby, *bird watching*.

As I sat there listening, not conversing, but listening, she promised to teach me the difference between the common collared

Pratincole and the less common, black-winged Pratincole and she also said if I were careful, she would let me observe them through the 7x50 mm Dienstag Carl Zeiss binoculars her grandson had purloined from the *Kriegsmarine*. None of what she said made any sense to me, however I did promise to spend some time with her watching the black-winged Pratincoles through her grandson's stolen binoculars. Unfortunately, I never had a chance to make true on my promise. A few days after our arrival she left to visit relatives and never returned. Frau Degenhardt cleaned out her room and sent her belongings, including her grandson's prized binoculars, to her family in Munich. So much for *bird watching*.

After our new arrivals had finished their breakfasts, they both rose from the table and settled in the adjacent sunroom to read. After they had left, Doktor Mueller looked over at me. "How would you like to live here with Frau Degenhardt? That is, until we can find a place of our own to settle as she has graciously offered us her spare rooms until then." Although I didn't look forward to Frau Stoffregen smothering me with her bird watching stories at breakfast every morning, I did look forward to spending more time with Uncle Otto. "I'd be delighted to stay," I replied.

## Our New Life Begins in Rottach-Egern

Once Doktor Mueller and I were alone, I got up from my seat at the breakfast table, walked over, and sat down in the chair Frau Degenhardt had recently vacated, as I was curious to learn how he had worked his magic in such a short time and found us a place to stay. He patiently explained that he and Frau Degenhardt had made an *Anordnung*, an arrangement, and he said it in a way that hinted he needed to leave it at that.

I wasn't too sure what he had meant by that and I was admittedly a bit jealous of how quickly she had managed to wiggle herself into our lives, however, what happened between Doktor Mueller and Frau Degenhardt was obviously between the two of them, and I never did figure out exactly what type of *Anordnung* they had struck. Although the three of us wound up living under the same roof for several years, Doktor Mueller and Frau Degenhardt always maintained separate quarters. Of course, what they did behind the closed doors of their separate quarters wasn't any of my business.

I never observed any *romantic* gestures between the two of them; no hugging, no kissing, no hand holding, however their conversations often inadvertently slipped from the more formal "*Sie*", to the more personal "*Du*"; the language two intimates might be more likely to share.

As the emotional distance between Doktor Mueller and me widened, it was becoming less likely that we'd ever find the opportunity to have the much-avoided conversation, the one I desperately needed to have. At the beginning, I had hoped that once we had settled in somewhere, we might end our little charade and move on with our lives, but now we apparently had assumed the roles of our pretend characters; they were now our real personas, not our make-believe ones.

Although the war was inching closer to Rottach-Egern day-by-day, everything changed on April 30th 1945; the day Radio Hamburg announced Adolf Hitler's death. See, I can say his name now because I can include his name and the word "death" in the same sentence. The radio announcer said that Adolf Hitler was killed in Berlin as he fell "at his command post in the Reich Chancery fighting to the last breath against Bolshevism and for Germany". Of course, that turned out to be a lot of bullshit. Forgive me if my language offends you, but the cowardly little bastard had just killed his dog, watched his new wife die before his very eyes and then he took the easy way out; he put a gun to his left temple, bit on a cyanide capsule, and blew his brains out. I wouldn't call that 'fighting to the last breath', I'd call that 'a coward's way out'. He had led his adopted country into a war they never wanted, had murdered millions of innocents, had sacrificed their beautiful towns and cities, then had turned out the lights, leaving the doors open for the Russian hordes he had originally said he would crush in a few weeks to come in and destroy everything in their path. I say 'good riddance'!

From that day forward, life in our town clicked back on, as though someone had flipped a giant switch. Of course, May 7th 1945, was even more of a red-letter day. That was the day Germany finally capitulated and signed an unconditional surrender, and it was also the day the dreaded swastika-bedecked flags and banners magically disappeared from Rottach-Egern, and although we had yet to even catch a glimpse of our conquerors, that however, that was about to change.

Our conquerors finally appeared on May 18th. Frau Degenhardt later told us she had just walked out of the local *Apotheker* when she began hearing loud cheers and applause coming from around the corner. Soon, a US Army jeep flying an American flag came around the corner, turned, and drove down the main street towards the center of town as people stopped in place, waved, cheered, and applauded as it passed by. As the sound of applause rippled down the street, people came streaming out of nearby buildings to see what the commotion was and they, too, joined the growing crowd following the slowly moving jeep down the street.

When the jeep and the curious crowd reached the town square, the jeep stopped, and the crowd finally caught their first glimpse of their new masters; a 1st Lieutenant and his sergeant translator; an unimaginable victors' entry. The Germans had valiantly fought this horrible war, had been soundly defeated, and probably expected their vanquishers to come marching into town, armed to the teeth, following a marching band. Instead, they only got one jeep, one lowly 1st Lieutenant and his skinny, buck-toothed sergeant. Go figure (Meyer's favourite expression). War *is* strange, isn't it?

Fortunately, Frau Degenhardt was among the crowd, so we got a first-hand account. She told us the 1st Lieutenant stood up on the jeep seat and began to read from a sheet of paper he held in his hand as the sergeant standing next to him tried to adjust the volume on his *Megafon* and kill the annoying squeal it had started making when he first turned it on. Frau Degenhardt said everyone in the crowd immediately put their hands to their ears in protest and she hoped they would be able to hear what the 1st Lieutenant finally had to say. Although she couldn't recall his exact words, it was something to the effect that Germany had unconditionally surrendered to the Allied Forces, and as such, the Allies had assumed provisional control of the country and would set up an office in the near future to help the town recover and rebuild. With that, the two Americans sat back down in their Jeep, the crowd parted, and they sped away. That was it, such an anticlimax as the crowd quickly dispersed and continued their lives as though nothing had happened.

When she had mentioned they would help the town recover and rebuild, Doktor Mueller and I looked at each other in amazement; the war had completely bypassed the town and other than rebuilding the tourist industry, there was nothing else to recover, or rebuild.

From that day forward, I noticed Doktor Mueller began to change, as though he now had something to hide. He rarely went into town, never went near the office the Allies had eventually set up, and he totally avoided conversations centering on the war and what roles the returning veterans had played. As the defeated German troops who had once left town full of hope and visions of a quick victory trickled back into town and began to resume their interrupted lives, life in Rottach-Egern appeared to return to what I had expected normal life to have been before the war. The coal supplies improved as did the petrol supply, the food supply, and the telephones even worked better, if that's possible. In addition, Radio Hamburg was quickly replaced by Radio Free Europe as the most listened-to broadcast network.

Slowly, the tourist industry began to recover as the tour boats, once again, started taking tourists on Lake Tegernsee for lunch cruises, and when winter came, we began to see an influx of skiers eager to challenge the Rottach-Egern/Wallenberg ski resorts and the nearly one-thousand metre vertical drop the expert skiers craved. As the tourist industry slowly recovered, Frau Degenhardt's boarding house once again returned to its former role; one of the finest tourist houses in the area.

Doctor Mueller gradually assumed the role of innkeeper and sometimes handyman, while Frau Degenhardt spent most of her day in the kitchen making those wonderful meals that kept the tourists returning, year-after-year, however, I'm not sure what role I assumed. Even though Doktor Mueller and I still maintained our somewhat fragile relationship, I slowly became a lost and forgotten child. It seemed as though only Uncle Otto was interested in what I was doing, and what I was *doing* was becoming fascinated with the different languages I had begun to overhear from our visiting guests. English, Italian, French, Spanish, a mélange pleasing to my ear. When I casually mentioned this to Uncle Otto, he invited me to join him on one of his daily trips to the local library, the beginning of a journey of amazing discoveries that continues to this day.

## Professor Krumpfelder's Magic Library Desk

One beautiful day in early autumn, I reminded Uncle Otto that he had promised to take me to the library. He appeared surprised that I was still interested as perhaps he thought I had agreed to accompany him just to please him, but I hadn't; I seriously wanted to visit the library with him.

When we had finished our breakfast, he carefully picked up his handkerchief 'placemat' from the table, inspected it for crumbs and when he was satisfied there were none, he carefully folded it, and placed it back into his suit coat pocket.

After finishing his morning ritual, he looked at me. "Shall we?" he said.

I knew he was toying with me, "Uncle Otto. Have you been eavesdropping?"

"Indeed I have, Fraulein. Your little word games with Herr Mueller fascinate me and I'd like to join in, if you don't mind."

"Shall we?" he repeated.

"*Gerne (With pleasure),*" as I played along.

He and I walked down the sunny street towards the local library. It wasn't far; just a couple short blocks and we could definitely sense autumn's approach. It would certainly be a welcome change after the hot summer we had recently endured.

When we walked through the library's front door and approached the front desk, the librarian looked up and warmly greeted us, "*Guten Morgen*, Professor. I notice you've brought a guest with you."

"Indeed I have, Frau Zimmerman. Please allow me to introduce my newest student, Anna Mueller."

Frau Zimmerman reached over the desk and shook my hand. "Welcome, Fraulein. Please allow me to see if Professor Krumpfelder's desk is ready," as she got up and disappeared between the fully-stocked library shelves.

"You have your own desk?" I asked in amazement.

"Of course. What good is a library if you don't have somewhere private and comfortable to enjoy your reading?"

Soon, Frau Zimmerman returned, "Your desk is ready, Professor. Please enjoy today's adventure."

Uncle Otto took my hand and led me between several bookshelves, around a couple of corners, through more bookshelves, and finally into a small alcove tucked away in a quiet corner of the library, and it was obvious he had made this expedition quite often.

This was the first time I had ever been in a library and it was an amazing experience! Everywhere I looked there were books; books stacked neatly on the shelves, books on the long reading tables, books stacked on the floor, books, books, books, everywhere! I wanted to stop and examine each one, however Uncle Otto was in a hurry to get to his destination, so he hurried me along and it didn't take long to get to the little, hidden alcove he called his 'office'.

A small lift-top desk, two chairs, and a reading lamp were snuggled comfortably in the alcove. "My office," he exclaimed as he turned on the reading lamp and pulled out my chair for me. He then lifted the desktop and removed two pencils and a notepad, which he set on the desktop in such a precise manner that I immediately recognised it as part of his daily routine, something I hopefully, would be able to observe during many future visits.

With a twinkle in his eye, he asked, "Fraulein Mueller, what is it you'd like me to teach you?"

I hadn't expected that question, so it took me a while to answer and as he patiently sat there, I tried to think about what it was I *did* want him to teach me. Although I had a general idea of what I expected, it was difficult to find the right words to express myself. Finally, I decided to attempt an answer. "Uncle Otto, when I hear our guests speaking in languages I don't understand, I'd like to know their words so I can understand what they're saying."

Uncle Otto chuckled aloud, "Well, Fraulein, I'm amazed you're already able to understand the difference between vocabulary - *words*, and *language* - how we use those words to form thoughts and ideas. It's such a simple concept, but one I frequently had to browbeat my university students with to get it through their thick skulls; the difference between *vocabulary* and *language*, which you seem to already know. That's wonderful, and it makes my task much simpler as it presents me with a starting point to begin our lessons."

Thus began our marvelous journey through the amazing world of vocabularies and languages. Our first lesson began with Professor Krumpfelder's engaging discourse on vocabulary and language and his thoughts and ideas were so brilliant, so well-spoken that even I, a young girl, saw the beauty in his explanations. He then arose from his chair and soon returned with a book in hand which he handed to me and commanded, "Read it!"

I opened the first page expecting to see a language I understood, most probably German, however I was shocked to find a language totally unknown to me. "Read it!" he repeated.

"I can't, Uncle Otto. I don't know the language," I answered, somewhat frustrated.

He continued his probing. "Is it because you don't understand the *language* or is it because you don't understand the *vocabulary*, the words?"

Now I was thoroughly confused. Hadn't he just complimented me on knowing the difference? "Both, perhaps." A question more than an answer.

"Well, you're partially correct, however the main reason you aren't able to read the book is because it's written in French. Even if you *could* read French, without knowing the *language,* it would mean nothing to you. You may understand the *meaning* of the words, but without the magic of *language*, they could just be a list of ingredients for making a tasty oxtail soup. To me, words in a printed book are attached to the pages with little springs. Lifeless, boring, meaningless; that is, until you apply the magic of *language*. *Language* gives *energy* to the little springs; the better the words are strung together using *language*, the more *energy* they have; the more *energy* they have, the more they fly off the page in an avalanche of *language*. When I take a well-written book from one of the library's shelves, I can sense that energy as I hold the book in my hands and the anticipation those words must feel waiting to fly off the page as I read them. Vocabulary - *words*; language - *energy;* energy - *power*."

I had always wondered why Adolf Hitler was able to hypnotize an entire country with his words and his mesmerizing use of the language. Now I know why. He knew the *words*, he knew the *language,* and better than anyone else, he knew how to use their *power*.

Although Uncle Otto's description was rather flowery, I completely understood his concept and his love of *language*; however, I first needed to learn the French words, its *vocabulary*.

"Where should we head off now?" he asked, breathless from his impassioned first lesson.

"Why don't you teach me French, Uncle Otto?" I asked, as though it were that simple, however we had to start somewhere.

"Good idea," as he took back the book he had just handed me and turned to the first page. It was Victor Hugo's *Les Miserables* and he began to read aloud: *"En 1815, M. Charles - François - Bienvenu Myriel était évêque de D - Il était un vieillard de soixante-quinze ans, il avait occupé le siège de D - depuis 1806."*

Although I couldn't understand a word he was saying, I can repeat it now almost word-for-word, even in my sleep. A French dictionary, a pencil, a notepad, and *Les Miserables* occupied us for the entire upcoming year. Fortunately, Uncle Otto could speak French, so I had the luxury of hearing him speak it, however, many of the languages we learned in the upcoming years were unfamiliar to both of us, and we had no idea how to pronounce many of the words we learned, and we used to sit for hours laughing as we argued over how to pronounce some of them.

For example, Polish being my natural tongue was never difficult for me to read, speak, or understand. However, when I tried to teach Uncle Otto how to read and speak Polish, he just couldn't get over the fact that *Łódź* was pronounced *Wodz,* and *czerw* was pronounced *surf.*

Whenever I became frustrated with his reproaching me for incorrectly pronouncing a new, difficult word, I'd go to the library's children's section and retrieve a copy of the Polish children's book *Kajtuś Czarodziej* and I'd hand it to him. "Your turn to read aloud," and then I'd sit back and giggle outrageously as I listened to him mangle my mother tongue. Several times Frau Zimmerman had to scurry through the library shelves to deliver her stern warning; after all, we *were* in a library.

Professor Krumpfelder was a great admirer of the German-Jewish historian and writer, Alfred Rosenberg, and he often used his ideas to explain to me what made different languages so different from one another. In fact, he always kept a couple of Rosenberg's books handy on his desk as he said they were important manuscripts we should all learn from, and he was always referring to them. To remind me, he would often read the following passage from one of his books which I finally wrote down in my journal to save him the time and trouble.

Here, I'll read it to you. *"I am convinced that the different races have their different rhythms – in character and conduct, in music, and in the dance. A certain type of music or of the dance cannot be carried over from one race to another because it would not suit the other. It is exactly the same language. The rhythm of one language cannot be applied to an entirely different language. One country has its folk songs in major keys, another in minors. This is no mere accident, but corresponds to an inner rhythm of the soul."*

Remember I told you how rhythmic Professor Krumpfelder's speech was? Well, Alfred Rosenberg certainly hit the nail on the head, didn't he? A wonderfully thought out theory that was, unfortunately, hijacked soon after Professor Rosenberg had announced it when Dr. Gerd Cehak of the Biological Institute of the Reich Academy for Sports and Gymnastics, himself, announced that each race *does* indeed have its own characteristic speed of walking, talking, and moving in general.

Alfred Rosenberg (a Jew and avowed Communist) certainly played into the hands of the Nazis and their theory of racial superiority when all he was trying to do was explain the differences in how different cultures had developed their own unique languages of speech, music, and dance. Looking back on it now, I wish he had used the word *culture* instead of *race*. The word *culture* certainly better describes our differences, in my opinion anyway. It encompasses so much more than the word *race* does.

After I had mastered French and was able to read all five volumes of *Les Miserables* from cover-to-cover with passable comprehension, we soon embarked on an ambitious plan. We decided I should learn two new languages each year. The first six months would be spent with Uncle Otto teaching me a language he already knew and the next six months we would learn a new language, together.

Overall, by the time I was eighteen years old, I could read and write German, Yiddish, Hebrew, French, Spanish, Swedish, some Russian, some Greek, and some Latin. In later years, I learned Vietnamese, Cambodian, Thai, and Japanese, however it wasn't until Meyer and I had immigrated to Israel that I finally learned 'proper' English like the British speak, so unlike what you Americans claim as your own. Perhaps you could learn some manners from the British especially how to speak *their* language.

Our little lessons sitting at Professor Krumpfelder's magic library desk in the hidden alcove became the gateway to my lifelong passion for languages and it's the only reason I was able to come to New York to work as a translator at the U.N. and, finally, for several major publishing companies. I often sat at our apartment window on Lydig Avenue in the Bronx looking out over our new neighbourhood and marvelled at my incredible journey from a small, backward farm village in Poland to one of the greatest cities on earth. What a journey; what a life!

## Doktor Mueller's Dilemma

It was April 20th 1948, my sixteenth birthday, when Doktor Mueller and I finally got around to begin the discussion I needed to have ever since that fateful night in 1942, however, he shut the door as soon as I had attempted to open it.

Frau Degenhardt had baked a special cake for me, an angel food cake (my favourite), and the four of us were sitting around the supper table enjoying it. Besides Frau Degenhardt, Doktor Mueller, and me, Uncle Otto was there as he said he wouldn't miss my party for the world.

Eventually, the conversation came around to what had happened since the war ended and how its conclusion had only split Europe, rather than mending it. The Cold War was currently at its height and unbeknownst to us, the start of the Berlin Blockade was only two months away and it was a very dangerous world, indeed.

It all began innocently enough when Uncle Otto asked Doktor Mueller what he had done during the war. Doktor Mueller had carefully avoided this topic up until this time and it took him a few moments to answer, but finally he said, "I didn't participate in the war, Professor Krumpfelder. I was a merchant living in Poland and even though I was still considered a German citizen, somehow I avoided being called up into the German Army. Just pure luck, I suppose."

Although both Frau Degenhardt and Uncle Otto accepted his explanation at face value, I almost fell off my chair. After the two of them had excused themselves and Frau Degenhardt had cleared the table, Doktor Mueller and I retired to the sunroom. I had noticed his relationship with Frau Degenhardt had cooled lately, although they still ran the tourist house as a team; however, I never pried into their business, as I never thought it was my privilege to do so, but I noticed something was bothering him.

After we had gotten comfortable, I decided to try, once again, to broach the dreaded subject. "Father, when Uncle Otto asked you what you did in the war, you weren't honest with him, *were* you? Why did you answer him that way?" I asked.

"Anna, what did you want me to say? Should I have told him *I* was an SS doctor at Auschwitz and *you* are a Polish Jew I had rescued from the selection line? Is *that* what I should have told him?" his defencive retort.

His blunt answer caught me off guard. "No, I didn't ask you what you *did* at Auschwitz, I merely asked you *why* you answered his question the way you did. Please don't get so *defencive*. You have nothing to be ashamed of, *do you?*"

Doktor Mueller crossed his arms in front of him and assumed a very protective posture, "To be honest, Anna, I don't think it's any of their business what I did in the war or why you aren't my real daughter. You know the Jews are hunting down what they call *war criminals* and are bringing them to justice. Do you want one of them to knock on our door and take me away?"

"Why would anyone in their right mind want to call you a *war criminal*? You *helped* the sick Jews at the camp, didn't you? Nobody could ever call you a *war criminal* for *helping* the Jews, so I don't think you have anything to worry about. Is that what's been bothering you lately?"

I could sense his growing anxiety by the way he reacted to my question. "That and a lot of other issues. I thought once we had finally reached safety and could settle down, you and I could begin to build a new life together. A life free from outside influences, unending conflict, and the constant need to be fleeing from danger. It's been almost three years since we arrived here, and *yes,* we have settled down, and *yes,* we have begun to build a new life, and *yes,* we're free from war's danger, but *I'm* restless, my *soul* is restless. *Our physical* flight from danger may have ended, but *my emotional* flight from what I did at Auschwitz has yet to come to a peaceful conclusion."

That was a lot of information to dump onto a sixteen-year-old girl. He and I had never had what I might have called an *adult* conversation about such serious topics, and I didn't know where to try to steer this conversation. Perhaps it would be better to take a detour and revisit this topic later, so I slightly changed the subject away from him, and more towards me.

"Father, why did you take me out of the selection line that horrible night in Auschwitz? I always thought that perhaps I was someone special, someone who reached out and touched you in a meaningful way."

He closed his eyes as though he was replaying the scene in his mind, "Do you want me to be honest, Anna, *brutally* honest? You might not like what I have to say."

"Please, Father, I need to know the answer," as I braced myself for what was to come next.

"Remember when I told you we had recently lost Anna right before she was due to arrive at our home in Auschwitz? Frau Mueller was falling apart and I didn't have the time to console her, so I picked you out of the line as a gift to her, a way to mend her broken heart. I hate to admit it, but there wasn't anything special about you, nothing about you that reached out and touched me, it was just a spur of the moment decision."

In an instant, with those cruel words, he ripped my heart out and threw it away. All the time we had been together, I felt he had chosen me because I was special, when I just turned out to be a spur of the moment folly. He could have picked any of the thousands of young girls he had thoughtlessly sent to the gas chambers, and I was completely and utterly crushed. That certainly was a conversation-ender, and I ran out of the sunroom up to my bedroom, leaving a path of pain and sorrow trailing behind me.

Curiously enough, Doktor Mueller never apologised for confessing that to me nor did he reveal what he did at Auschwitz, and it wasn't until much later that I was finally able to pry it out of him, albeit grudgingly. After that, our relationship was exceedingly strained and for the life of me, I couldn't figure out how the man I had grown to love had so suddenly turned bitter and hateful. Something terrible must have been bothering him and he had turned his umbrage towards me. Where had it all gone so wrong?

Life after that wasn't the same. Although the three of us still lived in the same house, we were always at odds with each other and there was always a sour feeling hanging in the air. Although Doktor Mueller and I continued attending Mass at St. Laurentius Church every week, it felt as though the words of penitence we dutifully recited didn't matter anymore; we were merely going through the motions of pretending to be good Christians. Of course, deep down, I was still a Jew, so perhaps I shouldn't criticise him for going through the motions when I was doing the same thing, myself.

Eventually, we both stopped attending Mass as he said he didn't feel comfortable being in the congregation, instead, he felt his calling was on the other side of the aisle; he said he wanted to become a priest. A real priest, not a pretend one like before. He said it gave him great comfort when he had worn Father Tadeus' garments and he desperately needed to feel that way again.

So, on Wednesday, September 29th 1948, Doktor Mueller packed his bags, walked out the front door, and took a bus to the seminary in

Munich. It wasn't a pleasant farewell and it was several years before I saw him again.

## Doktor Mueller, In Retrospect

Perhaps this is a good time to talk about my feelings for Doktor Mueller; now that I've come to a place in my story where he walked out of my life, at least for the time being. Perhaps this entire story may be more about him than it is about me, and in a way, that might be true.

It's more a story about the two of us, two people who collided in the midst of a stormy time; a time where individuals' paths crossed for a fleeting instant and then diverged forever. Think about it. Think about two soldiers whose eyes meet right before one of them pulls the trigger and kills the other or two lives who intersect for a brief moment as one of them walks to the gas chambers and the other one walks home to dinner with his family. Life's all about momentary intersections and although Doktor Mueller's and mine was more than just a fleeting intersection, that's the way it began that terrible night in Auschwitz.

Someone recently asked me about Doktor Mueller and although I'm certain time has softened my opinions; it once again started me thinking about him; *who* he was, *where* he had come from, and *what* he believed in. Strangely enough, I still can't figure the man out as he has continued to be an enigma even after all these years.

I hate to admit it, but if I discarded all his bad attributes and only kept the good ones, there wouldn't be much left of the man, sadly to say. Don't get me wrong, I'm sure he had some good attributes; however, they were certainly overshadowed by his bad ones.

[289]

# Innocence Lost - A Childhood Stolen

If I were to attempt to describe him now, I would say he was distant, unemotional, detached, and obsessive/compulsive. The only time I *ever* saw him cry was when the bridge collapsed on our way into Germany and I don't know if his reaction was from fear, relief, anger, or sheer frustration. When we were sitting on the park bench in Auschwitz and he told me about Anna being killed in a bombing raid, he reported it to me matter-of-factly, as if he were discussing the weather. Likewise, the day he returned home and found Frau Mueller lying in their bed, dead, wouldn't you think he would have shown some emotion such as grief, sorrow, anguish, much like any normal person would have? However, he didn't. I could go on and on recounting many other times any normal person would have broken down and cried, but he never did.

Although he was a good conversationalist, he often had a difficult time with people who didn't understand him or the point he was trying to get across. He often treated them contemptuously, as though he knew something they didn't as their viewpoints always fell short of his standards and quite often the conversations turned ugly when he chided them for their lack of knowledge on the subject.

One of his worst faults, however, was his authoritarian behaviour. He ruled the world around him with an iron fist as it was *his* way or no way at all. Although he often asked my opinions, I felt as though he did it out of courtesy, not as an attempt to listen to my ideas, and that part of him I secretly came to despise.

Now that I mention secrecy, that word also describes him to a tee. He and I always had our little secrets, things we couldn't share with others and I know some of them made sense; some we needed to keep to ourselves as we fled across Europe; however, his need for secrecy extended well beyond that. Like the time he revealed that he and Frau Degenhardt had struck an *Anordnung*, but he couldn't tell me about it because it was a secret. Everything was a secret, secret, secret! What other more sinister secrets was he keeping from me?

Often, his paranoia got the better of him. After the war had ended and we were living in Rottach-Egern, he frequently talked about the Jews who were hunting down *war criminals* and everywhere he looked, he saw Jews hunting *war criminals;* behind every bush, driving every car that passed by, every guest that stayed in Frau Degenhardt's tourist house. If he noticed one of our guests had checked in with a Jewish-sounding name, he would do his best to avoid them even if his behaviour bordered on sheer rudeness. Often, he would take a roundabout way into town just in case someone was following him, as he was certain his name was on the top of the *war criminal* hunter's list. If someone approached him on the street to perhaps ask for directions and he didn't recognise them, he'd turn around and briskly walk away.

I often wonder, myself, how I could ever stay with such a person, however his personality wasn't revealed to me in one emotional outburst. It took some time before I realised who he truly was. To begin with, when he pulled me out of the selection line with the excuse of repairing Alinka's tattered arm that was, to me, an act of kindness. An act of gentle kindness, accompanied by a protective one as he put his arm around me as though to shelter me from the unfolding drama, and then he took my hand as we walked down the street towards his house. Those actions touched my heart, especially after the rough treatment we had only recently endured since we left Warsaw.

His teaching me how to read German, taking me into Auschwitz and sitting on the bench by the river, and all the times he protected me as we fled across Europe; I thought those were kind acts, acts truly from his heart. Now, I realise they weren't acts of kindness at all; they were just part of his self-fulfilling performance, a role he played to satisfy his own perverse needs. Likewise, no matter how many times he told me he loved me, I never felt the same kind of love like I had from my parents or my family. It was as though professing his love for me was more for *him* than it was for *me* as I'm sure just hearing himself say the words "I love you" must have been some kind of personal reassurance that he could feel love for another person without necessarily having to show it.

I'm not a trained psychiatrist; I'm just talking about how I feel about Doktor Mueller; however, I'm certain a psychiatrist will have a field day when they read my story. They'll probably want to attach some scholarly, technical label to him and to our relationship; abuser/victim, sociopathic tendencies, abandonment issues, anger, etc. etc., and I'm sure some, or all of them may be applicable, but it wouldn't change who I am or how I feel, now would it?

What more can I say other than I truly loved him, and in a way, I'm sure he loved me, too. He often told me that he loved me, and there were many times where he showed it with his actions; actions any loving parent would display towards their child. Once again, a psychiatrist might say it was just an abused person's reflexive response to their abuser, however if that were the case, how would a ten-year-old Polish peasant girl even begin to understand those dynamics? I just loved him despite his many quirks and countless flaws.

Many times I tried to throw my love out to him as a lifeline, a way for him to pull himself up and out of the depths of his despair, but he never grabbed onto it. Perhaps he didn't want to, perhaps he didn't feel the need to, or perhaps he didn't know how to, but regardless of the reason, he never did.

I do have to admit that all the love I felt for him, all the kind things he did for me, all the good times we had, these were all irreparably shattered when he revealed I wasn't someone special he had rescued from the selection line. I was merely a random choice. It was as if someone had reached into a huge jar filled with marbles and only pulled one out. I was just another marble, plain and no different from all the other marbles in the jar; just a random marble in a sea of identical marbles. Nothing special, at all.

These are just thoughts of a seventy-eight-year-old woman who has an advantage *you* don't yet enjoy as there are still many unwritten chapters in my story you need to read. These later, yet-to-be-written chapters involve remorsefulness, forgiveness, taking responsibility for one's acts, and the ability to turn one's life around and make amends. However, the following chapters in my life are about the beginning of my new life without Doktor Mueller, how I truly felt about him, and how he had managed to deceive me for all those years.

## My Eighteenth Birthday Party

Once Doktor Mueller had left for the seminary, life at Frau Degenhardt's tourist house returned to as normal as could be under the circumstances. Frau Degenhardt and I were eventually able to patch up our relationship; however, I never had the nerve to ask her about the *Anordnung* she and Doktor Mueller had made. I suspect they were an 'item' as my grandson would say, and perhaps that's why he had left so abruptly that September. Maybe things just hadn't worked out for them.

I did have a brief conversation with Doktor Mueller right before he left and we reminisced about our motorcar trip and the good times we had enjoyed, and I expected him to apologise for the remarks he had made about my not being special, however he didn't and I didn't force the issue.

During our conversation, he tried to explain why he was forsaking life in Rottach-Egern for life as a Catholic priest and some of what he explained to me made sense, and some didn't. He talked in vague terms; something about his *soul* being restless, feeling more comfortable wearing *priest's garments*, and wanting to make *amends*. Vague references like those, however he was never very specific as he just tended to ramble and he sounded confused, conflicted, and tormented. I suspect it had something to do with his work at Auschwitz, but every time I asked him about that, he always changed the subject. Later on, when I learned the truth about his role at Auschwitz, I was better able to understand his motives for entering the seminary.

As I watched another year come and go, although I hadn't told anyone, I had already made plans to leave Rottach-Egern as soon as I was able. There just wasn't anything there that captivated my interest enough to make me want to stay there for the rest of my life. Uncle Otto's wonderful language lessons continued, Frau Degenhardt's tourist house was having its best year ever and one or two of the local boys had eventually taken some interest in me. Unfortunately, I never reciprocated, their interest soon waned, and then died. I guess my soul, like Doktor Mueller's, was restless too, but for different reasons.

It was Thursday, April 20th 1950; my eighteen birthday. Frau Degenhardt had once again baked her special angel food cake for me, and Uncle Otto was in fine form, dressed 'to the nines' and regaling us with humourous stories about his student days at Heidelberg University, Class of 1883. He talked about late afternoon barge parties on the Necker River where the beer flowed like water and more than one rowdy student had to be fished from the river. We all laughed because neither Frau Degenhardt nor I could begin to imagine the very proper Professor Krumpfelder ever attending a drunken, riverboat beer party with his college friends.

Since it was my eighteenth birthday, Uncle Otto gave me a very special present; a first-edition copy of Immanuel Kant's *The Groundwork of the Metaphysics of Morals*. I thought it was an appropriate present, especially with what I was about to divulge and Uncle Otto presenting it to me provided me with the perfect opening.

"Anna, now that you've come of age, what are your plans for the future," he asked politely.

I took a deep breath, counted to five, and replied, "I'm leaving for Munich the day after tomorrow."

My announcement was met with dead silence; my birthday dinner partners just sat there speechless. Finally, Frau Degenhardt composed herself, "Why *Munich*, Anna? Of all places, *Munich*? This seems like such a hasty decision. Have you taken the time and thoroughly thought it through? You're still a young girl, too young to leave here and go to Munich alone. You are going alone, aren't you?" she asked.

"Of course I'm travelling alone, Frau Degenhardt, and my decision isn't a hasty one either. In fact, I've been seriously thinking about moving to *Munich* ever since Herr Mueller left for the Herzogliches Georgianum Seminary there. Although I haven't discussed this with him, I thought it stood to *reason* that having him nearby might prove to be helpful in a time of need." I felt it important to include the word *reason* as I knew Uncle Otto would probably raise that issue as he and I had frequently discussed Kant's philosophy during one of our many trips to the library. In fact, *The Groundwork of the Metaphysics of Morals* was the book he had used as our textbook when he introduced me to the finer nuances of the German *language.*

He smiled across the table at me as he knew exactly where I was headed. "So, Anna. You've learned your lessons very well. In fact, you've literally taken them to heart. That's the *reason* I have given you one of my most prized possessions. I have carried it with me since *my* eighteenth birthday and I know you'll take proper care of it. As we have discussed many times in the past, Kant professes that morality is based neither on the principle of utility, nor on a law of nature, but on human *reason.* He tells us that *reason* tells us what we ought to do and when we obey our own *reason,* only then are we truly free. If you thought you'd sneak that one past your Uncle Otto with your sly inclusion of that word in your announcement, you are sorely mistaken."

Frau Degenhardt sat there listening to his discourse, however I'm sure she had no clue of what Uncle Otto was talking about, or even who Immanuel Kant was.

She made a vain attempt to keep up, although I'm sure our conversation had outpaced her long ago. "Why do you want to leave here, Anna? I've lived here all my life; it's such a wonderful place to stay, perhaps to raise a family, although Herr Degenhardt and I never had the opportunity. I wish you'd reconsider your decision; it seems so hasty."

I understood her concern, "It's not a hasty decision, Frau Degenhardt. It's something I've been struggling with ever since Herr Mueller and I began our flight from Auschwitz. Ever since then, I have constantly been under someone's wing, someone's protection, someone's supervision, and I'm grateful for that, however I need to stand strong and be myself. It's time for me to be true to myself. When Uncle Otto and I were learning English, we read Margaret

Mitchell's recently published *Gone with the Wind* to learn the English *words*, but we read Shakespeare's *Hamlet* to learn the English *language*. One passage in *Hamlet* truly reached out to me when Polonius says to Laertes, — *To thine own self be true, and it must follow, as the night the day, thou canst not then be false to any man —*."

Uncle Otto politely clapped his hands. "Well done, Anna. I see our lessons didn't go to waste, did they? I'm truly amazed that you remembered that beautiful passage. It's such an eloquent example of the power of *language*, although not quite as stirring, one of my favourite quotes is — *Every blade of grass has its angel that bends over it and whispers grow, grow. — (from the Jewish Talmud)*," as he gave me a knowing wink, once again reaffirming our shared secret; one I zealously guard to this day. "And I encourage you to grow; grow strong in your convictions, grow strong in your principles, grow strong in your desire to do well. I know you have the strength to accomplish these tasks and much more, and I commend you for your decision. Have you thought about what you'll do in Munich?" he asked.

I was eagerly awaiting that opening as I produced the letter I had been hiding in my lap the entire time. Waving it proudly above my head, I shouted, "I have a job!"

"A job?" they both simultaneously exclaimed in amazement.

"Yes, a job; a real job. The International Red Cross has recently set up some new Refugee Aid Centers in Munich. I read about them in a copy of the Munich Abenzeitung newspaper at the library and they are desperately in need of translators. With what the press is calling the Cold War, there has been a flood of refugees fleeing the Soviet-bloc countries: East Germany, Estonia, Latvia, Lithuania, Romania, Poland, Czechoslovakia, Russia; all speaking different languages. I sent the Red Cross a letter offering my services and they sent me this letter in return. Not only have they asked me to join them, they also sent me a railway ticket and one-hundred marks! The letter says they'll also provide me with shelter, food, and public transportation. It's truly a dream come true."

When Uncle Otto leaned back in his chair and folded his arms across his chest, I could tell he was proud of me. After Frau Degenhardt had left the room, he confided that Frau Degenhardt was probably extremely jealous of my moving to Munich as he said *that* had always been *her* dream.

## My Journey to Munich

A couple of days later, Frau Degenhardt drove Uncle Otto and me to the Rottach-Egern railway station. Our trusty Mercedes had long since died and we rode in her brand-new, 1949 Volkswagen. There was barely enough room in her new motorcar for the three of us and my luggage, although I had only packed one moderately-sized bag. Uncle Otto suggested we place it in the motorcar's trunk, however when he opened the trunk, I was surprised to see the engine instead. Whoever thought of putting the engine in the trunk and the trunk where the engine was supposed to reside? I just chalked it up to German engineering. However, even the 'trunk where the engine was supposed to reside' trunk, was too small for my luggage, so I had to ride with it in the motorcar's cramped rear seat.

It was a beautiful spring day. The local ski areas were enjoying an exceptionally fine spring skiing season and Frau Degenhardt's tourist house was fully occupied with rosy-cheeked skiers fresh from the slopes, enjoying their après-ski drinks, and bragging about their terrifying trips down the nearby, steep ski slopes.

# Innocence Lost - A Childhood Stolen

Rottach-Egern had been my Bavarian home for more than five years and although I hadn't made many friends there, I knew I would miss it the moment the train pulled away from the station.

When we arrived at the railway station, Uncle Otto attempted to retrieve my suitcase from the rear seat, but to no avail. However, between the two of us, we were finally able to extract it after much pulling, twisting, and shoving. So much for German engineering!

We three walked out onto the railway station platform and waited for the train to arrive. Standing there, I thought about how many of my journeys had started and ended with a train ride as I remembered the Passover trip to my grandparents' apartment in Łódź, our dangerous escape to Warsaw with our counterfeit ID cards, the tightly-packed and dehumanising cattle wagons that had frantically deposited us in Auschwitz, and now this.

Except for the trip to Łódź, the other two had been one-way; both into dark unknowns teeming with danger, however I was now on another one-way train ride, also to an unknown future, but hopefully one filled with good fortune and endless opportunities.

Like before, I heard the train's approach long before it came into view and I waited anxiously for the smoke-belching locomotive to appear, but imagine my surprise when I saw the train being pulled by a sleek, new kind of locomotive I had never seen before. I later learned this was the *Maiden München's* first trip using her new, sleek, diesel-electric locomotive.

As I stepped up onto the train, I turned and looked back at Frau Degenhardt and Uncle Otto and I hoped the looks on their faces expressed their love and pride for me and my new adventure. After I had taken my seat in the comfortable coach, I looked out the window just as Uncle Otto blew me a sweet kiss, removed the monocle from his left eye, reached into his suit coat pocket, retrieved his 'placemat' handkerchief, and dabbed the tears from his eyes. That was the last time I ever saw him and the vision of that dear, sweet man standing there bidding me farewell and dabbing his eyes with his handkerchief will remain with me forever.

Soon, the locomotive blew its air-horn and slowly began to move away from the railway station. Its throaty, muscular sound was totally unlike the friendly little 'toots' that had so annoyed me back in Auschwitz. It was as though it was proudly announcing the *new* Germany and its optimistic future, now attempting to forsake its dark past.

The train ride to Munich was a short one; less than an hour and as we rode along the eastern shore of Lake Tegernsee, I looked out the rain-streaked train window and remembered the day Doktor Mueller and I had driven our derelict Mercedes down the road paralleling the railway tracks. That was probably the last day we had truly worked together as a team; our destination was in sight, we had arrived safely, and we no longer needed to depend on each other like we had before. Of course, we didn't realise it then, nor did we think about it at the time, however it was definitely the beginning of our eventual disconnexion.

Now, I was on a train headed to Munich where he currently lived at the Seminary. Was it just a coincidence that drew me there or was it something deeper, perhaps something more sinister that pulled me once again closer to him?

As the train pulled into the München Hauptbahnhof railway station, I could feel the energy radiating from this historic German city now that it had shed its Nazi cloak and had started to rebuild itself. Munich was the *Hauptstadt der Bewegung*, the Capital of the Movement, the birthplace of the Nazi Party and had figured prominently in the Party's history. Because of its sordid past, the

# Innocence Lost - A Childhood Stolen

Allies had unmercifully attempted to bomb it out of existence with more than seventy air raids over a period of six years as the city paid dearly for hosting Adolf Hitler and his gang of thugs back in the 1920's. Now, however, that was in the past as the city had already begun rebuilding itself.

As with other German cities that had been reduced to rubble, Munich was faced with the challenge of whether they should bulldoze the city and start over, or restore the city to its former architectural splendor. A community-appointed commission voted by a single-vote margin to restore the city. Using old photographs and with the establishment of strict building regulations, a renewed Munich began to rise from the debris and a vibrant, new energy engulfed the city. That was what I felt the moment the train pulled into the Munich railway station; *energy*, one of Uncle Otto's favourite words.

I took a short cab ride to the International Red Cross refugee center on Tegernseer Landstraße next to the building that would eventually become the Polizeipräsidium München, the main police headquarters. For the time being, however, it was a large, mostly vacant building that had suffered moderate damage during the war and they were now in the process of rebuilding it. The Red Cross had converted some of its restored rooms into dormitory rooms where they could provide temporary shelter for the streams of refugees that flooded into their office every day, and my two-room apartment was in a separate part of the building, facing the street. The building was in an ideal location; easy to get to, near the center of town, and on a busy thoroughfare.

After someone had shown me to my new apartment, I followed them to the main office. What I had expected to see and what I actually encountered were two different worlds. I had expected to walk into a controlled environment, efficiently organised, and calm,

[301]

however what I walked into was sheer bedlam; a disorganised, dysfunctional mess. The waiting room was crowded with refugees speaking loudly in a cacophony of different languages, kids were running around the room unsupervised, people were sleeping on the floor, and some were even eating on blankets spread out on the floor; utter confusion.

As I made my way through the crowded waiting room, a diminutive woman opened the administrative office door and stepped out into the bedlam. "Janica Doubrova? Is someone here named Janica Doubrova?"

The announcer appeared quite frazzled. Her hair was piled on top of her head, however whatever she had used in a futile attempt to keep it in place, had given up long ago. Perhaps in her early twenties, she was quite attractive, or could be if she had taken some time to compose herself.

When she saw me approaching, she asked, "Are you Janica Doubrova?"

"No. I'm Anna Mueller, your new translator."

"Oh my, I wasn't expecting you until tomorrow. Well, go through that door over there and wait in the first office on the left. I'll be right in," she said. Her voice calling out, "Janica Doubrova? Is someone here named Janica Doubrova?" followed me as I walked through the door and waited for her.

Within a few minutes, she returned, "My apologies, Fraulein Mueller, things can get crazy around here sometimes. I'm Geneviève Daigneault, the director of this den of insanity. I'm sure you noticed that when you first walked in."

I knew from the first moment I met her that we would be great friends and within minutes, we were talking as though we had known each other for years, just Anna and Jen, two old friends.

It didn't take long for her to introduce me to her assistant, Horst, who led me into his office to begin my training. He patiently explained there were three phases in helping place the DP's. First, there was the intake process; interviewing the displaced persons (they seldom referred to them as refugees, often shortening their description to DP's), second was making short-term arrangements to meet their immediate needs for food and shelter, and third, was helping them make long-range plans for their permanent resettlement. That meant working with other worldwide organisations in order to find local sponsors who were willing to assume responsibility for them in their new countries since many countries wouldn't allow DP's into their country without a sponsor. Many of these conversations would test my linguistic skills in the months to come and quite often Uncle Otto's words would ring true in my ears, 'It's one thing to know the *words*, but it's another to know the *language*.'

## Munich

If I thought my job as a translator would have anything to do with translating, I was in for a huge surprise as I quickly learned on my first day at the Red Cross center. I had to take a crash course on how to become a babysitter, surrogate parent, comforter, counselor, confidant, Father confessor, and nursemaid. It was far more challenging than I had ever expected, however my life had always challenged me, so I took it all in stride.

I was fascinated as I listened to the DP's stories since they were something I could relate to. They all appeared to have common themes: most of them had been displaced from their homes either by war or acts of terror committed by their Soviet occupiers, they had fled to an unknown destination seeking safety, they had very few resources along the way, and they were weary of their travel. It all sounded so familiar to me, after all, that fairly described Father Heinrich's and my journey across Europe. Fortunately, we had the use of a motorcar and a great support system thanks to the Catholic Church. Perhaps my previous experience was why I was able to be so helpful; I could feel their pain.

Although I truly enjoyed Geneviève's mentoring, I especially treasured her friendship. Growing up, I didn't have any friends other than my immediate family and what I missed most was having a sister, and that's what she became to me; my sister.

I felt we had a lot in common, however we were really about as unlike as two people could be. I guess what attracted us to each other was that we shared a common love of life. To us, each moment was a treasure to be valued, not wasted.

Geneviève told me she had grown-up in a well-to-do Parisian family and had enjoyed all the privileges that went along with the family's social position; trips to the Palais Garnier, the Louvre, lazy picnics along the River Seine, and motorcar trips to the beautiful outlying chateau country to enjoy their world-famous wines and hospitality. That all changed on June 14th 1940, when the city capitulated to the Germans in order to save it from destruction.

She told me she and her father had stood on the tree-lined Avenue des Champs-Elysées and watched as the German occupiers marched past them with the sounds of their hobnailed boots echoing off the nearby, historic buildings. She said it was the only time she had ever seen her father cry. On the way back to their comfortable townhome in the exclusive Arrondissement de Passy, she said her father had turned to her and said, "I *must* do something." That 'something' turned out to be organising a citywide resistance to their much-despised German occupiers.

After that, her life, and her entire family's lives, had instantly changed from that of a very well-off Parisian family to a life of intrigue, danger, unsavory underworld characters, and secret meetings in the catacombs and sewers that crisscrossed under the old city. She said it was quite exciting, but extremely dangerous. Since she was only a ten-year-old girl, she became her father's most important courier as she rode her bicycle through the streets of Paris carrying secret messages hidden within its hollow handlebars. If she were ever stopped, searched and the hidden documents discovered, dozens of Parisian resistance members, including her father, could lose their lives.

She said she feared for her father's safety more than anything else and although she tried to live the normal life of a ten-year-old, she lived in constant fear. Every knock at their door, every unknown car or truck that parked outside their townhouse, every German soldier that seemed to pay extra attention to them as they walked down the street, all these simple daily events filled her with dread, and she found that she couldn't sleep at night and her health soon began to suffer. Finally, her family sent her to live with relatives in the outlying Parisian suburb of Vincennes and although removing her from her life of intrigue ensured her immediate safety, it didn't remove her from the constant torment of worrying about her family's safety, and she returned home to be with her family.

Of course, she was telling me these stories thinking I was a German citizen who had grown-up in Rottach-Egern as I had yet to tell her *my* true story. She would often stop during our many discussions and apologise for hurting my feelings as she relentlessly insulted the city's German occupiers. I would eventually reveal my true self to her; however, it took some time before I felt she was ready to hear *my* story.

What struck home was when she told me how brutally the Germans had treated the city's Jewish population. Beginning in 1942, all Jewish citizens residing in the city had to wear the dreaded, yellow Star of David on their outside clothing. As she was telling this to me, I felt their pain just as my family had and how my grandfather had told my father to wear it as a badge of honour, not a badge of shame.

Furthermore, to insult the Jewish population, they were forced to ride in the last car of each subway train on the Paris metro. However, what actually distressed me the most was when she told me that the pro-Nazi French authorities had rounded up more than thirteen-thousand Jews, mostly from the predominately Jewish suburb of Marais, and had transported them to Auschwitz, where they were immediately murdered. When I asked her when that was, she said it was in July 1942.

July 1942? *I* was living there in Auschwitz in Doktor Mueller's house and my thoughts immediately raced back to being awakened in the middle of the night by that *verdammt* train's incessant tooting, and now I knew many of those trains were delivering those same terrified, French Jews to their deaths. *I was there!*

This is the first time I've mentioned that Auschwitz was also a death camp since I wanted to talk about it within the context of Doktor Mueller's involvement. However, since I've now mentioned it, perhaps this would be a good time to discuss it.

Although I was a young, Polish peasant girl, I wasn't naïve. When I was living in Auschwitz with Doktor and Frau Mueller, I suspected the camp was more than just a resettlement camp, however I truly loved and trusted Doktor Mueller, and above all, I *wanted* to believe him, I *needed* to believe him in order to survive. I know it's difficult for anyone to understand how I felt, but he had just yanked me out of the selection line as I watched my entire family disappear into the misty darkness on their way to uncertain destinies and if I had thought for one moment they would soon be murdered and I'd never see them again, could I blissfully continue my life as though nothing had happened? No, I needed to hope against all hope that I would see them again and that we would soon continue our rural lives reunited once again as a family on our new farm somewhere in Russia.

I would often lie in Anna's bed at night wondering where they were and the visions of my little brother, Chaim, and my mother walking hand-in-hand to collect eggs in his little wire basket and the friendly little wave he gave me as they disappeared walking hand-in-hand to their deaths that night in Auschwitz, frequently came back to haunt me. Often, when Meyer and I walked hand-in-hand through the streets of Munich, I would suddenly stop, and think of Chaim and my mother walking hand-in-hand just like he and I were. He'd ask me if there was a problem and I'd cheerfully make up some excuse such as I had a pebble in my shoe or some other lame excuse, but walking hand-in-hand always meant something more to me than just a casual, thoughtless act. To me, it was an act of true love.

Many people don't realise that the Russians, not the Americans, actually liberated Auschwitz shortly after Doktor Mueller and I had fled to Bavaria, and it was one of the first concentration camps to be exposed. However, the Russians downplayed its true nature, perhaps because of similar crimes committed at their own Majdanek concentration camp, perhaps because of competing news about the Allied summit meeting at Yalta, or perhaps they just wanted to downplay the Jew's suffering for propaganda purposes, or perhaps a combination of all three.

# Innocence Lost - A Childhood Stolen

When news of other Nazi concentration camps began to appear and their roles as death camps were exposed, I hoped that since the Russians had downplayed Auschwitz's true nature, perhaps there was a small chance it had been different, truly a resettlement camp as Doktor Mueller had frequently reassured me. Once again, hoping against hope, however it wasn't until I had met Meyer that I discovered how terribly foolish I had been, all along.

Geneviève and I made a wonderful couple, if that's what you'd call us as we enjoyed each other's company, both at work and at play. Munich was in the midst of an energetic revival; full of hope, yet to be fulfilled promises of the future, and youth. Young people flooded into the city, including Geneviève and myself, drawn there by its golden promises; the golden ring on the carousel. It was a heady time, indeed.

Even though we both enjoyed the city's energetic resurgence, we still had to deal with the DP's we helped every day. Although we were surrounded by Munich's newfound prosperity, we couldn't overlook the fact that many of the city's newest residents were homeless, destitute, and needy as she and I would often search the nearby Perlacher Forest looking for their hidden camps. Like any modern city today, Munich's homeless had to struggle with many everyday necessities we often take for granted; shelter, food, and safety. Munich in 1950 was no different from New York City in 2011; the homeless needed a support system, and that's what the Red Cross attempted to provide on a limited basis with a stretched-thin budget.

Geneviève and I frequently struggled to overcome our daily challenges and after we recognised the need for better organisation and took the appropriate actions, the resettlement process became easier. Notice I've used the words *'resettlement process'* in what I think is their proper context; unlike the Germans at Auschwitz, we actually *resettled* people, not murdered them.

It was Thursday, June 7th 1951, and it had started like any other hot, summer day at the Red Cross; however, it would end up being one of the most important days of my life.

## Meyer Cohen

I had just walked into the lobby of the International Red Cross office. I was a bit late; I had overslept, and I had rushed to get ready, and then I had to walk through the already oppressive summer heat to get to my office. I really looked a mess.

As I walked through the front door, Geneviève had just stepped out of the administrative offices, clipboard in hand, and she gave me a knowing smile acknowledging my penchant for sleeping late, something she had reproached me for several times in the past.

"Sorry," I exclaimed as I rushed past her and headed towards my office. Just as I was about to close the door and get caught up on the backlog of cases already beginning to accumulate on my desk, I overheard her shout above the din of the crowded lobby, "Meyer Cohen. Is there someone here named Meyer Cohen?"

Meyer Cohen, Meyer Cohen. Where had I heard that name before? Then, like a lightning bolt, it struck me. Could it be the same Meyer Cohen my brother Lev had joined when he fled Uncle Addam's Warsaw apartment as the German soldiers were banging on the door?

I turned and rushed back into the lobby just as an extremely handsome young man approached Geneviève and was about to follow her into her office. "I'll take this one," I breathlessly announced as I grabbed the clipboard from her hand.

"Okay," she said, stepping back a pace or two, surprised by my bold move. "He's all yours."

All mine. *What an interesting way to put it*, I thought, as he followed me into my office. He certainly looked familiar, although it had been more than eight years since I had last seen him. The first thing I noticed was the cute little dimple smiling at me from the center of his chin, and the second thing I noticed was his smile; a charming smile that immediately captured my heart. If I had known who Tom Cruise was at the time, I would have called it a 'Tom Cruise smile', but at the moment, I just called it a 'yank the beating heart out of my chest' smile.

Meyer sat politely opposite me as I read his intake sheet.

- Age: Twenty-six.
- Place of birth: Warsaw.
- Occupation: Unemployed, but looking.
- Place of Last Permanent Residence: Dresden, Germany.

I tried hard to contain my excitement. The only two things I could confirm were his age and his birthplace, while the other two I would have had no knowledge of, so I decided to dive right in, "So, Mr. Cohen, what brings you here today?"

"Meyer, please. When you call me Mr. Cohen, you make me feel like an old man," his smiling reply.

"Okay, Meyer. What brings you here today?"

"And you are?"

"Anna. Anna Mueller."

"Well, since we're now on a first name basis, Anna, I guess I can take you into my confidence. I want to immigrate to Israel, but I don't have any papers."

"Israel? That's an interesting choice, Meyer. Why not the United States like everyone else?"

He smiled his million-dollar smile at me, once again, "First of all, I'm proud to tell you, Anna, I'm Jewish, and my Jewish soul wants to connect with its ancient heritage in its homeland, Israel. I'm sure you're well aware that Israel is once again a country with its own government, borders, and internationally recognised status, so should it be any surprise to you that I would want to live there?"

"I suppose not, Meyer. It's just refreshing to hear a destination other than the United States and I envy your desire to connect with your heritage," I honestly replied. Of course, I had completely repressed *my* Jewishness, and his mentioning connecting with *his* heritage made me feel somewhat ashamed that I had disconnected from *mine*. "Why don't you tell me a little bit about yourself and perhaps we can help you reach your destination, Israel?" I continued.

He appeared to relax when I expressed my apparent interest in him. "I'm not too sure what you are looking for, but I was born in Warsaw, Poland and grew up there in a predominately Jewish neighbourhood. It was a pleasant place to live until 1939 when Germany invaded Poland, but I'm sure you're fully aware of *yours* and *my* country's history."

His referring to '*my* country's history' rankled me; it was as though he was blaming me for his miseries without knowing exactly who I was or what my origins were. I was from Poland, not Germany as he had apparently assumed, however he had yet to discover that.

He continued, "As the war progressed, the Germans began treating the Jews in my neighbourhood as though they were animals unworthy of sharing the same planet with them. They treated us poorly, and they kept jamming our already overcrowded neighbourhoods with other Jews, outside Jews, ones that may have shared our same religious traditions, but perhaps not the same values. Eventually, they built a wall around our neighbourhoods, a virtual cage to contain the wild animals as they now viewed us, lest we escape into the other parts of the city and devour its non-Jewish residents. It was absurd and terribly demeaning."

I interrupted him, "I'm so sorry to hear that, Meyer. It must have been awful," without revealing that I, too, had lived in that 'cage'.

"It was more than awful, Anna, it was horrible. Of course, I'm sure you never had to go through anything like that yourself, so it's probably difficult for you to imagine those feelings, but take it from someone who has lived through it, it's nothing you'd ever want to experience."

I just nodded my head in agreement.

"Finally, some of us had enough and we decided that instead of cooperating with our occupiers, we'd defy them; show them we were their equals, if not their superiors. How many times did I hear them refer to themselves as the Master Race? The Jews walked this earth long before *their* fair-haired, Aryan hobgoblin ancestors did. Master Race? Hah. Of course we knew from the beginning our uprising was a futile one; just a handful of ill-equipped Jews against the overwhelming might of the entire German Army, but it was a protest, not a military campaign."

I sat there entranced by his soliloquy and the power of his *language* as I eagerly waited for his confirmation that he was, indeed, *the* Meyer Cohen I so needed to talk to. I had been there in the Warsaw ghetto, too, however the magnificence of his language far exceeded what would have been my feeble attempts if I were to describe to him what he had just described to me.

"One-by-one, they cleared the neighbourhoods of the caged animals until there was hardly a Jewish soul left in sight. A deathly quiet then enveloped the neighbourhoods as the few of us left hidden behind anxiously awaited our fates. We knew that once the neighbourhoods had been cleared of the ferocious Jews, the Germans would undoubtedly come in and level all the buildings, which they did. We did our best to thwart their attempts, but they ruthlessly tracked us down like rats in a sewer, which we were literally becoming. Fortunately, I was able to flee and make my way out of the neighbourhood; it was just a lucky break that I discovered a sewer exit not guarded by the Germans."

Before he could say another word, I interrupted him. "You just said you escaped through the sewers? Was there anyone else with you?" I asked, knowing his answer would reveal his true identity, one way, or the other.

"There was, but we parted company right before I escaped."

"You say *he*; did *he* have a name?" I asked holding my breath.

"He *did. Lev Kabliski.*"

I sat there, stunned. That was the first time I had heard my brother's name uttered in more than eight years and I wanted to jump up out of my chair, run over to Meyer and hug him, but I refrained for the moment.

He must have noticed my surprised reaction. "Did I say something wrong?" he asked. "You act as though you may have known him. Did you?"

I lied. "No, I didn't know him. It's just that I realised how a decision made in a fleeting moment could so drastically change a person's life. You obviously made the right decision. Do you know if Lev Kabliski successfully escaped as you did?" I asked, hoping to hear good news.

"No, probably not, although I don't know for certain. For all I know, they probably tracked him down and killed him as there were only a handful of us who escaped the German's pursuit, and he wasn't among us. Sadly, I never saw him again after we had parted in the sewers."

When I heard Meyer say Lev had probably been killed, hunted down like a rat in a sewer, I couldn't help myself, and I began to cry. Meyer was so sweet; he took a clean handkerchief from his pocket and handed it to me.

"I apologise for upsetting you so. I hope I didn't offend you," he offered apologetically.

"No, Meyer. It's such a sad story, a touching story that I couldn't help but react the way I did," not wanting to tell him he had just delivered confirmation of the first death of someone in my family; my dear brother, Lev. The other confirmations would eventually follow, but not right now. "Please tell me more about Lev Kabliski; he must have been your friend."

"Lev was more than a friend; he was truly my brother. He wasn't a city boy like me; he grew up on a farm somewhere in Poland and he always made me laugh as he recounted what it was like living on a small farm. They had a horse, chickens, a cow, rabbits, and some sheep. Nothing I could relate to. He told me that sometimes the Christian families would invite the family over to share a roasted pig. Pork? I'd ask him. You eat pork? Well, he'd just smile and say, 'Leviticus 11:6 says the Jews shouldn't eat pork; the animal is unclean. Of course, I'm not sure if Leviticus, whoever he was, ever lived on a subsistence farm like we did.' He'd then crack up as he continued, 'When I mentioned this to my father, he'd say, 'Sorry, Lev, even if they scrubbed the big, fat hog up extra clean, you'd never catch anyone in our family eating pork.' So, you ask me if I knew him. What more can I say?"

His humourous answer dried my tears with my laughter as I could just hear my father say "Even if they scrubbed the big, fat hog up extra clean, you'd never catch anyone in our family eating pork."

When I glanced at my watch, I was amazed to see it was already lunchtime. Somehow, the time had passed us by as we talked about Meyer, his life and his friend. "Would you care to join me for lunch, Meyer?" I asked.

"Sure. I have nothing better to do," smiling that unforgettable smile.

## Our Courtship Begins

Meyer and I walked down Tegernseer Landstraße on our way to lunch as we continued our conversation. The ancient linden trees lining the street were in full blossom and the dainty, white flowers' fragrance followed us all the way to the little outdoor café where we were headed on our first date. Of course, he didn't know it was a date, he just thought we were going out for lunch, however if I had anything to do with it, it would eventually wind up being called our 'first date'.

The café was quite crowded and we had to wait a few minutes for an outside table. We could have been seated at an inside table right away, but I wanted to sit outside, somewhere where I could see his handsome face, not at some dark, secluded corner table; although later, that would become my preference.

When the waiter finally led us to our table, Meyer raced him around the table to make sure *he* was the one pulling my chair out for me. It was rather humourous watching them jostling one another for the best position, and I'm glad when Meyer finally won.

Once we were seated, being the gentleman he was, he immediately attempted to steer the conversation away from himself and in my direction, instead. His curiosity posed a real dilemma for me. Although I was flattered, I wanted to be up-front with him right from the beginning as too much of my life had already been spent living lies, and it was important for us to start what I hoped would be our new relationship on an honest footing. Our new relationship? I *was* being rather forward, wasn't I? For all I knew, he might be married with a large family waiting for him to return from his visit with good news.

"What would you care to know about me, Meyer? My life doesn't sound nearly as interesting as yours." and with that mundane first question, we began our lifelong conversation.

"I don't know, Anna. It seems as though I've done all the talking since we first met. Now, I'd like to know something about you, if you don't mind," he asked through his million-dollar smile.

What to reveal and what to hide?

"Meyer, I don't mind spending a couple of minutes talking about myself, but I *do* need to know more about *you* since you're the one who has asked me for help. There isn't much to tell. I spent most of my teenage years in a Bavarian town called Rottach-Egern just south of here, and that's where a wonderful retired professor taught me the love of language. That's why we can sit here and speak in Polish; it's all possible because of dear Professor Krumpfelder."

Meyer interrupted, "I wondered why you speak Polish so fluently, especially since you're now telling me you grew up in Germany."

I smiled, "I'll take that as a compliment, my being fluent in Polish, that is. Now let's talk about you, Meyer." As I hoped that I had just revealed enough to satisfy his curiosity, for the moment, anyway.

"I'm not sure what you'd like to know; however, I don't think we have enough time today to hear my entire story. Perhaps we can meet again. Would you care to order?"

The remainder of our lunch 'date' was spent talking about Munich, the Cold War, and other pleasantries, and before we knew it, it was time to return to my office. When we parted at the front door, he asked if he could stop by the next day and being a Saturday, perhaps we could take a leisurely walk through the nearby Perlacher Forest. He said it was a popular destination because of its many kilometres of walking and biking paths; which I already knew. I tried to appear as though I reluctantly agreed, although if he hadn't asked *me*, I would have asked *him,* instead.

The rest of the afternoon was like any other afternoon, with one exception; I couldn't wait to see Meyer Cohen the next day. Not only did I want to learn more about my brother, Lev, I also wanted to learn more about Meyer. Was he married? Did he have a girlfriend? What did he do after he escaped Warsaw? Of those three questions, only two truly mattered to me.

We agreed to meet in front of the Red Cross building at noon the next day and when I walked out a few minutes early, I was surprised to see he was already sitting there holding a small bouquet in hand.

The moment he saw me, he got up, and walked briskly towards me. He handed me the bouquet with a smile, "Hi, Anna. These are for you; I picked them along the way. I just couldn't resist. So, are you ready to take a stroll?" he asked.

I took the bouquet and held them to my nose, *"Chciałbym (I would like to),"* I replied. Like the day before, our walk down Tegernseer Landstraße was a pleasant one as the linden's marvelous fragrances followed us as we casually strolled, lost in conversation. Like us, there were other people walking down the boulevard's broad sidewalks and they were just as engrossed in conversation as we were. Within a couple of blocks, we finally arrived at the forest's main entrance at the corner of Tegernseer Landstraße and Münchner-

Kindl-Weg where there were a few wooden benches set back in a small grove of evergreens, private yet near the main thoroughfare.

"Shall we?" he asked as he led me over to one of the benches. Of course, my first instinct was to come up with some clever reply as I used to do with Doktor Mueller, but all I could say was, "*Dobrze (Okay)*." Our little word game would have to wait until I got to know him better.

After we had sat down, he turned to me. "Tell me more about yourself, Anna. You hardly told me anything about yourself yesterday. It was all about *me,* and I'd like to know more about *you*; get to know *you* better."

I didn't want to talk about myself as I had already revealed everything I was willing to reveal during our lunch 'date' the previous day. "Meyer, I'm sure we'll have plenty of time in the future to discuss my rather boring life, but yours is so interesting, so intriguing, and I'd like to hear more about your life in Warsaw. You told me yesterday that you had a friend named Lev Kabliski. If you don't mind, I'd like to know more about you and him. Where did you meet him? What kinds of things did you do together? What was it like to fight the Germans in the ghetto? Things like that; things I can't even begin to imagine."

"Anna, you appear to be quite interested in Lev. Is there any particular reason you're so interested in *him*?"

"Not really, Meyer. He just sounds like a brave man and since he can't speak for himself, perhaps you could speak for him," my quick-thinking reply to Meyer's thoughtful question.

"Anna, it's funny you should call him a man; he was barely sixteen-years-old when I first met him. He was more of what I'd call a gangly teenager, someone barely on the brink of his manhood, but he was tough. I guess life on the farm suited him well and I've never met a person with such strength, both physically and emotionally."

How true his words rang in my ears as I don't think I could have described my beloved Lev any better than Meyer just did; him chopping wood by the barn spoke to his physical strength, however the family greatly depended on him for his moral character, his courage and wisdom that far exceeded his years; those spoke to his emotional strength.

Meyer continued, "He and his family fled their farm after the Germans came through their village and burned it to the ground. They eventually wound up living with his grandparents in an apartment in Warsaw, next door to my family."

I was curious about what else he remembered about my family. "You said he fled to Warsaw with his family. Do you remember any of them?"

"Well, I remember his parents, his little brother, and his cute little sister named Mira, however I didn't get to know them as well as I got to know Lev."

So, I was Lev's cute little sister. Wouldn't he be surprised if he knew he was sitting next to her at that exact moment!

He continued, "We all realised the Germans would eventually force us out of our homes and take us away like they had already done in other nearby Polish cities, only we just didn't know when. We learned through friends that some neighbourhood men were forming a group to commit acts of resistance against the German occupiers, and Lev and I were one of the first ones to join. We were lightly armed; it was a resistance of small acts meant to frustrate rather than defeat the Germans. It wasn't until the *Powstanie w getcie warszawskim (The Warsaw Ghetto Uprising)* a year after Lev's family left, that it truly became an armed rebellion."

Just hearing him talk about it brought back terrible memories of our last days in Warsaw. "You said Lev's family left Warsaw. Did Lev remain behind?"

"He did, however I shouldn't have said his family had *left*; I should have said, instead, they were forcibly *deported* to Auschwitz and we never heard from them again. Both Lev and I fled the apartment building just as our families were being brutally dragged out of their apartments, loaded into trucks, and taken away, however the Germans didn't deport everyone in the ghetto at the same time. Instead, they dragged it out over many months, one terrified block at a time. I'm not too sure why they did it that way, however living with the fear that *your* block might be the next one they cleared out, was excruciating. You didn't know until the trucks pulled up in front of your building that today was the day. Can you imagine the torture of living with that dreadful anticipation, day-after-day?"

His raw emotions touched me as that must have been what my parents and grandparents had talked about in hushed whispers; they had made it through one more day, but what about the next day? I have to admit they did an admirable job of hiding it from us children; however, hearing it now drove pangs of anguish through my heart.

"Meyer, I can't even begin to imagine living with something like that on a daily basis." Although I had been there, my family had effectively sheltered me from the fear. "You said you and Lev remained in Warsaw for almost a year after his family had been deported. How did you survive on your own?"

Meyer abruptly stood up and stretched. "Anna, I'm getting a little stiff sitting here. Why don't we continue this conversation as we walk?" I had to agree as we fled this 'bench of sorrows'.

## Our Walk in the Forest

As we began walking down the path into the forest, I could feel Meyer's hand innocently probing for mine; however, I quickly stuck my hands into my pockets as I wasn't ready to make that commitment, not yet anyway. He didn't say anything; he just took it in stride as he also stuck both his hands back into his pockets. Although his acknowledging my reluctance was a small gesture on his part, over time I came to know him as one of the most sensitive human beings I've ever met; always tuned into my feelings.

After a few moments of awkward silence, Meyer continued our walking conversation, "Anna, you asked me how Lev and I survived on our own and I have to tell you that it wasn't easy. Finding shelter was no problem, after all, there were literally hundreds of nearby empty apartments; however, the biggest challenge facing us was finding food. At first, although the newly evacuated residents' larders were usually sparsely stocked, we had no problem rummaging through their contents. However, since there wasn't any refrigeration, fresh food soon rotted and we had to content ourselves with eating any non-perishable items we could find. Mostly crackers, hard cheese and things like that, however over time, not only did we have to compete with the remaining, starving ghetto residents who were also searching for abandoned food, we had to start fighting the rats. The rats were huge, gigantic, and often when we opened a closet door in an abandoned apartment looking for food, we'd find dozens of huge rats fighting one another for the last morsels. It was awful."

I couldn't imagine having to fight rats in order to survive. Although food had been a nagging issue during Doktor Mueller's and my flight from Auschwitz, we could always look forward to a hearty meal when we stopped for the night. Having to scrounge for food amidst overly-aggressive rats was something I couldn't begin to relate to.

I interrupted, "Meyer, I can't even begin to imagine how difficult life must have been for you and Lev, but why didn't you try to get away, flee somewhere where you could both be safe?" An obvious question, I thought.

"That's an interesting question, Anna, and one that I frequently get asked and I only have one explanation; commitment to our mutual cause. We all had agreed that we needed to remain in the ghetto to the last man and harass our occupiers as much as possible. Many of the other ghetto residents went about their daily lives as though nothing had changed; only their freedom to move about the city had been hampered. Big deal! They apparently didn't realise how dangerous their situation was becoming, or if they did, they didn't do anything about it. If I have to compliment the Germans on one thing, it was that they were masters of deception, perhaps understanding the Jews' collective psyche better than the Jews themselves and they played them like a fine instrument."

His eloquent words rang true. I, too, had often wondered why our Warsaw neighbours were so complacent; so willing to climb into the waiting trucks without protest, so willing to be shoved into the cramped cattle wagons without protest, and finally, so willing to stand in the selection line also without protest. His words about the Germans understanding the Jewish psyche suddenly made me realise they had been priming the Jews, and the entire world, for their ultimate extermination ever since they had come into power in the early 1930's. The *Final Solution* had been their unspoken goal from the beginning and they were such masters of deception that by the time the *Final Solution* truly became *final*, the Jews had no other choice other than to willingly comply.

I truly abhor what the Germans did to the Jews, *my* people, and I don't want to imply that in any way they bore any of the responsibility for the cruel treatment at the hands of their tormentors. It was despicable, inhumane, and morally unjustifiable and they were, are, still a proud people, however they were as much the victims of mass psychological manipulation as were the German citizens. To me, Meyer and his friends became the small, yet effective protesting voice of the ghetto's Jews; barely a whisper, yet, still a voice.

When we finally came to a small, sunlit clearing in the forest, Meyer pointed towards it, "Shall we?" he asked. Oh boy; I was so tempted to provide a clever reply; however, I held my tongue as we sat down in the warm grass.

Meyer leaned back on his elbows, his handsome face illuminated by the warm, summer sun. "Am I boring you, Anna?" he asked. "It seems as though all I talk about is the Jews and their problems. I'm sure it's difficult for you to relate to what I'm telling you not being Jewish yourself and I'm certain there weren't many, if any, Jews in your town. Were there?"

"Just two," I answered, but I wasn't ready to reveal the two Jews were just Professor Krumpfelder and me.

"Just as I thought," Meyer reacted to my statement. "That's why I feel it's important for me to speak to you as a Jew. I'm sure *you* were the victim of the German's loathsome propaganda as much as the Jews were, but on the opposite side. That's why I'm taking the time to present *our* side; maybe help you understand why it's so important for me to go to Israel. I want to be among *my* people; I want to breathe the same air *they* breathe, feel the same sun upon my face *they* feel, and worship the way *they* worship; all without the fear of hearing hobnailed boots on the street outside our apartment."

I reached over and gently laid my hand on his, "Meyer, that's kind of you to tell me about your feelings. They are so heartfelt and meaningful to me, so much so that it makes me want to do everything I can to help you achieve your dream of going to Israel and your story is so moving that it makes me feel as if I were there myself. However, although you obviously survived your ordeal, at least you didn't starve anyway, how did it finally end? What finally caused you and Lev to flee through the sewers?" as I desperately needed to connect with Lev's final hours.

It was obviously something Meyer needed to talk about, however I sensed his hesitation. Finally, he began speaking about the final uprising, "When the deportations from the ghetto first began, the resistance members were still under the impression that the Jews were being sent to labour camps or were being resettled somewhere in Russia. However, by the end of 1942, word had gotten back to us that they were being exterminated, not resettled, so we decided it was time to take action. We had some minor skirmishes with the Germans in January 1943, but on April 19th, Passover Eve, the Germans entered the ghetto in force, and we knew it was finally time to strike back. Unfortunately, we were only lightly armed and we knew right from the start that we'd be no match for the Germans. Between us we only had three rifles in each area, some pistols, minimum ammunition, some homemade Molotov cocktails, two land mines, and one submachine gun in the entire ghetto.

That was it; our brave army of about two-hundred lightly-armed souls against the might of the entire German Army's tanks, machine guns, artillery, and heavily-armed troops. However, we gave them one heck of a fight, we did. From barricade-to-barricade, street-to-street, building-to-building, and room-to-room as they relentlessly pursued us. I later heard that Jürgen Stroop, the German commander, paid us tribute albeit in a roundabout way. Although he referred to us as 'Polish bandits', he, himself, admitted we had fought a brave, though losing battle. By the way, he was arrested after the war's end and hanged from the gallows in Warsaw in 1952, not far from where the so-called 'Polish bandits' had so frustrated his troops."

I sat there totally engrossed in his recounting the ghetto's final days using such eloquent language, however I still needed to hear more about my brother, Lev's, final hours. "I'm sure what your group experienced must have been terrifying, but I *do* want to know more about what you did; you and Lev."

"Well, somehow in the confusion of the ensuing battle, Lev and I managed to separate from the others. Although we had started fighting as a group, one-by-one the group splintered off into smaller fighting units as it was our strategy to make the Germans also split their forces as they pursued us. Perhaps we would have a better chance fighting them one-on-one instead of one entrenched force against another. So, Lev and I ran down a narrow alley and ducked through a door into the basement of a deserted apartment building where we had lived for the past few weeks. Perhaps after we had escaped the ghetto, we might be able to join up with one of the outside resistance groups. We already had our rucksacks packed, ready to flee and right before we left the basement and headed to the sewers, Lev reached into his pocket and pulled out two, now worthless, thirty-złoty coins. He handed one of them to me and said that although we were now *brothers*, it was time we needed to go our separate ways and these coins would be what would bind us together, forever; a reminder of what we had suffered together and how we had now truly become one *soul*. So, we briefly hugged, and then we headed to the sewers. If you don't mind, Anna, I'd like to continue my story, but sometime later. Why don't we just sit here and enjoy the beautiful sunshine."

It was apparent that he, like me, was becoming weary of talking about the war, so we just sat there in the warm Munich sunshine and made casual conversation, including the next time we would meet; which I hoped would be soon.

## An Accidental Admission

Meyer and I met several times after our first walk in the forest, however I intentionally steered our conversations away from the war and focused more on lighter topics, one we could enjoy, rather than endure. Several times I sensed he wanted to tell me more about his war experiences, but like the first time he had tried to hold my hand, I withdrew my attention and successfully managed to change the topic.

We had so much in common and he often mentioned he couldn't understand why a Polish Jew like him could feel the same way about most issues as I, a German Christian, did. He said it was uncanny, as though we shared the same soul. Little did he know but we did; a common, ancient Jewish soul.

The more time we spent together, the more I began having very strong feelings for him although I had never experienced true love before, he was my first, and I do have to admit that my feelings for him must have been what true love felt like. In later years when my women friends and I would get together for idle chit chat, I was amused to listen to them talk about their first 'boy crushes' and their teenage feelings of giddiness, overwhelming desires, and how their priorities were hijacked by their overpowering longings to be with their boyfriends.

It might seem strange, however I never felt that way about Meyer. Our love, right from the beginning, was based on mutual respect and understanding. Of course, I was physically attracted to him as I'm sure he was to me, however I told him right up-front, the first time I'd share his bed with him would be on our wedding night. As I think back on it now, I'm certain he must have thought I was proposing to him before he even had a chance to propose to me. I only had two other rules; the first was that I wouldn't tolerate anyone who abused alcohol like Doktor Mueller did, and secondly, we would always be honest with each other. I know. I was breaking that rule right from the beginning, however, I don't feel I ever lied to Meyer, I just didn't fully reveal the truth at the beginning. Is that truly lying, I ask you?

We enjoyed many long walks (hand-in-hand), dinners sitting at secluded tables in our favourite restaurants, and hours just sitting and talking. We never seemed to run out of things to talk about, however, we carefully skirted the one topic we had avoided since our first walk in the forest.

When I finally did broach the subject, I don't know why I picked that particular moment. Somehow, I just sensed it was the proper time to revisit that conversation. Perhaps my curiosity just got the better of me, or perhaps there were still some missing pieces in Meyer's puzzle. For example, what had happened between the time he had escaped from Warsaw and the day he walked into my life at the Red Cross office? If we were going to be a couple, where we were obviously headed, I needed my husband to be a completed puzzle, not one missing a few pieces here and there. I needed to know and although I'm certain Meyer was surprised by my apparent ambush; it had been well planned.

I had spent the past couple of days laying the groundwork as it took me some time to assemble all the ingredients I needed to prepare my 'ambush' dinner. Geneviève had even graciously shared one of her precious bottles of French wine she had brought back with her from her recent visit to Paris to see her parents. Before Meyer's arrival, I prepared the main course in the community kitchen the Red Cross staff shared, and then I brought it back to my small apartment where I intended to keep it warm on my small hot plate. A card table I borrowed from the recreation room was set with the only two complete sets of plates, glasses, and silverware I owned. When Geneviève and I visited and shared some of her magnificent wines, she always served them to me in water glasses, so I'd just tell Meyer that was the way they did it in Paris if he questioned why I was serving him that way.

Imagine the look on his face when he walked into my tiny apartment and was confronted with my little surprise. "Anna, what's the big occasion? Why the fancy dinner setting?" His attempt at flattery was pleasing to my ears.

"Meyer, it's our first anniversary. It's been one whole year since we met. Did you forget?" I asked, with a counterfeit pout on my face.

"No, Anna, I didn't forget. I thought *you* had," as he deftly produced a bouquet from behind his back. "I picked them along the way. I hope you like them."

Meyer was such a sentimental old fool; he knew how much more I appreciated a handpicked bouquet than a store-bought one, and he always seemed to know exactly what I was thinking, but he didn't have a clue this time.

My dinner was a complete success beginning with the homemade *haluski* right down to Geneviève's wine. Well, the *haluski* wasn't entirely handmade; I did use store-bought noodles, however he didn't appear to notice. After graciously acknowledging his accolades over my culinary skills, I cleared the table and we just sat there at the small card table enjoying the rest of the wine.

I moved the small vase with Meyer's bouquet off to one side so I could better see his face when I finally started my long-planned conversation. In fact, I had rehearsed my opening lines quite often. "Meyer, it's been quite a while since we talked about it, in fact, it's been almost a year." I watched as he slightly cocked his head to one side in puzzlement. "However, I think it's time now to finish the conversation we began on our first walk in the forest. You left me hanging just as you and Lev parted in the sewers. What happened after that?"

"Anna, I didn't think you wanted to know about that. To be quite honest, I didn't think you were interested in the rest of my story. Why now?"

I knew he was going to ask that question, so I had also carefully prepared my answer, far in advance. "It wasn't because I wasn't interested in you and your story, it's just that I wanted to connect with the man you are now, not who you were back then, and now that *I love you*, I need to know what made you the man you are today." There, I had finally said what had been on my mind for several weeks!

"I'm sorry, Anna. Did you just say that you love me?" his startled reply.

"I did, Meyer Cohen. I just told you that I love you, and I have for quite some time now, *you 'Polish bandit'.*"

"Oh my," as he reached across the table and took my hands in his (one of the other reasons I had moved the flower vase). "I've been meaning to tell you the same thing for weeks now, but I didn't know how you'd react. To tell you the truth, I was more afraid of you than I was of my German pursuers in Warsaw. Anna Mueller, *I love you*, too," as he stood up, placed my hands to his lips, and sweetly kissed them just as Uncle Otto had done when we first met.

Although it was one of the sweetest moments in my life, it would have been magnified tenfold if he had called me Mira Kabliski, instead. When he sat back down, still holding my hands across the table, I continued our pleasantly interrupted conversation. "Like I was saying, I want to hear your story beginning with your escape through the sewers up until the time we met. It's important for me to know everything there is to know about the man I love."

He leaned back in his chair, withdrew his hands from mine, and crossed his arms across his chest. Whenever Doktor Mueller did that, I knew he was becoming defencive and I hoped the man I had just professed my love for, hadn't just as suddenly withdrawn from me. However, as I came to know Meyer even better, I discovered it wasn't a defencive move; rather it was his way of concentrating when he needed to focus on a particularly troublesome problem.

Meyer slowly began to slide the missing puzzle pieces into place. "When I emerged from the sewers, I expected to be met by a German firing squad, but instead, there was no one nearby except for some of my resistance friends running across an open field towards nearby woods. I soon caught up with them and we ran as fast as we could, expecting to hear the sounds of German troops pursuing us, but strangely enough, we were never followed. I'm sure they were more interested in crushing the rebellion rather than acting like hounds chasing hares. The Germans are that way you know, once they have their mind made up to do something, there's no stopping them."

I had to laugh; he had just perfectly described Doktor Mueller, Frau Mueller, and Frau Degenhardt in one sweeping statement.

"We wandered aimlessly for days, foraging for food where we could, sleeping at night where we could; always looking over our shoulders to see if the hounds were pursuing us. Finally, we were able to join a small band of resistance fighters near a Polish town called Łódź."

The mention of my grandparents' town immediately caught my attention, and for a moment I wondered if we had been there at the same time, but I soon realised that was long after we had been deported from Warsaw.

Meyer continued. "We wanted to go into Łódź to see if we could join up with other resistance fighters as we were tired and we needed food and shelter; however, we were told that the Jews living there had been rounded up and trapped in a ghetto just like Warsaw, so we continued on by foot."

"When was that?" I asked, now curious.

"I'd say it was sometime in the summer of 1944. Perhaps early June, if I had to guess. We didn't have a calendar; we just had to rely on the weather and when the sun rose and set."

As he talked, I tried to figure out where *I* was living as he and his band of resistance fighters made their way across Europe. If it *was* June 1944, I was living with Doktor and Frau Mueller in Auschwitz.

"Our band never stayed in one place too long as it was too dangerous and we had to rely completely on the goodwill of the local residents, however, we never knew when we approached someone where their loyalties lay, so we often resorted to thievery. If the Germans wanted to call us 'Polish bandits', then we'd gladly oblige them. We were truly amazed at the destruction as we travelled across Poland as every village had been destroyed, burnt to the ground, with nothing left; not even a kernel of corn in the silos. It wasn't until sometime in December when we finally found comfort. That's when we joined up with another band of resistance fighters in their camp just outside a Polish town called Bielsko."

Bielsko? A partisan's camp? *"Nikolas!"* I shouted, knowing the instant I said it, I couldn't take it back.

Meyer abruptly sat up straight in his chair. "Anna, did you just say *Nikolas*?"

That was something I hadn't planned for, not in my wildest dreams. "No, Meyer, I think you must have misunderstood me. That wasn't what I said," thinking quickly.

"Anna, if you didn't say *Nikolas*, what *did* you say?" he pressed.

"I don't know. Maybe it just sounded like I said *Nikolas*. Let's move on," I anxiously suggested.

"Anna, tell me the truth. Did you just say Nikolas, because if you did, we have a lot more to talk about other than what I did after I left Warsaw? Anna, I love you, but I don't sense you're being honest with me. Look into my eyes and tell me you didn't just say Nikolas."

By now, he was standing up, his hands placed firmly on the table, and leaning forward in my direction. I knew I would eventually have to let him know who I truly was, however I hadn't planned on it being that night. "Meyer, please sit back down, you're frightening me. I'll tell you the truth, but you have to promise you'll calm down and wait until you hear my entire story. Promise?" He nodded his agreement as he sat back down.

"I know Nikolas' name because I was there."

"Where?"

"At the partisans' camp outside Bielsko."

"*You* were in the partisans' camp? That's impossible, Anna. Utterly impossible. You said you were living in Rottach-Egern then."

"No, Meyer, I didn't say that. I said I spent my *teenage* years there. I was being very honest with you when I told you that. Truly, I was."

"I don't believe a word you're saying, Anna. Tell me, if you *were* there, when was it?"

"I think I was there the same time as you, Meyer."

"It can't be, Anna. The wine has gone to your head and you're speaking nonsense. If you were *really* there, what else can you tell me about the camp?"

I was struck by the absurdity of our current dilemma; was it even possible in my wildest dreams that Meyer had been one of the partisans in their camp at the same time we had been there?

I continued. "I remember we hadn't been there for more than a day when we fled the camp because the Germans were approaching. We tramped through a dense thicket to another camp hidden deep within a rugged swamp. It was truly an exhausting journey and Doktor Mueller carried me on his back most of the way."

Meyer brusquely interrupted me. "Wait, Anna. You must have heard that from someone else who was there. Perhaps from one of the refugees you helped. Anna, it can't be true. There weren't any women in the camp," and he crossed his arms in front of his chest, however this time I sensed it was now a defencive, not a pensive, posture.

"Meyer, I *was* there. Believe me, I *was* there. Remember when a group of Polish refugees arrived in the camp right before the Germans overran it? There *were* several women in the group and I was with them, but I was just a little girl then. Remember now? It was *you* that offered to help me down off the cart when we first arrived in the camp. That was *you*, Meyer, wasn't it?"

He just sat there stunned, speechless, looking confused. Finally, he looked right into my eyes, "You mean you're *that* Anna Mueller; *that* little girl who rode into the camp with the other refugees? I can't believe it; you're not being honest with me, Anna!"

I figured it was now or never. "Yes, Meyer, I'm the same Anna Mueller that you offered to help down from the cart, but I'm *not* Anna Mueller."

"I'm sorry, Anna. You say you're the same person, but you're not. I'm terribly confused. So who *are* you?" he loudly demanded.

"*Mira Kabliski!*" as I stood up and shouted out my name for the first time in many years.

"You're, you're," he stammered. "You're *Mira Kabliski*?" as he got up from his chair and rushed towards me with his arms outstretched. This time I didn't refuse his offer as I had in the partisans' camp, I rushed into his arms. "Yes, I'm Mira Kabliski, and I love you, Meyer Cohen, more than you'll ever know."

## The Bench of Two Sorrows

We just stood there by my little gaily-decorated 'ambush dinner' card table, hugging, not saying a word. It was such a huge relief to be able to reveal my true self to Meyer after all that time and I just stood there in his arms, shaking with a mixture of relief, anticipation, and a fear of how he might have reacted.

Finally, we separated; he took both my hands in his and looked at me as I stood there anxiously waiting to hear his next words. His tone of voice when he began speaking was comforting. "*Mira*, what you've just said is so overwhelming that it's hard to comprehend. I fell in love with a German woman named *Anna Mueller* and wound up, instead, with a Polish Jew named *Mira Kabliski*."

I quickly interrupted him as I didn't know where he was headed, "Meyer, I'm the same person you fell in love with; I just have a different name, my real name; that's all."

"Don't take me wrong, *Mira*. I'm not disappointed, sweetheart, I'm thrilled. However, your stunning revelation has made me feel somewhat foolish."

"Why, darling? You shouldn't feel that way. You've done nothing foolish," as I tried to comfort him.

"Oh, but I have. I think back on all the times I lectured you about how the Germans treated the Jews, assuming all the while you were German. How *you* couldn't even begin to understand *our* suffering, the brutal treatment *we* endured, how *we* struggled, how *we* fought our oppressors, and how *we* died defending our heritage. You sat there and listened patiently while all along you were one of *us; you* suffered too."

I took Meyer's hand and led him to my bed where we sat cross-legged, yoga-style, facing each other and spent the entire night talking about our lives, the struggles we had overcome, and marvelling at how our two Jewish souls had searched for each other until they finally connected in a small apartment in Munich.

Obviously, my revealing my true self to Meyer was a huge relief; however, I still had to maintain my Anna Mueller persona for everyone else, including Geneviève and the Red Cross staff. Of course, I just had to tell her about Meyer and our budding romance since there was no way of hiding it, although I was forced to conceal the true circumstances.

Although Meyer and I enjoyed our personal time together, I continued to work on the reason he had originally come to the Red Cross; obtaining a visa to emigrate to Israel. After the conclusion of the *Milkhemet Ha'atzma'ut (Israeli War of Independence)* in 1948, the new Israeli state witnessed its largest-ever immigration of Jews. This came at a time when Israel was in the throes of its greatest struggle for survival and continued throughout a period troubled by both security concerns and economic hardships.

Fortunately, the Israeli immigration authorities gave the Holocaust survivors first priority when issuing visas along with the Jews living in Muslim countries like Yemen and Iraq who needed immediate evacuation. The first immigrants to reach Israel were not only survivors of the Holocaust, they also came from DP camps in Germany, Austria, and Italy and some came from British detention camps in Cyprus. Even though the Jews were spread out throughout Europe and Russia, Israel had now become a vacuum cleaner lovingly drawing them back to their long-denied Promised Land.

When I had applied for Meyer's visa, unbeknownst to him, I also applied for *my* visa. There was no way I was going to allow him to leave Munich without me, however it was quite tricky since I had to apply as Anna Mueller, a supposed Holocaust survivor, without letting on who I truly was and without the Red Cross staff finding out. I was shocked and surprised when my visa was granted before Meyer's, however I didn't let him know, that would have to come later, and I wanted to surprise him.

The months flew by as we both waited patiently for Meyer's visa to be approved. Since he hadn't been in a concentration camp, he wasn't classified as a survivor; he was classified as 'other', a catchall phrase for the remaining Jews who wanted to immigrate to Israel and it was quite frustrating as we both watched a mass exodus of Jews head from our Red Cross office to Israel. Finally, in early October 1953, Meyer's visa was approved and I couldn't wait to share the good news with him.

It was Saturday, October 3rd 1953, a beautiful late summer, early autumn day in Munich. Since it was a special day, I thought it important to end our Munich relationship and start our Israeli relationship where it had begun — Perlacher Forest.

When we turned into the forest, he led me towards the benches where we had first sat that fateful day. When I saw where he was headed, I stopped, "No, Meyer. I can't sit there, that's our 'bench of sorrows'. Let's just leave it that way, okay?"

He tugged at me, "No, Mira, we have to sit there, there's something we need to get out of the way if you and I are ever going to find happiness together."

I reluctantly sat down next to him not knowing what it was we needed to talk about, although I perhaps suspected what was to come. I sat patiently next to him waiting for him to begin. Finally, the beginning of the long-avoided conversation began. "Mira, darling. If we are ever to find happiness together, we need to be honest with each other, *brutally* honest." Where had I heard *that* expression before?

"Do you remember when we sat up all night and talked about our lives?" How could I forget? "You told me then about how Doktor Mueller pulled you out of line when you first arrived at Auschwitz?"

"Yes, I remember, Meyer."

"Do you also remember telling me how they separated the arrivals into two lines?"

"Yes."

"Where did you think those two lines wound up?"

"Doktor Mueller told me the line on the left went to the showers to get cleaned up before they resettled them and the line on the right went to the hospital for medical treatment. I've always believed what Doktor Mueller told me, so why do you ask?"

"Think about it, Mira. If that were true, why did they send your father to the line on the left and your Uncle Addam to the line on the right? Does that make any sense to you? You told me your father had suffered grievous injuries when the German soldier hit him in the mouth as you were boarding the trucks in Warsaw. Shouldn't he have joined the hospital line on the right instead of the, so called, resettlement line on the left?"

The incongruity of what Meyer had just pointed out didn't register. "I don't know why, Meyer. It was just so confusing and none of us had time to think about it, we just followed orders. The left line went in one direction, the right, another. The lines' destinations were never revealed to us when we were separated, we just followed their orders."

Meyer sighed, a sign he was about to tell me something I didn't want to hear. "Mira, you know I truly love you and you're the last person in the world I would want to hurt, however when I tell you what I'm about to, please remember it's the truth that will hurt you, not me. Are you all right with that, Mira?"

"Meyer, I'm not sure what you're about to tell me, but I do love and trust you," I reassured him.

"I know you've told me on several occasions how you longed to rejoin your family someday on a farm in Russia. If we are going to be lifelong partners, I can't live with someone who constantly longs for that reunion because that reunion will never happen, Mira, because there are no resettlement farms in Russia. That was all a lie, a terrible lie; your family isn't waiting for you in *Russia*, they're waiting for you in *Heaven*; they're all dead. Didn't Doktor Mueller tell you that? Why didn't you make him tell you the truth?"

Suddenly, my world collapsed around me. "Meyer, you're lying. That can't be. Doktor Mueller assured me repeatedly they were safe and living on a farm in Russia. Why would he lie to me, Meyer? Why would he lie?"

[338]

"Mira, that's between you and Doktor Mueller, but I'm speaking the truth, please believe me," as he protectively put his arms around me as I broke down sobbing.

I have to admit I had always suspected Auschwitz wasn't a resettlement camp, however I needed to hold onto the slim chance my family *was* still alive and now I had to acknowledge the truth; they weren't. Forgive me for not mentioning it before, but I had confronted Doktor Mueller many times about where my family was and he constantly reassured me they were safe and healthy. It's just something I didn't want to talk about until now; our quarrels were just too painful to discuss with you. Finally, he told me he wasn't going to talk about it anymore and he angrily slammed my bedroom door in my face. I covered my head with my blanket and cried myself to sleep as he had truly hurt my feelings. When I confronted him the next morning, he apologised and told me he would help me find my family after the war had ended. That was the last time we had talked about it, however, after we had moved in with Frau Degenhardt, I would often overhear the conversations our guests were having about the camps. Some said they were horrible and the Germans would forever have that guilt hanging over their heads, while others said it was just Zionist propaganda aimed at getting support for a new Jewish state in Palestine.

It seems as though I had pushed the obvious signs into the back of my mind and had ignored them. *Why*, for instance, were there two ominous smokestacks in the distance that continuously belched greasy, black smoke, *why* did Doktor Mueller have the overwhelming urge to wash his hands when he came home from 'work', *why* had my father joined the line on the left when he was the one needing medical treatment, but most telling, *why* had the trains always arrived crammed with people and then had *always* left empty? *How* were the 'resettlers' getting to Russia? That was a long journey, so *why* the empty, departing trains?

We both sat silent with me surrounded by Meyer's love and him surrounded by the sadness he felt for having to tell me about Auschwitz; hurting the one he loved the most. Elisabeth Kübler-Ross once spoke of the five stages of grief and I went through each of them three times; so for me, there were fifteen stages of grief. I'm over it now; that was a long time ago, however reliving it now is as painful as hearing it the first time.

After a while, Meyer stood up, took my hand, and said, "*Idziemy? (Shall we?)*"

"*Będziemy (We shall),*" I replied, the ending of an old game Doktor Mueller and I used to play on our dash to safety across Europe and, now, the beginning of a new, lifelong game with Meyer.

By now, I'm sure many who read my story are asking why I wasn't angry when I finally learned the truth about my family's fate and that's a fair question to ask. I can only say that I *do* carry an ever-lasting fury deep within and sometimes I wish I could reach in, take hold of that fury, rip it out, shake it until it surrenders, and then throw it away.

But honestly, as hard as I try, it somehow always manages to elude me and sometimes I lie awake at night and admonish myself for being such a weakling, and yet, I'm always able to convince myself that it comes from being strong, not weak. To me, a weak person would have given up long ago and surrendered and if I had surrendered, I would have perished like my entire family.

Did I know all along what had really happened to my family? Of course; I'm not stupid. After the war was finally over and the world finally become painfully aware of the atrocities the Germans had inflicted on the Jews and other innocents, how could I not realise they had all been murdered that horrible night when we had first arrived at Auschwitz? However, as the saying goes, I was 'hoping against hope' that somehow they had survived. You have to remember that I was just a little girl at the time; a traumatised and abandoned, little girl. Unless you were there, you can't even begin to understand the terror, the confusion, and the unbridled hatred directed towards the new arrivals.

I know. Some may want me to direct my anger at Doktor Mueller, but you have to understand that he had become my saviour, my lifeline, my father-figure, my family; all that I had left. If I were to direct my anger at anybody or anything, it would at the *system* and the people who didn't rise up to protest and I don't really want to get into that; it's way too painful. You can try to sanitise it by calling it whatever you want; *Ethnic Cleansing* or *The Final Solution*, but you really need to unmask it and call it what it really was; the senseless murder and torture of millions of innocent people.

Earlier, I told you about Meyer's concept of God versus mine and I do have to admit that I'm finally beginning to understand and accept his point-of-view. If *my* caring God did exist, why would He allow these horrible things to happen? Perhaps, as Meyer pointed out, God has populated His planet Earth with something He calls His children; us. Perhaps it's really an experiment; an experiment to see how we all get along and if we are successful, He'll spread humankind throughout His Infinite Universe, but if we aren't, *"I, the Lord, will show no mercy or pity when that time comes. In my anger I will destroy the earth and every sinner who lives on it."*

## The Bench of One Happiness

As we got up to leave our 'bench of sorrows', he led me to its next-door neighbour. "Sit!" he commanded in an attempt to be light-hearted.

"Why?" I asked.

He tugged at me, "Sit down, Mira; there's something I need to tell you."

When we had finally settled comfortably on the bench, he took my hand and paused to catch his breath. "Mira, I've been thinking about us. It's been more than two years since we met, and I've come to love you more dearly than any man should be allowed to, however my undying love for you has created quite a dilemma for me."

That wasn't exactly what I had expected to hear. Was it possible this bench would turn out just like its neighbour, the one we had just departed; another 'bench of sorrows'? I waited anxiously for him to complete his thoughts, although I dreaded their possible destination.

"I know it may still take some time for the Israeli Immigration Bureau to issue my visa, however I'm confident they eventually will, and I'm willing to wait until then, but," he paused mid-sentence as my heart literally stopped. Where in the world was this conversation headed? I already had more bad news than I could tolerate, and I anxiously waited for him to finish his sentence.

I'm sure Meyer sensed my lack of enthusiasm to hear what he was about to say as he smiled that million-dollar smile, "But I can't leave here without you, and I *won't* leave here without you," and his beautiful, coal-black eyes pierced my soul as he looked directly into my eyes and asked, "Mira Kabliski, will you marry me?"

That wasn't the destination I sensed his thoughts were struggling to reach, and I was more than mildly surprised, to say the least. "Of course, I'll marry you, Meyer Cohen. Life without you would be empty, not worth living," as he took a necklace out of his pocket, one with a thirty-złoty coin hanging from it and lovingly placed it around my neck; my engagement necklace!

I've noticed you admiring my necklace from time-to-time, but until now I didn't feel it appropriate to reveal its true meaning. This is *that* coin, that *same* thirty-złoty coin my brother Lev gave to Meyer as they parted.

When Meyer gave it to me, he said it was the most meaningful thing in his life, and he wanted to share it with me, just like Lev had shared it with him before they had parted in the sewers beneath Warsaw. I've never taken it off since then, not even when I was in the hospital delivering my babies, and my family knows I still want to be wearing it when they bury me.

Before he said another word, I reached into my purse, "And I have something for you, Meyer," as I handed him both visas. "We're going to Israel, Meyer. Both of us; you and me."

"Our new 'bench of happiness'," as we kissed our first kiss as a newly engaged couple. However, I only had one piece of unfinished business before our upcoming departure for a new life in Israel and it was one I truly dreaded.

## The Long Overdue Confrontation

After some research, I had discovered that Doktor Mueller had taken a new name when he was ordained, he was now Father Anthony, and he was the Catholic priest in a small German town in southwestern Bavaria. Of course, I was filled with great anticipation and dread as Meyer and I pulled up in front of his church on our way to the ship waiting to take us to Israel. It was the first time I had seen the church, and it was smaller than I expected, or maybe I should say it was smaller than I had hoped. We sat there knowing my meeting with Father Anthony would be difficult, however it was one Meyer and I had discussed at length. If he and I were going to continue our new journey, Father Anthony's and mine had to come to an end before Meyer's and mine continued.

Finally, Meyer turned to me, "Do you want me to come in with you?" he asked.

Having him there with me would have been a great support, however I *started* this journey with Father Anthony on my own, and I needed to *end* it that way. "Thank you, Meyer, but this is something I need to do by myself," as I reached over and squeezed his hand, three times, of course. He leaned over and gave me a sweet kiss for courage as I got out of the motorcar and walked up the cobblestone pathway leading to the church.

The front door was open, so I walked in not knowing what to expect. Like most other Catholic churches we had visited, there was a cross hanging over the altar with a man I now knew to be Jesus hanging from it. There were two or three *babetshkes* sitting alone in the plain wooden pews, their heads covered with scarves, bowed in reverence, praying. There was no one else in sight.

There was a door at the rear of the sanctuary, which I assumed to be the door to Father Anthony's office. I tried to be quiet as I walked down the center aisle towards the altar and when I reached the stairs leading to the altar, I genuflected as I had seen Father Heinrich do so many times before. Later, when I mentioned this to Meyer, he told me I was crazy; Jews never genuflected, especially in a Catholic church. However, I had to remind him that whether it was a Jewish synagogue or a Catholic church, it was still *God's* house and my gesture was to *my* God, in *His* house, and to *my* God alone. It was just a continuation of the many conversations Meyer and I had about religion and our differing opinions on the subject.

When I got to the door, I gently knocked. "Come in," a familiar voice from behind the closed door greeted me.

I took a deep breath and slowly opened the door. Father Anthony was sitting at a small table eating a bowl of soup and when he saw me standing there, I thought he'd spill the soup all over himself as he dropped his spoon on the floor and jumped up to embrace me.

It had been several years since I had last seen him; in fact, I hadn't seen him since he had left for the seminary. He had aged considerably and put on some weight, too, his hair had turned completely white, and he had grown a goatee, which looked silly perched on the end of his chin. However, I immediately noticed his beautiful hands; those long fingers with perfectly manicured fingernails. Surgeon's hands, pianist's hands, artist's hands; I would have given anything for hands like his.

We embraced and as I buried my head in his cassock, I was immediately transported back to that fateful day in St. Mikolaj's Church when he had first stepped out of Father Tadeus' closet clad as a priest. Only this time, he was a real priest, not an imposter.

"Please sit," as he pulled out the other chair at the table. "Have you had anything to eat? Would you care to join me for lunch? It isn't much; I'm trying to watch my weight as you probably noticed."

"No, but thank you. My fiancée, Meyer, and I stopped on the way here to get something to eat."

Father Anthony picked up the spoon from the floor, casually wiped it on his cassock and continued our conversation between sips. I was startled by his actions having watched him so meticulously wash his hands every night after he came home from "work". What else had changed since I last saw him? "So you're engaged? That's a pleasant surprise. So, tell me, what have you been up to lately? It's been so long since you and I have been in touch, and I'm sure there are lots you want to tell me, especially since you have a new man in your life. How are you and Meyer doing?" he asked as the conversation we both dreaded having, began on a simple note.

"Meyer and I are doing well, thank you for asking," as he sat there smiling at me, a familiar face with an unfamiliar name. Although there was so much I wanted to tell him, the reason for my visit had one goal only, and I didn't want idle chitchat to get in the way. Perhaps I could find a way to begin our conversation, the one we had avoided for almost a dozen years. So, I began on a friendly, probing note, "Father, how did you choose your ordained name? I thought Father Heinrich suited you well."

"Ah, I wondered if you were going to ask that question. It's something I've been asked more than once. Perhaps you already know Saint Anthony is the patron saint of wayward souls, lost souls if you prefer. *Lost*, as you and I were as we wandered across Europe trying to find *our* sanctuary. Almost like the Ten Lost Tribes of Israel you told me about and how they wandered aimlessly trying to find *their* sanctuary after they were deported from the Kingdom of Israel. Even Moses, himself, wandered in the desert for more than forty-years trying to find *his* sanctuary, too. Of course, you and I didn't wander in a real desert on our journey; it was perhaps more of a *moral* desert, if you will."

Perhaps he had just given me the opening I was looking for, a way to begin the conversation I needed to have with him; the real reason for my visit. "It's interesting that you mention lost souls wandering in the desert looking for their sanctuary; a place for them to feel safe and secure. Although you may feel *your* journey to *your* sanctuary may have ended, *mine* hasn't, although the destination may be in sight. When Meyer and I leave here today, we're going to take a ship to Israel." There, I had said it and there was no taking it back.

"*Israel!*" he exclaimed in a typical Doktor Mueller tone of voice. "That's quite a shock to hear. Why Israel? Frau Degenhardt wrote to me and said you had a good job in Munich. Why in Heaven's name would you want to live in a godforsaken place like *Israel*? It's in the middle of the desert; no trees, no mountains, no greenery like here in Bavaria. It's the last place I'd ever want to visit."

I chuckled to myself. Hadn't Jesus been born in Bethlehem and wasn't that in ancient Israel? Wasn't that the holiest of holy places for Christians? I tried hard to suppress a smile since this was the beginning of a serious discussion. "You, yourself, just mentioned Moses, and how he led the Israelites out of bondage and persecution in Egypt in search of their Promised Land, *Israel*. A place where they could live in harmony with their neighbours and worship *their* God without interference. Well, the Promised Land has been officially returned to the Ten Lost Tribes of Israel. Israel is now a legitimate, recognised country, and Meyer and I want to live there."

He nervously tugged at his goatee. "I'm not too sure it's a good idea for the Jews to have their own country; after all they're the ones that started the last war and I'm sure they'll start more in the future."

At last Father Anthony had opened the door that needed to be opened, and I stuck my foot into it before he could close it. "Father, I know we've had this conversation many times before, however it never comes to a conclusion that we're both happy with, at least not me. I desperately need that conclusion before we leave here; it might be the last time we'll have a chance to talk about it."

When he tipped his almost empty soup bowl and slowly took his last sip of soup before answering, I knew him well enough to know he was just buying some time to think about his answer. "What do *we* need to talk about? I think I've made *my* position on the matter perfectly clear. What is it you want to know?"

Okay. This was it. "I want to know why the Germans murdered millions of Jews and why you didn't tell me my family was among them? Auschwitz was an extermination camp, not a resettlement camp. There never were any resettlement camps, were there? They were all extermination camps, weren't they? And you were part of that genocide, weren't you?"

"What do you mean *extermination camps*? Who put that silly notion into your head?" he answered quite gruffly. I could tell by his sharp rebuke that I had just stepped into territory that had been up until now, forbidden territory.

"Father Anthony. I truly love you like a real father, but I really need to know what *you* did at Auschwitz. Meyer and I have discussed this at length, but he didn't want to tell me. He said the words had to come out of *your* mouth, not his. So, tell me, Father. What *did* you do at Auschwitz?"

As I sat there patiently waiting for his answer, he appeared to shrink right before my eyes; the way my father had reacted when the stranger had ridden into town and told the villagers that Germany had just invaded Poland. I know now that I had just put him in a terrible position; however, I thought it was a subject he had dealt with long ago. Obviously, he hadn't.

He bowed his head and began softly sobbing as he finally revealed the truth to me. "Auschwitz wasn't *just* an extermination camp. It was a *work* camp, too. Do you remember when you arrived on the train at Auschwitz, and we separated your group into two lines? One line to the right and one to the left? The ones on the right went to the *work* camp."

"And where did the ones on the left go?" I asked, already knowing the answer; however, I wanted to hear it from him.

He put his head down onto the table and said in a soft whisper, "To the gas chambers."

He was beginning to get me angry. "I didn't hear you. Where did you say they went?" I asked in a much louder voice.

More loudly now, "To the gas chambers."

"And then where?"

"To the crematoria."

"And then where?"

"What do you mean, then where?"

"I meant what happened to them after the crematoria?"

"They pulverised their ashes and spread them in a nearby field!" he shouted.

His answers came so rapidly it was difficult to understand them. "Say it! Say it all in one sentence. I want to hear you say it all at once!" I demanded.

Father Anthony kept his head on the table, his hands clenched behind his head, his arms shielding him as though protecting himself from invisible blows as he shouted out. "They went to the gas chambers, then they took them to the crematoria, then they ground up their ashes, and then they spread them on a field behind the camp! There, I've said what you've been waiting to hear all these years!"

"What you're saying is that you killed my family, burned them in an oven, and then spread their ashes in a field. Is that what you're saying?" I shouted at his shielded head as my face started burning with anger.

"*I* didn't do any of those things to your family. *They* did! Not *me!*"

"*Who* did that to my family?"

"*They* did! The *others!* I was just a small cog in the *'process'*. Nothing more; just a small cog."

"A *'process'* you call it. A *'process'*? How dare you insult me with your semantics? It wasn't a *'process'*, it was *'pre-meditated murder'*, and whether you *personally* put a gun to my family's heads, or you *personally* dropped the Xyklon B pellets down the ventilation shaft and laughed as you heard my family desperately pounding on the locked doors screaming with their dying breaths as they choked on your poisonous gas, you're just as guilty as *them*, the ones who actually did it!"

Father Anthony suddenly sat straight up and looked directly at me. "No, no, you don't understand. I didn't have anything to do with that. I was just doing my job; following orders. I didn't make any of those decisions, someone higher up did. We were all just following orders; every one of us."

"Just following orders, you say! So, if Pope Pius ordered you to sacrifice one of your parishioners on the altar, would you do it?"

"Of course not, that's different."

I could see him beginning to get uncomfortable. "Why is that any different? An order's an order, right?"

"I don't know, it's just different. Pope Pius would never ask me to do something *immoral* like that."

"Ah. So, it's a *moral decision*. Right? When someone gives you an order that presents you with a dilemma and you have to make a *moral decision*, you should have the right to obey or disobey that order. Shouldn't you?"

"I guess so, if you put it that way."

Fortunately, our heated discussion had slowly begun to cool down somewhat, and I hoped we were just beginning to have an adult conversation that would strike at the heart of my own personal dilemma.

"You knew what was happening at Auschwitz, and every time you sent someone down the path to the gas chambers, you made a decision; a *moral decision*. Didn't you?"

"No. That decision was already made for us. Women, children, the infirm and elderly; they went to the gas chambers first. That was the rule. Someone else made that rule. I was only asked to make sure the adult males were healthy enough to go to the work camp. Nothing more."

"I hope you don't think that somehow absolves you from your *moral decision*, because it doesn't. Your participation in the whole '*process*', as you call it, should have posed a huge *moral dilemma* for you. Shouldn't it?"

"I don't know. It all made sense the way they presented it to us back then. The *Jews* were the problem, and the '*process*' was the solution."

"Didn't you for once think about what you were doing? How could you look those people in the eyes and not betray the fact that in a few short minutes, they would be dragging their lifeless bodies out of the gas chambers and burning them like trash in ovens. Didn't that bother you at all?" as I hoped Father Anthony could finally see the point I was trying to make.

"I guess I did at first, but over time I just got numb to the whole situation. I guess I could have protested, but to whom, and what good would it have done anyway? Would it have saved anyone from their fate? I don't think so. What do you think I should have done? Run up to the front of the line and warn everybody, or maybe just yell STOP! It just isn't as simple as you might think. You didn't understand *then*, and you don't understand *now*. You'll *never* understand. So, I ask you, what would you have done?"

His unexpected question puzzled me. "I don't know, but you blame the entire situation on the Jews, and I'm sure that makes it easier for you to justify what you did, but nothing justifies it. It was some crazy megalomaniac that started this war, not the Jews. They were just an excuse. It was just a convenient way to get you and the others, to follow him like the Pied Piper, and what did it get you in the end? The blood of millions of innocent victims on your hands and the death of many innocent civilians, including your beloved Anna. How many *Annas* did you send off to the gas chambers?"

The minute I said it, I knew it was the wrong thing to say, and I would have taken it back in an instant, if I could have.

Father Anthony stood up and angrily pointed his finger at me. "Leave Anna out of this! She had nothing to do with it. How dare you blame me for her death! I didn't send any *Annas* to the gas chambers. The ones we sent to the gas chambers carried the Jewish seeds we needed to eliminate before they grew into weeds; weeds that would only strangle our pure Aryan nation. I think you better go now," as he pointed at the door.

I just stood my ground. "I'm sorry, Father. It just slipped out. Please forgive me, but I'm not going to leave until I've had my say."

Father Anthony sat back down in his chair, his face red with anger.

I asked, "May I continue?" as he nodded his head, but didn't look at me.

I continued, "When I came here, I had hoped our conversation would be simple, as I hoped you would have already dealt with these issues by now, but obviously you haven't. You may wear the cloth of a priest, but you don't have the heart of a priest. Not yet anyway. I feel as though you're hiding behind your priest's garments because you're hiding from the *truth*. My entire motive for coming here was to hear you tell me the *truth* in your own words, not someone else's. Nothing more than that. Now I realise that you, yourself, haven't even begun to deal with the *truth*, let alone confess it to someone else like me, to someone you have unremittingly professed your love for. I've long since grieved for and accepted my family's cruel fate, believe me, I have, and it wasn't easy, but the *truth* is, what you did in the past, regardless of *why* you did it, was wrong; terribly wrong, and you need to come to grips with that."

Father Anthony looked straight at me, "I hear what you're saying, but before I can even start to come to grips with those issues, I need time to think it through; try to get things straight in my mind. Ever since I was a teenager, I was taught to hate the Jews. Hitler didn't teach us to hate the Jews; he just fanned the embers of hatred that were already there until they finally burst into flames. What he said made sense. After all, he had taken a broken, defeated Germany and turned it into a leading world power. What he did healed the wounded psyche of the German people, and if we needed more living space, so be it. If the Jews had to be eliminated, so be it. Anything he wanted, so be it. But now I *know* he was wrong and I *know* you speak the truth, child, but I don't know where to start. It's all so confusing to an old man like me."

"Maybe, Father, you could start by apologising to me and asking for my forgiveness. Maybe that will start you on the road to your salvation," as I looked straight into his eyes now clouded with tears. "Can you say you're sorry?'"

He looked at me and said in a seemingly humble voice, "I'm sorry, Mira. Truly, I am. I'm sorry for not being honest with you, I'm sorry for all the hurt I may have caused you, and I'm sorriest for the role I played in the mass murder of innocent Jews," as he ran around the table and hugged me in his arms. "I've asked God for his forgiveness many times, but I didn't know *why* I needed His forgiveness. I always thought I was doing the right thing, so I just tucked it away in the back of my mind and left it there to wither and die. Now you've unlocked that door and shown me the truth, and I'm so ashamed. Now I know why I need His forgiveness. I love you so much. I knew you were special the moment I saw you, and I'm so lucky to have had you in my life."

His thin lips curled up into a slight smile. "The tables have turned, haven't they? Once I was your saviour and now you're mine."

I ignored his lie about knowing I was special the moment he first saw me as he had already broken my heart when he had confessed that I wasn't special at all, but he had just called me Mira! He hadn't called me that in years. I had been his Anna ever since we had left Auschwitz, and I remembered he had once told me when it came time to discover who I truly was, I'd know the right answer. Was he trying to tell me this goodbye would be the ending of one journey and the beginning of another? A journey to discover who I truly was?

"I forgive you, Father," as I hugged him back, but did I truly forgive him? I still struggle to this day with whether I completely forgave him or not.

I guess we had said everything we needed to say about Auschwitz, so we spent a few minutes reminiscing about our motorcar trip across Europe in *EselKoń,* and then I remembered I had one more question to ask him. "Do you remember the hitchhiker we picked up along the way? When he told you he had killed the camp doctor, by the way you reacted, I would have thought maybe you knew him. Did you?"

He reached into his cassock pocket and pulled out a handkerchief to dry his eyes. "Yes. Very well, in fact. He was my roommate in medical school. We were best friends, and the last time I saw him was right before he left for Sobibor. My wife and I had dinner with him and his family, and then he left the next day. He had a wonderful family, and he was such a dedicated family man. He hated this war as much as I did, however we both had to follow orders. So sad."

Now I finally understood why he had reacted that way. "I'm sorry to hear that, Father, but why didn't you say something at the time? When you let the hitchhiker out of the motorcar, you gave him some bread and cheese and you even sent him off with your blessing. That just doesn't make any sense to me, especially when he had just confessed to killing your best friend."

Father Anthony paused for a moment. "Maybe I had seen enough killing. What good would it have done to kill the hitchhiker in revenge? Would it have brought Erich back? Of course not. Don't you think the killing has to stop somewhere? Why not with me?"

We sat for a few more minutes, knowing our final farewell was quickly approaching and when it was apparent our conversation was ending, he said "Just a minute. I have something for you," as he got up and left the room. He returned shortly, holding something behind his back.

He walked over to where I was sitting. "Did you forget something?" he asked as he deftly produced Alinka from behind his back and held her out to me.

"Frau Degenhardt sent her to me. She said you had left her behind, and I even finally mended her arm. Sorry it took so long; I'm not the greatest tailor, so forgive my clumsiness. I did the best I could with what I had, however I'm sure she won't mind now that she's whole again and is finally reunited with you."

I reached out and took Alinka from his hands. To be honest, even though she had been one of the most important things in my childhood, in the intervening years I had totally forgotten about her and I hoped she didn't think I had abandoned her.

Father Anthony walked Alinka and me to the front door of the church. The three *babetshkes* were sitting in exactly the same places as when I had first arrived. We stood there for a few moments saying our goodbyes, and then I turned and walked back to the motorcar where Meyer was patiently waiting. I looked back at the church just as one of the *babetshkes* was leaving. Father Anthony spoke briefly to her and then touched her forehead in blessing. Then, with a casual wave of his hand in our direction, he turned and walked back into the church. That was the last time I saw him, and I hoped our conversation had done him some good; maybe reconcile him with the God he so frequently prayed to. At least our final conversation had answered many questions for me, however it never answered why so many had suffered.

When I got into the motorcar, Meyer looked over at me as I clutched Alinka tightly to my chest just as I had when I first arrived at Auschwitz. "Is everything all right?" he asked.

I leaned over and kissed him lightly on his cheek. "I'm ready. Let's go."

I wish I could say this final chapter in my story will leave its readers reaching for a tissue to dry their eyes; tears of joy and happiness now that my story has drawn to a tidy conclusion, but it hasn't. I'm sure many expected a "Hollywood" ending; all the loose ends tied up neatly, a final collision between the protagonist and antagonist in one tear-jerking moment that leaves the audience teary-eyed as they watch the credits slowly roll up the screen; however, that's not the way things happen in life; not in mine anyway.

Although I had heard the words from Father Anthony's lips, I hadn't heard them from his soul. They sounded so shallow, so impenitent; they were words he wanted me to hear, but merely words, spoken, not heartfelt. I had come to know him well enough by that time that I was well aware of his deviously manipulative personality to know better than to take his words at face value.

I'm not certain he ever truly faced his demons. Perhaps he was the ogre in my nightmare, that shocking monster who swallowed my entire family in one fiery mouthful, or perhaps he was one of the leather-clad whip crackers I saw driving the Jews to slaughter; perhaps not, but he certainly wasn't the magnificent, white-robed spirit with the star-filled satchel over his shoulder who showed me the beautiful valley from the mountaintop. That he wasn't, for sure.

Doktor Mueller has haunted me all these years, and I can't for the life of me understand why I still love him so, even with all his faults and the role he played in sending my entire family to their deaths. I think it was the English poet, William Blake, who wrote, *"Without contraries is no progression. Attraction and repulsion, reason and energy, love and hate, are necessary to human existence."*

## My Long Journey Ends and a New One Begins

When we finally departed the ship in Haifa and got into line to meet with the Immigration officials, Meyer took my hand, "Be brave, Mira, be brave." Where had I heard that before? I had to reproach him; my papers said I was Anna Mueller and I was born in Germany. He just squeezed my hand three times and smiled at me; that million-dollar smile, the one that had melted my heart the first time I met him.

I knew when it was my turn to be questioned I'd have to make a life-changing decision on the spot. *Who* was I? *What* was my story?

*Where* had I come from? A challenge Doktor Mueller had presented me with many years before.

When I approached the Immigrations Official sitting behind the desk, I handed my papers to him. "Name!" he demanded.

I proudly pulled myself up to my full height. "Miriam Ruth Kabliski," I answered in a loud voice as Meyer gave me a curious look.

"Nationality?" he asked in a slightly bored voice.

"Jewish."

The Immigration official smiled. "I meant, where were you born, Miriam?"

I fidgeted a bit as I thought I had given him the answer he wanted. Finally, I realised he was asking my birthplace, "Poland!" I said proudly.

The official off-handedly stamped my papers with a loud clunk without even looking at them. "Welcome to Israel, Miss Kabliski."

As we left the Immigrations Building, I tossed my counterfeit Anna Mueller ID papers into a nearby ashcan, turned, and left them all behind, every one of them; Mira Bednarczyk, Bernadette Schneider, Anna Mueller, and I, *Mira Kabliski* — holding my future husband's hand — walked proudly out into the sunshine to freedom and a new life.

# - The End -

# Innocence Lost - A Childhood Stolen

**Author's Note:** *Meyer Cohen and Mira Kabliski were married in a traditional Jewish wedding soon after arriving in Israel. They eventually settled in a small town outside Jerusalem where Meyer attended The Hebrew University of Jerusalem and earned his law degree. Over a number of years, he was able to build a successful law practice and served three terms in the Knesset, Israel's ruling body. They immigrated to America in 1962 when Mira went to work at the U.N. as a translator, and they settled in the Bronx on Lydig Avenue in a traditional Jewish neighbourhood that greatly reminded them of their neighbourhood back in Warsaw. As in Israel, Meyer started a successful law practice until his retirement in 1995. After retiring, they moved to Sebring, Florida where they lived until Meyer's death in early 2003. After Meyer's death, Mira moved next door to my mother in Fairway Oaks, an assisted living facility in Venice, Florida.*

*After we had finished our last interview, she handed Alinka to me. "I want you to have her. She's now yours, so please take good care of her." Although I protested, she insisted. So, as I type this last paragraph in her story, Alinka is sitting on a shelf above my computer. Unfortunately, Mira never lived to read her story. She died on April 20th 2012, on her 80th birthday and her family buried her next to Meyer, along with her thirty-zloty engagement necklace prominently displayed around her neck. Now, Alinka sits there and looks down on me; a constant reminder of a remarkable woman, a remarkable life, and a truly happy ending.*

*Philip Sherman Mygatt, Englewood FL, November 15, 2018*

The author's email address is: *pmygatt@msn.com*

## My Research — Did Mira Really Exist?

Although I know that this story is a work of fiction and that Mira wasn't a real person, I was always haunted by that fact that I felt someone looking over my shoulder as I wrote her story. One day while I was having lunch with my good friend and fellow author, Dr. Edith Fiore, I happened to mention that I was writing this book and that I felt as though I was actually seeing the events unfold as I was writing them; as though I was being guided by Mira, herself. Dr. Fiore, who has had a very successful career as a psychologist specializing in past-life regressions and spiritual possessions, said that she had no doubt that Mira *was* guiding me and she encouraged me to do some research to discover if Mira was indeed a real person or just a figment of my imagination.

As Mira's story unfolded, it became obvious there were many parts of the story I could corroborate. For example, did Miriam Kabliski Cohen ever exist? Are there any immigration records showing that she and her husband came to the United States? Using a map, could I find the places in Europe she mentioned? These all presented challenges, but, fortunately, having access to the Internet provided immeasurable help. My major concern, however, was what if she was a real person, and what if she still had family living in the United States, or somewhere else? Would her family allow me to tell her story, or would they object? So, it was important to not only try to find out if she ever existed, it was also important to discover if she had any living relatives. If so, could I track them down?

When Mira first introduced herself, she called herself Mirka Kabliski, originally from a small village near Zelów, Poland. Later she corrected me and told me that her name was actually Miriam, Mira for short, not Mirka. Unfortunately, she never mentioned the name of her village, if it even had one. Since she claimed the Germans destroyed it in 1939, would it be possible to find a pre-1939 map of Poland and then compare it with a current map to see if there were any villages that existed in 1939 that don't exist on a modern map?

So, I decided to check all the villages within thirty-kilometres of Zelów, since her father often traveled there and back in one day. If he was driving a horse cart, thirty-kilometres would be about as far as he could travel in one day and return before sunset. This was an arbitrary judgment call, but I had to start somewhere. This might seem like a simple task, however, the borders of Poland have been extremely fluid and have changed many times during its long history. Unfortunately, after I had researched many different websites, I was unable to locate any pre-1939 maps that had enough detail to pinpoint tiny villages, and I had to admit that I had probably come to a dead-end.

Then, using Ancestry.com as my starting point, I tried to locate any records for someone named Miriam Kabliski who had been born in Poland in 1932. My initial research turned up both a Mirjam Kabliski and a Miriam Kabliski, who were born in 1933 in Krakow, Poland. As it turned out, they were the same person with different spellings of their first name; a common occurrence in genealogical research. When I checked the other household members' names, they were listed as Bronia and Izydor Kabliski; probably her parents. This most certainly wasn't the Miriam Kabliski I was looking for. I wasn't discouraged. After all, in her story she, herself, claims she had tried to find her birth records, but, if they had been recorded, they had probably been destroyed when the Germans burned her village in 1939.

The records I found for Mirjam Kabliski were from the archived Krakow Poland ID Card Applications for Jews during WWII. Perhaps I could search the ID Card Applications in other cities especially Łódź

[361]

where she and her family had initially fled. Then, I recalled she claimed her father had made them fake ID cards identifying them as non-Jews, so that didn't lead anywhere.

Perhaps I needed to try another approach. If she and her husband, Meyer, did immigrate to the United States sometime after 1950, there had to be immigration records somewhere. When I checked, what I did find was intriguing. There were, indeed, several immigrants named Miriam Cohen who were born overseas in the early 1930's who had immigrated to the United States, however, their information didn't quite match what was in her story; although they were tantalizingly close.

What about Meyer Cohen? I did locate a man named Meyer Cohen, born in Poland in 1927 who had become a United States citizen, however, it didn't record the date he was naturalized. This was the closest match I could find anywhere for a person named Meyer Cohen born in Poland. There were several men named Meyer Cohen who were born in Russia and then immigrated to the United States, however, Meyer's actual birth place is never revealed to us. There were quite a few other men named Meyer Cohen living in New York who had also become United States citizens, however, the only information for them was a name and a number on an index card; not much to go on.

As her story progressed, Mira mentioned very specific family names of her parents, brothers, grandparents, aunts, uncles and cousins. Could I track any of them down? Lev, Chaim, Ania, Adiya, Aaron, Efrayim, Emanuel and Schmaiah Kabliski. Were there records for any of them?

I found several Levi Kabliski's, but no Lev Kabliski. Was Lev short for Levi? There were also several Chaim Kabliski's, however, none of them seemed to match the Chaim I was looking for. The small boy in the photograph of the Jews being forcibly removed from their Warsaw apartments was tentatively identified as Tsvi Kabliski. Was this just a coincidence? Further investigation was unable to uncover any persons named Addam, Ania, Adiya, Efrayim, Emanuel, Schmaiah, or Aaron Kabliski; although there were some close calls, but no exact matches.

I then searched the names listed on the United States Holocaust Memorial Museum database and although I found several close matches, none of them matched who I was looking for. Another resource I searched was a list of Auschwitz victim's names as presented in testimony submitted to Yad Vashem, Israel's official memorial to the Jewish victims of the Holocaust. There *was* a Sigfried Kabliski listed and he was from Łódź. Could he have been a relative?

The Auschwitz/Birkenau Memorial and Museum was the next source I checked. Although there were thirty prisoners listed with the surname of Kabliski, none of them were the same names mentioned in the story. Unfortunately, the Nazis destroyed most of the documents they created and a list with the names of all Auschwitz victims just doesn't exist anywhere. So, it doesn't surprise me that, once again, I came to a dead-end because only her Uncle Addam supposedly joined the line headed towards the work camp, the rest headed straight to the gas chambers, and wouldn't have had their names recorded.

If I couldn't validate Mira and her family, what about Doktor Mueller? Did *he* even exist? Interestingly enough, there was a very prominent man named Heinrich Mueller who was the head of the feared Gestapo and was the highest ranking Nazi never to be traced after World War II. However, a search of the names of doctors who worked at Auschwitz/Birkenau, didn't turn up a Doktor Heinrich

Mueller; perhaps the list was incomplete, for obvious reasons. Another roadblock.

If I couldn't validate names, could I validate places? That turned out to be a lot easier than researching names. Even though I was unable to locate Mira's village on the pre-1939 maps, all the cities, towns, and roads mentioned actually did exist the time. I was even able to use *Google Earth* and zoom in to where Mira claimed the rock and dirt barricade blocked the road and to my utter surprise, it appears there is still some evidence of its previous existence.

I was skeptical from the beginning and I'm still skeptical, however, Mira seemed to be a real person to me, even though I couldn't prove whether she or any of the people in her story ever existed. Perhaps her story is just a figment of my imagination, or perhaps it's a composite of many Holocaust victims' stories yet untold. Perhaps, it's entirely possible that I accidentally tapped into some collective consciousness and this story has turned out to be many stories woven into one. Instead of Mira's story, it might be a combination of stories about real people, real places, and real journeys of those who are no longer here to tell us in person. In any case, I hope this story took you on a fascinating journey, whether you believe Mira existed, or not. After reading it, I'm sure you have an opinion, one way or the other.

If she has a living relative, I would welcome them to come forward and perhaps shed more light on this mysterious spirit. Until then, I will take everything at face value and just enjoy this wonderful experience.

## Appendix A

The original German caption reads: "Pulled from the bunkers by force." The SD trooper pictured second from the right, is SS-Rottenfuehrer Josef Bloesche, who was identified by Polish authorities using this photograph. Bloesche was tried for war crimes by a Polish court in 1969, sentenced to death, and executed in July of that year.

The little girl on the left has been identified as Hanka Lamet, who is standing next to her mother, Matylda Lamet Goldfinger (the woman second from the left). The boy carrying the sack has been identified as Leo Kartuzinsky, and the woman in the front has been identified as Chana Zeilinwarger. Numerous people have identified the boy in the foreground as either Arthur Domb Semiontek, Israel Rondel, Tsvi Kabliski or Levi Zeilinwarger, but none of these identifications can be conclusively corroborated.

Made in the USA
Columbia, SC
13 May 2020